# NO PRESENT LIKE TIME

# NO PRESENT LIKE TIME

## Steph Swainston

GOLLANCZ

LONDON

The right of Steph Swainston to be identified as
the author of this work has been asserted by her in accordance
with the Copyright, Designs and Patents Act 1988.

First published in Great Britain in 2005 by
Gollancz
An imprint of the Orion Publishing Group
Orion House, 5 Upper St Martin's Lane, London WC2H 9EA

10 9 8 7 6 5 4 3 2 1

A CIP catalogue record for this book
is available from the British Library

ISBN 0575070064 (cased)
ISBN 0575076410 (export trade paperback)

Typeset by Deltatype Ltd, Birkenhead, Merseyside
Printed in Great Britain by
Clays Ltd, St Ives plc

www.orionbooks.co.uk

To Brian

Thank you to Simon Spanton and Diana Gill. I am incredibly grateful to my agent Mic Cheetham for her help and support. Many thanks to M. John Harrison and to Richard Morgan for giving me time. Thank you to Stuart Huntley of The Schoole of Defence for some of the moves in the Chapter 1 duel. Thank you to Chris Jackson and the crew of MV *Chalice* for minke whales and sea eagles. Thanks to Lynn Bojtos, Cath Price and Gillian Redfearn for hanging out at the Castle. Love and thanks to Brian for everything – touché!

They change their clime, not their frame of mind,
that rush across the sea.
–Horace

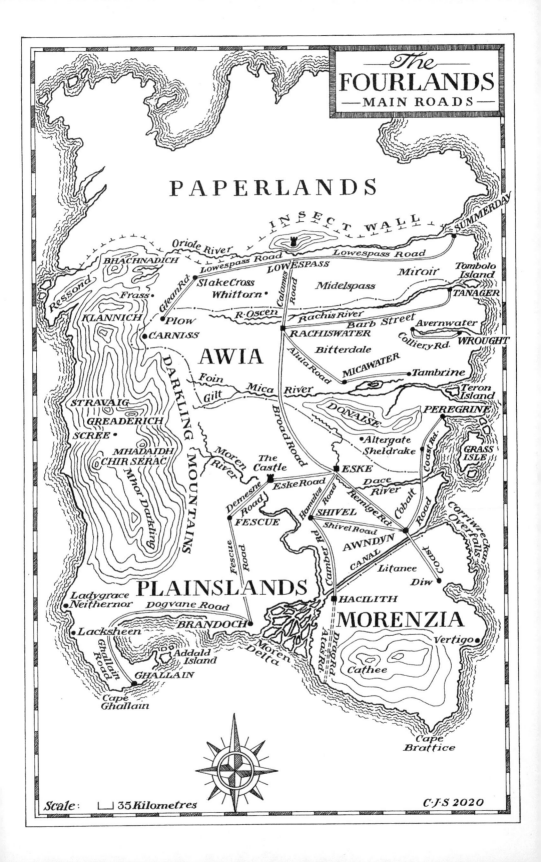

# CHAPTER 1

**January 2020**

On this soft night I followed the Moren River valley, flying back to the Castle, hearing the chimes of clock towers in the Plainslands villages as I passed high above.

The night air was shapeless. I couldn't sense any current. I concentrated, flapping steadily on, marking distance by time, marking time by going through all the songs I know. I lay horizontally, looking down around me, cruising with stiff, shallow beats. I felt the air rushing between my feathers on the upstroke. Then I pulled my wings down again, the feathers flattened, the tight muscles moved around my waist.

Thermals were dissipating as the sun set. I was dropping altitude to find them and the work was getting harder. Fog was forming, low in the pasture and along the river bank. The tops of the valley sides were dark shapes rising from the mist like islands. Beyond, I could see parallel hills all the way out to the beginning of Donaise. Hedges and drystone walls looked like black seams separating fields of clean, lapping white mist. There was no sound, just the skeleton zip of my wings peeling back the air.

I spotted a point of light in the distance, like a city, and checked my compass – bearings dead on for the Castle and hopefully there would be some supper left. The speck resolved into a cluster of lights, then each cluster separated again, and distances between them seemed to grow as I got closer. Lights slipped from the horizon down towards me, until I was over Demesne village. Street lights shone up, picking the mist out in flat beams. Denser wisps blew past, curling, and the fog began to take on a shape of its own.

The fog changed everything. Fog covered the river's reflective surface, meandered to the water meadows. Fog poured between the cultivar yew plantations and spiky poplar coppices where tomorrow's bows and arrows were painstakingly being grown. Fog drifted over the roofs of the village where most of the Castle's staff live. It pooled on the carp ponds, stole into the tax barns and settled on the market's thatched roof. It cloaked the watermill, the aqueduct's dark arches, Hobson's stable and the Blacksmith's yard. Fog overran the Castle's outermost boundaries. It advanced through the archery fields, lay in the tilting lists, rolled over the tennis courts. It muffled the concert hall and the bathhouse complex.

One of the Castle's spires was silhouetted against a white light, which suffused into the mist in an immense grisaille sphere. The floodlights were on in the amphitheatre. They only illuminated the sharp Northeast Tower, its black sarsen stone striking in the whiteout. Features became visible as I closed the distance. The Castle's vast bulk was obscured. Occasionally angular roofs and the crenellated tops of walls appeared, fragmentary, through the mist. The square base of the round tower was submerged two metres deep into a sea of fog. I flew through thicker patches – then it looked as if it was receding on the plains. On a whim, three hundred years ago, the Architect had encrusted her studio in the turret with sculptures. Eagles, storks and eels loomed out of the mist, with her company's logo and the tools of her trade in stonework blackened by kitchen smoke. The windows bristled with deep, tangled marble ivy so realistic that birds were nesting in it.

Fog cold in my eyes and throat like clouds. A smell from the kitchens of wood smoke, roast beef and dishwater had caught in it. A faint scent of lavender from the laundry house tainted it. Burnt whale oil from the floodlights saturated it, turning the fog into smog.

Storeys and gable roofs and towers rose behind towers. The spaces under the buttresses were filled with tracery. The Carillon Courtyard had a lawn mowed in wide stripes and a roof that had been covered in scaffolding for eight decades. On the steeplejack's walkway was a wooden treadmill twice as tall as a man, used to raise loads of Ladygrace stone. Its basket hung from the rope wound on its axle.

Two centuries ago, I thought the North Façade was a cliff face formed by the power of nature. I had tilted my head until I thought I would fall over backwards, but I still couldn't see the top of its spire. I had crouched on the hard grass a few hundred metres away, looked up and realised – all the crevices are carvings. The cliff ledges are parapets. Statues of idealised immortals, pinnaform spires embroidered with vertical lace. The glory of the Emperor, god's governor of the Fourlands. It had made my neck ache.

I flew an assured path around walls flaking masonry, mottled with moss. I passed pinnacles decorated with ball flowers. The Finials, a memorial sculpture, was a row of scalloped arches resting on free-standing black marble shafts. It carried the signatures of Eszai, people who through their peerless talents have won immortality, a place in the Circle, and reside here. Graffiti scarred the arches, the names of immortals past and present; I had incised *CJS & TW 1892* in a love heart on the highest topstone.

Now invisible in the mist, the gravel courtyard at the foot of the Finials encircled a statue of Dunlin, recently the King of Awia. I had ordered it to be placed there with the statues of other great warriors so that he would always be remembered.

The tall Aigret Tower seemed to drift in the mist and I sheared through it. It was the Slake Cross Battle cenotaph, square openwork, completely hollowed out to a lantern of air. At every level its pillars were thicker at the top than at the bottom, so they looked like they were dripping down – melting. It had no walls, its pillars were backed by those of a second and third tower nested inside; through its worn bird-boned latticework I flew without breaking pace.

Small, indistinct groups of people were heading along the avenue in the direction of the duelling ground. Some carried oil lamps; their golden light-points bounced away into the distance. Next to the floodlights' white glare, a whole crowd of lanterns was gathering. I must take a look and see what's happening. Standing on one wing I bent my knees and turned. The ground tilted sharply as I dropped onto the Castle's roof-forest, like a wasp into a very ornate flower. I swept in so low over the barbican that my wingtips touched, made a sharp right, narrowly missing the lightning rod. Airstream roared in my ears as I dived towards the duelling ground, wondering if I could see well enough to land safely.

Fog drifted with me over the low roof of the adjoining gymnasium, and a second later poured from the open mouths of a dozen gargoyles carved in the shape of serene kings like chess pieces, which leaned out, face down, over ornamental gardens. I flew through one of the streams, taking a shower in the damp fog. As I glided in on fixed wings, vortices curled off my wingtips so I left two spiral trails.

The duelling ground is inside a large amphitheatre with high, half-timbered walls topped by flagpoles. The fog had not yet smothered them but it rose up the outside like water climbing around a sinking ship – the oval building looked as if it was sliding down into the invisible earth.

Four floodlights stood at the edges of the amphitheatre, on ten-metre-high iron scaffolds. I circled the nearest floodlight, feet dangling, and settled onto its metal housing. I shook wisps of fog from my wings and pulled them around me, stood cloaked in long feathers.

The shade was very hot. I shuffled to the front and perched on the edge. The only noise was the oil lamps' hissing. Above and around, all was dark – but the pitch below was bathed in light. Two figures in the centre were swiping at each other with rapier and dagger.

There was Gio Serein, the Circle's Swordsman. When I was growing up in Hacilith, he was the immortal with the biggest fan club. Every child who wielded a stick pretended to be Serein and plenty of teenagers had aspirations to fight him. This could only be a Challenge. I peered closer to see who could possibly go a round with him. It was a young Awian lad, who kept his stubby dark wings folded so as not to present a target. His flight feathers were clipped in zigzags, the current fashion, making them lighter. Short brown hair was shaved at the sides and stuck up in sweaty spikes on top. For agility, he wore only a shirt and breeches. His sweat-patched shirt was fyrd-issue, dark blue of the Tanager Select infantry. He wore a glove on his left hand, grasping the rapier hilt. He moved as if he was made of springs.

Serein had his knuckles upwards and thumb on his rapier blade to make strong wrist blows. The stranger caught one on his dagger, thrust it wide, went in underneath with dagger and rapier. Serein struck back, low, with a cry.

The newcomer swept it aside, made a feint to the face, jabbing twice, and again Serein gave ground, keenly aware of his body's position. Then he ran in and scuffed up some sawdust with his leather pump. The Awian was wise to that trick; he parried the thrust. Metal slid over metal with a grinding swish.

I glanced up and the size of the crowd held my attention. The twenty-tier-high banked stands were crammed to capacity and more people arrived every minute, blowing out their lanterns, shoving a path down the walkways to sit on the steps and lean against the posts. Gazing around, I couldn't see any space where I could join them.

Directly opposite was a canopied box with the best view of the ground. The Emperor San was seated on a chair in the centre, watching the two fighters impassively and completely without expression. One thin hand rested on his knees, the other was curled on the armrest. His face was shadowed by the gold awning, thin magisterial features framed by white hair that hung loose to his shoulders. If San was out of the Throne Room this must be really important. I folded my wings neatly so the tips crossed at my back, and bowed my head in case he was watching.

On the Emperor's left, Tornado, the Castle's Strongman, was so big he filled that side of the box. He peered out from under the awning that bulged over his head. On his right, Mist, the Sailor, stood with a great big grin on her face, her hands on wide hips under a white cashmere jumper. Rayne, the Doctor, sat with her assistants on a bench at the side of the ground, ready to intervene if anything went wrong. I recognised many of my fellow immortals scattered through the crowd, all intent on the duellists. Well, I thought, it wouldn't be a new year if Serein didn't have another Challenger, but usually his supporters in the crowd bellowed and cheered and hissed. This time there was a breathlessness in the air.

The duellists walked in a circle, marshalling their strength. Watching tensely. Both had their sword-tips horizontal in third guard, daggers in their right hands held out straight to the right side. Footprints turned the sand dark in a ring where they trod. They must have been at it for ages; their clothes were wet and the sand was damp with sweat.

Serein thrust, knees flexed. The Awian traversed sideways and Serein's swept hilt nearly caught on his tightly taped sleeve. They never lost eye contact; I knew what that was like. Head up and body in balance, keep all the moves in your peripheral vision no matter how bright the steel is, cutting round your head.

Serein made his slicing arc too wide. The Awian jabbed at his stomach. Serein was forced back. The Awian jumped forward, thrust sword arm and leg out, aimed for the hamstring behind Serein's knee. Serein parried but his blade sloped. The Awian's rapier glanced off, he directed it to Serein's calf. Serein moved away fast. Top move! Yes! Eat your heart out, Serein! I bounced up and down on the floodlight housing until the whole thing shuddered.

Sorry.

They set to circling again, obviously exhausted but trying to see what chinks might open in each other's guard. They tried to spot any recurring foibles, to predict and use them. They were perfectly synchronised, reading the timing from each other's eyes. Seeing through the feints. Every time Serein sought a way to break out, the newcomer was with him, close like a shadow through every strategy.

Serein shifted into second guard, spun the dagger so the blade was below his hand, took a swipe across the Awian's face. Crash, crash! They moved apart. Serein has spent his life studying the art of killing. Why hasn't he won yet? His footprints on the sand traced out one of his geometrical charts. He was using every trick he knew and he was getting nowhere.

Some people climbed up on the roof and lit the last floodlight. If the duellists registered the white glare intensify, they didn't react. They concentrated on thrust and parry, leant in with both hands at once, dagger blocking rapier. A spray of sweat drops flew from Serein's fair hair as he flicked it back.

My floodlight was a good vantage point. Moreover, being half Rhydanne I could see movements faster than the flatlanders can, so I saw Serein's cuts; to the other spectators they must be a blur. This was Serein slowed by fatigue. I knew how impossibly fast he moves when fresh, because he's beaten me black and blue with a buttoned rapier before now.

Serein was two metres tall, his substantial arms were hard with tired muscle. He bared teeth in a snarl as he screamed at himself inwardly: concentrate! Even at this distance I could read the frustration in his pale eyes: why won't you yield? Why can't I hit you? He kept turning hatred into big, angry slashes that his opponent just leafed aside with dagger, his rapier in front narrowing the angle of attack. They were both as good as it was physically possible to be. The outcome depended on who would slip up first, or simply stop, ground down by exhaustion. Perhaps Serein was slightly more cautious than the boy, because he had more to lose.

Serein made two crown cuts to the boy's head, lunged for his feet. The boy tried to catch the blade in his dagger quillions, missed.

This kid has been around, I decided. He fights like an immortal. I had been flying on my own for days and my whole body was alert to their moves. I had been in remote Darkling, which made me conscious of the crowd.

There was the Archer. Lightning stood closest to the duellists, leaning on the crush barrier staring raptly at them. A wide Micawater-blue scarf was draped around his shoulders and a quiver of white-flighted arrows at his hip. He has the physique of a cast-bronze statue. The willpower of one, too, and to be honest their sense of humour as well. This century he is less glacial than usual, because he has been enlivened by another hopeless love affair. It was easy to see him; the surrounding crowd kept a respectful distance. Though they all stood shoulder-to-shoulder, Lightning was on his own.

I swept off my perch with my wings held right back, down to the edge of the pitch and landed neatly next to him. 'Who's the Challenger?'

Lightning smiled without turning. 'Welcome back, Jant. How was the road from Scree?'

'Very foggy. Who is he?'

'That young man is Wrenn, a career soldier from Summerday. He left the Queen's guard and made his formal Challenge to Serein last week.'

'Is that why the Emperor called me back?'

Lightning looked at me for the first time. 'No. Don't mention it in public – San has work for us. I was also recalled, and I am not at all happy about it, since I had to leave my betrothèd's side.'

(Lightning is the only person I know who still puts the è in betrothèd.)

'Wrenn looks like a fyrd captain.'

'He is. He made a name for himself in the town. He's working his way up through the ranks, and I think being such a fantastic swordsman has made him quite unpopular. Courtiers scent rumours and seek him out to prove themselves, but Wrenn refuses to know when to lose. He gave Veery Carniss more of a flaying than a duelling scar. If he was nobility, he could have been promoted higher. It's a shame; I suppose he was frustrated by the cut-glass ceiling which is why he's trying a Challenge.'

'They both look tired.'

'Jant, they started at six o'clock.'

'Shit!'

Lightning gestured at the crowd, 'Long enough for the Eszai and the whole of Demesne village to join us. Hush now. He's such a short boy, I don't know how he keeps going.'

There was no blood on the sawdust. 'Four hours and they haven't touched each other?'

'They've broken a sword each, though. Sh!'

Wrenn had obviously trained in broadsword techniques as well as the ideal figures of fencing. An overhead blow down to the face, a thrust to the belly, adapted to the rapier – duellist's weapons designed by humans for settling disputes between themselves in their city.

Winning is all. The Castle's constitution is simple: two men on a field and by the end of the day one of them will be immortal, and the other may as well be down among the dead men.

They used identical rapiers, damask steel blades with the same length and heft, issued by the Castle to ensure the Challenge is fair. The Challenger is allowed to set the time of the competition, but the Challenged immortal decrees the type of contest. Serein was formerly a fencing master; he had popularised the art across the Plainslands and Morenzia. Three centuries ago, he won his place in the Circle by broadsword combat but since then he has usually stipulated that Challengers use his accustomed rapier and poniard. Wrenn was so thickset that I could tell the long blade hadn't been chosen to favour

7

him, but he had no problems wielding it. He cut straight at Serein's chest.

Serein flung both hands up and bounded back. He landed in high guard, with both blades pointing at Wrenn's face. Wrenn ducked below them to attack – he flattened himself to the floor, one leg out behind, lunged forward with the rapier at arms' length.

Serein got low to thrust, but Wrenn was quick to his feet. Serein stood still, parried with dagger, thrust with sword. Wrenn pulled his cut to keep out of distance. He thrust under Serein's arm.

'That's three from the left,' muttered Lightning. 'He'll change now.'

That's what Wrenn wanted us to think. He attacked from the left. He traversed to the opposite leg and changed dagger grip, so the blade was down below his hand. He leant in, back straight, made a wide sweep, but too close and almost ran onto Serein's rapier. The crowd inhaled, expecting a double kill, but Wrenn, off balance, gave ground and the two began to circle again.

Wrenn launched a heavy cut to Serein's shoulder.

If this was me, I would—

Serein jumped and stopped it with just his dagger before it gained momentum.

Well, I wouldn't do that.

Then he tried to kick Wrenn in the balls.

Wrenn leapt away, threw his weight back and returned a reverse thrust at the same time.

I gasped. I'd never seen a fencer move that accurately before.

Serein couldn't turn inside the thrust, and retreated, face sallow. He allowed his rapier point to drop from guard for the first time. It gave Wrenn time to rally; he tried a cleaving blow. Serein beat it aside, turned his sword and cut at Wrenn's exposed hand. Wrenn backed off just fast enough to keep his hand. He parried, the dagger coming up beneath his rapier for support. He lifted Serein's blade, but Serein snatched it free. Wrenn faced Serein squarely, his whole body curved into a hollow, his middle held away and his left foot down securely.

They found new strength, remembering that they're fighting for immortality. San forbids his immortals to kill their Challengers, although genuine accidents happen now and again. Serein looked furious at how long this was taking, he was channelling all his brilliance at getting first blood from the young man.

Of course, no money Serein's novices could offer him would lead him to reveal his finest moves. He never taught his students enough for them to Challenge him. But it seemed that Wrenn had reinvented all Serein's techniques from scratch, and added his own innovations.

Serein deliberately made an out-of-distance attack, trying to draw Wrenn in. Wrenn was having none of it, he kept his body well away. Serein tried a better angle, this time Wrenn's dagger parried low. Serein's rapier drove straight at it. The blades shunted together. Serein punched his swept hilt at Wrenn's fist. The dagger shot from Wrenn's stunned hand like a dart.

Wrenn did not look for it but changed his rapier to his right hand, wringing his fingers. He was at a serious disadvantage. Serein's eyes tracked Wrenn's expression as he deigned a smile.

'It's only a matter of time . . .' Lightning said.

Wrenn knocked Serein's rapier up with his sword's forte, sliced across Serein's stomach. Serein kept his arms out of the way. His confidence peaked; he didn't need to give ground. He could just wait.

'Serein will stick him like a pig.'

Wrenn made a straight thrust in *quarte*, Serein turned it easily. Everyone watched Serein beating Wrenn back across the releager, step by step until they were right underneath the Emperor's box. Wrenn was beginning to look from Serein's rapier to dagger, and I could see his mouth was open.

Serein was lining up a way to end this. He feinted with the dagger, swung his rapier round in an outside moulinet for force, straight down at Wrenn's head.

And Wrenn stepped into the blow.

He caught the inside of Serein's hand on the grip with his own wrist, forced it aside. His rapier arrested Serein's dagger and he stretched that arm fully to the other side. He tilted his blade; the tip lowered to Serein's throat. Serein struggled, stopped. Face to face they were so close their chests almost touched. Wrenn looked Serein straight in the eyes, made an almost imperceptible movement of the point and a red trickle ran down below the Swordsman's larynx, between his collar bones into the front of his shirt. First blood.

Wrenn punched both arms into the air. 'Yes!' he yelled. 'I did it! I really fucking did it!'

For a second there was silence, and I could tell the same thought was running through every mind in the throng: how brave have you got to be to step *into* a cut in prime? Wrenn was prepared to die if his trick failed. Knowing he has to die sometime, he risked it for the ultimate reward. Serein had lost that mortal determination – well, all us Eszai are living on borrowed time.

The crowd erupted. A lady next to me put her hands over her ears, the cheering was so loud.

'What timing,' Lightning breathed. 'What bloody timing.' He vaulted the low wall and sprinted across the pitch. I got to the duellists first, saw Lightning throw a brotherly arm around Wrenn's shoulders. Wrenn lowered his rapier, swayed on his feet. He was about to faint.

I was suddenly at the focal point, and almost deafened by the crowds. Outside the lit ground the stands were invisible but the applause was like a wall of sound. A chant caught like city-fire and spread through the stands: 'Wrenn for Serein! Wrenn for Serein!' Fyrd swordsmen stamped their feet on the wooden benches; the thunder went on and on. Soldiers in civvies began to spill out onto the pitch. I clapped my hands until the palms stung.

'Yes!' yelled Tornado, with one fist in the air. He stuck two fingers in his mouth and gave a long whistle.

'Well done!' Lightning exclaimed. 'Well done, my friend!' He turned Wrenn to the yelling crowd and raised Wrenn's shaking arm. 'The victor!'

Serein, beaten, opened his hands and let his dagger and rapier fall to the trodden sand. They smelt weakly of disinfectant. He looked around for a place to lie, knelt down, then curled up from humiliation and sheer exhaustion with his hands over his head.

Wrenn seemed frightened. He looked more terrified the more he realised how many people were out there. His face had a lustre from the grease smeared on his forehead to stop sweat running into his eyes. He was beyond the limits of mental and physical endurance; he stumbled. Lightning walked him towards the Doctor's bench, but the crowd swallowed them in and then hoisted up Wrenn in the centre, hands on his legs and backside like a crowd-surfer. They carried him high above their heads, into the square passageway and rapidly out of the fencing ground. The floodlights highlighted tousled wings and assorted backs as they ebbed away from us. Serein and I were left alone.

The sea of fog breached the far wall and poured down, slipping towards us at ground level.

'That's it,' the Swordsman murmured. 'Is that it? Am I out?'

He gradually got to his feet, shoulders bowed, head lowered.

'Serein,' I said. 'It comes to us all in the end.'

He looked at me resentfully, but I couldn't tell whether he was sighing from overexertion or bitterness. 'Once I've left the Circle I won't want to see you again,' he admitted. 'Don't visit me, Jant – I don't want you to see me grow old.' He put a hand to his throat, rubbed it, and gazed at his red palm. The blood flow had practically stopped, but he was sticky with it chin to waist.

He looked up to the hulking empty stands. 'It's the fear that takes it out of you.' He rested his hand on my shoulder for a second. Then he picked up his rapier, broke it over his knee, and walked off the field.

# CHAPTER 2

I climbed the spiral staircase to my tower room. The murals on its walls became more lurid and grotesque towards the top. I don't remember painting them; I must have been really stoned.

'Hello, lover,' I said, emerging from the doorway.

Tern was waiting in the lower part of the round split-level room, her hands on her hips. Anger spiced her voice. 'Look at you! All windswept! God, you look like a juggler from the Hacilith festival! Out of those flea-bitten mountain clothes and into a suit . . . Here, wear this one; it's elegant.' She gave me a light and unusually demure kiss on the cheek. I looked around our untidy apartment that my wife had colonised with architectural drawings, cosmetics, rolls of fabric and an enormous wardrobe inside which I am sure a Rhydanne couple could live quite happily.

My carefully stacked letters slid into each other under Tern's discarded dresses. All my specific piles of correspondence had formed one mass like the Paperlands and reeked of her expensive perfume. She saw my look of horror and said, 'I tidied up your mess.'

'That was my filing system! The letters I've read go on the table, noteworthy letters on the floor under the desk. The ones I haven't read are on the fireplace next to the pine cones . . . Where have they gone?'

My alphabetised books were spattered with used matches and sealing wax. Shed feathers littered my collection of old broadsheets. Tern's gowns covered the chaise longue where I like to lounge; dress patterns were taped on the posts of our bed. Her underclothes were scattered in mounds. She had even disturbed the dusty table on which stood my precious distilling apparatus, although I had reassembled the glass retorts and condenser solely for the production of barley sugars.

Tern wore a bustier of chartreuse-green satin; its pleated sleeves wreathed her small black wings. At her throat, her wide jet heirloom necklace looked like a collar. 'This is all the rage,' she purred. 'Well, I say it is.'

'How do I unfasten it?' Her bare shoulders made her all the more tempting. I tried to undo her hair but her usual loose dark waves were pulled back into a complicated chignon.

My wife's town was reduced to brick shards and ashy rubble by the Great Fire of 2015. Of her black stone manor house only one single outside wall still stood. Slug-trail slicks of molten glass hardened from its pointed arched windows; lead roofs lay in solidified pools. The stumps of scrubby trees in her woodland were burnt flat to the ground. Every building and foundry in Wrought was destroyed, none of her possessions escaped the flames. Wrought was her birthplace and the scene of our honeymoon; Tern now aspired to rebuild it completely. Luckily, her designer fashions sold well on the Hacilith catwalks and as far as she was concerned Wrenn joining the Circle was a opportunity for trend-setting. She caressed my wings as I peeled off my tight trousers and changed clothes. Long wings are considered the most attractive, and as feathers need a lot of preening, Awians look after their high-maintenance bodies with care.

'I didn't see the duel,' Tern said. 'I needed the time to get ready. I heard from Rayne that the Challenger gave Serein a good nick to remember him by.'

'It was a first-blood duel,' I said. 'Those were the rules, so Wrenn had to.'

'I hear that Wrenn is scrumptious,' she commented. I shrugged. I seated myself in front of the mirror and let her brush my black hair that reaches to my waist, removing all the tangles caused by flying. It was agony. When she finished I crossed feathers through it like windmill sails and underlined my eyes.

'Listen.' Tern raised a finger at the clatter of coaches vying for space in the courtyard far below. 'I hear some ladies inviting themselves to his reception. Those can't be reporters or they would never have managed to sneak past Tawny at the gate.'

'We have an hour. I've been on my own in Scree for weeks. I want you.'

Tern pulled away – so as not to ruin the painstaking work of art she has made of herself. I gave her the full benefit of my cat-eyed look that she found so exotic. 'We should clear a space to sit down . . . Perhaps lie down.'

'Come and join the clamour,' she said.

Tern, you and your diamond self-sufficiency.

Unlike the stately homes of Awia, the Castle's sarsen outer bastions were thick, sturdy and unassailable. The Castle's purpose was defence of the entire Fourlands; it protected every manor, growing gatehouses and curtain walls while they bloomed balconies and arched dance halls, ornate turrets and painted bartizans.

The ground around the Castle was thrown into immense earth-works to ward off Insects. A channel of the Moren River was directed into a double moat around its man-made hill. The twin exterior walls that ran round the Castle's eight sides were strengthened by huge cylindrical smooth stone-faced towers decorated with crenellations and with shallow pointed roofs. Along the walls flags rustled and furled; the heraldry of the Fourlands' current sixteen manors and two townships. Fifty pennants flew under the Castle's sun, each with the sign that an Eszai had chosen for his or her position.

The Emperor's palace fitted inside the Castle like the flesh in a nutshell. Its marble towers stretched up from inside the impenetrable curtain wall. The Throne Room spire was the tallest; farmers who worked the demesne saw the sun glint on its pinnacle and they knew the Emperor occupied his throne beneath.

As Tern and I walked from our austere tower we saw only glimpses through the cold fog; its attendant hush muted every sound, drawing all the lustre from the palace. We saw lights shining behind sash windows and the oculus ovals made to look like portholes of the Mare's Run wing where Mist had her rooms. A stone-balustraded balcony ran along the length of its top floor, like the gallery on a ship. The Mare's Run was built between the outer walls and the palace five hundred years ago; it filled some of the space where gardens used to be. Several other buildings were shaped to fit into the western side of the gap: the dining hall and a theatre with its scalloped bronze dome topped by a white wood lantern-turret.

I did not take the rooms owing to me as Messenger in the palace's Carillon Courtyard when I joined the Circle. I preferred to move into the unused apartment at the top of the Northwest Tower on the outer wall because I found it easy to launch myself from its height. My window gave a view for a hundred kilometres of the river, the playing fields and white goalposts; red dock stalks sticking up from the green rough ground of Binnard meadow. Tern has never persuaded me to move back into the palace.

Tern shivered and I reached out with a wing to give her a pat on the shoulder. Tern's wings are much smaller than mine, as are those of all Awians, because although they are the only winged people, they are flightless. I am the sole person ever to be able to fly. As I am half Rhydanne my light, long-limbed build and mountainlander's fitness, when added to Awian ancestry on my father's side, gave me my ability.

Hand in hand Tern and I walked down an enclosed passage over a flying buttress that spanned from the outside wall to the palace. It was a narrow, vertiginous bridge that soared over the roof of the Great Hall, stretching thin and tenuous in the air. Below us, we could only see the glow of lamps in niches outside the hall and on four stone steps that rose to double doors with opulent panelling. The deeply carved decoration inside its triangular pediment was even more ornate: two flamboyant white Awian eagles flanked the Castle's sun emblem.

Our buttress walkway crossed above the head of the marble statue that topped the pediment, a slender woman bearing a sword and shield, her luxuriously feathered wings outstretched. Sometimes I land on the roof, providing a sudden perspective – she is twice my size. The hall was built by architects from Micawater, and Lightning is the only Eszai who would remember what the statue actually symbolises. It could be anything: freedom, justice, the wet dreams of a hundred generations of Awian adolescents.

As I walked with Tern I thought the whole building seemed smug, as if it had soaked up the atmosphere of too many whispered indiscretions at formal parties and was simply waiting for the next.

We descended to a small cloister. A colonnaded corridor ran round the misty lawn; we walked along two sides. Outside the Throne Room its stone ceiling was elaborately carved with fan vaulting; bosses hung down like leafy stalactites. Instead of curtains the drapes that framed the Throne Room portal were sculpted from amber.

The Throne Room seemed even more massive after the narrow narthex. Tern and I walked in down the long aisle past the screen and bowed to the Emperor. The Emperor San was first to be present, according to his custom. This was an important occasion, so he wore the tall spired platinum crown that Awia presented to him when the First Circle was formed. San normally wore no crown at all. We settled on one of the front benches, because they were closest to the sunburst throne and I wanted to hear what Wrenn had to say.

On this side of the screen, the benches faced each other and were gently stepped as in an auditorium. I watched in silence as the other Eszai walked in and gradually filled the seats. Most of the women gazed at Lightning, but some looked at me. I doubt that I cut a fine figure at court, since the fashion's long gone for looking pale and dishevelled, but there's no denying the effect I have on them. I may not command the battlefield but I can put the best spin on the outcome. I might not be a keen huntsman but I can gut a weekend newspaper. At sparring, I prefer words to swords, and I used to shoot drugs not arrows, but I'm free of all that now.

Wrenn entered the far end of the Throne Room, tiny below the huge rose window. It was symbolically important that he came in alone. He looked all around nervously and jumped as the doors closed behind him with an enormous crash. Then he began to walk, stiffly and obviously aching all over, towards us down the length of the scarlet carpet that was far more terrifying than any fencing piste. The Imperial Fyrd archers on the gallery with their pulley compound bows watched him carefully.

'That's the new Swordsman,' I whispered to Tern. 'This ordeal will be worse for him than the duel.' My initiation was an awful trial. 'Before this is over, he may well wish he'd died out there.'

She leaned forward to watch him. 'It depends how much he has to hide.'

Wrenn passed us slowly, giving the curious eyes of all the Eszai time to take him in. His short hair was wet from the bath or the steam room. His clothes were clean, but the same dull blue with thread holes on his sleeve where his fyrd patch used to be. He only looked straight ahead to the Emperor's dais – though not, of course, to the Emperor himself. He reached the platform's lowest step and knelt.

'My lord Emperor,' he announced. His voice gave way. He tried again: 'I humbly petition to join the Circle and I claim the title Serein, having beaten Gio Ami Serein in a fair Challenge.' He thought for a second, eyes aside like an actor trying to remember his lines – but also because it meant he didn't look at San. 'I intend to serve you and the Fourlands every minute of my life.'

San regarded Wrenn and the members of the Circle in silence. Even at this distance I felt the scrutiny of his incredibly clear and intelligent gaze. San always wore white – a tabard with panels of colourless jewels over a plain robe that reached to the floor. The pointed toes of his flat white shoes projected from under them. The style of San's clothes had remained the same since the year he created the former Circle, four hundred years after god left. His whole body was covered except for his thin and ringless hands.

The sunburst throne also remained a symbol of permanence. An ancient broadsword and circular shield hung from its back. They were a keen reminder that if us Eszai finally fail him in the Fourlands' struggle against the Insects, San will again direct the battle himself. In the Castle's stables a destrier is always reserved for him, never ridden, never used.

San rose and approached the front of the dais. 'You have selected yourself for the Circle. You have humbly placed your talents at the world's disposal. I thank you. Every successful Challenger must complete one last observance to become immortal. You must tell me everything about your life so far. Relate all that you think is significant from your earliest memory to the events that brought you here. You will not lie. My Circle will hear your testimony but they will neither interrupt nor judge. Nothing you reveal will ever be repeated. Only a refusal to speak will jeopardise your entrance into the Circle, not what you say. You have already won.

'The ceremony continues with your reception afterwards: for one hour the other members of my Circle may question you as they wish. You will always reply with the truth; they will neither criticise nor condemn. They are not permitted to repeat your words at any time or place. If anyone ever reveals what he or she learns, he or she will be rejected from the Circle. During the following hour you can question the other immortals about themselves. Likewise they are obliged to tell the truth and you must never disclose what they say.'

It's the only chance you'll ever have, I added to myself.

San looked expectant. Wrenn hesitated. He suffered in the intense silence, and so began, 'My name is Wrenn Culmish. I'm . . . I am from Summerday bastide town. Insects killed my mother when I was a infant and my father brought me up. He was a fyrd soldier given land for his service, and he taught me to fence . . . I surpassed him in skill when I was fifteen . . . But he proudly organised bouts with the other townsmen. I learnt from them and soon I always won. So I had a faint dream of trying for the Circle.

'The year after, a soldier turned highwayman picked a duel with my father, who knew his identity. The robber waited on the road for him on the way back from the pub. My father did not return. I searched for him – I never stopped – but three days later the river washed his damaged and dirty body onto the sandy bank right in front of the governor's house. It was so badly beaten that we could not tell how he died.

'I borrowed some rich clothes to disguise myself and I went looking for the highwayman. I rode up and down the Lowespass Road until he held me up. I disarmed the swine in a minute and he knelt, begging for mercy. Before I handed him over to the magistrate – he was hanged – I . . . I cut him . . . I took him apart. Until he told what he had done to my poor father.

'The first night he buried the body in the woods outside town. He could only scrape a shallow hole because tree roots blocked the soil. The following day he fretted that a passer-by might find the grave and unearth his crime. So the second night, in raw weather, he dug it up, carried the body to the Miroir moor and buried it in a deep hole. But then the idea tormented him that the moorland peat would preserve it forever and the disturbed grass would reveal the grave. So the following night he dug it up again. He threw it into the river from the top of a rocky outcrop. The river's flow brought the broken remains straight to Governor Merganser's door . . . I am sorry for what I did to the highwayman . . .'

San made no comment, so Wrenn continued. 'Anyway . . . when I knew that I was alone, I decided to travel south. If I had stayed in Summerday I would still be there now, gradually forgetting everything I dreamed of. I went to Tanager and joined the ranks of the Select Fyrd. I helped clear Insects from Rachiswater and the land around the River Oscen. I conducted myself well, I'm proud to say, and when Skua was killed I was made division captain. Then I saw the future stretching out, always the same. I was thwarted. I sparred with all-comers. I gave the gentry scratches but they came back wanting more, unable to believe they had lost to a smallholder's son. In the end I beat them all. Well, yes, I resent them . . . But that doesn't matter now, does it? I've done something they could never do.

'My dreams of the Circle returned. Thank god, my skill rather than my background is what matters to the Castle, I reckoned; there's a way out of this circus. For five years solid I spent all my off-duty time training. I was full of doubt and hope. I thought I was a dupe and a wretch to consider fighting the Swordsman. I nursed the idea for years and did nothing about it, then one night on a mad impulse I sent a letter to him. He chose to fight using rapier and dagger, which is my forte . . . Um . . .' Wrenn's speech filled the hall and it seemed to him that his voice droned on. 'I am twenty-five years old,' he whispered, looking at the backs of his hands. He stuttered and fell quiet. He realised that in a few minutes he would be twenty-five for ever and their appearance would never change.

'Answer my questions,' said the Emperor. 'Have you ever fought Insects alone?'

'Yes, my lord. I've killed Insects one at a time in the Rachiswater amphitheatre and hunted a couple found lurking by the town.'

'Have you ever felt fear?'

Wrenn hesitated, wondering what the best answer was. I knew that doubt well; in my initiation I had to confess all kinds of crimes to the whole Circle. I saw from his panicked expression that we seemed more forbidding and the Throne Room door looked tempting. I thought he was going to make a dash for it.

'Yes . . .' he said eventually. 'I have never been as frightened as I am right now. But I master my fear.'

San asked, 'Do you have a partner to bring into the Circle?'

Wrenn shook his head. He tried to smooth over his exhaustion with confidence but it could still be seen like the shape of wings under velvet. 'I've made no time in my life for girlfriends.'

There is no way you can lie with the Emperor's gaze on you; it's impossible to hide anything. Wrenn squirmed uncertainly and stared at the floor. 'You want me to tell? I spent my nights in the brothels instead. Well, it's easier. I've been planning this Challenge for years; I couldn't afford the time to have relationships.'

We all privately remembered how terrible it is to speak alone in that vast space and felt sympathetic. I had witnessed the ceremony as an Eszai three times before, firstly when Tern joined at my wedding, and most recently when Ata Dei became Mist. I glanced at Mist; she looked shifty, probably recalling how during her initiation she tried to lie but instead found herself confessing that she murdered her husband for his place in the Circle.

San stated, 'You swear to serve me, in my service to the Fourlands, in god's name, for as long as I give you life.'

'I swear,' said Wrenn, forcefully.

The Emperor raised his right hand, bony fingers and prominent joints. 'Come forward.'

Wrenn climbed the dais steps, wondering at the great transformation about to take place. I could practically hear him thinking: *this is it.* He braced himself for immortality as if it would burn through him. It's nothing like that. It doesn't hurt, in fact when it happened to me I could feel no sensation.

The Emperor extended his hand to Wrenn. Wrenn grasped and pressed his lips to it for a second. The Circle took him in.

Wrenn looked up finally to the Emperor's eyes. San announced, 'Now you are the Swordsman. Your name is Serein.'

A smile broke slowly over Serein's face. He dropped to his knees at San's feet, in silence. Then as if he could not bear such close proximity to the Emperor and aware that the rite was over, Serein quietly backed down from the dais, turned and passed the benches. We all stood as he passed. Lightning and Rayne glanced at each other; they had felt the ripple in the Circle as San made the exchange: one out, one in. After the transfer they'd feel Wrenn's presence as slightly different from Gio's, like a new person joining an inhabited room. Serein walked down the aisle, seeming to diminish in size, and left the Throne Room by himself. Lightning would join him outside; he made it his responsibility to greet new immortals and give them some much-needed advice. One by one we bowed to the Emperor, who was always last to leave the court, and followed Serein. As I passed through the door I grabbed two pocketfuls of confetti and glitter, swept up my hands and threw it over our heads.

A babble of a hundred conversations hung in the air of the Great Hall. I wanted to climb up to my rafter where I customarily sit, legs dangling, to watch the party. But I couldn't do that with my arm around Tern. I led her through a dozen conversations.

'Is he here yet? I want to meet the boy. I've questions to ask him . . .'

'He's twenty-five, bless. How rare it is to be so adept so young.'

'Try the smoked venison, it's excellent.'

'Eleonora? Busy revitalising the kingdom. She's good, by god, I only hear praise.'

'But the court's full of scandal. What she does with chambermaids, I—'

' "For an Eszai everything is easy." Ha! How can they think that?'

'Look! There's Comet. He's back! *Hais-gelet*, Jant?'

The Emperor was seated at the high table on a raised stage. He did not touch the feast before him. Tern swayed her skirt a little to the music – a young lad slammed away at the piano, lissom women in jasper red played fiddle reels.

Confetti on the carpet, candelabra; people leant on the oak panelling, kissed under the arches. Frost was building a cantilevered bridge out of forks and salt cellars. Rayne and Hayl played chess with marzipan pieces on an enormous pink and yellow cake shaped like a chess board.

What platters and plates and bowls of food! There were sugared almonds, edible stars, spiced wine, iced wine, spring water, wheat beer and cream liqueur. There were flambéed swordfish, sliced lengthways on silver trenchers.

There were packets of Cobalt cigarillos on the table for those who wanted them. Boar pies – speciality of Cathee, charcoal-roast mush-rooms, fat onions, saffron rice from Litanee, steak that juices-up your mouth. There was peppered asparagus and kale from the Fescue fields; squash, tomatoes, baked potatoes cracked and oozing butter, Shivel cheeses like crumbly drums with fat blue veins. There was fruit: glazed, glacé, covered in cream.

There were warm loaves, soft inside and smelling sensual, lobster claws pickled from the Peregrine coast, poached pike from the river. Northern exotics like pinnacle rabbits spirited in from Carniss, eels from Brandoch, Awndyn salmon and sundry seafood.

East into Awia, the spices were wilder – fenugreek and turmeric dhal, moist cake with nutmeg and cinnamon sultanas. The best coffee from Micawater, prime grapes plump with juice, olives like slick jewels, floury chorizo sausages in net bags, artichokes you had to be Awian to understand, pizza, prosciutto, ciabatta and more olives.

Tanager crispy duck, all kinds of little birds, larks in pastry, magglepies, dumstruks and starlings caught on lime and cooked on the branch because Awians consider falconry insulting. There were peacocks couchant looking haughty with their skin and fan-tails replaced. There were crackling hogs with grafted wings and bemused expressions. Bustards were stuffed with turkeys stuffed with pheasant stuffed with partridge stuffed with quails stuffed with chestnut – cutting into it revealed layers of meat like tree rings and was more than I can face. A swan glided up the high table, by gingerbread with silver metallic icing that the Emperor quite ignored.

Eat, eat, eat. Immortality in gluttony. Watch out for checkmate on the marzipan cake!

Lightning noticed us and remarked to Serein, who was gorging sliced beef and fruit sauce in a wood bowl. His chest was broad and his arms well-defined muscle. He held himself tensely, trying not to dissipate under the tide of strange things, expressive people. Serein's regime of training had not prepared him for the duel's aftermath – he was the centre of attention but he still felt alone. If he wished himself back in Summerday now, he would feel much worse when he bore the responsibility of command on the battlefield.

Aside from his skill in archery Lightning has cultivated many social talents. It was said of him that if he was in the building no woman would ever have to open a door. He was dapper in black tie and a raised-and-slashed celadon silk shirt, his wings sticking out the back. Some people say that wings have become smaller over millennia because they can't be used and as Awians, especially non-aristocratic ones, intermarry with humans. Whatever the truth, Lightning's wings were distinctly larger than Wrenn's.

'Serein Wrenn,' Lightning said, 'may I introduce you to our Messenger and Lady Tern? Comet can fly; I think that's because he takes things too lightly. He will carry your letters anywhere in the Fourlands, and will help if you need translations, so don't hesitate to ask.'

The frontier boy bowed, steering back his sword hanger with his left hand and staring at me. I tolerated the usual scrutiny. People don't notice the subtleties straight away but they find my leggy proportions jarring. I shook his hand. 'I'm impressed – nobody can be taught to fight like that.'

'Comet Jant Shira. Lady Tern. It's an honour to meet you,' he said, looking as if he meant every word of it. His eyes were so wide I could see all the whites round the blue irises. He was wired on anxiety. He could not put a foot outside the narrow sphere of etiquette for fear that he would say or do something dreadful and be rejected from his hard-won place in the Circle, without ever knowing why. His fear was unfounded because only another Challenger could replace him, but he was almost frozen by the manners he imposed on himself.

A servant passed by, carrying a salver of champagne flutes. I took the whole tray from her, balanced it on one hand. I swept it low in front of Serein. 'Take a drink.'

He declined, uncomfortably.

'Go on,' said Tern.

'I don't drink,' he said, reddening.

'No, really? Tonight of all nights!' I pushed the tray towards him. 'One glass of champers to celebrate?'

'Sorry, no, Shira – I'm not used to it. If I took a drink now, I could never rise at six to practise.'

After a duel like that, who would anyway? 'Sleep till midday,' I said. 'Your first day as an Eszai. That's what I did. I sprayed champagne everywhere; I love being soaked to the skin in it.'

Lightning was enjoying this. 'The Swordsman doesn't drink alcohol, so leave him alone.'

'Shira, if I slip up and lose my edge a Challenger will get the better of me.'

Every time he said 'Shira' I bit my teeth together and they were starting to hurt. I said, 'Call me Jant. The name Shira really signifies I belong in the lower caste among the Rhydanne. It means "Born out of wedlock" – I can't translate it better than that.' Well actually I can, because it means 'bastard', but I'm not putting ideas in his head.

Wrenn had caused offence already and he was appalled. His face moved awkwardly; he was over-aware of its every feature. 'I'm sorry.'

'Worry not.' I waved a hand. I make my body language expressive to compensate for the difficulty most people have in reading my cat eyes.

Wrenn shuffled his feet as if they took up too much space on the carpet. I wanted to tell him, I understand how daunting this is, but lighten up, you won't be out on the street tomorrow. You'll still be here, immortal, staring at the backs of your hands like a fool.

He was frantically searching for something to say. Every word sounded loud and momentous to him; he picked them carefully, knowing they would be permanently impressed on his memory. I remember when I was in his position, in my reception when I was surrounded by Eszai – I had heard of every single one before through tales or monuments to their work. They were all here, in one place, and they talked to each other! I had been a novelty to them. I tried to get to know them all in one night, but the Eszai I most wanted to speak to was the Comet I had displaced. I practically pinned Rayne against a column and gabbled to her excitedly about chemistry and the latest research into Insect behaviour. I told her far too much about my past, without realising she understood, and that in describing the slums of Hacilith I had reminded her too much of hers.

I could offer Wrenn advice and he might bring something new and interesting to the Castle. I began to understand why Lightning took newcomers rapidly under his wing. I said, 'Serein is your stage name; you'll be grateful for it. You can make Serein whoever you want and Wrenn, your real self, will be safe.'

Serein glanced across the hall and suddenly gaped at a gossipy cluster of extremely beautiful girls. They saw him watching and wafted their plumed fans, parading themselves. They were mortals – Zascai – only fleeting names; they stood on the outside smiling, craving to be chosen and drawn in. Tern eyed them stonily. 'That's just the beginning. Next time, when word gets round, there'll be crowds.'

'Look,' said Lightning urgently. 'Be careful of those ladies. You need to learn how to discourage them.'

'Have fun,' I said vaguely. He could choose a different gold-digger every night; no need for whores.

Tern snorted. 'Seduction's their job, Wrenn,' she warned. 'They've studied it. If you give them an opportunity they'll eat you alive. They will try anything to marry into the Circle.'

'They only want immortality,' Lightning added. 'Don't wed the first one you meet just because she shows interest in you. You should wait for one who loves you for yourself.'

The eldest girl was about twenty and she had a driven look that no make-up could mask. She was hungry for the chance to peel away from her rivals and address Wrenn alone; a social climber eager to find footholds in the flaws of his character. An expert seductress, Eszai-good, if there had been a place in the Circle for seduction. She had started young and become an expert in her teens. Well, that kind of dedication was necessary to win the ultimate prize.

Tern wagged her finger at the Swordsman. 'For god's sake don't tell them anything. You'll be reading it in the gossip columns for the next six months.' She smiled and I pulled her closer. She instinctively knows how to flirt with anyone. The problem with having a trophy wife is that you have to keep re-winning the trophy.

'There is Tornado,' Lightning said. 'Wrenn, come and let me introduce you to the Circle's Strongman.' Wrenn found himself shepherded expertly between the dancers, who turned to glimpse him at every step, so he was always the centre of a space surrounded with people, all smiles and for the most part slightly taller than him.

'That golden boy is going to get his orange juice spiked if he's not careful,' I muttered.

Tern giggled and curtsied. 'May I have this dance?'

We danced. Her hand draped on my whipcord upper arm. My hand clasped below her shoulder blade on the silk, basque-wired like a lampshade. My lace shirt cuffs hid my fingerless gloves. She followed my steps in quick time like a snappy reflection. We had practised this; we felt good. I felt great, only Tern can keep up with me when I go so swiftly. And underneath all her clothes she's naked. She was giddy already from the room spinning about us. All those faces. Our bodies together, shoulders apart; my hips rubbed just above her waist. 'I'll lead, you can spin.'

'Easy!' Her skirt twirled; she was laughing.

The music ended; Tern leant forward, hands on knees, little cleavage in danger of escaping. 'Oh, Jant,' she said breathlessly in her carnal voice. I rubbed my cheek on her cheek and kissed her eyelids. I kissed her lips, and deeply her mouth.

We were still snogging when Mist Ata appeared and nodded curtly. She carried a candle in a holder and her forehead was creased with worry. 'Jant, come with me.'

'Later, Mist,' I murmured.

'This can't wait any longer.'

I disentangled myself from Tern and placed a finger on her nose. 'Soon,' I promised.

'Soon,' she repeated, as if from a distance.

I followed the Sailor. 'You were brave to ask San for leave,' she said. 'Mind you, I could tell you needed a holiday.'

'I was improving my flying. And besides, no one else ever goes to Darkling so I bring back news for the Emperor.'

'Yeah, right. Lucky, lucky; I haven't had any leave for five hundred years.'

At the quiet end of the hall Lightning waited by the camera obscura, leaning against the door with his big arms folded. Mist beckoned us inside.

'Oh, so you found a hiding place to avoid Wrenn's questions?' I said.

Mist replied, 'Jant, you don't even know the *type* of reason why you're here.'

The camera obscura was a tiny, black-painted room with a pinhole in the door that shone a circular image of the hall onto the far wall. The entire party was pictured inverted there – minutely detailed figures crossing the lit screen. I examined it. There was the tiny piano and musicians upside down. Miniature people waltzed past a section of the long trestle table. A blurred servant trudged behind them with a leather blackjack jug. I squinted to see the Emperor below the sun shield in the centre. I spotted Tern; she was talking animatedly to someone whose image stepped forward onto the screen. I contorted trying to view them the right way up. It was Tornado, an unmistakable giant of a man. Tern put her hands up to his chest. He bent down; she kissed him lightly on the cheek. His hands embraced her hips, far too closely in my opinion, and together they danced off the edge of the projection.

Oh, no. I wanted to run straight to Tern, but Mist blocked the doorway, setting her candle on the floor. Her shadow hid the screen.

'Can we get this over with?' I said, annoyed. I craned to see the figures now dancing on Mist's blouse and face. My wife was out there, chasséing with a man who had enough muscle in one bicep to make three warriors.

Lightning said, 'At least choose a more comfortable lair for your conspiracies.'

Mist said, 'Jant, what would you say if a land existed far out in the sea about which the Empire knows nothing?'

'I'd say that if you want philosophical debate in a stuffy cupboard you can ask another Eszai. It's not like me to miss a party. Especially important parties.'

Mist delved in her shoulder bag and brought out a thick book with crinkled pages. Her hands were pockmarked from her pre-Castle life as a milkmaid and butcher's delivery girl on Grass Isle, rowing her skiff every day to deliver cuts of beef to the islanders and cutting remarks to the sailors who wolf-whistled.

She gave me the book. 'This is the log of the *Stormy Petrel*. I have discovered an island, named Tris, reached three months out of Awndyn harbour on an east-south-east bearing.'

I said, 'Where? Three months? No, that's not possible; nothing's that far away.' I glanced at Lightning. 'You're being very quiet.'

'I'm not going with you, Ata,' he said.

'Going where?' I exclaimed.

Mist said, 'The Emperor requests that you and Lightning sail with me to the Island of Tris.'

'No! . . . Look, slow down, this is a lot to take in. San knows of this island?'

'Yes. I returned from my voyage last month. I kept it very confidential though I wanted to sail in triumph into port. I told San everything and he has ordered a second expedition that you two must join.

'But . . . I don't believe you. My duty's here; I have lots of work to do in Wrought. You won't need a messenger on a caravel; yes, I could be of more use working for you here. I—'

'You hate ships, we know. Tough.'

'Ships are fine as long as I don't have to be aboard them.' I caught a glimpse of the projection, on which numerous Eszai by the long table were asking Wrenn questions, but I couldn't see Tern. I was sure that I was being made the butt of a practical joke. I tried to give the impression that I was amused but was willing to see how far I could push Mist's invention. 'So what's it like on this island?'

Mist handed me the notebook. It began with the co-ordinates of the Awndyn coastline, the edge of the chart off which she had sailed. Her round feminine handwriting encircled a sketch map: 'The Island named Tris by its inhabitants,' I read, and: 'The town drawn from the harbour. The natives say "Capharnaum", this must be the town's name? Another settlement due south, name unknown. Triangulated height of mountain approx. 3000m.'

'Natives?' I said. 'You mean the island is populated?'

'Aye.'

'Who by? Plainslanders?'

'Some are human, some are winged people, living together in the town. As far as I could see there is no Insect infestation whatsoever.'

The island was shaped roughly like the head of an Insect, being rounded with short, spiny peninsulae. Mist had recorded the inlets and promontories with customary precision. The land rose up a gentle concave slope, poured off a sizeable river, and then soared into a massive peak. No details were marked, and the east coast was just a dotted line. 'I didn't sail that far, it's only an estimate,' she explained.

'I was interested in the natives. I couldn't understand their language; that's why I need you, Jant. I wrote some of the words down, see?'

'Can I study this?' I said enthusiastically. I would soon learn if it was a practical joke or not.

'That's just what I want you to do! If the knowledge alone doesn't satisfy you, there's more than enough rum to wash it down with. Their accent gave me quite a shock. I think the corsairs used some of those words, who infested the Moren delta when I was a girl.'

I leafed through the logbook. Mist's entries for each day were brief: '5 June. Distance travelled, 240 kilometres, lat. 29°S long. 129°E. Fresh gales and cloudy, good visibility. Sounding 100m, black sand with small shells. Ate a number of flying fish.'

'Flying fish?'

'Yes. And I have seen a place where oysters grow on the branches of trees.'

I shrugged. Well, why not? 'You left *Stormy Petrel* stuck in Oriole River.'

'Aye. Frost's company raised her. I spent last year refitting her for a deep sea voyage.'

Lightning spoke: 'There have been explorations before. They found nothing.'

'Saker, the ocean is a big place.'

'It's not possible,' I said finally. 'I don't believe it.'

'Where the fuck do you think I've been for the last six months?'

'Keeping your head down and escaping embarrassment!'

Mist gave me a candid look, which was a sure sign not to trust her. 'I have but recently rejoined the Circle, and this venture will prove my worth to those who would Challenge me or mutiny. This is not just another Grass Isle project seeking Shearwater's Treasure. I'm serious! There's nothing for me on the mainland, is there, since I lost Peregrine?'

Lightning looked at her mildly without replying. He opened the door a chink because we were all starting to suffocate, and muted music seeped in from the party outside. I lowered my voice. 'How did you know which direction to sail?'

Mist said, 'By chance. Yes. Well, there might be many—'

'No, there are not!' Lightning was quietly furious. 'God founded the Castle to protect the world. If the Castle doesn't know about this island then how could we fulfil our purpose? Insects might run rampant over it and we'd be none the wiser.'

'It might not fit with your ideology but all the same it's there.'

I thought, maybe the Fourlands isn't the only land and maybe we're not the only guardians god left behind. I examined the scale. It was big – four hundred kilometres in circumference. 'It isn't an island like Grass Isle at all, more like a chunk of Darkling out in the ocean. Tell us, what's in the town?'

'I don't know. I didn't leave *Petrel*.'

'Convenient.'

'I wanted more than anything to put ashore! We had weathered storms with ten-metre-high waves. *Petrel* lost half her caulking and cladding because Awndyn's shipbuilders are so shoddy. You would not believe the trouble I've had with the unions. Her sails were torn, the rudder splintered. Most of my men were sick, some with scurvy, and we were desperate for fresh water. I took on supplies from the natives' canoes but I didn't land because the governors of the town didn't permit me. They have many governors.'

'What?'

'I'm telling you it's true. People came out in big canoes and surrounded us. I sketched them, there.' *Stormy Petrel* dwarfed the canoes, looking like a goose with her goslings, and none of the vessels had details since Mist was a poor artist.

I crouched down in the cramped space on the parquet floor by Mist's feet. The sea was not my element; boats bring on a phobia that I can never rid myself of completely. My fear was reasonable because if I ever tried to swim, the weight of waterlogged feathers would drown me. I also had a sneaking idea that everybody was acting and deeper lies were readily being believed. 'I'm not going. I might be the only Eszai who can crack this language but you can choose mortals from the university who have just as good a chance.'

'Don't mistake me; I hardly want you there, Jant. The last thing I need is dead weight and winged liabilities on my ship. If I had my way, I'd be doing this on my own! But San picked you two from the whole Circle to accompany me and we're obliged to obey. Here's his written command.' She passed Lightning and I small envelopes with the familiar crimson insignia. 'If you want to appeal, go ahead,' she added.

'I will,' said Lightning grimly. 'I would love to see the result of my investment and your method of operation. I would like to be the first from the Fourlands to trade with Tris, but I am repairing Micawater and I should be there.'

'You knew? Damn,' I moaned, beginning to have the feeling that the conspiracy was against me.

'Yes, although I wish otherwise. The *Melowne*, the supply ship to be taken on this voyage, belongs to me. I have the Queen's permission to send it so that *Stormy Petrel*'s crew will not suffer hunger again. And in return I have a quarter-share in whatever goods we bring back. But that doesn't mean I must accompany the expedition, Mist. I will be a passenger on your ship if the Emperor decrees it. No more, no less.'

Lightning was rebuilding Micawater to look exactly the same as it did before the Insects damaged it five years ago. He obsessed about every detail in the restoration of his palace outside the town, believing it an inviolable duty to his family. He wanted to fulfil the trust they had placed in him to conserve the palace: he matched masonry, sourced silks, kept both its wings as symmetrical as the day it was first completed. I thought the fact he was tinkering with it and not helping Tornado and Queen Eleonora clear the remaining Paperlands that the Insects had built in northern Awia showed he had time to spare.

Mist addressed him: 'You can't sulk for a whole generation. Do you want your world view to become obsolete and eccentric like the portraits that hang in your house? Jant, listen to this: Lightning's family portraits have been repainted many times, about every two hundred years once they start to fade. The artists try to be accurate but scarcely perceptible changes creep in accidentally, flattering trends to the ideal of the era. Next time, those alterations are copied along with the rest and new ones are made. His portraits are as idealised as his memories. Saker, how can you tell what's real and what isn't when you rely on the past? If you don't want to know of new discoveries, how long will you last as an Eszai? Suppose the island has better bows than Awia? A better type of wood?'

'Without Insects to inspire them, I doubt it. Let them come with their Challenges.'

The camera obscura was growing even stuffier and I was gasping for air. I nudged the door wide, looking for my chance to escape. Serein Wrenn caught sight of us and strolled over with a limber gait. I wondered what he thought, seeing three Eszai in an alcove. When everything else at his party was so perfect, we stood out as a great anomaly. 'What are you talking about?'

'We beg your pardon,' said Lightning. 'This is a private discussion.'

Wrenn bowed and was about to leave us to it, but Mist sized him up. 'No, wait . . . What time is it? We have to tell the truth for an hour.' I could practically hear her mind calculating. She took in his shirt buttoned down the left side showing his strong torso off to the best advantage, his small round stand-up collar and sharp-styled hair, the worn cherry-red leather thigh-boots with the tops folded over his knees.

Out came her travel-worn notebook again. 'You need experience.

You'll find this interesting,' she said, and set her plans on him like wolves.

The others blocked my view of the party, so I turned again to the pinhole image. The beam angled by the half-open door illuminated the wall next to me, unfocused and with washed-out contrast. Fuzzy figures rippled over the uneven surface, so small that their activities looked quaint but nonetheless unsettling. I checked them one by one: Gayle exchanging a few words with the Emperor, Frost crammed into a ball gown and wearing steel-toed boots. I couldn't see Tern. Where was she? Why wouldn't Mist let me out? I tried to edge away from the stifling corner but Mist stood firm, talking hotly into my face, toes pressing against my toes, only the logbook between me and her ample breasts. Tern's figure must be in my shadow, but though I inched forward I couldn't see her waltzing on the wall. The perfume on Mist's long white hair tickled my sinuses; there was also the pong of Wrenn's gravy breath. His shoulder was up against mine and the bright love of adventure in his eyes would enthuse the entire fyrd. It was even worse to think I would be on the ship with him.

'. . . so the Empire must explore Tris,' Mist concluded eventually. Lightning glared; he rightly thought that we were making unnecessary problems for ourselves.

'Are you worried?' she asked Wrenn.

'Nothing worries me,' he said.

'Nothing!' I said. 'Poor lad, there's quite a lot of it out there.'

He stared at me. 'I haven't even unpacked my rucksack. I'm ready to go.'

'Aye, thought so. Gentlemen, you will be discreet and keep this a secret. You must go out into the party with knowledge that no one else in the whole world has. Smile; you'll find it hard. I will see you at Awndyn by the end of the week; the *Stormy Petrel* is ready to sail.'

Lightning beckoned a butler and said, 'Go down to the cellars and bring me a bottle of Micawater wine. The oldest you can find.'

The party sashayed and shone around me. I walked through it, dead to the heart and scarcely seeing Tern in a clumsy two-step with the Strongman.

I ran out to the balcony and jumped to the balustrade, threw myself off. Beating hard and yelling with fury I reached eighty k.p.h. between two spires, just brushing stone with my wingtips. I zigzagged close to tightly packed walls near-missing by a centimetre on every familiar turn. I exploded out of the fog, still climbing to the clear starry sky. The tallest towers poked though the mist's cotton blanket like black sea stacks; lights flickered deep among them. I reached the top of my trajectory, for a second hung there. Somersaulted. Fell, head first, masonry soaring past, the mist's surface undulating.

I splashed through it, silently.

I flew circuits of the Castle until I slowed down and my anger wore off, turning into hopelessness. I landed on the sill of the Northwest Tower, bounded down into my room, sprang onto the four-poster bed and ripped its curtains together. In its gloomy, ivy-entwined brocade cave I sat and thought. Drugs, that's what I need. Drugs.

# CHAPTER 3

Next morning I decided to seek an audience with the Emperor and appeal against the terrible orders that he had given me. I left Tern sleeping in the four-poster bed; I had pretended to be asleep when she came in late. I dressed, ate breakfast and shut the door as the Starglass struck ten. I ran down the frescoed spiral steps three at a time, at a speed that may well be the death of me one day. I ignored the thick rope that serves as a handrail and opened my wings for balance as far as was possible on the dizzying staircase. I hurtled round the last corner and crashed into Lightning, who was climbing up. 'Huh? Get out of my way, Micawater.'

'Jant! I have to talk to you. The Emperor's just asked me to put Gio out of the Castle!'

'Who?'

'Gio Ami. The Swordsman for four hundred years until last night.'

Gio was from Ghallain, a bleak town on the tip of an inhospitable cape. His wealth and acumen were entirely self-made. Three-letter names were often used among the coastal Plainslanders, a tradition dating back as far as the Emperor's birth. Like Awian names, they're not gender-specific. I thought, Gio really belongs in sixteen thirty-nine. What the fuck is he going to do out there, in the twenty-first century?

We walked towards the Simurgh Passage on the extreme eastern side of the palace, and along past Lightning's rooms where pale watercolour paintings covered the walls completely, their frames touching. The Archer said, 'Gio refuses to leave. I have sometimes seen defeated Eszai act this way. He has lived a long time in the Castle; he may fear the outside world although he'll never admit it. It has changed since he was last mortal.'

I remembered Gio's arrogance and said, 'More like he can't accept that anyone could beat him.'

'Yes, I agree.'

'Well, I hope he isn't armed.'

'Oh, of course he is armed. That's why I need your help to evict him.'

We walked up a flight of steps to the attic of the passage and the quarters traditionally appointed to Serein. Bucklers were displayed on the walls outside his doorway, with dusty bullfighting cloaks and wood-and-leather dusack swords for practice. Broadswords and falchions were arranged in circles and fans, next to sail-hilted daggers and Wrought katanas with naked blued steel. There were ceremonial two-handed swords with curlicued quillions and flamberge blades inlaid with gold wire, and several portraits of Gio. Servants passed us, carrying boxes and suitcases down to the ground floor. One wore a sallet helmet and the others had shirts wrapped around their heads.

Lightning and I peered into the awkwardly shaped room, which had a sloping ceiling. It looked like the den of a sports-obsessed teenager. It smelt of rubber-soled shoes, canvas ingrained with sweat, the wooden grips of polearms smoothed and varnish worn away with use. Twinned rapiers in cases and practice foils in holdalls were stacked along the wall, under a shabby dartboard with a fistful of darts jammed into the bullseye. A beautiful schiavona cut-and-thrust sword with a basket hilt and a sharkskin grip hung in pride of place on the opposite wall.

In a big glass tank at the far end of the room enormous yellow koi carp cruised back and forth, their mirror scales glinting like plate armour. Two servants were indiscriminately stuffing the clutter into boxes and moving it out.

Gio Ami was sitting on the divan, slouched against the wall with despair. A foil with a round guard lay across his knees. His long, old-gold-coloured hair hung in twists to his shoulders, he had a single ring in one ear. His face was somewhat lined and worn, hollow cheeks offset by a broad chin, which now had fair stubble. His bare chest and taut belly showed under his unfastened frock coat. It was of Awian manufacture because it had wide slits up the back that were empty and looked peculiar without wings. His pale blue breeches matched, but laces trailed from his open boots. A number of Diw Harbour Gin bottles lay discarded on the floor.

Gio still had the quality of those who are great at what they do, an intense concentration unknown to most people. His coat's rich embroidery was testament to his affluence, gained through running his fencing *salles d'armes* since the turn of the seventeenth century. Branches of the Ghallain School had been opened in Hacilith and the majority of Plainslands manorships.

Gio had taken the dressing off the wound at his throat, which gaped

33

a little, pink and clean. He must be trying to make it scar. He noticed us standing in the doorway, 'What do we have here? A lonely aristo and a gangland killer.' He looked from Lightning to me. 'Neither high looks of authority nor smart words will make me leave.'

Lightning sighed. 'Gio, if you don't go now, Jant and I will put you out of the Castle bodily.'

Gio spun the hilt of the foil, making the sword roll up and down his thigh. I watched it, well aware that he was still the second-best fencer in the world. His voice slurred slightly. 'Don't call me Gio. I am still Serein.'

'You were outmatched.'

'I have just said goodbye to the Sailor, the Cook and the Master of Horse. All my former friends are abandoning me.' He gestured at the servants. 'And the new Serein will have my rooms, as well as my title and my immortality.'

'We're not deserting you,' I said.

'All immortality belongs to the Emperor,' said Lightning.

Gio gave him a dirty look. 'Yes, you nobles are great at knowing who owns what. None of you will stand by me now I've fallen from grace. Why should I be cast out? It wasn't a fair fight!'

The oldest servant began to pack Gio's combat manuals. 'Bugger off,' said Gio, and threw *The Academy of Defence* accurately at his head. 'The floodlights in the amphitheatre are useless. I demand a retrial.'

I thought for a while. 'You can Challenge him in a year's time, that's a rule of the Castle.'

'Challenge him as a mortal? Try to regain *my* title from *him*? Damn! I still don't understand the move he made. He tricked me with an unorthodox caper,' Gio spat contemptuously. 'No one will want to be instructed in my method now, the techniques I spent my life recording. My school will empty like the court of Rachiswater and then what will I do for a living?'

'Having been in the Circle will bring you fame enough,' I said in a conciliatory tone.

'Fame as a has-been.' Gio pointed the foil, working himself up. 'Why did I ever aspire to such a corrupt little world? Wrenn killed me in that duel! All right – so I might die forty years from now of old age, but he has killed me. Ruined by a non-fraternity fighter, opportunist, someone who never studied! A coarse recruit from a frontier town who wasn't even listed in the top five hundred swordsmen. He never competed in the annual tournaments. I hadn't even heard of the insane kid before he turned up!'

Gio did not realise how hidebound he had become over four

centuries. He had systematised the art of fencing and relied so much on his perfect knowledge that Wrenn's irrational move confused him completely. Immortals who are afraid to risk their lives are as useless against the Insects as those who become lazy or overconfident, solitary or debauched. San's rules for the Circle are wise; fresh blood will take our place if long life causes us to lose our edge.

'You've gained a year and you can try again.'

'A year for what? A year to practise?' He gestured at a wall-chart of footprints coding positions for rapier exercises. 'To shape up, lose weight, gain stamina?' He bent a sinewy arm until the long muscles knotted.

I took Gio's point that clearly he was in the best fitness and still got beaten, but none of us could know what effect the following year of renown and a six-month sea voyage might have on Wrenn's condition. The Castle has lost all Gio's knowledge now, replacing him with someone who is expert but inexperienced. It struck me as wasteful; I wished they could all be saved. I wondered why the Emperor refused to widen the Circle to accommodate more warriors; we would never pose a threat to San because we would never accumulate enough experience to be as wise as him.

I said, 'Gio, the Empire needs you too. We don't want to lose you.'

'The Castle's already rejected me. Though I devoted my entire life to its service . . . I defended Hacilith in the last swarm.' His voice was drained of its usual energy. He would take days to recover from such an intense fight. 'I felt the Circle dropping me. I knelt down and couldn't get up. You bastards. But now I don't feel much different, I suppose because I'm only twelve hours older. I think mortals feel like they're twenty-one years old all their life, though their body gets slower and then they die. I'll provoke a few duels before I die, though. I'm going to send a few of them ahead of me.'

Gio picked up his predecessor's book, *Treatise on the Art of Fencing*, and weighed it thoughtfully in his hand. 'What happened to the Serein before me? When I displaced him from the Circle he went mad and hung himself.' A downward twist of his lips showed what he thought of a Swordsman committing suicide. He spun the book through the air and swore when a servant ducked and it hardly clipped him.

Lightning said, 'We are nowhere near restoring Awia and people already gripe about the necessary austerity. We need your imagination, not to mention your leadership.'

'Saker Micawater, what the rich fuck do I care about Awia now?'

Serein Wrenn, in his fyrd fatigues, hurried into view down the corridor. He made as if to enter the room but Lightning spread his blond wings across the doorway. The youth blinked at him, bewildered.

At the sight of Wrenn, Gio leapt to his feet, the foil loose in his right hand. Wrenn swept his rapier from its scabbard. Great. Now I was trapped between the best and second-best swordsmen in the world.

'No!' said Lightning. 'You may not fight.'

I took the knife from my boot and pressed the button for the blade.

Gio eyed me. 'Nice. A Rhydanne with a flick-knife.'

Lightning said, 'Put it away, Jant.'

'If you think I'm afraid to keep duelling, you're wrong,' Wrenn called.

'Every single year until one of us is dead,' Gio spat.

'You were wide open with that moulinet. You bloody deserved it!'

Lightning repeated, 'You may meet in twelve months. You may not fight now.'

'Step aside, Archer.'

Lightning stared at Gio, arms folded and wings spread.

Wrenn stretched out in a broad ward stance, an action that seemed to say: come on, stab me in the chest.

Gio shook with fury. 'I swear, Archer, get out of my way! Or I'll cut every tendon in your bow arm! I'll have my title back within an hour!'

'Honour demands a respite.'

'I'm mortal, I'm going to die anyway! Where's the honour in that? I've nothing to lose!'

Wrenn watched guardedly through the gap between Lightning and myself. He was calm, in control, just as I am aware of every centimetre of my body when I prepare to fly.

Gio flourished the foil. 'I'll die famous by running you both through!'

'Jant,' Lightning said eventually. 'It looks like we need Tornado's help to close this situation. Go to his room and fetch him; quickly, please.'

I hesitated.

'I can skewer you all on one blade!'

I nodded, ducked past and sprinted away. Gio watched until I reached the stairs and then he threw his foil aside. He pushed past Lightning and Wrenn, head up and haughty eyes averted. I stepped out of his way; he descended the staircase and walked out swinging his arms, across the wet grass of the quadrangle towards the Dace Gate and the Castle's stables.

Lightning exhaled and rubbed his forehead. 'God,' he said. 'Such an worthy adversary.'


Memo
To: Tern
From: Jant. You know, your husband. Tall, cheekbones, black wings . . . Yes, that one.

Tern, darling

Where are you? I wanted to say goodbye. The *Stormy Petrel* sails Friday – Mist has ordered us straight to Awndyn and I doubt I will be coming back. It is bound to sink, and I shall drown. Or be lost, becalmed, and starve. Besides, the sea nourishes monsters far worse than Insects. If you feel the Circle break, think of me, and open the letter I left with Rayne.

NB I borrowed a thousand pounds from the Wrought Restoration Fund. Hope you don't mind. If we return in six months' time, I'll make enough money to pay it back with curios from 'Ata's Island'. Love you. Goodbye.

Jant.

# CHAPTER 4

A shower of sleet fell at dawn, covering the stable courtyard with lumpy, slushy ice. Shallow puddles in its gutters looked grey as laundry water. Darker clouds smeared in the overcast sky above the large square forecourt. The sparrows that infested the eaves and stalls shouted out a dawn chorus. Warm air steamed from three pairs of thoroughbred horses harnessed to a gleaming coach. Lightning's carriage was waiting to carry him and Wrenn to Awndyn. It would take them three days to reach the coast, so they had planned to spend the first night at Eske manor, enjoying the hospitality of Cariama Eske.

There was a clock tower on an arch above the main gate. I landed in front of its peacock-blue dial, which showed eight a.m., and watched Wrenn and Lightning sheltering from the rain inside the nearest stable while their belongings were loaded onto the coach. Mist had said we could bring no more than one sea chest each, but my rucksack and Wrenn's small knapsack were so meagre – since I travel light and Wrenn was poor – that Lightning allowed himself more luggage.

The coachman stooped to check the bits in the mouths of the dapple grey mares and ran the reins through brass rings on the centre bar. His scarf and thick buttoned coat made him look portly. He held the coach door open; Wrenn jumped up and struggled inside. Wrenn obviously didn't know about the steps, which Lightning kicked out from under the polished splashboard. Wrenn settled himself on the seat and removed his woolly liripipe hat. He was obviously feeling self-conscious; I doubted that he had ever been in a coach before. He had changed his clothes – the ones he wore in the ceremony were discarded to show his entrance to a new life. The coachman slammed the door and pulled a leather strap to lower the window. He leaned in, exchanged some words with Lightning, then climbed up to his bench, took the whip in his left hand and flicked the reins. 'Hoh!'

The whole heavy rig rolled forward with the clop of clean hooves, a hiss of water from the wheels. The mares with braided manes shook their heads trying to see round their blinkers. They walked to the gates; I saw their six broad backs, then the dark red shining lacquer of the coach's roof loaded with wooden chests pass beneath me under the arch. The wheels sucked up sleet from the ground, spraying it into the air above them, leaving two tracks of paving clear from slush.

Wrenn twisted round to stare at me through the back window, one elbow on the tan leather. I wished that I could hear their conversation on the journey. Lightning paid Wrenn more attention than he paid me, offering the same time-refined advice. But I wanted to reach Awndyn before the coach did. I jumped off the clock tower.

My wings' muscular biceps, as thick as thighs bunched together, creasing the middle of my back, then separated as I pulled my wings down in the laborious effort of sustained beating. My long wings are pointed and fairly narrow, good for gliding but taking off is as hard as sprinting. I can usually settle into a rhythm that uses less energy but it's still like running a marathon.

I love long-distance journeys; I can stretch out along the route. I relaxed and leaned into the first of the long kilometres. The coach-and-six sounded hollow over the stable's wide drawbridge across the second moat and out of the Castle's complex. They passed the paddocks with steaming dung heaps and soggy ploughed fields, joining the Eske Road and entering the oak forest that comprised most of that manor.

I flexed my wings in and rolled once, twice, risked a third although I fell fifty metres each time. I opened my wings hard against the rushing air. High above the coach I rolled wing over wing, watching the even horizon turn a full three hundred and sixty degrees.

Then I set out for the coast. Diagonal lines of sunlight slanted down, patchily highlighting the level, loamy fields of the plains around the Moren. When flying from manor to manor I find it useful to follow one of the straight military roads that the Castle commanded to be built between towns for the movement of troops. But to fly cross-country I pick a point on the horizon, a notch or a hummock, and head directly towards it. The notches become vales, the hummocks turn into hillsides. When I become tired I fly a more convoluted route to find and climb onto thermals to rest.

At a height of two hundred metres I don't see individual tree tops, just a mass of twigs and pine needles. The slate roofs of the towns are scaly patches that look flat among the forest's green-brown froth. The houses built from local stone were camouflaged in the landscape, and I passed over hunting lodges without seeing them. Towns all seem the same from the air; I hardly distinguished between them. My travels have taught me that people everywhere are intrinsically the same: well-disposed to me as Comet.

The same would not be true for Tris. I considered the events of the last two days as I flew. No one could predict what the Trisian people would make of us; I hoped that I could communicate with them. I was terrified of the hated uncharted ocean. The things that swam and slapped suckers on ships' sides beggared any description – behemoth serpents and sentient giants amassed from the rotting bodies of drowned sailors.

I wondered what to do about Tern. At this very moment she could be stroking Tornado's wingless back, hewn muscles, shorn head, and I had to leave on some damn godforgotten ship! I imagined her sitting on the palm of his hand and he lifts her up to kiss her. Away at sea I was powerless to stop this latest outbreak of her infidelity; it might deepen and then what would I find on my return? Tern married into the Circle through Tornado, myself divorced and having to live next door to my beautiful ex-wife for all eternity?

I knew every landmark – the white fences along the 'racehorse valley' racetracks that Eske is famous for, their stables where destriers are bred. A line of tall poplars by Dace River; further on in the forest smoke straggled from a charcoal burner's shack. I concentrated on keeping the horizon level to fly straight, but in the evening I was grounded by a heavy hailstorm and, annoyingly, had to spend the night in the Plover Inn on the Remige Road. If this was a routine journey I would sleep in the woods because, since I'm Rhydanne, temperatures have to be much below freezing before I start to feel cold.

By the following afternoon I could see the faintly lilac-grey Awndyn downs in the distance. Cobalt manor's hops fields and oast houses dotted the downs; a bowl-shaped pass resolved into the coast road. Finally I crested the last hill – and there was the sea. The grey strip of ocean looked as if it was standing up above the land, ready to crash down onto it.

Every window in Awndyn-on-the-Strand was brassy with the setting sun. The town's roofs slanted in every crazy direction. The manor house stood on a grassed-over rock-and-sand spit jutting out into the sea. It had tiny clustered windows and tall thin octagonal chimneys with diagonal and cross-hatched red brickwork. I glided down through another sleet shower so strong I had to close my eyes against it, and landed on the roof of a fish-and-chip takeaway. I waited till the squall stopped spitting wet snow, then climbed down from the chip shop and walked into town, crossing the shallow, pebbled stream on a mossy humpbacked bridge. The Hacilith–Awndyn canal ran beside it into an enormous system of locks and basins packed with barges.

A creative cosmopolitan atmosphere hung over Awndyn, with a smell of cedarwood shavings and stale scrumpy. It was the only Plainslands town to prosper after the last Insect swarm, profiting from the merchant barges that paid tolls to navigate the locks and carracks with full coffers anchoring in the port. It was well positioned to make use of all their raw materials. Swallow, the musician governor, had encouraged a bohemian community; artists and craftsmen were welcome in the tiny crumbling houses and ivy-shaded galleries. Artisans' slow and friendly workshops overhung the shambling alleys; glass-blowing and marquetry, cloisonné and ceramics, leatherwork, woodturning and lapidary, musical instruments and elegant furniture were crafted there.

I was prospecting for drugs, just as a gold miner follows rules to find deposits. Scolopendium is illegal everywhere except the Plainslands – in Awia the laws have been tight for fifty years and counting; in Hacilith's deprived streets the problem is at its most serious; and at the Lowespass trenches its use is tackled very severely. But centipede fern grows wild in Ladygrace, the sparsely populated foothills of southern Darkling. The governor of Hacilith tried to pay the Neithernor villagers to burn the moorland hillsides and destroy the plants but thankfully they never succumbed to the offer. Scolopendium extracted from the fern fronds flows out of Ladygrace together with more well-known drugs, and addicts' money is sucked back in along the same routes. The ban is almost impossible to enforce.

To find scolopendium in a town look for boundaries, for example the edge between rich and poor districts, or between streets of different trades – where houses begin at the edge of the market or where at night people empty from cafés into clubs. The prospector should investigate places where newly arrived travellers are lingering. Longshoremen with cargoes from Hacilith are the most promising, because a handful of cat hidden in a cabin is worth twice as much as a richly stocked hold. When I was a dealer I witnessed even the most scrupulous merchants give in to greed. I determined not to buy from the pushers at the dockside, but they would only be a couple of links down the chain from one of the more powerful traffickers I know.

Buildings give clues: dirty windows and peeling paint in a rich district, or a tidy house in the middle of a slum. This is because they are houses where business is done. When I'm hooked, I read the signs subconsciously; a sixth sense guides me to a fix.

I walked past clustered half-timbered buildings with warm red brick in herringbone designs. Stonecrop grew out of the walls that were topped with triangular cerulean-blue tiles and bearded with long, grey lichen. The town looked like a grounded sunset.

Following my rules brought me to the quayside. Awndyn harbour was a mass of boats. At low tide they all beached, propped up against each other, and fishermen walked across their wooden decks from harbour wall to sand spit. At full tide they all sailed together, a flotilla of bottle green and white, Awndyn's dolphin insignia leaping on prows and mastheads. As dusk fell, I watched them unloading, passing metres of loose netting in human chains to the jetty, where boys rocked wooden carts on iron wheels back and forth to get them moving on the rails. The boys were paid a penny a half day to shunt the heavy carts to a warehouse where fisherwives unloaded the catch into crates of salt and sawdust.

After dark it began to drizzle sleet. The road was plastered in a thin layer of wet brown mud. I walked along the seafront and passed the Teredo Mill, a tall cider mill with peeling rose-pink window frames, dove-holes in diamond shapes in its ochre-coloured walls. It was roofed with white squares cut from sections of Insect paper. Last harvest's apples had been pressed so the intense sweet smell that hung around the mill in autumn was replaced by the heady reek of fermentation.

A group of young apprentice brewers were sheltering in the underpass where a path ran under the waterwheel's cobbled sluice. The wheel was raised from its millstream and clean water flowed along the conduit above their heads. They were smoking cigarettes after a day's work. One of the promenade street lamps cast my shadow long across the road. The brewers regarded me curiously. The youngest had dyed purple hair, baggy chequered trousers and a black coat that reached the floor. I checked him out for the marks of an addict, drew a blank. Well, I haven't hit gold but I'm very close. We fell into the quiet of mutual examination, until he nudged his friend and bowed. He walked over the road to me. 'Comet?'

'Yes?'

'It is . . . it is you?' He looked back to his friends, who all made 'Go on' motions.

I didn't want their presence to scare away the sort of character I was really looking for. I was about to tell him to get lost but something of my Hacilith self was reflected in him. He didn't know what to say – there was awe in his eyes like tears. His co-workers crowded round with eager expressions. They were a little too well-heeled to be true rebels. 'So you've met the Emperor's Messenger,' I said. 'How can I help you?'

'Did you see the duel between Gio and Wrenn?'

'What's the new Serein like?'

'Tell us the tactic he used!'

'Tell us if he's married,' a girl said. Her lanky body had a passing resemblance to a Rhydanne woman and momentarily I had to control myself.

'I just flew here . . .' I said.

'Is it true there's never been a Swordsman as good as Wrenn?'

I tried, 'I've just returned from Darkling. Let me tell you—'

'I don't believe Wrenn taught himself. He must be a genius!'

'My name's Dunnock,' said the boy with purple hair. 'I study music – in the governor's arty set, but she demands a lot of her circle.'

Wonderful, I thought; other Eszai have the Fourlands' best vying to be trained by them in the Select Fyrd; I attract gangs of disaffected youths. I tried a simple approach. 'Actually the Governor sent me to find a man called Cinna Bawtere. I've been ordered to arrest him. Have you heard of him?'

'What if we have?'

'Why do you want to arrest him?'

I rounded on Dunnock. 'Show me where his lair is these days.'

The brewers, now quiet, ushered me through the underpass. My leather-soled boots squeaked on the tiling; then we turned left on Seething Lane away from the sea, past the puppet-maker's shop and into the artists' quarter.

Shop signs projected above doorways: CROSSBOW CLOCKWORK LTD and FYRD RECRUITMENT LOWESPASS VICTORY HOUSE, APPLEJACK AND FINE TEREDO CALVADOS. Bleak graffiti sporadically decorated the walls between them, declaring, '*Ban the Ballista*' and '¡*Featherbacks go home!*'

The local resentment of Awian refugees was worse than I thought. It made me angry – they weren't to blame for being made homeless by the Insect swarm. In fact, I thought guiltily, the swarm had largely been my fault. I knew that Tern was trying to persuade the Wrought armourers back to continue their vital tradition in her manor. Her blacksmiths worked extremely hard wherever they had been forced to settle.

The Swindlestock Bar was dead centre of the artists' quarter. It was built inside the mouth of a gigantic Insect tunnel, like a grey hood with a rough, deeply-shadowed papier-mâché texture. The tunnel had been cut from the Paperlands and shipped south for building material; the nightclub's front projected from its opening, with two storeys of green-glazed bricks and black beams. Paper curved down to the ground, looking like a huge worm cast. Windows had been cut in it. Outside the door, a sloughed Insect skin hung in an iron gibbet, its six spiked legs sticking out. It was transparent brown and gnarled; it revolved slowly, a dead weight in the sea breeze.

I know some clubs in Awndyn that could be described as meat markets. This was more of a delicatessen. Green light so pale it was almost grey reflected on the water pooled between the cobbles. The vague and eerie light came from cylindrical glass jars by the club's open door – larvae lamps – lanterns full of glow-worm larvae. The doorman picked one up and shook it to make it brighter.

The brewers nodded at the doorman and walked straight in. Inside, the floor was malachite-coloured tiles, the decor ebony with a matt shine. In a deep fireplace sea-driftwood burnt with copper-green sparks. A lone musician up on the stage was salivating into a saxophone. He played exceptionally; he must have been one of Swallow's students. The larvae lamps emphasised his sallow face as he leant across their shifting light. He paused, recognising me, and his eyebrows sprang right into his hairline, then he started up another low, sexy drone, playing his very best as if I was a talent spotter.

The brewers vanished into the press of bodies around the stage. Dunnock turned to me and pointed at the ceiling. 'Check upstairs. They ask to see track marks,' he added, agitated. 'You're not wearing a sword.'

I raised a hand to calm him. 'I don't need a sword to arrest the likes of Bawtere.'

'Wow. They're never going to believe this back at the vats.'

'Keep it a secret!' I said. I elbowed through the dancers' slow jazz wave to the stairs. They creaked as I climbed them. At the top, a bullseye lantern swung in front of my face, startling me, and a voice rasped, 'Oo's that? One for Cinna?'

'Yes,' I said.

'Oo is it?'

'His boss.' I deliberately looked straight at the lantern because I know that my Rhydanne eyes reflect. Cinna's flunky must have seen them shine as two flat gold discs. His chuckle stopped abruptly.

'All right, Comet,' he whispered. 'You want t'see Cinna?'

'Of course,' I said.

'Just . . . wait a minute, please . . . Shit, a fucking immortal . . . He's a fucking immortal . . .' The voice trailed off, and then returned. 'Come through, Comet.'

He beckoned me along the dingy corridor, then through a beautiful door inset with opal to a big black and white room. In the middle of the square chamber stood a vast carved table. Its rectilinear designs were echoed on printed six-panel paper screens that folded like concertinas along the dim walls.

Cinna Bawtere had no friends, only collaborators. He was fat but suave, with a receding hairline and flabby, incandescently red lips like a couple of cod fish lying in the bottom of a boat. He had a duelling scar like a dimple by his mouth, suggesting that long ago his skin hadn't been pasty, his belly protruding and his chin double. But these days Cinna could get out of breath playing dominoes. People worked for him now, and his big hands had lost all the cuts and calluses they had when he was a sailor. He was a tactless, feckless, reckless individual with an ego the size of Awia and a conscience the size of a boiled sweet. Cinna's extras included a cutting-edge understanding of chemistry as it applied to narcotics, and of the law and how to break it. His wings were speckled; every fifth feather had been bleached. He wore new blue jeans and a patterned cherry silk dressing gown. Like so many ugly men, he was fond of good clothes.

I sat in an engraved chair and hooked my wings over the low back. 'How great a sense of hearing do the walls have?'

'It's all right. We're totally alone.' Cinna gave me a hard stare from the other side of the table. Eventually he said, 'You haven't visited for a long time, Comet.'

'Four years isn't a long time to me.'

He creased into his chair. 'By god, and you look Just The Same as you did when I first saw you, twenty years back.' He gave a little smile. 'I thought you'd forgotten me, because I hadn't heard any word since the Battle Of Awndyn.'

'So how is business?'

Cinna raised his hands to indicate the shadowy room. 'As good as you see it.'

'Cinna, I'm here to tell you that I won't turn a blind eye to your dealing any longer.'

His round shoulders sagged. He scooped a packet of cigarettes from the table, poked one out and lit it. 'I'd been expecting this. So it's finished? The game's over?'

'If you continue and you're caught, you can't invoke my name; I won't help you. If you keep selling contraband to Mist's sailors and she complains to me, the next time you see an Eszai he'll be with a fyrd guard to seize you.'

'Now, Jant, how disappointing after all this time!'

I shrugged. 'I want you to go back to legitimate trade. Why not?'

Cinna placed both hands flat on his polished table. 'Because it's Not That Easy! This latest "paper tax" from the Castle caused an uproar in Hacilith. You should hear the merchants muttering. All the money's sent to Awia.'

'You know there's a worthwhile cause. We need to break down the Insects' Paperlands there.'

'Well, why can't that kingdom look after itself?'

'For god's sake, they're doing all they can. Awia will repay its debts in full; you mortals just can't see the long term.'

'Oh, I understand,' said Cinna. 'But I hope Eszai realise how quickly Plainslanders forget Insects once the immediate threat cools off.'

'Look, you have to stop dealing. In Hacilith now, the punishment for pushing cat is death. I've seen dealers broken on the wheel. In Awia they just jail them for life.'

He nodded. 'Well, ergot pastilles are all the kids want these days. They have no taste.' He wallowed over to a side table where there was a decanter of port and some crystal glasses. He poured one for me.

'To the Emperor,' I said, and drank.

He topped up my glass. 'And another toast. To all the kids who ever sang protest songs against the old king's draft.'

I put the glass down. 'It's the Empire's war,' I said evenly. 'Let's talk business, not nostalgia. I know how you feel about the past but I have to obey the Emperor's command.'

'You singled me out and saved me because I was an Independent, Deregulated Pharmaceutical Retailer,' he said. It was true; I wanted a dealer and I found Cinna trustworthy, who owed me his life and his livelihood. Once I got my fingers round the edges of his ego, he was a business partner more loyal than a fyrd captain. 'Do you know it's twenty years ago almost to the day, when you appeared with a handful of draft notices,' he continued. Worry lines on his forehead came and went as he talked. 'Nailed on the lifeboat house door – lists of families to contribute to Tornado's division. My mother wanted to hide us but I knew how relentless you were. She showed us a trapdoor to the coal cellar, but, god-who-left-us, what use is that against someone who knows every Trick In The Book?'

I swirled beeswing in the glass, embarrassed on his behalf that he would rather hide than fight.

'You took my brother. He was killed at Lowespass. All they could find of him to bury was a handful of feathers; the Insects cemented the rest into their Wall.'

'Many people die in Lowespass.'

Cinna grimaced and picked at one of the spots around his mouth. 'Jant, I remember we had to line up in the courtyard – you were there checking names off on a list. You looked younger than me and I hated you, the way schoolkids hate swots. You looked as calm as a merchant checking sacks of corn, a buyer at a livestock market—'

'As if I'd done it a thousand times before.'

'Yeah. It made me want to strangle you, and you looked so frail I was sure I could. My brother knew what I was thinking; he elbowed me in the ribs and said Comet's Two Hundred Years Old! Knowing that I wouldn't stand a chance. Then he climbed onto the cart bench with the rest of the stevedores and that was the last I ever saw of him. Taken away to the General Fyrd. Every one of the five hundred men in his morai were slaughtered.

'Well now I've witnessed Insects flatten Awndyn I can understand why we need to keep the Front – but back then I'd never seen one and it took me fifteen years to recover. Your frozen age is so misleading, it makes us mortals underestimate you. You can run faster than a deer, but you just looked like a Bloody College Kid.

'We know the effect scolopendium has on the people who trade it, let alone the users. I haven't sought friendship or lovers – just money – thinking that at any second the governor's fyrd could snatch me away.'

I glanced up from the mediocre port. Cinna was not known to be a man of great imagination. 'What are your plans?' I asked. I knew he would find it hard to relinquish his beautiful suite. He had become too much of a *bon viveur*. He was too fat to return to life as a sailor, honest or otherwise. 'Are you holding any now?'

'I've a quarter kilo of Galt White to sell, and that will be The Last Deal. Maybe.'

'Let me take it off your hands.'

'Oh ho!' He pointed a finger over the top of his wine glass. 'I thought there was another reason for this visit! Once an addict, always an addict!'

'That's not true, Cinna. Besides, it's not for my use.'

'Well, I don't know anybody else who buys in quarter-k quantities. Not even Lady Lanare when she's poisoning her whole family.'

'Are you selling or not?'

Cinna chortled.

'It'll be the last time I ever buy cat.'

Cinna chortled with wicked glee.

He unlocked a panel in the wall and scooped out a large white paper envelope. He gave it a shake to settle its contents, then pushed it to me across the table.

I rubbed it, feeling the fine powder inside. 'Go first,' I said.

He held his palms up. 'You know I don't do that. I can't stand the hallucinations.'

'This time you do.'

He dipped his finger in it. 'Damn you, Eszai.'

I knew that my tolerance would have decreased, so I took just the edge of a fingernail full and licked it. It spread on my tongue, tasted numb, slightly grassy with a crystalline metal-salt edge. This was snap-condensed. Fuck, it was good. I closed my eyes in shame as I realised what I'd done. It was five long years since I last tasted scolopendium.

'You look like the Archer tasting fine wines. It's Pure As Darkling Snow,' he assured me, hands wide in a ham actor's gesture. 'We make it using your technique, no one else can match the quality.'

'Yes, this will help. At least until we reach the island,' I said. Cinna gave me an odd look. I explained rapidly, 'No, not Grass Isle, I mean Tris. Mist told us a strange tale of a new island three months' east of Awndyn. She tells of a fascinating culture and mouth-watering fruit like, like apples that look like pine cones. Six months' leave from the Castle! Unless it's some kind of mirage caused by sailors drinking their own piss. Think what it means, and not just for bored Eszai, for everyone! . . . But, knowing Ata, we won't make it out of the bay before something awful happens.'

I huffed out a breath and stood up. The weight of the envelope seemed correct. I had a feel for it, like a long-time card sharp knows by touch how many cards are in a deck. I dropped it in to my satchel and reached for Cinna's packet of cigarettes, slid them towards me and pocketed them too. 'Thanks. Now may I have a lantern? I'm needed back at the manor house.'

'Ah-ah. That's a thousand pounds please, Comet. And unfortunately cheques drawn on the defunct Bank of Wrought are not welcome at Bawtere Unlimited Imports.'

I haggled down this outrageous price, that would only be right for Lowespass, to a more reasonable eight hundred and eighty pounds. I counted out nine hundred from my wallet and Cinna swept the money away.

I noticed that, out of the pound coins he gave me for change, the majority were Awian, embossed with Tanager's swan. From the other three of the Fourlands' mints, there was only one each with the Summerday scallop shell and Hacilith fist, and a couple of the Eske mint's 'daffodils'. Currency was supposed to be produced at the same rate throughout the Fourlands, as advised by the Castle. I hoped that Awia hadn't responded to its adversity by minting more money. It would be a typical Zascai way of thinking, a short-term solution that would just drag Awia further into the mire.

Cinna's bristle-chinned henchman returned with the bullseye lantern, muttering, 'Thought Rhydanne could see in t' dark.'

Cinna is one of the few dealers I know who has not ended up using. They take to it because drug-dealing is so wrong and they find that scolopendium is a very tempting, potent salve for all misdemeanours and open emotional wounds. However, Cinna had always stayed at the money-worshipping stage, a bit like myself when I lived in Hacilith. He was from one of the Morenzian villages and had worked hard to escape. I didn't blame him; the Morenzian industries, law courts and markets were all in the city. The intellect of the country was leached by Hacilith's University and its Moren Grand Theatre monopolised the fame, leaving the surrounding villages lacklustre and dull.

Cinna knew that everything he is or owns he has built himself on a precarious base. He is always waiting for the tiny push from an Eszai or governor that will send the whole card tower tumbling back into the dirt. 'Taking cat is a waste of all-too-precious time,' he said. He held the door open for me and added, 'But I have thought what immortality truly means, Jant. I'd do drugs too.'

I left the nightclub, crossed Seething Lane and went down a couple of slippery steps onto the hard expanse of the beach. The breeze blew stronger and colder here than in the sheltered town. I left no prints on the rippled wet sand. I won't get addicted again, I told myself; this is just casual use. The empty ocean was a sucking black space; there were no lights out there. I swung my lantern but it only just illuminated the lapping water's edge.

Far beyond the harbour mouth an obscure profile merged with the night, a motionless hulk like a premonition. It must be the *Stormy Petrel*. By god it was a huge ship.

I passed the quay, the only part of town that the governor bothered to maintain properly. Small vessels were roped together across the harbour mouth, each one bore a swinging lamp. Their yellow arc reflected in the gentle ripples; they made a silent blockade. A succession of boats was rowing out towards the *Stormy Petrel* from the quay. I dimly saw a man in each, straining at the oars. Every boat was stacked with barrels; the last stocks of fresh water were being loaded. Mist's night workers on the jetty stooped and rolled kegs, muttering in a smuggler's undertone. The first rowing boat blurred into darkness but I still heard with dread the rhythmic splashes of its oars distorted by the breeze. The rower gave a shout; at his familiar voice a passage opened through the blockade.

Mist had spread the word that this voyage of discovery was no different from the others she had attempted, but if you compared the current level of secrecy to the previous expeditions you would draw a very different conclusion.

# CHAPTER 5

The following day, the subculture of Awndyn was invisible in the bright winter sunlight. The black and amber crosstrees and crow's-nests of fishing cogs anchored in the harbour protruded above the houses as if the rooftops had masts. The harbour master's office had sculptures of caravels in shining bronze on its tower tops, complete with wire rigging.

I met Lightning and Serein Wrenn at the quayside. They were watching the procession of boats still plying out to a deep channel called Carrack's Reach where the tall ships were anchored. A crowd had gathered on the promenade. The air was cold but a glorious sun beat down, flattening the waves to translucent ripples that lapped up inside the harbour wall, hardly moving its heavy sheaves of green-brown bladderwrack.

Wrenn and the Archer descended to a rowing boat that was stowed with our belongings. Wrenn sat upright on the plank bench with his scabbarded rapier and sword belt gripped between his knees. Lightning leant on the gunwale, trailing his fingers in the water, with a distant smile on his woodcut face. He carried a bow and a quiver of exquisite arrows, and the circlet around his short hair glinted in a most annoying way.

I sprinted along the jetty, wings half-open to build up airspeed. I ran faster and faster still, towards the lighthouse at the end. I passed it, reached top speed; the jetty ended, I jumped off into the air. My wings met below me, I swept them up till the primary feather tips touched.

I flew over the waterfront that was lined with several hundred people. Some ducked, swearing. They had a glimpse of my boot soles and ice axe buckled across my waist. I heard their murmur of envy ripple like waves.

I leant with my wings held up in a V-shape to circle tightly, and began to rise on a weak thermal above the chaotic roofs. I reached the height of the buff sandstone cliffs and soared above, seeing their grassy tops. Then I turned out towards the ships; the sea's surface sped beneath me. I would miss Awndyn's homeliness. I had taken a pinch of scolopendium with breakfast and as a result I was less afraid of the ocean. When you're intoxicated, the balance changes between all the facets of your personality, making a different character. I was eager for Tris.

A group of people proceeded along the rough stone jetty. From high above I mostly saw their heads. The woman with a walking stick had long red hair over a green shawl held tightly closed; it was Governor Swallow, surrounded by her attendants. They stopped at the foot of the lighthouse and looked out to sea. Swallow began to sing. She keened, she swelled the dirge with all the force of her opera voice. The wind gusted the melody up to me; clear and high, it slid over eerie minor notes that prickled my skin. Her melancholy lament rose past the crowded quay, past the rowing boats to the caravels. The rowers heard it. Lightning heard it and looked back. The breeze blew it to Tris. I didn't know why she sang a dirge, but it seemed apt.

Outside the harbour, the boats began to churn from side to side. At least I don't have to sit in one of those little tubs. Colourful caravels lay at anchor, scattered some distance apart. As I gained height and my viewpoint widened I saw around thirty – like brightly painted models, some with windmills on deck to wind winches, some drab and barnacled, some with men sitting in the complicated cat's cradles of their rigging, all lashed to buoys with flags atop, and streamed out in the same direction by the flowing tide.

The fleet was a sober reminder of Mist Ata's talent. Her patience and will power could conquer the world. In the fifteenth century, caravels were developed from ungainly merchants' carracks, although since that time they had undergone many improvements. San recognised their use for bringing supplies and troops to the Insect Front, so he made a place in the Circle for a Sailor and held a competition that Ata's predecessor won. The first Sailor immediately tried to deter Challenges by forbidding any Zascai company to build caravels. It was a plan that the Emperor certainly didn't condone. Ata knew it, and ignored the ban. For her first Challenge in fourteen-fifteen she made caravels in sections, in Hacilith where the Sailor couldn't observe them. She had them dragged overland on a road she commissioned to be built, to a secret assembly yard made for the purpose at the coast. She sailed her new ships cockily around Grass Isle – their sudden appearance frightened her predecessor. That's the kind of determination Ata has, and joining the Circle had not affected her admirable ambition. She planted vast forests to grow elm and oak for future ships.

The *Stormy Petrel* was by far the largest caravel, sixty metres in length. No surface was left undecorated. At her rear was a high aft castle, painted red and spiralled with gold curlicues. The forecastle at her bow was slightly smaller, and between them was a low deck with the largest of her four masts. The black hull was very rounded, its sides slanted in steeply, giving her a teardrop shape when seen end-on. *Stormy Petrel*'s figurehead was a muscular young man with a folded breechclout. Above him projected a square prow that was heavily decorated with scarlet zigzags and the Castle's sun. A varnished spar jutted from it like a tusk, and at the waterline five metres below the prow a taut anchor cable ran from its port. The foremost part of the deck was a sort of promontory with cross-planking through which I saw the waves.

The Sailor must seriously want to impress the islanders with the Empire's ingenuity and riches. *Stormy Petrel* inspired confidence in me, too: Mist was pragmatic, so if she had spent money on decoration, the rest of the ship must be sound and formidable. She would be as trustworthy as the best Sailor in the world could make her.

A narrow balcony ran the *Petrel*'s length on both sides, three metres above the waterline. Baroque woodcarving clustered around the stern, picked out in the Castle's colours, red and yellow. The vertical dimensions of the fixed lanterns were tilted to the rear, and the entire top of the aft castle slanted backwards, so the *Petrel* looked like she was racing along even when she was sitting still. The diamond-leaded stern windows were adorned with ruby-stained glass sunbursts. The sun-in-splendour formed a sumptuous centrepiece below them, covered in dazzling gold foil. It scintillated with sunlight reflected from the waves.

Banners twined from the masthead, spinning on their cords like kites. Mist's plain white pennant was the longest. I also recognised the argent swan of Queen Tanager, and Cyan Peregrine's sleeping falcon. There was the black plough insignia of Eske manor, Shivel's silver star, and Fescue manor's crest of three sausages on a spike. Carniss manor must have sent funding too, because its flag was there, a black crescent pierced by an arrow. One hundred years ago I told a Rhydanne girl called Shira Dellin that she had just as much chance of driving the Awian settlers from the lower slopes of Darkling as she had of hitting the moon with an arrow. The settlers founded the manor of Carniss and they immediately took that image for their badge, which made it even more painful when they proved me right.

I made a controlled descent between the first mast and mainmast, and dropped with a hollow thud onto the deck. I settled my wings and folded them. Cinna's scolopendium was so good I couldn't feel them ache at all.

Lightning and Wrenn climbed aboard and joined Mist by the wheel. Wrenn grinned uncontrollably. He was brimming with excitement. Sailors began to stow the flags. Mist called, 'Make sail! Half-deck hands below for the capstan. Brace full the foresails! Send order, if you please, to Master Fulmer on the *Melowne*; we shall be underway . . . Welcome to the ocean, Serein,' she added.

With the *Melowne* behind us, we slipped past the ships in Carrack's Reach, black barrel buoys on our left side. An Awian racing yacht called the *Swift Shag* ran close to escort us; her bell rang in salute. 'They're wishing us luck!' I waved. I was completely high on the fact I wasn't afraid.

Ata leant on the wheel. 'How are you, Jant?'

'Yeah. Uh-huh.' I was staring at the carved mascle emblem on the bow of our sister ship. The *Melowne* was painted in the colours of Micawater, dark blue and white lozenges; she carried so much ornament she looked as if she had been decorated with the fittings from a bankrupt brothel.

'Tell me, what day is it today?' Ata asked.

'Mmm.'

'Let me see your eyes.'

I took off my sunglasses and looked at her. 'Well, OK,' she said eventually, but with some doubt.

The *Melowne* flew all the canvas she could, to match our pace and kept behind us on the right. Lightning didn't greet me, being deep in conversation with the Swordsman. He pointed to the great blue wedding cake of a caravel. 'She's named after my sister. Little Melowne . . .'

'Yeah,' I said. I leant over the railing and noticed that no two wave peaks were ever the same shape.

'She was the youngest of my family,' Lightning began. 'The youngest of nine. She died when she was only six years old.'

'That's a great shame,' Wrenn said.

'Oh, I'm all right. I got over it around the turn of the first millennium,' Lightning said staunchly. I heard that in the year one thousand, through the use of many economic pressures, he eventually managed to run the Avernwater dynasty into the ground and turn their manor back into parkland.

'It was a long time ago, you understand,' he said quietly. 'Melowne was the youngest of my family; she was full of life, happy all the time. My second-eldest brother, Gyr, was exceptionally fond of her. He tended to be morose and she brought out the life in him.

'They were playing, one morning in midsummer, while we prepared to celebrate godsloss day. A flowery parade headed by the July Queen came towards us down the avenue and the young maiden playing Queen was about to pass in front of the palace. People lined the streets to cheer her. Inside the palace we wanted a good view, so all us children ran up to the top floor. I found a roof window. Melowne and Gyr were just below me, out on the parapet. Melowne had daisy chains around her head and in the buckles of her shoes. She leaned right out over the balustrade as the procession passed below and he held the back of her dress. She was laughing with delight, pointing at the chariots and kicking her feet. She kicked Gyr under the chin accidentally and, in shock, he dropped her. I just saw her vanish.' Lightning pointed down over the railing.

'That's terrible.'

He nodded slowly. 'My little sister's death caused an uproar. Nothing was the same after that. My brothers hated Gyr . . . and I did too. He became enraged and silent; eventually he left us to found a new manor at Avern. I don't think I ever forgave him.'

I paced across to Mist in the hope of less sentimental talk. She watched the supply ship carefully before relinquishing the wheel to her second-in-command. I think she had appointed her sons and daughters to all the officers' positions. 'Gentlemen,' she said, 'let me show you your cabins.'

Mist explained that the *Stormy Petrel* had five levels, including the open-air decks and topcastle. The hold was the largest, where pinnace boats for exploration were carried in a dismantled state, and at the stern, an animal pen full of ruddy, bright-eyed chickens. We climbed down the hatch to the living deck, which was above the waterline and had small, sunburst-painted shutters from bow to stern. Every sailor had just forty centimetres by two metres' length to sling his or her hammock. I marvelled that Awians could force themselves into such a claustrophobic space. Rather than their leafy towns that nestled in countryside, and their small families in roomy houses, here feather-back men were crammed together without enough space to spread a wing. Mist's cabin cut into their quarters at the stern and extended into the deck above; I could almost stand upright in it. She had a bedroom and a study that doubled as a dining room, with a polished mahogany table quite incongruous on the ship. It seemed that she intended the *Petrel* to be her manor house.

Back above, she said, 'Jant, you have the cabin under the poop deck.' She opened a door onto an empty compartment with a sloping floor, one metre wide by two long, and a metre high. One hinged shelf was folded back against the wall above a hook for a hammock. Was I expected to fit in there?

'It's a fucking closet,' I said.

'I swear, it's the most luxurious passenger accommodation we have! Well, if you want to sleep outside, feel free . . . Come on, Lightning, let me show you the fo'c'sle.'

At least my cabin was furthest from the waves. I could lean out of the porthole and judge the level of water against the planks of the hull to determine how fast we were sinking. It had the best view, fresh air, and I could fly from the deck above. The motion of the waves swayed my cabin the most but that didn't bother me. I was anxious to be rid of Mist's smiling face so I folded myself into the tiny wooden box. What the fuck was I doing here?

Once noticed, the ship's movement was relentless. I could still fly home, but then I would have to face the Emperor. I was stranded between two terrible eventualities. I sat cross-legged, elbows on knees, head in hands, fingers through my black hair like a waterfall.

Footsteps boomed up and down the tilted ladders between decks and above me. Timbers creaked. On second thoughts, *Petrel* seemed extremely flimsy. The sailors adjusted something, the floor righted and, even-keel, she began to gather speed.

I shuffled further into the cabin, bolted the door and opened my razor. I started to divide up my quarter-kilo hoard of cat. I tipped out the powder on a book cover, cut it and made paper wraps of roughly a gram apiece. Why did I buy so much scolopendium? So that Cinna couldn't sell it to his victims? No, because I need enough to stay high for the whole voyage. With an ex-addict's ingenuity I hid the paper wraps in every possible niche, wherever they were concealed from view. I wedged them in the ceiling joists and between the floorboards. I taped them to the underside of the shelf, packed them into the lantern and the squat candlestick. I concealed wraps between the pages of books, in the whetstone pocket of my knife scabbard. I even sewed them into my coat lining.

An hour later I still had two hundred grams left in the envelope, enough to poison the entire crew of both caravels. I tipped a fingernail-full of cat into a beaker of white wine. It touched and dissolved like melting snow. I cut a line on the book cover and snorted it. My jaw sparkled. I threw the porthole open and threw up, monumentally, down the *Petrel*'s side.

Then I returned to the poop deck, dazzled by brightness. The fresh wind made me shudder. The mainland was ridiculously small and featureless – I could see the entire Cobalt coast, a pale green line edge-to-edge of the horizon, already turning blue. The Awndyn cliffs were a faint smudge less than half a centimetre high. In every other direction spread the indistinguishable ocean. I didn't want to look at it. 'It's as if we can see the whole east coast,' I said to Mist.

She laughed and shook her head. 'Say goodbye to it, Jant.'

I could fly back even now. I leant over the stern and stretched my wings to feel the wind under them.

'This is something you've never seen before?' The Archer asked calmly.

'It's horrible.' I hissed a breath. 'It's a travesty.' I always have to work in their world. Lightning has visited the mountains on adventurous expeditions and once when I needed help; but I defy any of them to trek to the high plateaux. I cross boundaries more vertiginous and worlds far more precarious than this, I told myself, but I didn't feel at all reassured. 'Are we in water deep enough to be attacked by sea monsters?'

Mist tutted. 'Jant, there is no such thing as a sea monster. I have circumnavigated the Fourlands. I have sailed past this longitude for six hundred years, so you can absolutely take my word for it. Monsters are just the tales of drunk, braggart harpooners. You might see a whale spouting in the distance, but that's about all.'

I sipped my doctored wine and watched the *Stormy Petrel*'s green wake curve out like lace from a loom. The horizon receded; I expected a clap of thunder or something when it merged with the haze and vanished. I stared in that direction for long after, memorising the position. In an hour's time *Petrel* would carry me too far to fly home.

I turned away from the railing. I had been looking out to sea for so long the size and bustle of the ship surprised me. My hands were weak, my glass was empty. I took a step and the deck tilted. Shit, if the others see my condition they are definitely going to know. I must reach my cabin, lock door, sleep it off. I edged along the railing to the top of the ladder, and felt about with one foot for the rungs. I can step down, it isn't so far.

I crashed heavily onto the half deck, shook my wings and arms to locate them. Yes, of course the floor is bloody tipping, I told myself; we're on a sodding ship. I clawed the cabin open, threw my coat down but it slid towards the door. I have taken too much. But it feels so good, oh god it feels good. The buzz and dislocation comes on slow when I drink cat. So I forget to be careful and I always drink too fucking much. It'll peak soon, I hope. I was clever to return to the cabin while I still could. Now there's no coast only sea no land to land on only sea. We must trust our memories that the Empire still exists.

I've taken too much. I lay on my quilt, curled up, eyes closed – can't observe the outside world any more, too much going on out there. Thoughts rush round my mind and cat begins to break them down to their constituent cycles. Consciousness is circular. Thoughts come in cycles. There are big, slow, infrequent cycles and fast rings repeat inside them. Words are made when sound cycles click the right combination. Consciousness is circular; thoughts come in cycles. There are big— It's happening to me! I think I'm dying. Don't worry, I won't die; this has happened before. I hate it when this happens. I'm probably going to Shift. And I haven't been to Epsilon for years. Epsilon. Words are made when sound cycles click the right combination. Oh, no, it's starting to happen – am I dying? Don't worry, I won't die; this has happened before. God, I hate it when this happens. I'm probably going to Shift. And I haven't been to Epsilon for years. Probably going to Shift. Last time, I almost died. Rayne said I was dying. Don't worry, I won't die. This has happened before. I hate it when this happens (it's happening to me; it's happening to me). I'm going to Shift. And I haven't been to Epsilon for years. Consciousness is circular; thoughts come in cycles. Haven't I just thought this? Words are made when sound cycles click the right combination (—to me, it's happening to me, it's happening to—) What is? This feeling of dying. Don't worry, I won't die, this has happened before. Words are made when sound cycles. God, I hate it when this happens. I'm probably going to Shift. And I haven't been to Epsilon for years (—me, it's happening to me, it's happ—) I think I just thought that (—ening to me, it's happening to me, it's happening to—) oo to me ahp ap hap happening oo fu tu to me see words are made when words are made words worr dd hut hur lur wur wor words are ay ma may dde words are made words are made ugh dug dur wer wur words arr are geh neh ney ay made words are made ur err are arr . . . ar . . . r

. . .

Shouts assailed from all sides and before me were market stalls running into stalls out to where the horizon met the orange sky. Constant Shoppers hustled and bustled, a little boy selling postcards of

Epsilon darted through the crowd. I recognised the Squantum Plaza bazaar.

I sat on the pavement cross-legged and concentrated, changing my appearance from just a pencil sketch of Jant to something more solid that looked like me, with a few improvements.

Having brightened myself up, I staggered to my feet. I swore I would never come back here and now I've broken my promise again. A small grey cloud appeared above my head and began to rain on me. 'All right,' I told it, waving my hands. 'All right! I'm not that depressed!' The cloud showered a few more desultory drops and dissipated.

There were market stalls of mildewed books, cloth and raffia, cakes and beer. Horse brasses, porcelain, thousands of gemstones spilled on velvet. Flat green grief toads sang mournfully in glass tanks. Stalls sold ancient sea-krait scales, barometz root – looks like a sheep but tastes like turnip – trained falcons apparently 'the best hunters in the Scarlet Steppe' and confused stacks of bamboo crates full of finches that cheeped and fluttered.

There were bonsai ents – little gnarled trees with root-legs stumbling around on a polished tray. A marsh gibbon capered on a stall's canopy. It had pale green silky fur and round intelligent eyes; its back legs ended in duck feet. I couldn't help laughing at it. The monkey pulled its top lip back in a bubblegum-pink grimace.

Now that I was trapped here for an uncertain length of time, I decided to enjoy myself. I went looking for the pair of golden shears that was the sign of the Bullock's Bollocks bar. It was no easy task because Epsilon changes constantly.

A crowd of nasnas with tour guides wended their way between the tables. Nasnas are men with one arm and one leg each. The two nearest me were heavy-set columns of flesh, and they supported each other, hopping along in a pair. The arm of each man projected from the middle of his chest, waving like a trunk. I studied their faces and caught my breath. Each had a big, single eye directly above his nose, all his features in a vertical line, a wide mouth and rough skin. The men turned their great round eyes on me as they passed. Their guide announced, 'This is the edge of the Tine's Quarter. Take special care on the road please . . . And if you see any Tine, *run*. Well, hop *quickly*.'

Behind the nearest stall sat a big, bear-like animal. Its fur was pure black and white splodges. Backward-pointing spines grew round its neck and down its back. The beast shook itself and its quills clattered. Its head was bowed; it looked so hunched and miserable that I stopped, intending to buy it and set it free. The stall holder was a greasy man with a glass eye. A parrodi perched on his shoulder, with colourful ruffled feathers. It rolled its eyes and copied his every gesture.

The stall holder saw that I was a tourist and delightedly shook the bear's chain. 'A porcupanda, sir! A highly prized delicacy. Not five hundred pounds, not four hundred pounds. Three hundred pounds to you only, sir!'

'To you only, sir,' drawled the parrodi.

I concentrated and imagined the right amount of money in the pocket of my suit. I paid the stall holder and freed the porcupanda. When I patted its head, it licked my hand then bounded away.

I walked on, to the central fountain built with stinguish technology out of solidified water. White cement could be seen between the transparent blocks. It made a wonderful three-dimensional matrix with beams of sunlight dancing through, cast by the liquid water lapping inside the fountain. A couple of wet thylacines barked and played in the great jets that fell like diamonds.

A bouquet of chloryll courtesans lounged beside the pool. The chloryll co-cultivate this quarter of the city. Their extreme beauty reminded me of Tern, slight and exquisite; their skin was ebony black. One had tiny fruits growing in her shining hair, piled on top of her head. Her floor-length dress rustled, it was made of living foliage; here and there tiny pink roses budded among the leaves. Vines wrapped around her arms like long net gloves. Behind her hung a trail of coiling tendrils, fronds and variegated ferns. These fruiting bodies were great to sleep with, but instead I wanted to have a good look around Epsilon after so long away.

The market continued into the Tine's Quarter, where a wide road paved with eighteen-carat gold formed one side of the market square. A shiny building with smooth pillars housed four tall rectangular machines that emitted a low vibration. The salt-copper, watery-rotten smell of the Tine's red liquid was thick in the air. A sign hung above the machines read:

TINE AUTOMOBILES, THE HEART OF MOTORING
**Driving the arteries of Epsilon, you can't beat the Carotid Café.
All tastes catered for: blood, beer, coffee. Next: ten miles.**

A girl sat in a low carriage underneath the sign. It was made of gold, so it must be of Tine manufacture. It was moulded in feminine curves, with bulging panels over its small, spoked wheels, doors as in a roofless coach but an upright glass window fixed at the front. It had no shaft for horses.

I vaguely recognised the girl inside. She waved. 'Hey, winged boy! Jant! Remember me from court? I was the Shark!'

'Tarragon!'

'Come over. Don't worry about the Tine.' A Tine was attending to her car. He was a carnivore like all his species, three metres tall, bursting with muscle. He was naked except for a loincloth, his sky-blue skin scarred and tattooed. His blank eyes were pupil-less, uniform blue. His eyebrows were two pierced rows of steel rings: the Superciliary Sect. I thought that he could live for a week on the meat stuck between his sail-needle teeth. His taloned hands held a black rubber tube which snaked down and disappeared under the ground. He was pumping the red liquid into Tarragon's gold automobile.

The whole floor hummed. I trod carefully, ready to sprint at any time. I kept Tarragon between myself and the growling attendant, but Tarragon was a Shark, or rather the Shift projection of a Shark, and she was just as dangerous.

Tarragon grinned with sharp teeth. Fins emerged from the middle of her back and the sides of her body. With a look of concentration she mastered her shape transformation so they retracted and her skin smoothed. She briefly became a beautiful woman rather than a Shark.

'Do you like my shape?' she said. 'I find that air-breathers are nicer and more obliging to pretty young girls.' Then, lost in thought, the changes gradually reasserted themselves, so that I was confronted with the difficult challenge of talking to a frothy blonde teenager in a strapless dress, with three rows of triangular teeth. Parallel slashes appeared in her neck; deep gills like black ribbons. They widened, inhaled, and vanished.

She concentrated on improving the shiny crimson dress wrapped round her body. A furry phlogista stole draped her shoulders. Phlogistas are rare and expensive; they're long, like mink, but dark red in colour with deep, sumptuous fur. It had a little lion's head, but instead of a mane its face was framed by a ring of fleshy petals. This feline flower-face formed the clasp of her stole, and its yellow glass eyes glittered. Phlogistas are resistant to fire; to clean a fur you place it in flames.

I offered Tarragon my hand, but she looked at it as if it was her favourite sandwich. 'You can touch the car, you know,' she said.

I surveyed the vehicle. 'It's not alive?'

'No, Jant. It's not alive . . . *Parts* of it are alive.'

It was made of a thin sheet of pure gold, and the complicated fittings inside were gold, too: a wheel where Tarragon rested her delicate hands, and a dial that looked like a clock face but wasn't.

'The car won't hurt you,' she said carefully. 'But keep clear of the Tine. They invented these sports cars to do their hunting and to make religious sacrifices, injuring victims in interesting ways for the purpose of their worship. They're keen on fast, fast cars, the faster the better, like this rocket; the best that meat can buy. To build speedy cars they need good athletes. You are an athlete, aren't you?'

I nodded.

'Tine will do anything to lay their hands on a runner as excellent as you. If they knew about Rhydanne you would already be dead. They need athletes, that's what makes these babies go,' she said, tapping a flipper lovingly on the steering wheel. 'Take a look.'

She pressed a button and a trapdoor popped open at the front of the vehicle. I sloped round and peered inside.

Lying under the bonnet, a mass of green-purple guts quivered and heaved. Clear rubber tubes ran red liquid round them. They stank of ripe meat. Diagonally across the centre were six big hearts, doubled up in a line. Solid red-brown muscle pumped in unison. I had an impression of the mighty strength they produced to drive the spoked wheels.

At the top two pale pink lungs inflated and deflated of their own accord like bellows. They were joined to the depths of the engine by a windpipe ringed with cartilage. Dark clots lay slickly around it. Nearest me was a blood-smeared glass tank of water; gleaming veins ducted it out to cool the hearts. I saw about twenty red-brown kidneys attached by a network of ligaments to a porous gold pipe that led towards the rear of the car. As I watched, hot yellow liquid spattered out of the pipe onto the forecourt making a steaming puddle; the car relieved itself.

'Ugh.' I shrank back. 'God, it's disgusting!'

'I bought it to help me in my search,' Tarragon said. 'I'm looking for a way to save the sea kraits. That's why I'm here in Epsilon instead of at home studying, basking and eating tuna.'

Sea kraits were the largest animal I had ever heard of, but I had thought they'd all died out centuries earlier in the worst disaster Insects ever caused. 'I don't understand. Why are you bothered about sea snakes? And anyway, aren't you a bit late? Their ocean dried up a long time ago – and good riddance.'

'Yes, but I have ways to talk to them. Sea kraits are intelligent animals with a sophisticated knowledge all their own. I think it's a great pity they died out. All their learning was lost, Jant; don't you care? I saw you free the porcupanda just now.'

'There's a difference between a porcupanda and a kilometre-long sea snake! The Shift's better off without foul, slimy sea creatures!'

'So says the Rhydanne. Take care you're not threatened with extinction yourself. The Tine will want to make sports-coupés out of you. Wait! Don't run away! Be a nice Rhydanne and look after my car for a minute while I pay.' Tarragon hefted a slab of succulent steak, which was lying on the spare seat. She jumped down from the running board and turned her shark's waddle into a very sexy walk as she strode into the kiosk.

I leant on the car's curved side, staring all round for approaching Tine. If Tarragon was right they would be waving cleavers and bent on my demise. She had called this vehicle a sports car, but I have never seen one play sports, and if you ask me it is quite unsporting, sitting in a car when one is expected to run.

Tarragon reappeared, unwrapping a chunk of the Tine's red water frozen to a flat wooden stick. She gave it a big lick, then offered it to me.

'No way!'

'Suit yourself. Weird air-breather. You shouldn't visit Epsilon, Jant; you don't belong here. It makes me so sad to see you poisoning yourself. I hoped you had given up drugs.'

'Well, I'm having a bit of a relapse.' I explained the island, my fear of the sea and my current predicament on board *Stormy Petrel*.

Patches of grey sandpaper skin blotched her body and faded. 'A voyage of discovery!' she said enthusiastically. 'Well, in that case I'll help. I fancy taking a look at your vessels. I'll follow them at depth for a while so you don't have to fear the sea. If anything untoward happens to your ship while I'm in the vicinity you should be relatively safe.'

'Thank you. Thank you, Tarragon. What can I do in return?'

'Learning motivates us Sharks. An edifying experience is reward enough. And although I'm cruising distant waters right now, it shouldn't take me too long to swim to you . . .'

I frowned.

'All the seas are connected. Actually all the oceans in every world are one ocean. The sea finds its own level across the worlds; you can reach anywhere if you swim far enough. As long as the water is to our taste, what matters it what sea we breathe?' She continued, 'I wish I could see the ocean from the outside – an immense orb of water hanging in vacuum, so my school tells me. That's one Shift I can't make.'

I thought about this for a while. The same sea that is surging into Capharnaum harbour laps on the beach at Awndyn, backs up the sparkling Mica River at high tide – brackishly flows into Epsilon market, glistens in Vista Marchan two thousand years ago, and is swept the next minute by Tarragon's fins in the deep abyss. The land changes, but the ocean is a still pool, a pool like a sphere, hanging in the universe.

I decided that Tarragon was making fun of me so I giggled and she gave me a contemptuous look. 'It's true. You don't think angler fish and manta rays originated in your world?'

I shrugged, not knowing the animals to which she referred.

The Shark sighed. 'Jant, call yourself a scholar? No real student would mess with their mind the way you do. Why destroy yourself? Do you want to be found lying dead, a stiff corpse with a needle in its arm? What's cool about that? I get here through study and you get here through pleasure. I can smell it on you. Pleasure is actually bad where I come from.'

'And what is good where you come from?'

'Little bits of fish.'

'I'm sorry, Tarragon. I Shifted by accident. I'm only here because the ocean unnerves me and I OD'd.'

'There are other methods to achieve enough disconnection to Shift.' She smiled triangularly. 'By pain, or the way us Sharks do it – by thought. Promise you won't do drugs again and I'll teach you! You may eventually be able to Shift at will, just as I can – but probably not as well, because air-breathers aren't very intelligent. For example you would never be able to Shift as far as my world. The degree of dislocation would certainly kill you. You must be near death to get this far.'

'Shift at *will*? How?'

'You can will yourself to wake up from a nightmare, right? This is no different. Your body's not here; you're a tourist, a projection same as me. If you must travel to Epsilon, do it by meditation – you need a relaxed state of mind to project yourself. Of course, it's easier to leave the Shift than it is to arrive so you can either meditate or force yourself back home. All I do is wake from my trance and I return to my sea.'

It never occurred to me that I could find a different way to Shift. I had thought travelling to Epsilon city was a side effect of scolopendium, and that I could only wake when the drug wore off. 'I don't think I can.'

'Oh yes. You can travel along what, let's face it, is a well-trodden path. It just takes patience – and concentration. I'll show you!'

She leant over the car's low door, grabbed my belt and shirt front, and pulled me into the car. Her strength was incredible. I sprawled onto the passenger seat, into the footwell. My long legs waved in the air as I thrashed about trying to find purchase to jump out.

Tarragon held me down effortlessly with one little hand on my chest. She pressed a pedal to the floor, released a lever. The car lunged forward with such power I was thrown back against the seat. 'Let me out! Let me out! Help!' I struggled. 'Tarragon, you bitch!'

'I'll teach you a lesson, Shark-style!' Her pert breasts heaved with laughter. She blew a wordless human scream on the car's larynx horn.

It moved faster than a racehorse, rushed at my flight speed along the ground. Tarragon talked loudly as she steered: 'Let me tell you the safe method to Shift – you should lie still and empty your mind, relax and think your way here. It might take a few years to perfect but you immortals have time to practise. Try now – think your way back to the Fourlands.'

I refused. I wouldn't risk returning to a drugged sleep. My consciousness must be kicked out to the Shift for a reason; perhaps to stop it being damaged by the scolopendium I keep pumping into myself. What if I returned to a body lying in a coma? I'd be rejected from the Circle, could age and die without regaining awareness.

Tarragon saw me shudder and exclaimed, 'You can do it! Let me show you!' She spun the wheel, swung the car round and accelerated down the Coeliac Trunk Road, into the Tine's Quarter.

The sky was dark, and lights on either side of the Aureate's road gave a golden glow; a chill mist made a diffuse halo around them. Skin-worshipping Tine worked by the roadside. Their arms were flayed to the elbows. Tattoos covered their skin and the shells on their backs were painted with spirals. Their muscular blue haunches were cut with lettering like graffiti in old tree trunks. They had the broken noses of heavyweight boxers and the thick arms of fishermen. They carried other bits of victims' bodies too that I couldn't identify.

An immense spoked wheel four metres in diameter turned unhurriedly and a needle rose and fell. Tine fed skin backed with yellow fat under the needle; it hung over the edge of the sewing machine's serrated gold platform. 'Is that Tine skin?' I asked.

'Oh, they're just embroidering it. They'll put it back on later.'
They snarled as we passed.

'Don't look,' said Tarragon. 'It gets worse from here on.' But she knew I would look, because curiosity motivates not only Sharks but me as well.

Shattered glass ground under our wheels. I turned my head with a disconnected feeling. We passed burnt-out vehicles at the roadside, smashed and overturned. Blackened Tine bodies lay between them, marking their experiments with engines. Long lines of automobiles had impacted so hard that they were all joined together. Metal crumpled back on itself. Tine assembled around them, carrying hoses, wielding axes. Water sprayed above them; in a flashing yellow light the drops seemed to fall slowly. Nightmare slow motion as water and blood pooled onto the road. Curtains of bloodied skin hung out of broken windows. One muscle tissue axle throbbed in pain.

We passed a gorgeous woman that the Tine had welded into her car. Her body was set into the seat as smoothly as a jewel in a bevel. Only the front could be seen; her face and neck, breasts and belly. Wreaths of gold tubes ran out of the seat into the sides of her body, completely obscuring her ribs and the sides of her slender thighs. Her hands had vanished; bulges at the ends of her arms were seamlessly attached to the steering wheel. Her long hair became a stylised immovable gold curve sweeping back to form the headrest. Her feet merged with the floor; its solid gold seemed to lap up her slender legs. She was part of the car.

'If the Tine catch us, that's what they'll do,' said Tarragon. 'Make this car grow through us. Would you like to be a passenger forever?'

'Let me go!'

'Think yourself home.'

Something terrible is happening down there. Something vast in the heart of the Aureate is pumping viscous liquid around the drains and dykes bridged with connective tissue. 'Let me go!' I shouted. 'I want out!'

'Think yourself home, I'm not stopping you.'

'But I don't know how!'

'If I call out that you're a gymnast, Rhydanne, you'd be spending the rest of your life as a car. Well, your guts will. The rest of you will make a good roadsighn. Look, there's one.'

The roadsighn whispered, 'i trespassed in the aureate, look at me, save yourselves, go home, save yourself, tarragon, where are you going, tarragon?'

His legs twined together were planted in the verge, and a

membrane road sign grew from between his outstretched arms. In the mist he was just a spindly écorché silhouette murmuring, 'oh tarragon, what have you brought us?'

As we passed I saw his sticky dark pink colour, stripped to pus and muscle, his face locked in a wide *risus sardonicus* leer; 'tarragon, who is that? where are you going?'

'We're going deeper,' she said to me. 'The Spleen is on your right. On your left you will see—'

'Am I a sacrifice? Let me out!'

Gold buildings loomed smooth and rounded, lobed against each other like internal organs. They were horribly organic, studded with empty ulcerous portals – foramina and fistulae. The Ribs were flying buttresses with nowhere to land. We skirted the Labyrinths of the Ileum and in the distance the Cult of the Oedemic Prepuce had erected a tall gold wrinkled spire with an onion dome. We drove down a rubber subway that stretched and sagged. We emerged from beneath dripping red stalactites through a puckered textured sphincter onto the shore of—

A lake. Against the black sky I could just make out its dark red liquid and hear the lapping as rare ripples ran over its stinking surface. Gold ducts of varying bores, hollow femurs and arrays of tubules sucked liquid from it and ran underground. Glomeruli like fleshy cups fountained in occasional bursts so the automobile wheels sank in ground made spongy by gastric juices. On the far side, spotlights picked out and roved over the highly polished gold shell of the Western Kidney. I tried all the time to wish myself back to the Fourlands.

'Tine are a most religious and honest people . . .' said Tarragon. Tine crowded the shore. It must be a feast day because hundreds had gathered. Most were Duodenal Sect; their intestines had been pulled out of a hemmed hole in their stomachs and wrapped around their waists, and I could see waves of peristalsis going round them. One was a Novice of the Flectere Doctrine, who snap all their joints to bend the opposite way. His bare feet lifted in front of him because his knees were bent backwards like a bird's. His pale blue palms were on the backs of his hands, his fingers curled outwards. 'You have to admire their devotion.'

A gold paddleboat that ran on striated muscle fibres and catechism ferried between the Islets of Langerhans in the distance. 'We're going deeper,' said Tarragon. 'Soon we'll reach the Heart and Lungs, and we'll drive the length of the backbone processional. The Heart! I want to show you the Heart of the Aureate.'

'No!'

'Then think yourself home!'

'I can't!'

'Or the brain, deep beneath the Transgressor's Forest. In the brain there's a temple where any creature drawn on the wall comes to life. Don't draw stick men, they have enough of those. It's sickening to see them, limping towards you dragging their misshapen limbs and squeaking.'

I couldn't feel the pull. It would be at least an hour before my overdose wore off and woke me. I tried to be calm, pictured my cabin on the *Stormy Petrel* and imagined myself back there.

'That's a good boy!' Tarragon exclaimed. 'I know you can do it!'

She gave me a Shark's grin but I didn't give it back. We drove along the lakeside and I screamed when I realised what was pinging out from under our wheels and rattling off the chassis: a gravel beach of kidney stones.

Tarragon called to a whole congregation of Tine kneeling on the shore, 'Hey, see my passenger? He runs marathons! He can sprint as fast as a car!'

The Tine paused and stared. They gestured to each other, howled and ran directly at us. 'Hurry!' I yelled. 'Hurry up!'

Tarragon stopped the car. 'Will yourself home.'

Through rising panic I forced myself to stay calm and yearned, forced, demanded myself back to my body. Tarragon tapped a finger on her forehead and repeated the dictum, 'Shift by meditation. Not sensation!'

The Tine were almost upon us.

The dark shore twitched in and out of focus, then a wave of distortion rolled through it. Tarragon's face and the gold vehicle belched into disturbing shapes. They dissolved to grey. To black.

My stomach creased with fear; I closed my eyes. And when I opened them again, slowly and stickily, I was back in my cabin, lying on the floor.

## CHAPTER 6

I woke with the green taste of bile in my mouth, curled up so tightly I ached. Shit, I almost got eviscerated. I clenched my fists. Tarragon almost had me killed.

I rolled onto my back and contemplated the too-close ceiling. A gentle sighing must be the wind on the mainsail, and that constant slap and hiss will be the prow cutting small waves. There were no other sounds, so it was probably night-time. These deductions left me feeling rather proud but I sensed that the cabin had become a little bit narrower. It had changed shape – it was also longer. There was not enough room to open even the tips of my wings. What the fuck was going on?

I lit a candle and held it up. The walls were painted blue, not black, the portholes were square with white borders. It was a different cabin. Could I have Shifted back to the wrong place? Panicking, I ran my fingernails between the planks, brushed my hand along the shelves: nothing. Where were my wraps? Where were all my fucking wraps? I saw my rucksack, seized it and rummaged through it. The fat envelope containing scolopendium had gone. 'Damn you, Ata!' I shouted. 'Damn you, damn you, damn you!'

There was a knock on the cabin door. 'Go away!' I yelled.

I rubbed the hem of my coat and felt nine hard paper squares still sewn in. Thank god, they had missed some!

Cold air gusted into the cabin as a stocky figure pushed the door open with his shoulder. I saw Serein's silhouette, a round head with spiky hair. Behind him, dull blue inky dawn clouds packed the vast sky. He sat in the doorway, legs out onto the half deck, huddling in his greatcoat. 'Comet,' he said. 'You weren't well.'

'Is that understatement a new type of sarcasm you're experimenting with?'

'For god's sake, Comet. You look like you've been dragged through a battlefield backwards. Mind you, I've been seasick. The sailors started laying bets on the number of times I would puke over the taffrail. Mist told me you don't get seasick. She explained about scolopendium.'

'I see.' I took a swig of water from my leather bottle. 'I suspect that I am on the *Melowne*?'

The Swordsman nodded. 'We rowed you across from *Petrel*. You were out cold.'

'What! A rowing boat? So close to the waves? What if it had capsized?' Drowning while unconscious was too awful to contemplate.

'Ata said you could have this berth because you filled the other one up with drugs. Drugs aren't an answer, Jant. What are you doing that for when you're an Eszai?'

'What happened to my wraps and the envelope?' I said threateningly.

'We threw them overboard.'

'Shit.'

The Swordsman sounded both disgusted and surprised that an Eszai would knowingly use cat. 'How much did you take?'

'As much as I could.' I wriggled out of the constrictive cabin and pulled myself up, water bottle in hand. I scraped a match, lit one of the cigarettes I had stolen from Cinna and sipped at it. I blew the smoke out of my nose and coughed. I was never going to be any bloody good at smoking. It doesn't agree with Rhydanne as they are accustomed to thin air. I only do it rarely, when I'm under extreme duress, because if I ever got hooked it would destroy my ability to fly.

Wrenn joined me at the rail, standing upwind of the smoke. 'Are you all right? Apart from being dark and moody, I mean.'

I said, 'I loathe this bloody floating coffin of a boat.'

'It's a ship.'

'*She's* a ship. Apparently it's female. I hope all her masts don't break off when they fuck in the shallows.'

The Swordsman fell quiet, looking at the midnight-blue water. The waves swept up into points, lapping and side-stepping. Their ridges looked like cirques of the Darkling Mountains. Apart from a sailor manning the wheel and a watchman at the prow, all was quiet. Only knavish sailors, rakish swordsmen and drug-addled Rhydanne are about at this hour.

'The *Stormy Petrel*'s close by,' he said, pointing forward at two faint lights, one red, one white, which rose and fell gently. The dawn clouds were gradually becoming paler, but the *Petrel*'s sails and hull were blurred, a drifting perse-grey shape. The ships creaked continually, and when they weren't creaking they groaned and flapped and sighed. They were like animals talking to each other.

'Hm. I'm surprised Lightning and Mist can bear being on the same boat.'

'Can you see who's at the helm?'

I glanced at him. 'Rhydanne can't see in the dark, Wrenn; that's just a story. In fact I have crap night vision. Rhydanne eyes reflect to cut out snow glare so I don't get blinded. It's not much of an advantage at sea level . . .'

'Really?'

'Yeah. While I'm putting to rest myths about Rhydanne, you should know that they don't turn into lynxes on their birthdays. They can't survive being frozen solid and thawed out again. And they're not cannibals, whatever Carniss may say.' I lit another cigarette with the stub of the first. 'As for the bit about shitting in little pebbles like goats do, I reserve comment.'

'I didn't mean to be nosy. I'm sorry.'

'You should be. I stay smooth-skinned, mind. It would take me weeks to grow as much stubble as you.'

Wrenn rubbed his chin. I turned back to the cabin thinking that I needed more time to recover. From behind me Wrenn said, 'What's it like up there? In Darkling, I mean. Is it true Rhydanne don't talk to each other at all?'

Much as I wanted a few hours alone, that made me smile. I said slowly, 'Oh, they say all they need to. But that's not much compared with flatlanders, for sure. Even Scree village was only built by accident – it started out as a cairn. There was a tradition that every traveller puts a stone on the pile when he goes past. So it grew, very gradually, into a pueblo with rooms and an inn. Rhydanne come to the village every winter, when any person can occupy any room. They all get snowed in and drink themselves legless. In summer, they leave the rooms empty. The conditions make Rhydanne very self-reliant; they can't act in large groups. When an avalanche destroyed my shieling I couldn't find anyone to help me . . . The cornices were hanging waiting for the slightest shock. Eilean was crushed by the barrage and the whole valley changed shape.'

*I hung onto a rowan tree's upturned roots as the mountainside liquefied and tabular ice thundered. The next day, the air filled with white powder snow, saw me scrabbling at the granite debris until my fingers split, trying to dig her out.*

I smirked. 'She's still up there under tons of rock, flat as a waffle.'

'That's terrible. I'm so sorry.'

I huffed and tapped ash off the cigarette. 'I hated them. I grew up too slowly for Rhydanne and in the end I'd no love of their way of life. But Darkling paled into insignificance when I went to Hacilith and fell in with the Wheel. They were named from their habit of nailing enemies to the waterwheels of the city. The weird thing was that I was happy as a chemist's apprentice and I didn't need a gang's protection until I joined them. The longer you live, the more scars you gather, see?' I traced my fingertip over the deep scarification on my right shoulder, a circle with six spokes, the initiation to the gang.

'Shit, Jant. That's terrible . . .'

*Felicitia pulled apart the hilt and suede sheath of a hunting knife until its long steel emerged. It was unbelievably sharp; Felicitia had a lot of time to spare. His hands shook and he fumbled as he traced the lines drawn on with lipstick. My washed-out feeling of suspense tipped into agony. Unlike tattoos it was not superficial; it was deep. It could not be dealt with lightly. I swear the first cut went straight to the bone. My hands were bound behind me to a cast iron chair in a beer garden. I struggled, and when I started screaming they gagged me.*

*I stumbled home, leaving a trail of blood that rats scented, scurrying out from refuse piled on street corners. I dressed the wound myself, though my fingers slipped into and through the lacerated flesh.*

'It didn't hurt as much as Slake in 'twenty-five though,' I said, pushing my T-shirt up so he could see the remains of an Insect bite, a sixty-stitch-long scar that curved into the left side of my belly, ending in a puckered mark where its mandible hit my lowest rib. 'I held my guts in with one arm. I crawled a metre, collapsed and started to drown in the mud.'

'God. Slake Cross Battle. I heard stories . . .'

'Well, I took all the cavalry but none of them had mounts. Every man was sliced to bits. That's why we introduced testing the ground with poles for Insect tunnels before we camp. The Doctor knew I was still living but god knows how she found me because she said I was nearly buried. She pushed all my innards back in and stacked my stretcher on the cart. Because the Circle holds us, we can gain consciousness with life-threatening wounds and no desire to witness them. That got me back on scolopendium again but it also won Tern's attention. I was in hospital for a year; I kept turning up the drip's dial and passing out until Rayne threatened to take me off painkillers. While convalescing I began to panic that I had lost the ability to fly. I tried to glide out of the hospital window and ripped all my stitches . . . Zascai were queuing up to Challenge me but, true to the rules, San held them off until I had recovered. Lucky you, Wrenn; Insect battles to look forward to.'

'I get it. You're scarred by living an adventurous life. The same will happen to me . . . You're brave, Jant.'

I am? 'Well, not so brave as to duel with Gio,' I said, and we stood for a while in an uncertain quiet. I found talking like this reassuring – I had almost forgotten about the Aureate.

I lit a third cigarette but simply held it. I wondered how long it would take for me to fill the entire sky with smoke. When immortals think those things we are not being entirely whimsical. 'Couldn't you sleep?' I asked. I was fully aware that Wrenn had been left here to keep an eye on me.

'No. I keep thinking about this island. Then I got too excited and had to come up here to cool down. I can't wait to see Tris.'

'Personally I think it's Mist's plan to take all her enemies on one ship and scuttle it. I warn you, she's very dangerous.'

'But gorgeous.'

I glanced at him. 'So Ata has her hooks in you already? She's certainly beautiful; it's all the more reason to be wary. Even Lightning was taken in by her deceit, her callous human inventiveness and her beauty. She probably put you here on *Melowne* so he can't advise you, or to preserve her mystique. She plans centuries ahead; you haven't been alive long enough to think on our timescale.'

I ground the cigarette into a flurry of sparks on the rail and flicked it into the sea. 'Do you want to explore this boat?'

'Oh, yes!'

I raised the grating and trotted down the open-plank steps, looking around. Wrenn followed with his lantern. The *Melowne*'s hundred sailors were asleep. They mumbled and stirred in white canvas hammocks that hung three deep on the left and right of the deck, leaving a clear walkway down the centre. Some of the Plainslanders were snoring. Awians sleep on their fronts or their sides so they hardly ever snore. The deck stank of sweat, damp linen and the brown-sugar smell of cheap rum; a bowl full of laurel leaves intended as air freshener just added its own scent to the reek. Five porthole shutters on each wall were bolted shut.

'Don't disturb them,' I whispered. 'Let's go down a level.' I tried to move, and couldn't. Wrenn was standing on my feathers, bending the quills over the edge of the steps.

'Oops, sorry.' He shuffled back. I put a finger to my lips and descended through the second hatchway. This level was pitch dark

73

but the air smelt better, heavy with camphorwood, pine sap, oak sawdust and quality leather. I investigated some kegs stencilled 'Grass Isle', and Wrenn reclined on a pile of sacks of dried beans and rice, swinging his lantern about. The deck was packed floor to ceiling with well-stowed sacks and oil flasks, as far as the light could reach. 'We're under the waterline here,' he said.

'Don't.' I shuddered, thinking how the sea's pressure might cave in the hull, squashing it like an eggshell.

'Mist says this is the orlop deck, for stores and dunnage. The hold's below us; that's the lowest level.'

'What the fuck is dunnage?'

Wrenn shrugged. I levered a lid plank off the nearest cask. 'Wine, Wrenn, look at all this wine! Half of Lightning's cellar must be in here.'

He picked up a chunk of cheese covered in wax paper. 'Breakfast!'

'This one's rum.' I dipped a rationing cup in another barrel.

'I've found salted meat, oranges, a barrel of sauerkraut. What's "portable soup"?'

We forced our way between the racks. I climbed on top of the hogsheads and walked along, hunched over, brushing the ceiling, but the deck was so crammed we couldn't go more than a few metres. Wrenn sat back on the ladder, I leaned on the wooden pump pipe next to it, and we nibbled handfuls of booty – me with chocolate and rum; Wrenn with dried fruit, bread and water.

'There's another grid,' I said. 'Let's go down again.'

'It's locked, see?' Wrenn crouched and turned over a padlock.

'I should be able to crack that,' I said, wanting to impress the Swordsman, although I was not sure why. I put a hand to the small of my back, selected one of the smallest secondaries, gripped it and pulled. Flight feathers are very strongly attached so I had to give it a hard wrench to pull it out, teeth gritted because it hurt. It dragged the flesh, just like pulling a fistful of hair. It came out leaving a hollow funnel of skin from which another pinfeather would grow in a couple of months.

The quill was old and did not bleed. I flattened its translucent-cream point, and jiggled it about in the lock, turning clockwise and pressing hard to poke the tumblers round. I remarked, 'People say I had a misspent youth, but no other Messenger has so many useful talents to place at the Emperor's service.'

I felt the mechanism give in the lock; it clicked open and we hefted the hatchway cover. Wrenn stepped down first with his guttering lantern. 'Check it out, it follows the shape of the hull.'

The hold's walls curved up on both sides, like being in a wooden bowl. The ship's ribs were clearly visible. The ceiling was two metres above and I could stand up straight for the first time. *Melowne*'s side-to-side rolling was not so obvious here; we were standing directly above the keel and the ship felt stable. More equipment had been carefully stowed between the ribs and lashed to each of the knees supporting the deck above.

The timbers for the pinnaces had instructions printed on them like model kits. There was an enormous amount of folded canvas and all sorts of tackle. There were metal buckets full of solid tar like warm black ice, chains, cord on reels, copper nails and many times the ship's length in coiled hemp cables.

'This is all spare rigging,' Wrenn said, as he kicked the shaft of an anchor twice my height and as thick as my thigh. He clicked a latch on a long oilskin-lined casket. He let the lid fall. 'Oh, my god.'

'What's that?'

'Arrows. Look!' About one hundred arrows with very sharp broadhead points filled the box, laid in leather spacers to keep their flights apart. Wrenn dug his fingers between them and they rattled. I looked up and realised I was staring at a wall of similar boxes. Wordlessly, we counted them and made a quick calculation, 'Ten thousand arrows?'

'At *least*.'

'If there's shafts there must be—'

'Bow staves,' I said, breaking the seal on a larger coffer. It was full of heavy longbows, all with fresh strings and the bowyer's mark stamped two-thirds along their length where the arrow was intended to be placed. 'A couple of hundred bows, one for every man on the ship.'

'Look, there are halberds,' said Wrenn. 'And shields!' They were stacked along the hull walls, covered with sailcloth. He unbuckled the straps of a huge sea chest with joyful abandon. 'I wonder if there are any swords? Oh, yes, look!'

The chest was full of fyrd-issue swords with double-edged blades and brown mass-produced leather scabbards. Their pristine hilts flashed in the light as he swept the lantern over. 'I'd like to test one. Here we are—'

'Put it back! Wrenn, the grid was locked for a reason! Mist doesn't want us to know what's down here!'

But Wrenn, happily ignorant of Mist's cruel streak, was not afraid of her. He selected a seventy-five-centimetre blade and stuck it in his belt.

'By god, what does Mist expect us to do to Tris?' I said.

'Maybe the islanders are fierce.'

'Don't be a fool. Mist said Tris has no Insects; they've nothing to be violent about.'

We went forward, seeing more of the same; the *Melowne*'s hold was a ship's chandlery and well-stocked armoury. I hesitated. 'Can you smell something?'

'What?'

A sharp metallic scent like spilt blood or cut leaves lay very faint beneath the hot greased-iron smell of Wrenn's lantern. 'Nothing. Forget it.'

At the bow a huge black tarpaulin hung floor to ceiling like a curtain. A skittering sound came from behind it, as of something metal not made fast. Wrenn took a handful and swept it aside.

A massive Insect launched itself at us.

I ducked. Wrenn yelled. The Insect crashed into the bars of its cage and drew back on six legs. Its antennae whipped round in frantic circles.

Its back legs slipped on the steel floor, scraping bright scratches. Its mandibles opened, a smaller set gaped inside and it jumped again, into the bars. An enormous knife-sharp foreleg stabbed out at us. It clicked and snapped; the bars boomed as it hurled itself against them. Wrenn went for his sword and dropped the lantern. Suddenly we were in total darkness with the red spots of the flare-out dancing before our eyes.

Wrenn and I thought the same thing at the same time. We bent down and pawed frantically around on the floor for the lantern, but we only felt each other's hands.

'Where's the— Ow! Damn it!' I burnt my fingers on the hot oil leaking out. I stood back, seething with frustration as Wrenn picked it up. 'Is it broken?'

'I don't think so.'

'Are you sure? There's all that bloody rum up there!'

'There's a sodding great Insect right here!'

Wrenn struck a match and his shaking hand rattled inside the lantern as he lit it.

I shouted, 'For fuck's sake! Give me it, you daft fucking feather-weight!'

He hauled his new sword from its scabbard; with the blade balanced in his hand his composure returned.

The Insect raked the bars with its foreclaws. It chewed them, mandibles clicking like shears. Strands of drool hung down and wrapped round its feet; glutinous bubbles stuck to the floor. The

Insect rubbed its back pair of legs together; it turned round and round furiously in its four-metre-deep cage. Its body hung from long legs jointed above like a spider's. It was one of the biggest Insects I had seen, the size and strength of a warhorse; it battered the bars in absolute desperation to reach us.

It tilted its head and tried to push through, but the bulbous brassy eyes wouldn't fit. It pressed against the bars until its stippled thorax creaked, reached out its mandibles and gnashed. The mottled brown jaws met and overbit; they were the length and shape of scythe blades, chitin-hard and so powerful they could bite a body in two. A foreclaw swept the air. Wrenn and I backed off. He said, 'What's it doing here?'

'I don't know. I mean to find out.'

The cage's sliding door was secured by another big padlock. Its roof was a dented metal sheet. Wrenn pointed to some scattered meat bones that the Insect had voraciously scraped clean. It had macerated some into a sticky white paste and dropped it into the space between the cage and hull wall. 'They make short work of marrow bones!'

I grimaced. 'I thought I could smell the magnificent beast.' I thrust the lantern at Wrenn, dashed aft to the ladder and pulled myself up much faster than he could climb. He struggled behind me, probably realising for the first time what I can do. I swung my knees between the rungs and bent them to hang on, leant backwards upside-down, face to face with Wrenn. I prodded his chest. 'Mist will regret her latest trick.'

I flexed back upright and swarmed to the orlop deck. I scrambled onto the companionway and emerged from the hatch onto the main deck. All the sailors were eating their breakfast and rolling up their hammocks. Mouths full of porridge hung open in astonishment as I bounded past.

'Comet!' Wrenn shouted. 'Eszai are all equal! Stop and—'

'Kiss it,' I said. I jumped off and flapped across to the *Stormy Petrel*.

Mist is, of course, an early riser; she was already in her office eating ginger biscuits from a toast rack and walking a pair of brass compasses across an expansive chart draped over the table. I touched down outside next to the red hurricane lamp. I pounced into her cabin, right onto her, bearing her to the floor, my knees on her belly. The biscuits and a cafetière went flying. Mist was in control of herself; she saw my expression and screamed, 'Saker!'

'No more deceit!' I spat.

'Jant,' she said. 'Uppers make you manic. Why don't you calm down, before I have you locked in the brig?'

Her long white hair spread out, finer than silk. Her right hand edged behind the table's baluster leg, reaching for a paperknife. I snatched it and clattered it away against the bulkhead. 'An Insect!' I said. 'All those boxes of halberds! Why is there a live Insect on the *Melowne*?'

Mist's fair skin turned paler, her amethyst eyes wide. 'An Insect?'

'In a fucking cage!'

She caught her breath. 'Please get off me.'

I didn't want to let her move. I could only see one course of action. 'We must sail back to Awndyn. Fulmer will turn these over-ornamented crates around and take us home. In the Emperor's name, with god's will and the Circle's protection, you can consider yourself under arrest. I'll bring you before San, at knife-point if need be!'

'Comet . . .' she said calmly.

'The only good thing about being at sea is we won't be eaten by Insects. And you bring one along! A huge one! I'll throw it overboard . . .'

She saw there was no point in dissembling. 'Aye, I thought you would pry into everything like a starved rat. Let me up and I'll explain.'

As I disentangled her cloak folds from round us, Lightning glowered into the cabin with a cursing eye. The sea wind ripped his fur-lined coat into billows. He grabbed me and pushed me away from Mist. I hit the wall hard and sprawled down in a winded pile by the joist. 'Damn it, are you fucking trying to break my wings?'

'*What* is going on?'

Mist held her upper arm as if I had hurt her. She conjured an expression of gratitude for the Archer and sobbed experimentally but it had no effect on him. 'Jant is such a junkie.' She shrugged. 'He's so screwed up I am tempted to Challenge him myself.'

'No! This is nothing to do with cat!' I can't escape my one failing; my fellow Eszai use the label to taint *everything* I do, even when I'm clean. With always the same friends, I can't move on and begin anew, my mistakes stagnate around me. I smacked my fist against the joist, to take the heat out of my frustration. 'Don't tell me it's a hallucination, because Serein saw it too! There's an Insect, hundreds of cut-and-thrusters, a hundred caissons of arrows.'

Lightning listened carefully and at the latter he held up his hand. 'I know about them. Of course, Jant, think about it. Stop flouncing around and sit still. Would you travel to an unfamiliar country without armaments? Our ships are our only means of returning home so they're worth more than the Empire to us now. We have to protect them.'

'Mist said the island was peaceful,' I said sullenly.

'On the other hand, shipping Insects sounds sinister in the extreme. What is it for?'

Mist kicked open her folding chair and regarded the coffee soaking into her sea chart. 'I have a licence. No, not the usual showground licence. A warrant you'll respect.' She unlocked a tortoiseshell casket and removed a paper with the Emperor's seal.

She passed it to me and I read aloud: '"Every item of cargo carried by Mist on her journey is required and permitted in my name. It will benefit the Fourlands at the present time and in the future. San, god's guardian of Awia, Morenzia, Plainslands and Darkling, 19 January 2020."

'That's all it says. It's the Emperor's signature all right. But does he know we have a live cargo?'

'Comet, I'm surprised at you, suggesting that I could keep information from the Emperor,' Ata said mildly. 'Aye, listen gentlemen. Tris has no Insects. Imagine their surprise, interest and fascination when I exhibit one. I will tell them: the Circle protects the world from these maneaters – see our benevolence. Even the fact that I have brought it such a distance alive will right well impress them. The governors of Tris can have the Insect for a zoo or a circus, or make soup out of it for all I care. I'll present it to them with all our Darkling silver and Donaise wine.'

'Bullshit,' I said and glared at her as only Rhydanne can.

Lightning said, 'I think Mist is telling the truth.'

'I'm going to hang her off the thingy mast on the doojah until she confesses and Fulmer can take us back to dock.'

Lightning said, 'We can't wrest command of the fleet from Mist. Anyway, Fulmer is not just captain of the *Melowne* but Awia's representative to Tris. Queen Eleonora's spy, in other words. If we turn back he'll make her a dismal report.'

The wind changed direction, the ship heaved, we lurched and Lightning shifted position woodenly, his coat hanging in limp folds to the floor.

Ata smiled and shook her head. She tied her platinum hair into a ponytail, making her strong-boned face look even more martial. She smoothed down her waistcoat with its frogging and brass-domed buttons. 'Don't worry. We won't risk enraging Eleonora. God, Lightning; I try to show you more of the world, but you just bring your own world with you.'

I was struck by a thought. If I was Wrenn, sincere and uncertain, or a sailor who witnessed my rapid departure from the *Melowne*, I would row across and try to eavesdrop on this conversation. I listened for any sounds outside the cabin and called, 'I can hear you; there's no need to bloody hide!'

Wrenn pushed open the glass-paned door and appeared, abashed. His shirtsleeves were wet with spray; water squeezed out of his soaked boot seams at every step.

I said, 'Great, why don't we invite the rest of the Circle in here and then we can have a party?'

'You could really hear me?'

'Not at all, but I thought it best to check.'

'Oh. Clever,' he said, downcast. He glanced around, taking in the leaded bay windows that gave a view over the stern, Mist's cot with its embroidered canopy, a stand of scrolled charts, the navigational instruments laid out on her ledger and ginger biscuits all over the floor. With a fencer's grace he had adapted well to the ship's dimensions and he was short enough to stand without stooping, whereas Lightning rested his head on his hand pressing the beam.

Wrenn was well aware of Lightning's one-night stand with Ata. It was common knowledge that one night Lightning comforted her a little too assiduously and now they have a daughter. Wrenn folded his wings submissively, their elbows at his backside and the wrist-joints just visible from the front, clasping his shoulders. He picked his way with care: 'My lord. Um. Lightning. I respect your experience but this is my first assignment as an Eszai. You know that's important. I don't want to return empty-handed only a couple of days after setting out. I'm dependent on Mist for success and I'm sure you don't want me to fail. Anyhow, we left with such pomp that all the matelots in Awndyn will laugh fit to piss if we sneak back.'

He slid his fingers into his rapier's swept guards and grasped the grip worn to the shape of his hand. 'When I was in the ranks Lightning's honourable ideas sort of filtered down. None of us ever deserted. Well, I think it's dishonourable to turn back.'

I scowled. Wrenn bit his lip but continued, 'I agree that ambassadors shouldn't carry weapons. "Weighted down with iron, weighted down with fear", the saying goes. If Mist intends to use the Insect against the islanders I'll kill it myself. But she has set her heart on exploring Tris. Jant, if you threaten her you will cross swords with me. One sword keeps another in its sheath, so maybe if I support Mist there will be peace. You should be ashamed of yourself for intimidating a lady.'

I said, 'She's scarcely a lady.'

Lightning eyed us pensively. He stroked the scar on his right palm and eventually said, 'Very well; we press on.'

'But—'

'Enough!'

Ata relaxed. 'Jant, you clown. Stir a mutiny again and I'll have you towed behind in a barrel.'

I said, 'I need some fresh air.' I walked out to the main deck, slammed the cabin door with my drooping wing. I climbed the whatever ropes to the top of the mainmast and sat up there for hours on the something spar, face into the wind, and let the sea air fan my anger.

# CHAPTER 7

## Wrenn's Diary

*29 February 2020*

Comet suggested that I keep a diary to record my exploits on this voyage. This morning I woke at six a.m. (bell eighteen), and did two hours of rapier-and-dagger exercises on the deck. I improved my time by a second or so on the 'wild boar' sequence. I have to be ruthless with myself in practice because a Challenger wouldn't spare me. Then jogged up and down the keelson in the hold until Fulmer asked me to stop. I would like to practise sparring but no one here is even half as good as they need to be to test my arm.

Lightning is the best fencer among them I'll ask him for a bout and in return he might teach me some archery. He puts target butts forward on the foredeck and shoots at them from the half deck. His arrows fly the length of the *Petrel*. It's great to watch when we run alongside, but Mist only lets him have a quarter-hour a day rather than the four hours he needs. It's amazing to meet Lord Micawater in person – and he treats me like an equal! I've always wanted to be like him. I wish Dad could see me now.

So even though we have been aboard for a month, we are as fit as we can hope to be. Comet is either holed up with his books or away flying. Every morning he slings a water bottle on his shoulder, takes off and flaps up into the sky until he is just a speck and I worry that Lightning might mistake him for a seagull and shoot him. I still can't get used to a man gliding. He must feel so free. It must be odd to see people from above. He can always tell who they are, I suppose he has got used to it. I wish I could fly – think of the fencing moves I could use!

I can't wait to fight Insects. As soon as I get back from Tris, I'm going to the Front. I have loads of ideas to rid Lowespass of Insects completely – such as filling the river with salt, so they can't drink it. But Lightning tells me they tried that back in 1170. When we return, I'll be surrounded by foxy girls and, by god, I need it. Who knows, Lightning might be pushed off the most eligible bachelor top spot for the first time in fifteen hundred years.

It's a shame Mist swept me away from my moment of triumph. I wish I could be back with all those girls who were longing for me. But Mist said my absence will make them keener. She's grateful that the best Swordsman in the Fourlands is at her side. Any time.

*1 March 2020*

The weather is lovely, very bright and a lively wind clips us along. Comet refuses to leave his cabin. I think he is ashamed. He is drinking doped wine every day now. I reported to Mist, but she says let him be, the remains of his cache that escaped confiscation won't last much longer. Why doesn't she punish him for bringing scolopendium on board? In the fyrd it's the most serious offence to be caught with drugs, especially if you deal them to other soldiers. Scolopendium is pretty mysterious and old-fashioned stuff. I don't know anything about it but, god, I can't accept that an Eszai uses it. I suppose since Comet can fly, in good weather anyway, he takes his success for granted.

Mist said that people like Comet were the most useful, just as crooked wood is handy to the shipbuilder because odd shapes can be made into parts that hold the rest together. I don't get that, really. I thought the Circle was of one purpose.

Rain showers make the boards slippery. The tars say they're chancing their lives every time they go to the latrine planks at the prow to have a crap. Great waves break over the beakhead so they chance to get washed off, or slip and fall five metres like a turd into the sea where the ship will sail over them. Being valued passengers, our latrine is a tiny cubicle with a hole in the seat, on a private balcony at the stern. If you get the angle right you can piss against the rudder. The whole gallery smells of Captain Fulmer's poseur aftershave. Fulmer took one look at Lightning's frock coat and said, 'Good grief. This isn't the eighteenth century.'

I went to Comet's cabin and disturbed his work. I lost money at cards as we chatted. Those flat-chested mountain girls are so wild their love-bites need stitches, he says. We talked about rapiers and the new spring-loaded daggers whose blades split open into three points to trap swords. They impressed Comet but I told him they are just for show and would be dangerous in a real fight. I said, if you see a man wielding one you know he is a braggadocio.

I slipped Wrenn's diary back under his bunk and returned to my cabin. I worked there during the day with my notebooks that are so pleasant to begin and to dent the neat paper with a fountain pen. Contrary to what Wrenn thinks, neither flying nor languages is instinctive. I have learned the shapes of the air; I have to think carefully about my moves when aloft and sometimes I make mistakes. And if I make a gaffe in jotting down a translation, it's just as dangerous as a botched landing.

Mist had noted Trisian words from her first expedition, although without phonetics or even context. I figured out most of the unknown words from their roots, working back from modern equivalents. A few remained tantalising. The Trisians appeared to speak a form of Old Morenzian, pre-dating the first millennium. Nothing of that language survives recorded, apart from dusty learned works in a weird thirty-letter alphabet, ten letters more than I was used to. It dated from before the time of the First Circle when the fricative Low Awian language became the common tongue of the Fourlands. At around the same time, to be fair in the standardisations, San advised that the Fourlands' currency should be based on Morenzia's system, which was far simpler than Awia's.

I knew that the Trisians would be expecting us. The canoeists and governors that Mist dealt with will have spread the news across the island. They'll know it's human nature for us to return prepared to a great discovery, to tease out every detail. When our sails appear on their horizon, whatever plans they have made will be set in action. The Trisians will scurry to receive us, but I could not predict how.

I will just keep working and if I do too much cat and collapse, the others might realise how much torment my constant thoughts of Tern are causing me. I doubt she's dwelling on me this much, back in the Castle with her lover.

'Damn it!' I said aloud. 'Just stop the waves for one hour and let me think!' I wished myself back in Darkling, where I would still be drinking happily in the Filigree Spider if Ata's message hadn't got through. I reverted to thinking in Scree, a good language to be misanthropic in, as it has no words for groups of people and no plural verbs. Best of all it lacks a word for ocean. The Rhydanne word for climb is the same as the word for run, and there are plenty of words to describe the various types of drunk.

The only pub in Darkling is in the centre of Scree pueblo, where the bare rock buildings merge shapelessly on both sides of the raised single track. The pueblo has a shallow, all-enveloping roof with a hatch for each room, to prevent winter snows sealing people in completely. The Filigree Spider was busy, as it was the height of the freeze season. The herders had arrived, bringing their goats down from the high pasture. A few hunters visited to rest; they were nomadic and they pleased themselves. Many were afternoon-drunk (drinking becomes moreish and you write off the day).

I sat on one of the benches by the low bar and ate bread with rancid butter and salted llama's cheese. A row of freeze-dried rabbits hung tacked up by their ears behind the bar – Lascanne catches them by hand. I pushed my cup across the counter again; he slopped more whisky into it with an exaggerated gesture. 'It is snowing and drifting,' he said, as if that was news. 'Want a pinnacle rabbit?'

'No, thanks.'

Lascanne was alone-drunk (everything seems vaguely amusing). I suppose I was slightly daytime-drunk (no matter how much you drink it doesn't seem to have any effect).

The walls and most of the slate floor were covered with bright flat-woven kilims with warm red and indigo geometrical designs. A big hearth was on my right, its chimney shared with the distillery. A hunter lay on the furs beside it, very occasionally murmuring. She was drunk (dead-drunk); her sharp face rested on her folded hands. A family of four slept piled together nearby.

Three or four howffs were stacked against the wall. Howffs are tents of thin leather attached to rucksac frames. They could be rolled out and propped up by the frames to form triangular shelters. There was the ladder up to the Filigree Spider's unfurnished second floor, where many people were lodging until the thaw season. Square, dark openings were the entrances of small passageways that lead to other parts of the pueblo, again to escape heavy snows. The pub smelt of peat smoke and stew.

The door crashed open and two hunters struggled through man-handling a heavy bundle between them. At first I thought it was a rolled-up rug. The hunters, Leanne and Ciabhar, dropped the bundle in front of the hearth and turned it over. It was an unconscious body.

Leanne Shira saw me. She paused with one foot in the air before placing it down slowly. 'Jant! Look what Ciabhar found . . . We would have left him but we thought you might be interested.' She darted over and bit me gently on the shoulder, for a kiss. I think she was working-drunk (just a light haze on your life that lasts for days). Her face was cold to the touch. I watched her sleek narrow body, hard muscle flowering under pale skin at every movement. Fast movement, a melting of potential, she was gracile but strong. Her rubbery sprinter's midriff showed between her crop top and short black skirt.

She had two pairs of snowshoes tied on her belt, one on each hip for herself and her lover.

'Bring some whisky,' Ciabhar suggested.

'No alcohol!' I cried.

'Idiot! You're supposed to give them hot water,' said Leanne.

'What about whisky and water?'

Curious punters clustered round, making helpful suggestions: 'Take his coat off.'

'Put him in a hot bath.'

'Or under the snow.'

'He looks weird; I don't like it. I'm off.'

Now that they had accomplished dragging him in, their effort fell apart into the typical Rhydanne unit of organisation – one. Ciabhar Dara stood back and stared. He was tall and so lithe I could see the muscle fibres through his tight skin and the hollows where they joined the bone. His black hair was wrapped in a ponytail. The nails on his long fingers came to hard points. His trousers were worn buckskin; bright ribbons criss-cross bound his woven shirt's loose sleeves close to his arms. A heavy three-stone bolas was wrapped around his waist – a bolas is the best weapon for mountain conditions, and Ciabhar was a very skilled and patient hunter. He blinked cat-eyes. 'This man is really ill,' he said lucidly.

I pushed through. 'Let me see.'

The handsome stranger's skin was so waxen he looked like a statue carved from tallow. His lips and nail beds were blue; his breathing crackled. 'Oh, god,' I said, feeling snow-wet hands and an ice-cold forehead. He was severely hypothermic, but the Rhydanne wouldn't know that. Leanne flickered to my side and tried to pour hot water into his open, frost-blistered mouth.

'I watched him for ages,' Ciabhar said. 'On the Turbary Track. Walking on, walking up, without crampons. He wasn't a featherback so I left him in peace. He was searching around but he never saw me. At the top of Bealach Pass his pony lay down and died.'

Leanne gave him a look meaning, 'Breakfast is sorted.' She sped out, leaving the door open. She ran without pause over the bridge across Scree gorge that was just a single tightrope with two handrail cords, then lengthened her stride and disappeared, sliding, down the gritty path. She ran over the crystalline swathes of erosion among the naked rocks. Distant peaks looked as if ice had been poured down from their pointed summits and sharp boulders thrown sporadically up their slopes.

I said, 'I can't do anything for him here! Stupid! You should have descended. Down-slope – towards Carniss.'

Ciabhar shrugged.

'It's the *altitude* that's killing him. You just made it worse.'

I thumbed open an eye, the iris brown, pupils dilated. The lids were dark and swollen. I handled him gently as I took his pulse, which was slow. He stopped making the effort to shiver, as there was no warmth to gain by shivering. His breathing rate was dropping back to normal – too exhausted to keep the rapid pace. He coughed once, dryly, and a bubbling noise began in his lungs as he breathed.

'We're at eight thousand metres here. When did you last see a flatlander in the Spider?'

'They don't come to the plateau,' Ciabhar mused.

'That's because they can't breathe! They can't get sustenance from thin air; even I take days to acclimatise. And they freeze easily. Ciabhar, you know nothing. Help me carry him down to Tolastadh.'

I wrapped more rugs around the man's jacket, and noticed a small ink-blue tattoo of Cobalt manor's fishing bear on his wrist. 'A sailor?'

'What?'

'He's travelled a long way.'

As we hefted him his body convulsed once, froth ran from the corners of his mouth, and he died. Ciabhar dropped him, gave up cooperating and sloped away. Some more (cheery-drunk, boisterous-drunk, and totally pissed) hunters appeared and eagerly began stripping the corpse's clothes but I chased them off.

I checked his pockets, finding a damp paper bag containing sugar-cake, a wet box of matches and a very damp and fragile white envelope. It wilted and started to disintegrate in my hands. I flipped it over, seeing a crimson seal. Behind me Lascanne dragged the body out, intending to drop it over the edge of Scree gorge. Outside in the mountains, the dead are left where they fall. No Rhydanne cares about the dead in Darkling, where the living have so much to contend with.

I went back to the bar and slapped the letter down on its stone slab. Chamois-fat candles guttered in their horn holders. The script read: 'To be delivered to the hand of Comet Jant Shira. From Mist, Sailor and Captain of the Fleet. Send to the Filigree Spider, Scree. Please note – this envelope does NOT contain any money!!!'

'Oh, bugger!'

Just a few degrees colder, or another half-hour out in the drifts, and

Mist's courier wouldn't have reached me, and I wouldn't be sitting here in a hot, weltering caravel.

I perched on the ladder between poop deck and half-deck, watching a severely freckled Serein do stretches below in the main area. In order to impress Mist, he had learnt the names and actions of every part of the ship. He thrust his rapier through imaginary combatants who obviously didn't stand a chance.

He took a break and trotted over, swinging the rapier. 'Hello, Jant. You look a bit spaced out. What are you daydreaming about?'

'Darkling,' I said. 'And Tern.'

'Don't blame you. I'd miss her too.'

'Oh, yes?'

'Yeah. You're very lucky. In fact one of my mates in the fyrd had her picture as a pin-up. Just a tatty etching, of course, on the barracks wall. Tern is much, much more beautiful in real life. She's stunning. I wish my mate knew that I'd met her . . . Jant, are you all right?'

'I will be, if you don't ever speak to me again.'

# CHAPTER 8

'Very well,' Lightning said to Wrenn. 'I will spar with you. But I am only ranked sixth best with the rapier in the world, so a duel won't last long before you win. Give me a few hours to organise these men' – he gestured at the main deck where the *Petrel*'s sailors were hard at work – 'to make a more interesting game for you. After all, Insects don't play fair.'

'Agreed!' said Wrenn. He drew his sword and eagerly poked the point into the Insect-paper caulking between the deck planks.

Mist looked up from her ledger. 'Good, Lightning. That's better than you and Jant spending another night getting pissed on Mica-water port in my office.'

'I blame Wrenn for not drinking . . . We had to finish the open bottles.'

'Ha. I have to leave you boys to it every midnight to check navigational readings against the stars; when I come back in you're still carousing and reminiscing. Well, entertain my deck hands by all means, they need some leisure time, but you had better not injure any.'

Lightning leant on the rail and nodded. He was enjoying the novelty. 'Then here are the tournament rules: I'll do my best to hit you. We'll use buttoned rapiers and flat of the blade only. Every sailor you touch will play dead. Mist will arbitrate. The whole of *Petrel* is the arena.'

'And the *Melowne*,' said Mist. 'I'll bring her alongside and rope her to *Petrel* to make a gam. Then I can spare up to one hundred sailors. How many do you want?'

'All of them, of course.'

That afternoon, I circled above the lashed-together caravels. The sails were furled on all but the rearmost masts, which Mist said were mizzen masts with lateen sails set to keep the ships' prows into the waves. I took her word for it. My shadow flitted over as everyone on the *Melowne* crowded at the railings and clambered into the rigging to watch the *Petrel*'s main deck.

Wrenn and Lightning faced each other in the most spacious area by the foot of the mainmast. They raised their swords in salute, turned to honour the audience and Mist. Then they began to circle warily, watching each other with deliberation. Wrenn trod cautiously but didn't strike.

'Don't be afraid, shorty,' Lightning taunted. 'Besides, call that a haircut? Allow me to improve it.'

Wrenn tested Lightning with a pass; Lightning deflected it. Wrenn realised that Lightning was good, very good. He ran straight in with a diagonal attack. Lightning parried, let Wrenn run past him, turned – thrust – missed.

They circled. Lightning stabbed at Wrenn's chest, a killing blow had it landed. Wrenn regained the initiative, made a prolonged attack but Saker forcefully parried the blows.

Lightning gave a shout. At the signal, sailors rushed from the edges of the deck and open hatchways, straight at Wrenn from every direction. They all brandished the new broadswords. Some held them two-handed. Wrenn gasped – ran to back himself against the ship's side. Men clustered close, their mint-condition swords gleamed but Wrenn's rapier danced around them with agility. He parried every single one on his rapier's forte to protect his lighter blade.

I wanted a better view. I glided down to the crosstrees, curled my bare toes around the thick wood spar and then settled on it, legs dangling. Ten metres directly below me Awians and Plainslanders churned about, pushing Wrenn back against the gunwale. He jumped to the top of the railing, grasped a rope with his free hand, swept his rapier, clashing off all their raised staves and blades. He touched the padded knee of a woman's breeches. She backed away to the forecastle where she sat down. A cheer went up from the eager audience on the *Melowne*: 'You got Sanderling! Get Lightning! Go on!'

The sailors moved back on one side as Lightning pulled himself up to face Wrenn on the railing. The sailors cut off Wrenn's retreat. He held his rapier over his sturdy shoulder and climbed with his free hand, up the rope netting towards me. Lightning tested his foot on the lowest taut ratline. He stretched up and slashed with his point but Wrenn reached his rapier down and spun circles around it.

Wrenn hauled himself onto the crosstrees. I slipped into the air out of his way and glided over the ship as he ran lightly along the spar and climbed down the shrouds at the other side. He swung himself down to the half-deck leaving the sailors behind but Lightning dashed sternwards, scaled the half-deck ladder and confronted him there. He attacked Wrenn with a cut to the left shoulder. Wrenn retreated behind the helm to catch his breath. Mist was standing at the wheel but she didn't flinch or move a muscle. Behind her back, Lightning lunged, Wrenn gave more ground and came up against a rack of fire buckets.

Lightning made strong cuts to Wrenn's head; every time Wrenn parried his sword blurred with vibration. The furious clangs rang out over the ocean.

Wrenn caught a blow on his rapier's tip close to the round leather button. He twisted, almost disarmed Lightning. Lightning stamped his foot to distract him, rushed in with a flèche aimed at the solar plexus but Wrenn dodged.

Sailors started to climb the ladder from the main deck. Wrenn struck the first one at the top; the man jumped down. Wrenn 'killed' the next two and the third became uncertain how to attack. Three men on either side of the main deck spread out, anticipating Wrenn's escape route. They braced themselves by holding the sail lines above their heads.

Lightning called, 'Hey!' Five men jumped down off the topcastle, two burst out of my original cabin underneath. Wrenn ducked behind the helm. They charged at him; he touched them dead in seven seconds, his blade moving too fast to follow. Wrenn whipped round, rapier arm at full stretch, and arrested Lightning's blade mid-thrust.

Mist grew exasperated with ten men cutting round her and the helm. She yelled at the sister ship, 'Fulmer! To starboard!'

At the *Melowne*'s helm, Fulmer jumped. He spun his wheel simultaneously with Mist. The sails on the mizzen masts swivelled, all their air spilled out. *Petrel* and *Melowne* lurched, braked and tilted left.

Wrenn and Lightning lost their footing and slid on their backsides across the deck into the gunwale. Wrenn scrabbled to his feet first, fled down the ladder, and poised in first guard by the mainmast. Lightning gave Mist an angry glance, then sped after him. They started fencing enthusiastically. The sailors who maintained their balance quickly clustered round. Their mates picked themselves up out of the wet gutters and scuppers, and joined to restrict Wrenn's retreat from Lightning's attacks. Wrenn pressed back at them; he deflected every blow and kept his balance with clever footwork. Lightning never slowed but Wrenn still found chance to kill ten of the nearest sailors, alternately striking them between parrying Lightning.

The caravels righted themselves with a crash. But, bound together, they idled in the water, sails limp. They drifted side-on to the waves, which hit *Petrel*'s right hull and threw spray onto the main deck.

I flew closer, lost sight of the duellists while I landed on the poop deck, tricky because the ships were drifting slowly round. Everyone watched Wrenn.

Wrenn almost touched Lightning. Lightning fell back and let his team of sailors surge forward. He pulled a silk handkerchief from inside his shirt and wiped his face with it. Sweat ran freely down Wrenn's face.

Wrenn touched two more sailors; they flopped down at his feet. He avoided a huge Awian hefting a capstan bar, darted under and prodded him on the belly. The burly salt refused to die. He tried to trap Wrenn with the bar against the railings. He bounced on his feet like a boxer.

*Melowne* tars booed and started shouting, 'You're dead, Smew! You old bastard, get down! Stop being a bad loser! Finish him off, Serein!'

Wrenn jumped rat-fast onto the covered water butt and gave Smew a resounding slap on his bald pate. The big man must have been mindful of his audience, because he died theatrically.

On top of the barrel, Wrenn lunged and touched two more sailors. His right, middle, left; three more fell. His rapier was everywhere. I was dying to join in. I picked up a broadsword. Wrenn was obviously a head case; the most berserk of the crew members didn't perturb him. I wanted to cut him down to size.

Lightning glanced at me and made a covert spiral gesture with one hand. I recognised the gesture – a strategy we arranged long ago for the occasions we fight Insects in the amphitheatre. Lightning engaged Wrenn while I ran silently down to the main deck and crept up behind him. All I have to do is touch his back.

Wrenn read from his opponents' body language that I was there; either that or he can see behind him like an Insect. He stepped back sharply to keep us both in sight, swooped a parry past Lightning and onto me.

I immediately hacked throat to waist, making the most of my long reach. Wrenn took a bound backwards as if he could fly. He landed and slipped on the wet deck. He steadied himself, stubby wings spread, looked for eye contact.

I stabbed straight for his nipple; he fended my blade far out to the side in prime, his hand down. He riposted back in sixte to my chest, got nowhere near – my fast sixte counter-riposte batted it away. Surprise flitted across Wrenn's eyes. No time to think in words but I felt satisfied. Don't underestimate me.

Wrenn beat my blade aside to the right, parried Lightning, then back to attack over my blade to my shoulder. As his rapier rose, I dodged and sliced across his stomach. He turned his blade down and stopped my cut.

Again with his blade flat he smacked Lightning's cut away and made a return blow to me. The sailors had no room to attack with Lightning and I working as a pair. We fell into step but I couldn't pre-empt Wrenn because he kept cutting away to Lightning on my left.

My speed worried Wrenn. He twisted left, bound and locked Lightning's blade. He shouted and freed his sword in a motion that left Lightning confused, stepped away and concentrated on me. He blocked my slices with a short economical movement, parried down and outwards, jabbed under my guard. I moved reflexively, almost on automatic.

He attacked to my face. I brushed it aside with a weak cut from the wrist. It was a feint. Wrenn pulled the blow, punched past my hilt. I felt a sudden sting on my knuckles. The grip slipped out of my grasp and my broadsword looped pommel over foible, over the ship's side into the water.

Wrenn breathed through open mouth; his gaze slipped away as he switched his full attention back to Lightning.

Being disarmed and out of the game, I retreated to the steps and watched the fight continue. Wrenn was tiring, but eighty out of the hundred men were down.

Lightning hallooed again: 'Hey!'

The last of the crew rushed out of Ata's cabin. Wrenn made as if to dash back but instead ran to the gunwale. He vaulted *Petrel*'s side and landed on the main deck of the *Melowne*. The audience there drew back with surprised cries.

Wrenn hurtled past them and up the forecastle ladder. *Petrel*'s crew followed him, climbing or leaping over the perilous narrow gap and the log fenders between the ships. Wrenn defended the lofty ladder so well he killed ten more before they forced their way to his level.

A sailor made a lunge so long he overbalanced. Lightning ran in on the advantage but Wrenn parried coolly. Dead combatants sat down dotting the little triangular deck. Lightning made a concerted effort but Wrenn with his back to the foremast was invincible. The last two crewmen fell on Lightning's left and right. Only he remained.

Lightning feinted once, twice, thrust at Wrenn's sword arm. Wrenn had anticipated it and bound Lightning's blade. They grated together with a sound like knives sharpened on a steel.

Wrenn angled his blade and thrust down; his rapier point bounced off Lightning's thigh. Lightning knelt but before he hit the deck the round padded button was under his chin. Lightning spread his arms wide, his sword loose in his right hand.

Wrenn froze. His blue Summerday FC shirt had turned black with sweat; his face was crimson. He looked at Lightning straight and whispered, 'You're dead.'

Bodies in white shirts sprawled all over the ships. A gust buffeted *Petrel* and *Melowne*; water sloshed under their bows. There was complete silence.

Lightning brought his hands together in applause. Wrenn saluted him with his rapier on which new scrapes and scratches shone bright.

Everyone began to cheer. The beaten sailors got to their feet, brushing down their clothes, grinning at each other and staring with envy and respect in Wrenn's direction. The Swordsman concentrated on stretching his back and robust limbs in his customary sequence. His rapier stuck upright between the planks.

I vaulted to the *Melowne*, climbed to the forecastle and shook his hand. 'You're amazing.'

Wrenn bowed to me, and the audience; drops of sweat fell from his hair to the deck. Lightning shook and flexed his sword arm. It must have felt like lead from the strain and vibration.

Mist clapped her hands briskly; her high voice carried over the ships. 'On your feet, crew, and to your stations. Double rations tonight of rum and beer if you drink to the health and genius of Serein Wrenn.'

Wrenn turned to Lightning and said effusively, 'Thank you. That was a great idea. Thanks for letting me show the Zascai my flair.'

'Indeed. I admit I've never fought on a ship before, but one thousand years ago I saw the then Swordsman take on *three* hundred men in the Castle's dining hall. Not just sailors, either; six lamai sections of a Select Fyrd division.'

Wrenn's smile faded instantly, his pride deflated. However I saw a teasing gleam in Lightning's eye; I think he was making it up.

Into the second month every sailor and passenger on the *Stormy Petrel* and *Melowne* started to become possessive about their property. I knew with detailed intimacy the few items I had brought on board; I mended and cared for them jealously. I put a keen edge on my axe. I polished my mirror. I kept my wings preened and oiled in perfect condition. The ocean yielded nothing so the neatness of my cabin and the conservation of materials took on a great importance. I protected my private space thoroughly; we all became territorial. Lightning acted as if he had condensed his entire palace into a ship's berth. He spent too much time talking to Wrenn and seemed not to have noticed that I was taking cat again.

As a passenger I felt powerless and incarcerated. There were few chances to be of use but Mist employed me to carry messages between the ships. Every morning I tried to instruct her in Old Morenzian but she wasn't comfortable with formal study.

Something about the precise figures in Mist's ledger, her neatly complicated compasses and the vermeil astrolabe fascinated me almost as much as the glassware and herbs in the chemist's shop where I once worked. She had a quadrant made of incised ivory, a shining brass sextant and a very accurate sea clock in a cushioned casket. For all Mist's expertise she couldn't see from the air as I could, so every afternoon I checked the coastlines of her portolan charts. The sheer distance we were sailing frightened me, but there was no way I could bring her to confess the danger we were in.

Every dusk I went below deck to check on the Insect. Immediately it saw me it attacked, crashing into the bars of its cage. I crouched behind my axe, enjoying the adrenaline surge, and watched until it tired itself out. Everybody knows that Insects can't be trained; if it had been any other wild animal I would have dedicated the voyage to bringing it under control. It didn't understand my signals. It only sensed me as food. It raged and starved.

One evening I managed to loop a leather strap around the Insect's foreleg, but it tore off the tether and ate it. It chewed bones and layered them onto the smelly hard white paste spread round the edges of its cage. The concretion grew thicker over days and weeks. When it reached six centimetres high, I realised that the Insect was building a wall. I think it wanted to find other Insects, after all they are animals that work together. Since it found it was inexplicably alone and trapped, it began walling itself into a cell in which it presumably felt more at home.

I hoped that the Insect didn't have the ability to call others through, from whatever Shift world it hatched in. I imagined thousands of Insects popping into the hold, the ship gradually lowering in the water with their weight. Or our Insect finding a path to vanish back into the Shift, leaving an empty cage. That would raise some questions.

Each night, I stayed inside my cabin with the door bolted. I tried to meditate into the Shift, but every time I was unsuccessful and extremely frustrated. I tried to relax and empty my mind but I couldn't concentrate for more than a couple of minutes before I started on another line of thought, for example Tern's infidelity. After a week, I gave up.

I put red and yellow wraps in my hair and threaded fat jade beads onto my dreadlocks. I swigged rum. I masturbated myself sore. I lived immersed in sensation for weeks on end until the scolopendium stashed in my paper wraps ran out. I tried to ration it but that just made the craving worse. Since I've been addicted in the past, my body recognises cat and knows how to use it. I knew I could become quickly hooked again and had to be careful, but it was the only thing that stopped me thinking of Tern.

I slid down the scrollwork to the orlop deck and started searching among the supplies. The strength of the craving is difficult to describe to someone who has never been an addict. It is like an intense hunger, the same deep, terrible need a starving man has for food. It gnaws all the time, from the moment of waking through to the night, a tiny whisper or a cold gale that will push you into the most bizarre behaviours. It made me creep down here to the lazaretto lockers at the stern. Most of my will power was spent on coping with the constant fear of floating in the middle of the ocean; I no longer had the strength to stand against my yearning for cat.

The ship's medical supplies were in a wooden trunk. Unable to pick the lock, I took my axe to it. I sorted through all the various pieces of equipment, steamed-clean scalpels, folded bandages and ointment jars, and came across a cardboard box with struts separating corked glass ampoules. I ran my hand over them and they rattled. I pulled one out and looked at the label. A little skylark logo; *Scolopendium. 3% aqueous solution. Do not exceed the dose prescribed. Export interdicted.*

Skylarks. I counted across a row and down a column; there were fifty tubes, a great deal too much for this ship to be carrying. I was convinced that the Sailor must expect a fight on Tris. There were also a number of slender glass syringes in clean paper packets. I tore the end off one and shook it out. It's a better rush than I've had so far. No! God, honestly, Jant, you have no self-control. I put it down, feeling as if I wasn't in my body, with denial so great I wondered if I were actually here at all.

I have a choice. I'll just use it once and then throw all these ampoules overboard. I gave in – yes, I'll do it – and a flush of relaxation spread through me, a warm feeling of relief as if I had taken the shot already. I hadn't even noticed how on edge I was, how tightly I had been holding myself.

I hurried back to my cabin, braced myself in the lowest corner with my sinewy arm across my knees and looked at the inside of my elbow. I was in great shape and didn't have to tie up, my veins were hard like cables under the skin.

I felt guilty, then rebelled. Why feel remorse? If any other man aboard knew, the skylarks would be long gone. On the street in Hacilith us kids skilfully used guilt to hold each other back. Like little Eszai, we tried for any opportunity with all we had. But those few who succeeded were brought down by guilt, because they knew their friends were still in the gutter. I'm doing this because I can. Who would say no to such intense pleasure?

The timbers creaked and I jumped. Every time a wave gulped under the hull I was sure it was about to split and spill us all into raging water. Mist told me that the boards are meant to yield slightly to make the ship flexible. In my mind's eye the planks buckled, leaks sprayed between them. Frothing water races from the bilges into the hold, erupts through the hatchways; the ship tilts and sinks dreamily intact down to the seabed.

My mouth was dry with anticipation and I concentrated so hard on measuring the dose that nothing else existed – no ship, no other immortals, none of the sailors in the rigging feeling the breeze through their open wings. I know what I'm doing is wrong. But just once, to get it over with, and that will be the last injection I ever take.

When I'm hooked, which I'm not, I try to keep a little scolopendium in my body all the time. Drinking it is fine, to keep the level constant, but if it runs out and I dip below the basic amount, then I'm more likely to panic and . . . do this:

I pushed the tip of the bright needle into my skin, which separated as the point sank in delicately; deeper. Dark red blood shot up into the barrel and started to diffuse. *I want that back*, I thought, and pressed the plunger down as quickly as I dared. I lay back with the needle in my arm. My hands spasmed. A wave of contortion passed over me – the ecstasy was almost unbearable.

We travelled on. The days became indistinguishable. The days smeared into each other. And the sun rose over and over again.

# CHAPTER 9

I woke up horrified to find myself still on the ship, and another whore of a day stretching out in front of me exactly like the last. I reached under the pillow for another phial and with the help of scolopendium managed to stall its inevitable onslaught for a few more hours.

April. Needle scars were making a calendar on my arm. I kept my long-sleeved T-shirt on to cover them. An occasional shower refreshed us and filled the barrels, but overall the heat was oppressive and all the deck hands worked barefoot and stripped to the waist. Our clothes were faded by the sun and mine were patched. I was slightly more shadowy around the eyes, but not so anyone would notice. It suited me, anyway, and cat kept my weight down. The first thing any drug abuse removes is the part of your mind that gives a damn about your health. And there's an advantage to addiction – cat was a protection. All my anxiety was concentrated on one problem so I dealt with the rest of the world without concern.

I went to lounge on the foredeck, seeing the ocean plunge away in all directions the same. Wrenn and I watched *Stormy Petrel* sailing as close to the wind as possible, canted with all canvas out, three hundred metres ahead of us on the right side. Lightning climbed up to her aft castle and waved to us from the rail. He was tanned, and the sunlight had bleached his fair hair.

He strung a gold-banded compound bow and flexed it, loosing an arrow that looped high into the air. Wrenn ducked and shouted, 'Look out!'

The arrow plummeted straight at me and appeared sticking out of the deck plank not ten centimetres away from my left hand. I sprang up. 'Saker! What do you think you're doing?'

He couldn't hear me. He waved cheerfully and pointed at us, then at the horizon.

'What is that flash bastard on about?' The arrow had a letter tied to it. I broke the thread and unspooled the paper that Lightning had wrapped tightly around its shaft.

*Comet*

*By Mist's calculations you should be able to see the Island of Tris now, if you fly to a height four times the main mast and stay close to the ships. Look due east. Come and tell us if you see anything.*
*LSM*

While I read it, Lightning, who now had Wrenn's attention, proceeded to show off. He shot an arrow skywards and Wrenn watched it describe a high parabola while Lightning rapidly took another arrow and sent it after the first, shooting straight out in a flat trajectory. As his first arrow came down the second one hit it, spinning it head over flights. A second later we faintly heard the crack they had made as they collided. Lightning did this again to prove the first time wasn't a fluke.

'He can hit an arrow in the air!' Wrenn said.

'Yeah.' Lightning had been passing the last couple of weeks by sitting on the crosstrees and shooting at albatrosses. He halved their feathers to make more arrows. Only the dwindling numbers of seabirds slowed him down. 'You should see his trick with an arrow in a cork and a wine bottle.'

I gave Wrenn the letter, spread my wings and arced up from the stern. I climbed steeply, forcing my fifty-eight kilos into the air. I sensed every ripple in the breeze *Melowne* distorted with her massive cream sails.

The ships diminished quickly. I was terrified of losing sight of them in such a vast expanse. I tried to stay above the mainmast of the *Petrel*, although there was no lift at all. I could easily outpace them, and then I would be crossing and recrossing the same area of ocean, trying in vain to find them, until I fell from exhaustion and drowned.

I searched ahead, and saw nothing but more water, so I flew higher until the ornate *Petrel* was the length of my index finger, trailing rainbows in her bow wave. The ships' wakes were two Vs around their prows and white veils stretching behind them for hundreds of metres. I glided into a shallow spiral to rest. Either Mist's calculations are incorrect, or the island does not exist at all.

I chandelled up, higher still, and looked out east. On the horizon, raised on haze, a dark green patch seemed to float. A mountain! A mountain in the sea! I kept climbing, aware that I was the second immortal ever to set eyes on Tris. The island emerged, summit first. I felt a firm companionship with it, as if it had been set there especially for me. Fluffy white clouds hung over it, and I could just see their shadows on the smooth mountainside. The crest was pale grey with distance.

There were some crags around the shoreline. Maybe they were cliffs, I couldn't tell. I stared until my eyes watered. The haze began to dissipate, the perspective suddenly clicked, and I realised I was looking at a town. The white buildings resembled a slope of scree, tumbling from the mountainside down to the coast and perching on what must be lower buttresses of the peak. It was incredibly beautiful, so wonderful I found myself laughing. I whooped, somersaulted in the air and dived down to *Stormy Petrel*.

'Oh, my god. Oh god, Mist, you're completely right! You're a genius, Mist. I take back all I've ever slandered. It's there, where you said it'd be, and it's magnificent. Magnificent! I mean, even Awia never had anything like this—'

'Can you see it?' asked Lightning.

'He can see it,' said Mist, hanging on the wheel.

I aligned myself in the wind flow, beside the railings, facing towards her. 'I've never seen anything like it! It's so pretty it's just not true. Like . . .' Like a piece of the Shift in the Fourlands. I paused, and described it more calmly. A scout is useless unless he gives sensible reports. At sea level, the heat was stronger; it annoyingly slowed my thinking. 'I can see the town, though at the moment it's just a speck. I can see the island's whole west face – actually Tris is a huge mountain growing up out of the sea!'

Mist carefully noted a compass reading in her ledger with a pencil stub, and snapped her telescope out from its case. This was utterly fantastic – a new part of the Empire we—

A gust nearly sent me into the waves. I was losing too much height. I gestured to Lightning, 'Chuck me that . . . and that,' pointing to a water bottle and a hunk of bread. He threw them from the back railing one at a time. I dived and caught them. 'I can't wait to scale the summit. I'm going for a closer look.'

'No!'

Try and stop me. I said, 'Don't worry, I'll be back before your heart beats twice.'

I half-folded my wings for strength, pulled them down through the air resistance. Mist had said the town was called Capharnaum. I repeated that word aloud as I cruised, the only wholly Trisian word I knew. I couldn't wait to speak to the islanders in their ancient language. That is, if they didn't run away at the sight of me. I was used to flatlanders staring, or their outright hostility. Once in a Hacilith café the waiter put a bowl of milk and a fish skeleton on the floor for me when I ordered beer and a sandwich. My gang returned the following night and burnt the café to the ground.

Nowadays I give Zascai something to stare at; I dress up to the role. But surely no Trisian would have heard of a Rhydanne before. I was very tempted to scare them on purpose. I'd have an eager audience, no doubt about that! They will just have to take me as I am, I concluded. After all, they're part of the Empire and I'm their Messenger as well.

Over an hour, the island grew larger and details appeared. Dark green bushes on the mountainside became twisted trees, an olive grove. A rugged shape in the centre of the town became an outcrop, and on its summit, fifty metres higher than the town's rooftops, a bright white complex resolved into a series of elegant, airy buildings with fluted columns, much bigger than I expected. It could be the manor house. The outcrop seemed to move across my field of vision faster than the mountainside behind it, so I could tell that it was a pinnacle standing out alone.

Black flecks on the sea became big canoes with five to ten men paddling in each, riding the surf with great dexterity. They even drew their paddles in and went flying down the funnels of the waves. A white strip underlining the town was a great harbour wall of admirable workmanship, nearly three times larger than the light-house quay at Awndyn. Rolling surf broke and peeled along it. Elsewhere on the coast, cypress trees extended right down to high-water mark, where the rocks were yellow with lichen and stained black by the sea. The trees were small and gnarled; the Trisians had no chance of ever building a caravel. Breakers boomed on the shingle, deep-water rollers thundered in parallel lines. Above their reach, an amber band of seaweed and a white band of shellfish striped the boulders.

Capharnaum was like a model. Closer now, and the model came alive, men and women in the streets. A winged lad in a straw hat cast a fishing line, and paid no attention as my shadow sped over him. I soared up, and marvelled.

A warm, delicious breeze blew constantly in from the sea, like the updraught from the hypocaust rooms in an Awian bathhouse. It's certainly difficult to find lift this good on the mainland. I was flying automatically, so occupied in staring around that I hadn't realised how little effort I was putting in. I rode the same current with several gulls, who watched with an attitude that said: You can't be serious. We whirled round each other, but they were the better gliders and they gained height. I peeled out of the thermal to look at the town.

I glided as slowly as I could without stalling and constantly made tiny adjustments with my legs acting as a forked tail, counteracting the air currents that now came from all directions. Even so I flew too rapidly to see much detail and I could only look down on the roofs.

Two main streets intersected in the centre of Capharnaum. They were surrounded by smaller roads that ran in a neat criss-cross pattern, like a grid. The houses were spaced very regularly; it was bizarre, completely different from Hacilith's sprawl and unlike the graceful curves in which Awians build. Cypresses flanked empty avenues leading north and south into the countryside. Roughly at five-kilometre intervals along the roadside there were tall black and white posts like gibbets, with short planks nailed at right angles to them. Probably some kind of flagpole.

At the edges the street grid lost coherence and the houses were jumbled together. Trees invaded between them. All the villas were exactly the same size, square and whitewashed, dazzling and clean. The terracotta tiles on their shallow roofs looked like overlapping feathers. Their square windows had alabaster screens instead of glass; their shutters were open. They had porticos surrounding square peristyle lawns or dark green gardens, some with statues. They faced out to sea. It was quiet, unlike Hacilith, it was tranquil. I could see no poor section of town, no slums, no kids standing on street corners. It did not resemble any town in the Fourlands, but maybe when Micawater was founded it looked like this. If I flew any lower I risked being seen. With an acute sense of unreality I wheeled above the town. It's a dream, I assured myself. It's all a damn dream.

Here the warm wind smelt of sage and thyme, herbs growing wild. Shrubs among the boulders bore yellow flowers. At the far north and south extremes of the island, on the gentle slope before the mountainside became steep maquis, there were two other towns, smaller than Capharnaum. Both seemed connected with the sea, but pale green terraced hillsides stepped above them.

Thin air at last, I thought. I had a brief glimpse of the mountain top – my god – is that snow on the summit? I wanted more than anything to investigate the white gleams and see if they were snow patches, and roll in them if they were, but Mist would not receive my report kindly if it focused on conditions at the peak rather than in the towns.

The mountain top was not a sheer arête as in Darkling – it didn't come to a point. It was a smooth, arid ridge that leant over into a big bowl-shaped hollow not visible from sea level. It was veiled with chutes of small grey stones. Clouds formed on the edge of the bowl and blew eastward.

That side of the island looked uninhabited, although it was too far to see any detail. Decaying cracks split the sheer sea cliffs, a drop of at least three hundred metres around which white birds swirled and dived. The black, denticulate reefs below them were like a half-submerged wolf's jawbone; churning water smashed over the narrow serrated molars and canine points. I determined to warn Mist. But calm and remote, far off in the eastern ocean, two other peaks of smaller islets emerged in a line.

Tris was fresh, quiet and, it seemed to me, content. My duty to bring news of the Empire to the island will probably be the most important task I will ever have as Messenger.

I winged back to the ships, which were still scudding stoically towards Tris. The weak wind did not affect the enormous rollers they rode. *Petrel*'s deck rose up to my feet as I landed next to Mist. 'Tris is an archipelago,' I said. 'I flew right over; there are more islands on the other side.'

'Did anyone see you?' she demanded.

'No. I saw ladies in smocks selling food from the porches of townhouses and boys drying green fishing nets on the harbour wall, but not one of the Capharnai saw me,' I said with dignity, coining an Awian word.

'When we arrive you must *not* fly. I don't want them to know; I mean, you'll only frighten them. Did you see any vessels other than canoes?'

'Don't think so . . .'

'What about signs of Insects? Any Walls? Paperlands?'

'No.'

'Fortresses?' Lightning asked. 'Bastions? Châteaux?'

'It's too big,' I said defensively. 'You have to see for yourself. There are plantations, vineyards, and goats on the mountainside.'

'Typical Jant, always thinking about sex,' Mist smiled, looking into the distance. A crosswind tangled her fine hair. The waves were reflected on the ships' sides as a moving mesh of light.

I returned to the *Melowne* in time to hear Fulmer complaining. The billows tossed the caravel every direction but forward. She ran headlong down a steep wave and pitched into the next rising roller. Puffs of spray burst off her keel and splattered back. We went up and down, up and down vertically on an irregular see-saw. Wrenn and I retreated to the poop deck.

Fulmer leant against the wheel's kicks. He was having a lot of trouble steering. *Melowne* jerked sideways every time she struck and wrenched the wheel from his hands. The broad ship had a massive drag; he couldn't keep her from sliding aslant into the troughs of the swell. 'Damn it,' he wheezed. 'Mist will just have to slow down for us, yes? Shit, she makes it look effortless. Get the flying sails in. Sea anchor back there and see if I can keep her prow half as straight as *Petrel*.'

From the poop deck we could see the back of Fulmer's head. Not a brown hair was out of place. As usual, and against all the odds, he looked pristine, still a court dandy three thousand, eight hundred kilometres from Queen Eleonora's entourage. Fulmer's genteel manner impressed me until I remembered that he had known about the Insect even before we set sail, and it was he who had been feeding it bones all this time.

Wrenn scrutinised the horizon. 'I can see it! I can see a tiny island!'

'In the next couple of hours you'll find it is huge.'

Up to the deck came barrels of wine, and bar silver was stacked in quadrilaterals. A forest of colourful pennants unfurled. As Tris filled our vision, the evergreen and pumice shore proceeding past, unbridled excitement overcame the crews. Mist and Fulmer found it difficult to keep the sailors working; men stared and pointed at houses, vineyards, the palace on the crag. They waved at tanned Capharnai fishermen in the first canoes.

Mist brought the ships in. She yelled commands to her crew, keeping them moving. I heard her from the *Melowne* three ship-lengths behind; the tension in her voice made me nervous. In contrast, Fulmer gave his orders in a quiet, assured style, politely addressing the hands. They copied every movement of the *Petrel*'s men, furling the sails in completely synchronised manoeuvres. Fulmer's ship sailed slick as fiddly clockwork in the *Stormy Petrel*'s wake.

The harbour walls pincered together on our left and right and formed a strait about five hundred metres wide. Dead centre of the channel was a flat-topped rock with a lighthouse on it. It towered above us, one hundred metres high, built on a square base half the *Petrel*'s length. As we glided past, the sailors became even more frantic. At first I assumed they were shocked by the lighthouse's great height, which was certainly surprising considering that the Trisians only have canoes. Then I realised they were pointing at the fire reflector: it was made of polished gold. The fittings of the beacon were all solid gold.

Fulmer called, 'Jant, do you see?'

'Yes, I do!'

'It's the most glorious thing I've ever seen.'

I muttered to Wrenn, 'What I don't like is the fact Mist never mentioned it before.'

I wore my purple scarf wrapped around my waist as a cummerbund, stripy black and white leggings under cut-off denim shorts. A black kerchief kept back all my locks and albatross feathers. The swell was making Wrenn look green but he was determined to watch the tumult on the main deck. He clung onto a network of ropes. 'It's all right to lean on the deadeyes. Sailors before the mast are going to reef the mainsail now, look.'

'Fascinating . . .'

'And lower it on parr—'

'Oh, shut up!'

He stared forward at the bow, which pointed like a pike at the town. 'Do you think there are ladies in Capharnaum?' he asked.

I glanced at him. 'Well, obviously.'

'No. Whores, I mean.'

'Oh. That kind of lady. They're human, well, they look it to me,' I regarded my fingernails in a secretarial gesture. 'So they'll have wine, women and song.'

# CHAPTER 10

As we crossed the harbour our ships fell under the lee of the mountain. The lagoon's surface was mirror-still; it reflected *Petrel* and *Melowne*'s images from waterline to masthead. Their sails went slack and they coasted in very slowly indeed, on the last of their momentum. Fulmer ordered the last sails furled and I looked up to see clear blue sky between the masts for the first time in three months.

Trisian men, women and children poured out of the town's façade and rushed to form a crowd on the sea wall and all along the corniche. The men's clothes looked quite plain – white or beige linen or silk tunics with coloured borders, and loose trousers underneath. Some of the girls wore pastel-dyed stoles over their double-layer dresses but none of their garments looked embroidered or rich.

Men pushed out dark wood canoes and jumped in, paddling towards us. The canoes had outriggers; blue and white eyes were painted on their prows. They moved very swiftly and were soon clustered around our hull. The Trisians shouted and pointed, held up all kinds of food and objects. Dozens of hands reached to the portholes, waving spiny fruit, enormous seeds, stoppered jars, dead fish on skewers, silver flasks. Our sailors hung over the railings eagerly offering anything to hand on the deck. They passed or threw down belaying pins, hatchets and belt buckles, the plumb line from the bow.

Fulmer's composure broke. He yelled, 'No trading! Stop it, fools, before you give them your vests and pants! No barter, till Mist gives the word! Hacilith law and punishment applies from now on.'

He glanced at me. 'The rash bastards will swap anything for curios. They'd pull the nails from the futtocks and even trade our instruments away if I don't watch them. We must beware of thieves, yes/ no? Even a fishhook from Tris is a novelty that will fetch money in the Fourlands now. Still, at least Capharnai are friendly.'

The *Petrel*, in front of us, glided through the reflections of Capharnaum's first houses, came alongside the harbour wall and docked. Our ship's salt-stained prow stopped just a metre behind the ornate windows of *Petrel*'s stern. Then two gangways slipped down and simultaneously locked into place. Wrenn immediately ran to the quay, where he stood smiling and waving, the first of our company to set foot on Tris. Native men and women approached him, asking questions that of course he couldn't understand so he just kept nodding in cheerful agreement.

There were no mooring loops on the wharf so Mist made her crew unload the stern and bow anchors of both ships and place them on the pavement with the ropes drawn taut.

Mist and Fulmer descended the gangways of their respective ships and met on the quayside. They shook hands politely in front of the astonished townspeople. 'We did it!' she said.

'I had every confidence in you, Eszai,' said Fulmer. He smoothed a couple of invisible wrinkles out of his suit sleeve with a spotless hand. The breeze opened his jacket and I saw a dagger swinging from his belt.

I descended to dry land at the same time as Lightning disembarked from the *Petrel*. He carried his strung longbow over his shoulder; arrow nocks protruded from the quiver at his waist. He glanced at the windows of every villa fronting the quay.

Wrenn bounded to a halt, panted, 'Have you noticed that none of the Capharnai have any weapons? Some of the fishermen have knives in their sashes but they look a bit odd.'

'It's true,' said Lightning. 'Jant, do you see?'

I said, 'I think the blades are bronze.'

Lightning said, 'But obviously there's no reason for Capharnai to know of swords. The Fourlands had no swords before the Insects arrived.'

'And then they were invented pretty quickly!' I grinned. I was loving the attention.

Mist gave me an expectant look. 'Make your introductions, Jant.'

I spread my arms and began to address the townspeople with a speech I had carefully prepared: 'Governors, ladies and gentlemen, thank you for receiving us from the Fourlands. We have brought some gifts as a sign of goodwill: casks of wine and silver ingots—'

The large crowd of people giggled as if I was mad. Mist and I glanced at each other. 'Keep going,' she said.

'We would like to meet the governors of Capharnaum to tell them of the Em—'

The crowd parted to let a man through. He walked forward until he faced us alone. I assumed he was the Capharnai's own representative. He was a tall old man, every aspect of his comportment upright and efficient. His eyes were the same dark brown as beer-bottle glass, hair every shade of grey, once so windblown it would never lie flat. He was dry as a ship's rib. His face was pinched; his mouth slotted in under his cheekbones. It looked like he was smiling wryly all the time, with a wicked grin that enticed me to smile with him, like a collaborator.

He wore a short cloak over a tunic with a deep hem border. His laced boots with open toes were so unusual Fulmer especially couldn't stop staring at them. No doubt Fulmer was wondering if he could start a fashion in the Fourlands for toeless boots.

The Trisian spoke slowly, giving me time to translate. The terms that I could not decipher, I left as he gave them. 'My name is Vendace. I was a fisherman, now elected to the Senate. They have sent me to thank you for coming here. Are you the same as the boat that appeared nine months ago?'

'Yes, from the Fourlands. Call me Jant. I can speak Trisian but please talk slowly; I don't know many words. My friends can't speak it at all; I'll translate for them.'

'What's he saying?' asked Mist, who was becoming very frustrated.

'He's welcoming us,' I said in Awian.

'Tell him I'm in charge and ask him to give his word that my ships will be safe here tonight,' said Mist.

I told Vendace, and added, 'We're here on peaceful terms.'

Vendace said, 'We saw your sails this morning – the Senate has convened in an emergency session to discuss our course of action. The Senate is still in progress and they have asked me to bring you to the House. Our constitution warns against contact with another land; our constitution is important to us.'

Mist tugged my arm. 'What's he saying?'

'I've no idea. He seems to be going on about their fitness.' I paused for a second to stop my mind whirling. 'He's offered to take us to the governors' house.'

Mist said, 'Well, at least ask a guarantee for our safety on land. I see some victuals being brought out. Thank him for giving me the opportunity to buy provisions and offer to pay with the bar silver.'

I stumbled over a translation to Vendace. The Trisians surrounding us all began laughing again. Even the fisherman couldn't keep a straight face – he smirked.

'Why are they sniggering?' Lightning enquired.

Mist asked, 'Are you actually saying what I tell you to say?'

I wished that she would stop hassling me. I hadn't had any chance to practise. I pinched the bridge of my nose. 'Well, I think so! Or I could have asked him to serve us a warm dog.'

Lightning said, 'They laugh when you speak of – of what?'

'The wine and silver,' I said.

Lightning said, 'Hmm. I should think they have wine of their own. And more than enough gold, if you remember the priceless lighthouse mirrors.'

I looked more closely at the crowd. 'You know, none of the Capharnai are wearing jewellery. But gold's available here; in fact it's abundant. Do you think it could be that Capharnai don't care for it?'

Lightning indicated a small girl who was sucking her thumb. A gold band held back her dark hair. 'That puts us on a level with their children. And I will wager that her crown is pure, refined gold.' He removed the circlet from his head.

Mist rubbed her eyes. 'But . . . Well, if precious metals are worthless we've no valuables to trade with. This island seems to lack nothing; what do we have that they could possibly want?'

'Steel,' said Wrenn.

Fulmer said, 'You clever, clever man! Yes, we can give them nails, tacks and chain links. Knife blades and hatchets were in demand; I saw the canoeists admiring them. How about halberds from the *Melowne*? The Trisians must use axes so they'll recognise halberds that are superior to bronze. They should be willing to accept what is better, yes?'

'It's possible,' Mist said guardedly.

Vendace remained unflappable but kept glancing at my eyes. He showed us a stone cistern on the quayside and Mist organised two squads of sailors to fill barrels with fresh water. She arranged another team to buy fruit, meat and vegetables from Capharnai merchants who were already approaching us out of the town, but she forbade them to barter for any other goods, or to buy items for their own keeping. Then she turned to her second-in-command. 'Viridian, tell *Melowne*'s bosun to obey my orders and follow them yourselves if you love me and your place in my fleet. Don't leave the ships unprotected. Move them only if you're threatened . . . And if we don't come back tonight, you know what to do.'

'Certainly, Mist,' she said. 'And good luck, Mum.'

Mist was dissatisfied with Vendace's appearance. She said, 'The Circle doesn't need a fisherman.'

'I was unaware we have the authority to recruit for the Circle,' Lightning commented.

Mist gave him a venomous look. I suppose she was right; it would be a stroke of luck if a leader of Tris excelled at some occupation and could join the Circle. She said quietly, 'This man is elderly enough to be very grateful for immortality.'

'Wisdom comes with age,' said Wrenn, vaguely.

'Maybe it does, here,' said Lightning.

'Aye, well no matter what venerable age he has reached, he's still a baby compared to us.'

Vendace had listened to their exchange without understanding a word. He smiled and pointed a direction through the crowd; we followed him.

The heat was like a barrier, and every rare midday gust of wind just blew hot air at us, into our skin, and offered no relief. It seemed to come in waves, each more stifling and cloying than the last. I unlaced my shirtsleeves, slipped them off and tucked them in my belt. The heat made the five of us walk slowly, with smooth, languid movements.

Fulmer said, 'I could quite happily live here. See the promenade, it's splendid, yes?'

'Yeah,' said Wrenn. 'I've never seen such sexy girls. Check out that honey with the short skirt.'

Fulmer selected a cigarette from a whale's-tooth ivory case and screwed it into a holder. He rubbed his short beard. 'I plan to come back and never leave at all, at all. I have no ties and our huntress Queen will gladly grant me permission. This is much better than Awia, which copies the Castle. We turn everything into a bloody competition, from maths to pottery, and we wear ourselves out. Here no one's the best and no one cares. See how happy they are?'

We were led from the harbour into a long, straight main boulevard bordered by white marble columns. Steles stood at regular intervals, topped with statues of men and women draped in cloth. I counted them, and noticed that after every ten statues an archway spanned the street. Smaller alleys led into the road-grid on either side of us, between the two-storey buildings. Small shops opened onto the pavement, with striped canvas porticoes: a confectioner selling pasties and pastries; sausages hung above smoked viands and a mess of octopus in a butcher's; a barber swept his shop.

Everybody was pointing things out and bursting with questions, far too many for me to translate. 'Look at the vines,' Mist said, enthralled.

They twined up a trellis on the last quayside house, heavy with black grapes, tendrils reaching to the terracotta chimney.

I surreptitiously peered over the green window boxes as we passed, seeing that the furniture in the lower room was slight and elegant. A small dog lay curled on a chair cushion. The cool walls were painted with a stylised frieze of pearl divers in an underwater garden. Trisian art seemed to cover everyday items rather than being framed.

'The knives,' Wrenn said. 'Ask him about the bronze daggers.'

'I certainly will not!'

Fulmer indicated a workshop where a canoe was being carved. Vendace said, 'We travel for hundreds of kilometres around Tris and the unoccupied islands.'

'Hundreds?' I asked.

Vendace nodded with enthusiasm for his profession. 'Easily, past the Motley Isles into the open ocean! Why do you question it? I'll speak slower if you want.'

Next we saw a large paved piazza surrounded by colonnades. Mist said, 'This must be a marketplace. Isn't it cute?'

A restaurant occupied the open, airy ground floor of the nearest block. About twenty Capharnai tumbled out and joined those lining the street to stare at us. A stout café proprietor wore a loose tunic, a single piece of material gathered at the waist by a sash. He beckoned. 'Come in, come and dine.'

Vendace raised his brown hands apologetically. 'Excuse me, Derbio, I must take our visitors to the Amarot.'

The round man giggled. 'Of course, but they're invited to drink tea with us afterwards.'

I was thrilled that I could understand a dialogue between two native speakers; my ear for the language was improving. I said, 'It would be a pleasure. What's tea?'

He seemed staggered. 'By Alyss, you are in for a treat!'

I listened to my friends' conversation. Mist was enthusing, 'The shops are so clean. No smoke, no grime . . .'

'No litter,' said Fulmer approvingly. 'You don't get that in Hacilith.'

I agreed: 'I thought something was wrong. No one's standing at street corners or porches. When I lived in Hacilith I never wanted to walk past threatening groups of lads.'

I translated for Vendace, who said, 'Youths don't wish to loiter. They are occupied learning the trade of their choice.'

'Not all the time, surely.'

Vendace said, 'In the evenings they discourse in the tea shops.'

111

'Wow. Tea must be powerful stuff. Doesn't Capharnaum have any crime at all?'

There was a hint of smugness in Vendace's voice. 'Of course there is, occasionally, but why should people break the law when they all decide on the laws?'

Wrenn whispered, 'That waiter was wearing a tablecloth.'

Lightning said laconically, 'What's odd about that? It's much more practical than the clothes we have now; you can put your wings through the back.'

'How do you know?'

'My mortal years were not so long ago that I don't remember them, Serein.'

As we walked through town, I noticed that the houses really were similar; apart from superficial variations in paint and plaster their furnishings were all equal. I wondered aloud, 'No one is poor.'

I elaborated for Vendace, who didn't understand me. He said, 'Our currency is based on labour. Every trade is paid the same, in days and hours. You can get more if you work longer, but people tend to work the same length of time. Time is the most valuable thing that exists, surely?' He unfolded some banknotes from his purse and showed us. 'That one is five hours. This one's the smallest – thirty minutes. What do you have?'

'Coins. Notes are small change for us. See here? Where we come from is similar because everyone in the Castle's given the same yearly handout – just a pittance. We can only ask for more money for appropriate projects.' I thought, If we give the Capharnai steel, it would be worth hundreds and hundreds of hours in their currency, as precious as months of lifetime.

Mist pressed me with more questions to translate. I waved my hands and glanced at the sky, trying to find words quickly, but Vendace stopped me: 'Please save your queries for the Senate. Then we can all hear and you won't have to repeat yourself.'

In the centre of town the road passed through a rotunda. The surfaces of its columns were covered with gaudy mosaics, squares of gold, blue sapphire and deep garnet; illustrated panels decorated the edges of its conical roof.

We approached the crag, and the street began to ascend a slope. The gradient became steeper with a series of long steps. We were heading for the columned halls high above. I pointed up to them. 'Lightning, aren't the buildings beautiful? Your pad looks a bit like that.'

He scanned them eagerly. 'The Tealean north front of my house emulates the style. It was a fashionable revival in the latter half of the sixth century.'

'A *revival*! Then how old could this be?'

'Sometime in the early four hundreds the Insects put an end to the people who originally built like this. That was before my time, but I'm sure I recollect my history lessons.'

Mist glanced at us. 'Yes, but we don't need one now! We are making history, gentlemen. Will you pay attention, please?'

Vendace led us along the magnificent boulevard, between the shuttered dwellings. Suddenly we emerged from the town, the red riot of roofs below us. The panorama extended to the ocean beyond the massive harbour walls which enclosed the lagoon and narrowed together either side of the beacon islet. The Trisians' canoes sheltered within it, secure from the breaking surf. Here and there between the sharp corners of the buildings I caught glimpses of a clean narrow river glittering until it merged with the ocean just south of the harbour.

'The Architect must see this,' I said.

Mist combed her pearly hair out with her fingers, pulled at the front of her strappy T-shirt and stared at the incredible view. 'We could easily get trapped up here,' she said. I was an unarmed emissary, but Lightning and Serein carried their customary bow and broadsword as respective signs of their status. Mist walked between them, knowing that with Lightning's lethality at a distance and Wrenn's invincibility at close quarters she was as safe as in a fortress.

I was wilting badly; I wasn't born for a temperature of forty degrees. My clothes clung to the backs of my knees, my armpits, chest. I was more uncomfortable even than Fulmer in his designer suit; I was desperate to stretch my wings. Mist had decreed that their strength would raise too many questions among the Trisians. I had folded them under my baggy shirt, which gave me an unattractive hump running the length of my back. The wings' elbows brushed behind my thighs and the wrists hugged at the level of my shoulders. My wings' leading edges were damp; from the wrist of each one to the small of my back the feathery patagium webbing cleaved together with sweat. The flight feathers stuck out from under my shirt.

'Don't spread,' Mist muttered.

'You don't know what this is like. I'm boiling!'

'Come now, it's no hotter than a Micawater summer,' Lightning said cheerfully.

The crowd of Trisians were not at all bothered by the sun. They kept pace with our party at a respectful distance and chattered together inquisitively, with curious and affable expressions. Children ran among them, peering from behind their parents' legs. A flock of white doves burst from a roof, wings whistling. I strained for refreshment from the faintest breeze, and I envied them. They didn't have to hide their ability to fly.

The street started to zigzag up, its steps closer together; it turned hairpin bends as the gradient steepened. It was immaculate with low walls on either side beyond which was open ground strewn with boulders under craggy outcrops. Blooms of butterflies rose and fell on lavender, wavered over planted hibiscus, lemon trees and bougainvillea, honey-drunk.

Then we reached the flat hilltop and entered the open courtyard of two dazzling white granite buildings. At the far end was the massive columned square edifice we had seen from the quayside, set edge-on to the sheer side of the crag's cliff. A second, longer hall of the same two-storey height adjoined it on our left. It had pilasters with scroll capitols set flat against its walls, a roof made of red pantiles. I was awestruck by the vibrant buildings; they were only the size of the Throne Room but somehow as impressive as the entire Castle.

The crowd trotted in behind us, and when we stopped they gathered round, watching Fulmer exhale smoke and stub out his cigarette in its amber holder.

'This is the Amarot,' Vendace proclaimed. 'From here, the Senate cares for Tris. Please follow me . . .'

'It's the hall of the governors,' I said in Awian. 'Come on.'

We crossed the courtyard that was one hundred metres square, paved with mosaics in copper, blue glass and black ceramic. Geometrical designs ran round its edge, and in its four quarters there were pictures: galleys, a weighing scales, a dolphin and Insects. *Insects*?

The mosaic showed a young woman with brown flowing hair, standing in a swarm of Insect heads and huge ant-like bodies. She held a wine-coloured pennant that streamed out behind her and the folds of her dress moulded closely around her breasts and thighs. She had flowers in her hair and an expression that looked more pained than noble.

Lightning recognised it at once; his eyes opened wide. 'I'm right,' he said. 'It's Alyss of the Pentadrica.'

'It must be a coincidence. How in the Empire could they know that story?'

'I don't know, Jant. I really don't know.'

Vendace led us through an open door into the long building. The air was cool and still, and we all stood blinking for a second until our eyes adjusted.

'If this is a church,' said Wrenn, 'then thank god's coffee break.'

Vendace said, 'This connects with the Senate House. I will show you the way. It is the library of Tris. A quarter of a million books have been collected here. Danio is the Senate member who takes special charge of it.'

'It's a library,' I translated.

'Then thank the librarians!' Fulmer took a cambric kerchief from his pocket and dabbed his forehead with it.

A library! I trailed my fingers along the cedar shelves as we passed, and my heart beat faster than in the Moren double marathon. A quarter of a million books! It may not be as extensive as the royal collection in Rachiswater, or the archives of Hacilith University, but I had been through most of those.

Vendace saw my rapt expression and chuckled. Every single book was unknown to the Empire and brimful with new information I could spend the next century piecing together. Some of the larger tomes were attached to their shelves with brass chains. They were bound in leather and their pages were paper or vellum. There were coffers full of codices and square baskets packed with papers.

The lower stacks were divided into pigeonholes storing scroll cylinders made of bronze. Some were green with verdigris and others polished by use. There were ledgers of loose leaves; slim volumes bound in boards, in violet and dark red buckram. There were folded maps and plans of every town on the island.

A few books lay open on a table where a reader had left them. One was actually hand-copied and beautifully illustrated with coloured ink. The rest were woodcut-block-printed, which again showed how far behind the times Tris was.

We passed bay after bay; each shelf had yellowing posters listing its contents but Vendace was leading too quickly for me to translate. All the same, I was beside myself with joy; I had found my treasure.

As we were led through the long room I began to grasp the enormous extent of the repository – it was floor-to-ceiling full of recorded knowledge. A few solitary scholars occupied chairs and tables in the bays. Fluid music drifted in from outside, a stringed instrument, but the windows were too high for me to see who was playing.

I tried to glimpse words on the covers and I lingered until I was trailing behind the group. Wrenn and Fulmer gave the books not one glance. Fulmer swung his walking stick as if he was taking a lunchtime stroll in Rachiswater Grand Palace. Wrenn's astonished gaze scanned everything without perceiving it. Mist was trying to communicate with Vendace and took no notice of the books. Lightning, however, had the gleam of fascination in his eye.

'It's wonderful, isn't it?' I said.

He nodded with the ardour of a collector. 'What an excellent discovery! I must have copies made and shipped back to my library. Of course it won't generate the profit Awia so badly needs, but the knowledge might help us. I think I can afford the payload-room for one or two shelves.'

I wondered if Lightning could see any work of beauty without wanting to own it. Sculptors and painters in the Fourlands vied for his patronage, knowing he would preserve their creations and provide the means to support them for life. 'We must curate this for the Empire,' he continued.

'It looks like the Trisians have done a good job of that already.'

'Jant,' Mist called back over her shoulder. 'Stop dawdling. Are you under the influence? Shall we maroon you here and pick you up in a couple of hundred years?'

The books on the nearest shelf seemed to be works of philosophy and natural science: *The Germ Theory of Medicine, Manifesto of Equality, Optics and the Behaviour of Light, The Atomic Nature of Matter and other theories by Pompano of Gallimaufry, Zander of Pasticcio's 'The Explication of Dreams', An Enquiry into the Uses of Saltpetre, Worlds Beyond Worlds: Transformed Consciousness, Some Descriptions of the Afterlife, Tris Istorio – A History of Tris*.

Superb. I whipped *Tris Istorio* from the shelf and behind my back. I shoved the little book under my wings into my waistband and pulled my shirt down over it. No one had seen me. Vendace was still talking to Mist.

We went along an open corridor that joined the library to the taller square building. Its entrance was an alabaster arch with an inscription engraved above it. Mist stretched up and swept her finger over the words. 'What does this say?'

I considered it. 'You're reading it the wrong way. They write left to right. Um . . . It says, "All men are the same."'

'You bet they are,' said Mist.

We found ourselves in a semicircular open area like a floor-level stage. In front and stretching up above us were rows of stepped seats on which around fifteen men and women sat, watching us. Some were young, some elderly. To our left, the columns were open to the air, the sheer side of the crag. The hall seemed to extend into space. We stood on the proscenium and felt the weight of the audience's scrutiny.

'What is this arrangement?' Lightning frowned.

I asked Vendace, who said, 'This is the Senate. Elected democratically—'

I waved a hand to slow him. 'I don't know that word.'

Vendace stopped and stared at me.

Mist said, 'What did he say?'

I struggled: 'There's no Awian analogue. It's – it's like the voting that takes place for mayors in Diw and Vertigo townships in Morenzia, or to choose a governor for Hacilith. But not just between influential families, for everybody. Um . . . rule by the people . . . That's what Vendace said.'

Lightning unslung his longbow and unstrung it. He bowed and whispered to me, 'This will do nothing but fray tempers and affect our judgement. We're depending on you to loose words as swiftly as arrows. Who's in charge of this court?'

'I think they all are,' I said.

Lightning concentrated on Vendace. For all the old man's gravity, he looked unsettled under Lightning's grey assured gaze. By now my throat was so dry it was sore. 'Can I have a drink?' I asked Vendace. After a while I was handed a green glass of water, cool and so pure it tasted of nothing.

A boy with a tray provided us all with glasses while Vendace continued to tell the Senate about our ships. I listened but was dimly aware of Wrenn sneaking out behind me, the way we had come, towards the library. I didn't know where he was going; I was concentrating too hard to worry about him. Our prestigious arrival was not proceeding the way I had hoped.

Vendace said, 'We are debating if we should let you stay, and whether or not we assent to any contact with the Fourlands. Our constitution advises against it, because we do not want your culture to damage ours, of which we are proud. Ours is a perfect society built on reason. There are myths that tell of others, very undesirable in comparison.

'The Senate is obliged to discuss every issue for three days before voting. So matters are considered thoroughly and no spurious motions are ever raised. We will let you know our decision in two days' time.'

I translated word for word. Fulmer almost laughed. 'Really, three days, the sluggards,' he spluttered. 'Imagine if on the battlefield you had to wait that long!'

'It sounds inefficient,' Lightning agreed. 'If we followed such a tradition the Insects would overrun us all the way to Cape Brattice before we made up our minds to fight.'

I grinned. 'Look, you two, be quiet!'

The senators murmured with curiosity, trying to figure out what we were saying. Mist hushed us, angered by her dependence on me. I marshalled my scanty knowledge of Trisian and introduced our company, ending with myself: 'Comet Jant Shira, the Emperor's Messenger, and you can call me Jant. We've come to tell you the fortunate news: you all have the chance to join the Circle and have eternal life, as we do. Time does not age us . . . Although I can't really prove it unless we sit here for ten years . . . Anyway, we want to remind Tris of its place in the Empire; we've come at the behest of the Emperor San, that your island and the mainland may no longer be adrift but firm allies—' I halted because at the mention of San the senators leant to each other and started talking.

Vendace turned to the fifteen men and women; they conferred together, speaking in complicated terms at a natural speed, much faster than I could hope to follow. They came to a consensus and informed Vendace, who motioned for me to continue.

'San makes us, and will make the best of you, immortal. We fight the Insects, but—' Another buzz passed between them, and I knew I had hit a chord. 'Insects, yes, like the picture in your courtyard.'

A young lady rose from the centre of the audience. She wore a short dress and a patterned stole wrapped around her body. Her sandal thongs criss-crossed her slender legs to the knee. Her features were light, her hair close-cropped. Unlike Vendace, she had wings; they were small, brunette and very pert. 'Danio, Bibliophylax,' Vendace announced. The library's keeper, if I understood him correctly.

Danio said, 'Insects are just a story; there's no evidence whatsoever. And how can people be eternal? You've taken old tales and you expect us to believe them? The threat of death defines humanity; nothing is as unnatural as an immortal.'

I translated, saying, 'Mist, they don't believe in Insects. I think it's your turn now.'

Through me, Mist spoke to Vendace, but everyone in the Senate assumed her words were also addressed to them. 'Sir, we brought an Insect to show you Capharnai – I mean Trisians. It's imprisoned on our ship, so if you come to the harbour I'll give you a tour of the caravels.'

Vendace said, 'What do you think, Professor?'

Danio paused, reluctant, then answered smoothly, 'Our visitors' colossal boats themselves suggest this isn't a hoax. Yes, this is truly a historic occasion. If they really have an Insect and if the myths I've spent my life discrediting are true, I want to see it.' She stepped down over the stone benches to the stage, approached me closely and looked at my face. A bitten-nailed finger brushed over my Wheel scar and then down to rest on my feathers, questioningly. We gazed at each other. She leant forward; humour danced in her strikingly intelligent hazel eyes.

Mist announced, 'Jant, tell them that anyone who desires can return with us to see the Castle. I'll show them the glory of the Fourlands; give them a great welcome and lavish ambassadorial treatment.'

Danio roused herself and turned away from me. Damn.

I closely translated Mist's offer but none of the Senate seemed impressed. Much of the island's adventurous spirit must be lost, because the few individuals who possess it in abundance could not be frozen forever at their optimum age. I resumed my speech: 'You don't understand. The Empire's hundreds of times larger than Tris. Our city of Hacilith could swallow Capharnaum ten times. Our fyrd's half a million men, our fleet of caravels like those two in the harbour is—'

Vendace cut me short: 'We are not interested. The Senate must consider for no less than three days, and you can not influence our debate because you are not an inhabitant of Tris.'

I ran a hand over my hair in exasperation.

From the corner of my eye I saw Wrenn scuttle out under the archway, holding a shiny object in both hands. He dashed rudely over to me and tapped me on the wing, 'Jant!'

I could stand no more. 'That's Comet to you! Can't you be quiet? This is a crucial moment, our first meeting with the Senate and you interrupt me! What do you think you're . . . ? Oh, what are you carrying?'

For a second I thought it was a Tine artefact and my reality slipped; I felt dizzy and disconnected. Wrenn held a chamber pot. It was identical to every other chamber pot in the Fourlands, except that it was shining metal: gold. It must have been very heavy.

Wrenn showed me. 'All the fitting in their privies are gold!'

'Bring it here,' I said. But the senator's stunned silence was breaking into embarrassed or inquisitive chuckles. Wrenn looked around at them and pointed to it, 'Have you any idea what this is *worth*?' he said in Awian, loudly and slowly.

The Senate may have worried that we were dangerous, or that we expected to be treated with obeisance. Instead, they saw that we were amazed by a simple chamber pot brought for some reason out of their bathroom. They thought we looked ridiculous. All the senators started laughing, and the tension in the air completely lifted. The ladies in cotton smocks or robes put aside their paper fans. The gentlemen unclasped their cloaks and craned forward to see us. Genial hilarity echoed around the spacious auditorium.

Wrenn thrust it at me, 'I can't believe it. Can *you* believe it? It's worth a caravel and it's a piss-pot of all things!'

'Put it down!' I said. 'Bringing the privy into the governors' hall! You're making us look really stupid!'

'Why are you interested in that?' said Danio.

I said coolly, 'Oh, it's nothing. I've seen pots before. We have them in our culture too. We are civilised, not simple . . . Oh, god.' I tapped it, and wisely understated, 'But we like this metal; we can use it. We would quite like to buy more.'

'Well,' Danio said. 'Jant, tell your delegation: if you love this . . . object so much, if you want this base material, please take it. It can be a gift from Tris, our first offering of goodwill.' Applause broke out from the senators on the stepped benches; appreciative exclamations supported her words. Danio laughed and offered the chamber pot to Wrenn.

'They're giving it to you as a present,' I explained.

Wrenn took it gratefully and said in awe, 'Shouldn't I give something in return? Oh, obviously,' He unbuckled the fyrd-issue broadsword and scabbard from his belt. He held it flat in both hands and presented it to Danio.

'Thank you,' she said. She accepted the sword and pulled the scabbard to bare a little of the blade, which she examined closely.

'Please be careful,' I said. 'It's extremely sharp.'

She gazed minutely at me again and asked the inevitable question, 'What are you, anyway?'

I shuffled one wing out of my shirt and opened it. *Duck you suckers* was painted in red on the inside but, shrewd as she was, Danio couldn't transliterate. 'I'm winged, see, just like you, well nearly.' I pointed to my face and took a sheaf of thick hair in the other hand. 'My mother was Rhydanne; they're a mountain people who look like this. I know that's new and strange but please don't worry – I'm not dangerous. My long limbs are from my Rhydanne side too. My good looks, I get from both sides.'

All fifteen senators accompanied us to the harbour with a surprising lack of pomp and ceremony. They walked without any attendants and just chatted to each other, waved at the townspeople with a familiarity that was nothing like Fourlands governors. The senators were dressed as plainly as the folk in the piazza and tea shops; they did not seem to be very far removed from them.

The Sailor conducted the senators onto the *Melowne*. I held the hatchway open and helped the ladies descend to the hold. I didn't see their expressions, but I heard their shrieks, and from Danio I learnt a whole ream of Trisian words that I won't be putting in any guidebook.

We tried to hide the state of the crews from the senators. The sailors had clearly contravened Mist's orders and discipline on board *Petrel* and *Melowne* had started to crumble. They had traded and squirrelled away every Trisian commodity they could lay their hands on, especially agate statuettes and the gold beads, chaplets and tiaras that the children wore. Only a few halberds were left unsold and the men had broken open the caskets of broadswords and started trading them. Every single man was completely drunk, some so legless they lolled as they sat dribbling the juice of exotic fruits, sloshing wine into cups or crunching on overcooked sardines. The carpenter retched and farted as Mist's boatswain sons dragged him down to be locked in the brig. He prattled, 'Capharnai might not want us – but their kids have made me rich!'

A bottle rolled round in the scuppers and bumped against my foot. I picked it up and sniffed it. 'Brandy, or something similar. The merchants are selling spirits to our men!'

'This is dangerous,' Fulmer confided. 'I must keep discipline. Lightning and Mist will stow a fortune in *Melowne*, under the noses of all our deckhands. I doubt I'll reach home without a mutiny.'

Throughout the second day, Mist and Lightning employed me to translate their deals with the merchants who waited in long queues. Capharnai carried books in their pockets and either read or stood in groups debating rarefied philosophical points. I yearned to spend the rest of our landfall in the library but the Sailor and Archer kept me hard at work with filthy lucre. My fluency improved, and I made friends with Danio, who taught me many new expressions before she was called away to the Senate. They discussed us non-stop through-out the day.

In return for the broadswords the Capharnai filled the *Melowne* with bales of cloves, tea leaves, sacks of peppercorns; we bought a cask of ambergris and one of frankincense. Our sister ship became a spice ship – I could smell it on the other side of town.

'Gold for steel, weight for weight,' Mist said smugly, examining the pale metal chamber pot. 'But that last silversmith – manufacturer of children's toys – kept the location of the mines a secret.'

Lightning said, 'No matter. I have gained a return of seven hundred per cent on the initial investment. This tea is too watery for my taste but, seeing as it will inevitably come to the Fourlands, it might as well come with me. And I've also discovered some excellent brandy.'

Wrenn used me to question every islander he met about sword fighting, and although I kept telling him it wasn't a Trisian tradition he was astounded to find that no one knew anything about the art.

'It seems to me they fight by talking,' I said.

Wrenn huffed. 'Yeah. But if Capharnaum becomes a manor the Castle will ask for its quota of fyrd for the Front. I'll be given hundreds of people to train from bloody scratch and I've a sneaking feeling they're not going to like it.' He disappeared into town with a party of midshipmen who were searching for a wine shop. The Senate permitted our men to leave the harbour only in small groups under the charge of Eszai. They didn't want the boulevard to be swamped with hell-raising sailors.

By evening I was sick of translating; confused with words swarming round my head until they lost their meanings. I was exhausted, but all in all it had been a fantastic day. As the sun set over the horizon where the Fourlands lay, Trisian canoes paddled in through the strait. After dusk the Capharnai entrepreneurs began to disperse and supper was served on board. The Senate retired and Danio came aboard to make notes and sketch the Insect. She was hypnotised by it, loitering in the hold, flinching every time it threw itself against the bars. When at ten p.m. Mist asked her to leave the ship, she stood on the quayside and stared as if insane at the exterior of the hull.

I told Mist that I intended to sleep on the mountainside. I walked out of sight of dainty Danio, who insisted on keeping vigil till tomorrow when Mist would let her back aboard. I took off and flew up, nap-of-the-earth in the pitch-black night, just a few metres above the mountain's contour. The lower slopes were olive groves, then dim rocky ground streaked along beneath me. I found a low cliff with an overhang and sheltered under it on the rough bare stone.

By lamplight, the *Stormy Petrel*'s crew lowered a spare mainsail and lashed the edges to two poles projecting from the portholes. The sail drooped into the warm water, which filled it, and the men started swimming in it. Men stood on the railing and dived in. I was too far to hear the splashes but I saw spray fly up in the flickering light of the yellow lanterns as *Petrel* rocked at her mooring.

Everything was delightful, and I lay alone. I have rarely been so happy. The air was cooler than at sea level; the rock conducted warmth away from my skin. It was a close night, so hot and humid that your balls stick to the inside of your thigh.

A light breeze cut through the cocoon of heat that moulded round me. It blew the smells of salt and peppermint into the rock shelter and carried occasional sounds from the town. Lamps were lit in the windows of Capharnaum's bizarre houses. I loved this scented island. I smiled and snuggled against the stone. I could think clearly now, for the first time in weeks. I no longer worried about the caravels, or Mist who wanted a hold on Tris that she could never be allowed to have.

I knew every road and air current of the Fourlands; now Tris was mine to explore. I could learn to discover like a mortal again and not a jaded Eszai. My sense of wonder was as strong as the first time I saw Hacilith city, when I was a foundling from Darkling with aching wings. In my first decade of life I had seen a total of just ten people, all Rhydanne. The city pulsed humans around its streets in a stream that terrified me. I could fly no further so I hid, amazed, among the mayhem for a year.

I suddenly realised that I hadn't been thinking about scolopendium. If I was on the ship, my body would be crying out for it by now. I laughed with surprise and relief. If I could spend a few more nights alone on the mountain, in the tranquil rock shelter, I could do withdrawal. If I could spend a few more days in this serene and secure place, I contemplated, my mind would never turn to scolopendium again. No more sliding down the OD ravine. No more cat. No need for coffee, ephedrine or myristica. Or whisky, papaver, harmine, veronal or datura. Thujone, digitalis or psilocybin; not any more.

I breathed the island deeply into myself. I wanted to take it in, inhale it, drink it, the whole island, until it became part of me. I felt organised and in control. Alone on the mountain I lost all sense of self, and the troubles that drove me to use cat went too. The Castle was an ocean away. How brilliant, I was still immortal with none of the risks. I wanted to stay alone on the mountainside forever, until eventually with no self left and no thoughts at all I would merge with the landscape. In my haven there was no need for language or communication. For a few hours I was free from the sickly need to identify, classify and name with words every single thing.

# CHAPTER 11

I returned to the *Melowne* very early next morning and had a wash with sponge and pitcher. I decided to go back to sleep until the call should come from Lightning or Mist to engage me in another day's frantic business with spice merchants and jewellers, and with the host of fishermen-turned-salesmen. They seemed determined to swap everything they owned for our damask steel or a handful of arrows.

I was woken by loud yells and battering on the cabin door. 'Comet! Help! *Quickly*!'

From the tone of Fulmer's snappy voice, I knew something terrible had happened. 'What? If it's a mutiny I'm on your side!' I stooped and wound a sheet around my waist like a sarong, then opened the door.

Fulmer stood on the half-deck, wearing only his trousers. Over his shoulder I saw the cloudless sky, the façade of Capharnaum's white villas, green shutters and balconies, the merchants waiting on the quay in a stunned silence, the lower deck. It appeared to be covered in tar.

Fulmer pointed. The Insect was poised on the gangplank. Between it and the quayside stood Wrenn. The Insect reared and struck, antennae whirling. Wrenn raised his rapier and dagger.

I dived back into the cabin and picked up my ice axe. Then I shoved past Fulmer to the rack of equipment beside my door. I snatched a long boathook and hefted it, at the same time yelling to Fulmer, 'Run down the other walkway! Go to *Petrel*. Wake Lightning and tell him to shoot it! You must knock *very loudly*. Quick!'

Fulmer slid down the ladder and slipped across the main deck. I saw bodies lying at unnatural angles and tightened my grip on the boathook as I realised the thick, dully reflective slick was congealing blood.

With a cold self-awareness I spread my wings, wiggled my ice axe into the folded top of my impromptu sarong, and found the right words to shout at the thirty or forty Capharnai: 'Run away! Go home! It will bite you!'

Holding the boathook shaft across my body like a weightlifter, I vaulted the railings. I plummeted straight down past the blue porthole shutters, reached flying speed and hurtled once round the ship's hull to build up momentum. I skimmed the figurehead and up over the forecastle deck for a straight run at the Insect. I jinked to miss the foremast, by pulling in my right wing and spinning right.

I swept over the Insect. I reached out with the boathook and put my full strength behind it as I swung.

The Insect's gold-brown compound eyes wrapped round its head and joined at the top with bristly margins. It could see in all directions. It saw me passing above and bent its six knees to squat down. It flattened its body flush against the gangplank, beaded antennae wavering and brushing the wood.

I missed and struggled to lift the hook as it glided towards Wrenn's head. I snarled, 'Fuck!' I turned downwind, dropping height and holding the pole out to the side, not upwards to tangle with my feathers. I flew over the merchants' heads so low my downdraught ruffled their hair. They all dropped to the ground in a wide swathe along my path. A few quick beats, and I veered round the stern of the *Petrel*, intending to circle the two ships and come in over *Melowne* for another swoop. There was no sign of Lightning in the frantic commotion on *Petrel*'s deck.

Wrenn had bare feet. He was naked but for shorts, the drawstring hanging down. The Insect stood higher on the gangplank, claws tightly gripping the edges. Wrenn blocked the route to the land, to its food. It struck at him. He blocked its mandible with his rapier and deflected its head aside. It swept its antennae back into their gutters, bore its weight on its hind limbs and slashed with its front legs.

Its hooked claws stabbed at Wrenn, who batted them aside. Its jaws closed on, then slid off, the rapier blade. Wrenn parried the tarsi feet in a sequence so rapid it was a blur. He had lost none of his skill – he was too focused to feel fear. But he couldn't predict the Insect's actions.

He followed the moves of its four claws and mandibles all at once, blocking every cut the Insect scrabbled at him. But his totally inadequate rapier clicked and slid over its cuticle – it wasn't heavy enough to bite into the shell.

He thrust his blade past the base of one antenna, then drew it back, slicing through the feeler. It severed and fell between the Insect's feet. A drop of yellow liquid like pus oozed from the hollow cut end and dropped on its eye, running over the curved surface. The Insect recoiled. Wrenn feinted, and its left claw swept the air trying to catch his blade. Wrenn lunged explosively and hit its thorax squarely, under its mandibles. His rapier tip pierced the chitin.

The Insect took a step towards him and the blade slid into its body. Fluid the colour and consistency of cream welled up around the blade and trickled down its shell but the Insect did not react. It crawled towards Wrenn, spitting itself on his rapier.

The sword point burst from its back, pushing out a length of cream-streaked steel. It forced itself down the blade until the hilt was flush against its thorax. It stooped to bite Wrenn's arm. Wrenn shook his hand free of the swept guards and jumped backwards, leaving his thin sword embedded through the Insect.

I cleared the height of the foredeck, came in fast.

Wrenn's face set in a grim expression. He cut with his dagger left to right, scratching the Insect's eye, but the blade skittered off, only etching a thin line over one hexagonal lens. It struck; he slammed the dagger into its mandible. The dagger blade shattered from tip to ricasso so violently that two long glittering steel splinters spun away from the gangplank in different directions. Wrenn was left holding the grip.

My wings shadowed his head. 'Here!' I dangled the pole from its very end. He had enough sense to drop his hilt and jump for the brass hook speeding towards him. I let go and passed it to him.

Our contact caused a drag that slowed me down too much and slewed me to the left. The quayside rushed up; I saw the pavement cracks. Too big, too close! I was going to crash! I leant right and beat down – my wingtips smacked a crate of oranges. The shock transmitted through my feather shafts and hurt my fingers. I pulled out of my dive; the crate tops scraped my knees and feet. I flapped, stubbing my wings. I banked up steeply, groaning with effort, my feathers rasping the air.

I glanced at Wrenn and saw him teetering, the pole held out for balance. He recovered, pointed the boathook at the Insect. It crouched to spring. It lowered its head and pounced at Wrenn, forcing him sideways. He swung the boathook and clubbed it weakly as it pushed past him. The spines fringing its legs lacerated his skin.

Its barrelling bulk threw Wrenn off balance. His boathook flourished in the air; he toppled off the gangplank and fell head first, spreadeagled. The soles of his feet vanished below the level of the harbour wall, into the strip of deep blue water. A second later I heard the splash.

I glanced at the crowd; their faces were full of doubt and disbelief. The Insect was real; this was no drama laid on for entertainment. It was coming down the gangplank. About half of them trotted backwards, still staring, then turned and fled for the streets. The rest seemed frozen. Those not gaping at the Insect were gawking at me.

'Go!' I yelled. A couple more people responded to the urgency in my voice.

The Insect landed on all six legs on the harbour pavement. At first it moved unevenly, angularly; it leapt and hobbled. It quickly became accustomed to freedom and the sailors' blood it had lapped up helped the hydraulics of its legs function properly. It ran as smoothly as it had done in the Paperlands and the people scattered before it.

They fled with screams, leaving one woman sitting alone. I recognised Danio instantly; at the water's edge near *Melowne*'s hull, in exactly the same place as I had left her last night, her bare legs dangling over the harbour wall. She remained transfixed a second too long, not knowing what to do. She pulled herself to kneel, then sprang up, all the while watching the Insect with a mixture of fascination and fear. She sprinted, arms outstretched, very fleet of foot. But she was too slow.

The Insect bounded after her. Its claws in the small of her back brought her down, face to the paving. She started screaming, high-pitched, struggling to turn round and beat it off.

The Insect dipped, sheared Danio's leg off at the knee and picked it up with its middle pair of arms. Its external mouthparts stripped the calf muscle from the severed limb. It held the dripping muscle with two sets of palps, which hung down like black sticky fingers. The maxillae behind its jaws guillotined up and down as well as left and right, masticating it into paste. Danio kept screeching until the Insect grabbed her round the hips, mandibles sinking deep, and tossed her into the air. She crashed full-length on the paving. The Insect jumped on her body and decapitated her with one powerful bite.

I flew low over them, frantically looking for a space to land. The Insect paused as my movement caught its attention. Its single elbowed antenna waved; the stub of the other one was covered with a yellow crust. Now all the Capharnai had gone from the harbour but a merchant in a tunic had stopped at a distance to look back at the abandoned goods, his chubby face white and eyes bulging.

Danio! I thought. It's killed Danio; what have we done? I found a clear gap between the baskets and boxes, but I was moving so fast I was in danger of breaking my legs. I stretched my wings back fully and flared off some speed. Gasping at the strain in my stomach muscles I swung my legs ahead and hit the ground braced, knees bent.

I put my hands down and somersaulted over and over, till I crashed into a crate of cinnamon bark.

Winded, I picked my axe from the ground and crawled to my feet. The Insect had reached the entrance to the boulevard. It had slaughtered the corpulent man and was standing on his body with front and middle legs. It ducked its head, its lamellar segmented abdomen high in the air. It closed its jaws until they clicked, cutting across the fat man's belly. It backed, claws skidding on the blood. It pulled taut a length of blue-green intestine, then ate it all the way back down into the man's body cavity. His sightless eyes and pale mouth were stretched open, rigid; I could see the inside wall of his ribs.

I thought, I must distract it till Lightning shoots it. Breathing painfully, I dashed across. As I ran, avoiding the discarded cloaks and piles of produce, I curved to approach from behind, thinking that the Insect would take a second to turn round and I could chop at its rear. But the Insect did not wait to be attacked. I don't know whether it recognised me or understood I was armed, but it crawled swiftly from the fat man's cadaver and leaped towards the boulevard. I swerved between it and the town and headed it off. I chased it. I lengthened my stride to sprint with Rhydanne instinct as if it was a stag. I closed in on the darting legs and aimed a blow at a hind femur, driving it to change direction.

The Insect slowed as it sensed a group of boatmen who, trapped against a villa's portico, prepared to use their paddles as maces. I made it switch towards the ships where Lightning should be, but it slashed a mandible at the last man, a thin teenager who fell clutching his thigh.

The Insect still carried Wrenn's sword through its thorax, the hilt like a silver badge. It had stopped bleeding. Its legs swept repeatedly fore to rear across its body. I aimed between them at a suture line that crossed its back like a joint in armour. I tore the glassy tips of its immovable little wings that projected from the middle segment, pressed close to its glossy shell. I tilted over and hit, but the blow nearly ripped the shaft from my hand, wrecked my running rhythm. I pushed hard at the ground to accelerate, change direction; to control the Insect.

My resounding strikes had more effect than Wrenn's clearly articulated technique. The Insect limped, but still ran rapidly on the bristly black pads under its slightly raised claws. I swung at the three small round eyes that formed a triangle between its compound eyes. But at this angle the plate of its forehead was too thick to crack.

The slabs cool beneath my bare feet; my ankles ached from the pounding. I panted the air. The Insect put on a burst and reached racehorse speed trying to escape. I sprang forward and kept pace with it although my leg muscles burned. I was exhilarated, keyed up with my own vigour. I sped my swiftest, desperate to snatch one more chance – I'll hook my ice pick into the copper striped abdomen and I'll bring it down.

I forced the Insect's route nearer to the glittering sea as we raced the length of Capharnaum's harbour. The last building had a blank stone wall. At its base was a semicircular drain opening as tall as my shoulder, edged with blocks. A shallow stream of dirty water flowed out of it into a channel, then over the side of the harbour wall. It was stained dark green and fuscous with flaking algae. The Insect sheered, rattled down into the sloping conduit and splashed straight into the black archway. I lost sight of it instantly in the darkness. I scrambled to a halt, scraping my heels on the verge.

The Insect had gone; no way was I going to follow it into the drain. In the confined space it would rip my throat out before I could even see it. I waited, on guard, feeling my pulse pounding in my neck. It quickly returned to normal but my temples hurt. I coughed a mouthful of frothy spit into the grey water and watched it flow into the sea.

Insects are at home underground and are not disadvantaged by the dark. When culling them in the Paperlands, the least popular operation is the task of channelling river water into their tunnels in order to collapse the deep, honeycombed structures. Fires are also lit on platforms at the tunnel mouths to draw air out and suffocate them, but Insects between the sizes of men and carthorses still burst forth to attack at full speed. I hated natural caves let alone Insect burrows and slimy sewers. If I went in there I would never come out. With terrible images playing in my mind, I loped back to the *Stormy Petrel*, past the merchant's bloated, half-eaten body with its ripped-open smock and Danio, headless, lying in a congealed red spray.

Lightning looked down from the *Petrel*'s highest deck, the back of the stern castle, an arrow at string, and wearing only trousers. Fulmer clutched the rope rail beside him. Mist's face peered out of an open window in the array directly beneath his feet.

The surviving sailors on the *Melowne* clung to her rigging. Wrenn was a tiny figure down at the waterline, steadily climbing a ladder of metal brackets up the rounded hull. His short hair was flattened; water dripped from his bedraggled wings. His feathers were completely tattered, split and peeled back to the shaft. His arse crack and leg hairs showed through his soaked white shorts.

'What happened?' Lightning shouted at me. He leant over so far that I thought the arrows would slip out of the quiver on his back. 'Was that our Insect? Where's Serein? Damn him, damn you! What were you bloody doing, perforating it?'

Mist yelled, 'Did it just get those three Trisians? How many of mine?'

Fulmer gabbled, 'Serein woke me up. I saw it massacre the sailors on the orlop. Master Mariner, I'm sorry. Serein said he would hold it off and took his rapier but it's no good against shell.'

Mist turned away abruptly and hurried out of view. A moment later she strode onto the main deck, staring around at the devastation on the quay. The wounded teenager had stopped crawling; I hoped he was just unconscious, rather than slain. The traders' goods were abandoned. The quayside was deserted by the living, but three or four faces crowded every open window and behind the bronze palings of all the waterfront houses, watching us with shock and outright terror.

'You didn't kill it!' Lightning raved.

I retied my sarong. 'I should have caught it, but it plunged down a drain. I wounded it and so did Serein, with his rapier. Stupid town swords. Fucking constables' swords. The idiot didn't have the right gear. It carried his rapier away! You— We must get archers to the tunnel as soon as possible. I need to know if it's trapped, so you can shoot it.'

'And if it's escaped to the town?' Fulmer whispered.

Mist shouted, 'Captain, to your ship! Why were all the grids open? I'll want to know! We can't discuss this outside,' she added *sotto voce* to me. 'Jant, speak to the Capharnai. Don't let them carry off their dead without an explanation. As soon as you can, meet us in the *Melowne*'s hold.'

Typically, I had the most difficult job. While I waited on the corniche to be confronted by furious islanders, the other Eszai disappeared into the hold, and from their exclamations I learnt that it was also strewn with carnage. I was very aware how alien I looked, wearing a sheet and with my long wings uncovered.

On the *Melowne*'s main deck the dismembered remains of six or seven men lay scattered, their limbs snipped at the joints and bodies gutted. The quartermaster's body drooped through the hatchway. Following Mist's orders, the sailors carried them to the land and lined them up by the anchor ready for burial because in a few hours' time the morning heat would be appalling.

Step by step, a group of Capharnai merchants approached me,

finding courage in numbers. I spread my hands down in the peace gesture and they seemed to understand. The first one, with an expression of awe and distrust, opened his arms like wings. I explained why I was the only man ever to fly, and told them it was nothing to be superstitious about. I repeated apologies as best I could and instructed them to wait in their homes and keep their children inside. Over the hiss of indrawn breath I continued – they should wait for word from the Senate that the Insect was dead. I asked them to bring down one or two goats for me to tether outside the sewer entrance and tempt the Insect out, but I suspected it was too replete for the trick to work.

I found myself talking over the wails and reproaches of families who had come to claim the Trisian merchant, the fainting teenager and Danio. I repeated that it was an accident and I clasped my hands and knelt, begging them to treat us kindly. When they saw that I couldn't meet their eyes, they understood my sincerity but they were chary. News spread up the town, causing a commotion and banging on doors, until it reached the Amarot and a deliberative silence descended.

Frightened, I retreated to the *Melowne*'s hold. 'I did my best,' I said.

'We believe you,' said Lightning. 'This disaster makes us all feel inadequate; it's far from the work we're accustomed to. Please attend to Serein and we'll consider what to do.'

Lightning had found a young Trisian man lying halfway down the ship, his lower face torn off. He returned to inspecting the victim. Behind us the buckled door of the empty Insect cage creaked as Mist opened and shut it again and again.

Wrenn sat on a packing case that now held cardamom seeds instead of arrows. I cleaned his grazes. I slapped on some comfrey ointment and tied gauze around his shoulder. His crenated wings slipped open like damp fans; his adrenaline high was fading. His shorts stuck to his stocky thighs and blood had dried on his bicep; he was peeling it off in tiny flakes. Grim determination was vicious in his face. 'Is this mine?' he said muzzily. 'It's all right. I don't think it's mine.'

I said, 'Yes, it is, but your scratches are superficial. Keep them clean and go easy for a few days. We can succumb to infection and serious disease as readily as mortals. In fact I can tell you quite a few examples of Eszai who've died from dusty wounds.'

'No, thanks.'

'Unfortunately it won't heal any faster, but the Circle will catch you and stop you being killed outright by little lesions and contusions.'

'Hey – what an advantage for fencing.'

I looked at him sternly. 'The only Eszai who survive centuries are those who know they're not indestructible. Zascai are relying on you not to get cut up.'

Wrenn lowered his gaze. 'I know; I was just keeping it at bay.'

'No one can slay Insects with a rapier,' I admonished. 'How many years has the Castle spent trying to develop the perfect weapon and now you try to use a *duelling foil?*'

Wrenn winced. 'I managed it once in the amphitheatre. My rapier was all I had to hand – Mist's sold every single broadsword on the ship and I gave mine to Danio. But you didn't do any better with your skier's axe. Ouch! Jant, have a care! I know I need experience. It was the biggest, toughest fucking Insect I've ever faced. And I failed; I'm sorry.'

'I'm sorry I didn't catch it,' I said.

Mist slammed the cage door. 'Jant, you showed the whole town that you can fly. We agreed to keep it a secret.'

'Did you expect me to let your pet devour Serein?'

'I can defend myself,' said Wrenn sulkily.

Lightning picked up a bronze Trisian trident that was lying next to the youth's body, and a purse made of soft leather. He approached us gravely. 'It seems as if our midshipmen were accepting bribes from curious Capharnai to look at the Insect. See?' He tipped the purse and a knot of fine gold chains snaked out into his palm.

'It must have broken out of its own accord,' Mist concluded. 'In response to them goading it. I wish I had commissioned a tougher cage.'

Lightning and I looked at her. She was well aware that we no longer believed a word she said. Lightning gestured at the cage. The Capharnai just regarded this as a freak show.'

'That's how they thought of us all,' I said.

Mist snapped at Wrenn suspiciously, 'Why were you up at five a.m.?'

He glanced around, admitted, 'I'd just got back. I spent the night in town with a local girl.'

'Oh, really?'

'I think she was called Pollan. At any rate, she kept saying "Pollan". She had world-class tits, I mean; you could get lost in there. Given last night's performance she could be selected for the national team, but any more mushy stuff and I'll relegate her to the second division—' Mist cuffed the back of his head. 'Ow!'

Wrenn ran a hand over his feathers, knitting their barbs together.

Missing vanes spoiled his zig-zag style. He was quite hirsute with feathers; a couple were growing on his back between his wings, since he had not been near a barber's in months. The pinfeathers were still wrapped in their transparent covering, like paintbrushes. Where the sheath peeled back and crumbled, the brown brush tip emerged.

Mist called, 'Fulmer?'

The dandy's shocked face appeared in the overhead hatchway. 'Yes, Master Mariner?'

'Help Lightning carry this body up to the quayside. We have to return him to his relatives and try to find some way of atoning for this incident. Comet, sally out to the Amarot and request the presence of Vendace, with companions if he wishes. The Senate might have finished their three-day debate about us and we need to know the outcome. *Fly* there, and tell Vendace to meet us at his convenience, all together in my cabin.'

She looked at Lightning, who was naked from the waist up with dishevelled hair; me in a sheet skirt and needle scars; and Wrenn, caked in gore with semi-transparent shorts. 'Not as you are.'

I flew slowly to the Amarot, taking no pleasure in seeing the citizens staring up. I grieved for Danio; of course I'd only known her for two days but she was the Trisian I had spoken to most, and with untold depths of wit and humanity she had shown the greatest interest in the Fourlands.

I stood alone in front of the Senate and explained everything. I offered our services to catch the Insect but they interrupted me with outraged cries. They seemed to surmise that the Insect was a ploy for us to stay longer at Capharnaum. The Senate agreed that Vendace should accompany me to the *Stormy Petrel*, to announce their decision to all us travellers at once. I waited as he gathered an escort of townsmen on the mosaic, but as we walked down the boulevard more men joined us from the houses, almost spontaneously, following closely without a word. They were armed with harpoons, their knives in their belts; one or two carried the halberds we had sold them. They were quiet, giving me space, but still I knew they were watching my every move. It was nerve-racking. I acted as amicably as possible, trying to alleviate the atmosphere. When we passed the piazza I saw the man in the tunic working in his restaurant. I smiled openly but he gave me a cold look and pulled the shutters closed.

I reached *Petrel* with relief, but Mist, after some negotiation, invited all Vendace's supporters aboard. The caravel's size daunted them, but twenty or so filed up to the main deck, where Mist and I convinced Senator Vendace to leave them and enter her office alone.

The long shade of the mountain had fallen over the harbour, and Mist's cabin was so dark she had lit candles. The smell of tallow combined with brass polish, tar and black coffee made Vendace even more uneasy. He surveyed the Sailor's gloomy office: the waxed panelling fixed between tough, roughly adze-marked timbers, the door with long flamboyant hinges across it, and the cassone in which Ata kept her clothes. The table bore a cafetière and a plate of yesterday's bread rolls. Its turned legs were bolted to the floor. In the corner was a basket full of Trisian bric-a-brac and wine cups. This ornate room was at odds with the rest of the ship and the sound of uneasy crewmen scrubbing bloodied footprints off the foredeck.

Vendace did not sit down until I begged, and then only reluctantly. Mist pushed a lidded glass of coffee towards him but he did not give it so much as a glance. He watched his companions waiting on the main deck through the small panes surrounding the door. He announced, 'The Senate has voted. Tris will reject all contact with the Fourlands' Empire. We've heeded the advice of the constitution of Capharnaum. Everyone voted that you must leave, with the exception of well-loved Professor Danio, who wanted to learn more. We agreed this morning even before your messenger informed us of the tragedy. We do not want you here. The slaughter of Capharnaum citizens, including her, simply reinforced their decision. We know that your boats are restocked. Take them home immediately and never come back.'

I translated for the others. I was leaning against the wall at the back of the cabin, one knee bent and the boot sole against the wood, head bowed, listening. I let them speak directly to each other, facilitating their conversation without interrupting it, whatever words were said. I took no side, simply letting my translation flow from the shadow, echoing their words and rejoinders in the correct languages: Awian to Trisian, Trisian to Low Awian.

Wrenn said, 'But Tris is part of the Empire too!'

'No, we are not. One man should not rule five lands. The Senate was shocked to find that one man has so much power. You have already tainted Capharnaum.'

Mist said, 'Senator, let us—'

Vendace pointed at her. 'On the occasion of your arrival last year, the Senate discussed the likelihood of more visits from your island. We were wary but we gave you the benefit of the doubt. Now we accept that we were wrong and the stories were correct. Although I personally have no idea what to do about the Insect, the Senate are making plans.'

The black moniliform antenna lay on Mist's desk beside her cafetière. Vendace pushed it around with his finger as he spoke. 'You say there are thousands of Insects?'

I said, 'Hundreds of thousands infest the north of our continent. We're sorry we lost this one. The tunnel was empty when I returned with bowmen and – um – harpooners.'

Vendace said, 'Jant, you can actually fly, and you can run . . . The merchants reported the speed you were flying!'

'I'm the fastest thing in the world,' I said. 'That's the only evidence I can give to prove that we're immortal.'

Vendace sighed. 'Some of the Senate believe you, but it makes no difference to us. Tris should be left alone by mortals and immortals alike. If you ask me, being able to fly is wonderful pleasure enough without heaping accolade and immortality on you as well.' He toyed with the antenna, asked plaintively, 'Why did you set an Insect on us?'

Mist said, 'We didn't. It was an accident and we're profoundly sorry. Please accept our apologies; mishaps like this will never happen again. The Insect escaped; we should have taken more care.'

'We'll hunt it down,' Lightning said solidly. His face had a bleak impassive expression. He stood by the door, occasionally checking Vendace's entourage. 'We're good at that; it's what we do. I will meet any proposal of compensation. At least allow us to give you advice and recompense for your people.'

'I'll go after it,' Wrenn volunteered.

'*Yes, we know; be quiet,*' I said.

Vendace said, 'The librarians are looking for charts. They've told me that the sewer drains the forum and branches throughout Capharnaum for six hundred metres. So you brought a legendary maneater as an object of wonder, and loosed it into the system under our town. I am astounded.'

'I can't translate this quickly,' I complained.

Mist asked the senator, 'If Tris communicates with the Caſtle even once again, we need a spokesman; a governor, you see. Tell me what you want.'

'The Senate wants you to leave.'

'No. Tell me what *you* want.'

Vendace turned pale, controlling his anger. He spread his dry palms like a scarecrow playing an accordion and said, 'I have learned some words of Awian: *Goodbye*.' He pushed his chair back and turned to leave.

Mist said, 'No, wait!'

She touched the chair asking him to sit down, though he looked very uncomfortable. She sighed and refilled her coffee glass. Without looking at me, she said, 'Comet, give us the benefit of your clever mind.'

'I say we stop insulting them. We should report to San and follow his instructions. I don't know about this town, but we're San's servants. I think he should make the whole Senate the governor; they seem to take decisions with one voice.'

'Don't interpret this,' Mist said. 'Forget the stubborn, overbearing Senate. The common man of Capharnaum will want something. I don't understand the desire that drives him.' She paced to the stern windows and looked out. 'Every people I have met want more than they can supply for themselves. In fact, every single person's greed is for more than he needs.'

'Not Rhydanne,' I said.

'Aye, a case to prove my point. Rhydanne are never drunk enough.' She nudged me as she paced back and nodded surreptitiously towards the casement. I peered through to see a crowd, mostly men, gathering on the quayside. Tridents glinted in their hands, with nets and the swords we had sold them. They stood in a passive silence that I found incredibly intimidating.

'Lightning, come here and take a look at this.'

Lightning muttered, 'They think the Empire is another little island.'

Mist said, 'Vendace, immortality's the most important offer your people could possibly have. The very opportunity will make you idle Zascai feel alive! Tris is so stagnant I feel smothered. We can tell that it hasn't changed for hundreds of years. You won't reject the Empire once you've seen its treasures – the sky-worshipping spires of Awia, mills of Hacilith! Everybody wants to be Eszai! Why turn the proposal down? Don't you wish to excel? Don't you want to know what the world will be like five centuries from now?'

Vendace was silent for a time, then he murmured something that had the rhythm of a quotation and sounded thoroughly resigned. He shot me an envious glance. 'It may be that we will not gain immortality, and we'll never be able to *fly*, but we all want to stay equal. We'll keep peace and our own pace. You have already threatened to upset the balance by coming here.'

'Give us a few more days,' Mist tried. 'We can buy another crate of gold. Serein will find the Insect.'

'The Senate's decision can neither be rescinded nor altered without a seven-day discussion. You must leave today.'

'I need to lay on enough water for the journey,' Mist countered. 'We'll leave tomorrow.'

'Yes, you will.' Vendace pulled his short cloak to his body, stood and left the cabin. Lightning stepped aside to let him go.

Mist gave a little scream and clenched her fists. 'Ah! Damn! Jant, I've one more chance,' she said in Plainslands. 'Follow him.'

'What did you say?' Lightning demanded. 'Don't exclude Wrenn!'

'It's private,' she spat.

On the main deck, Vendace's friends surrounded him. He looked reassured as they patted him on the back, and they began to file down the gangplank, Vendace shepherding them in front.

Mist caught the edge of his green-bordered cloak. The ex-fisherman tweaked it away and glared at her. She said, 'Jant, tell him this: I can give him eternal life. It doesn't matter whether we feel affection or not.'

She unnerved me. We must certainly be in trouble if Mist was prepared to play her last card. 'Do you mean . . . ?' I said doubtfully.

Her voice cleared of any vagueness, 'Aye! I mean marriage! A link through me to the Circle. Time is their currency, so immortality is my most priceless offer to one man.'

'I don't think that's a good idea.'

'Tell him, damn you – we don't have three days to mull it over!'

I repeated her words for Senator Vendace.

He was quiet, studying her for a long moment. His mouth twisted in disgust. 'No. How dare you bribe me to breach the Senate's resolution? To betray them! Just go! And never, *ever* return!' He strode down the gangplank without a backwards glance.

Over the next hour, the Capharnai melted away from the quay leaving an air of animosity. I watched the streets to the Insect through Mist's telescope, while the ships bustled with preparation to sail home.

'Well,' I said, embarrassed. 'You blew that, Ata Dei.'

She muttered, 'Next morning we'll set our backs and rudders to this bloody insular town.'

Nobody was present to watch us leave. As our sails filled and our figureheads pointed towards the open sea, I felt my trepidation mounting. I did not want to go out there again so soon. I contemplated that the Trisians may never raise their sights or be

138

forced into contest by a Challenger or by ambition as unquenchable as Mist's. Who here cared about the Castle's self-imposed trials? Half a minute's difference in racing time in a Challenge could literally be my downfall. A millimetre's distance on an archery target means life or death to Lightning. The Trisians will never know our accuracy or stamina but then they would never wear themselves out for a cause. By god, I liked them.

I sat at the stern, played a Rhydanne game of cat's cradle, and watched Tris shrink into the distance. The wind battered the clouds down to a thick bank on the skyline around it. Our caravels trailed a path back to Capharnaum harbour, but the waves distorted then covered our wakes as if the sea was determined to hide the trail we had blazed. I hoped that the spectacular failure of Mist's diplomacy would pass. I wished that Tris would eventually become a region like Darkling, which is part of the Empire but nobody expects it to get involved. The Rhydanne know vaguely that the Empire exists but really don't care; unfortunately the island of Tris has more to offer than Darkling.

That night I could see the lights of Capharnaum but not the land, so I became convinced the town was floating on the ocean. The next morning Tris had diminished so much on the horizon that I could put my thumb over it. By supper it was a speck; by the following day it had gone.

# CHAPTER 12

When we lost sight of the island on the evening of 10 May, I had nothing to do but cross the sea as an idle passenger. *Melowne* and *Stormy Petrel* sailed across the longitudes. We were two ships standing out proud on the ocean.

I settled into my sleeping bag on my cabin floor, with a jug of coffee and cat, and some liquorice root to chew. I filled my silver fountain pen, carefully propped the book on my sharp knees and began to read. I transcribed the first chapter of the small volume I had stolen from the library, *A History of Tris*, by Sillago of Capharnaum.

In the year 416 – a date that every schoolchild knows – galleys from the mainland arrived at our then uninhabited island, and anchored in the mouth of Olio River. During the following day, the settlement of Capharnaum was founded on the northern bank and the mighty galleys were brought upriver and set aflame, a remarkable symbolic act that marked the dawn of our present society.

Why did this flotilla of galleys leave the mainland and put their hope in the creation of a new country? In this book I will argue that it was due to the ingress into the mainland of a swarm of Insects. According to the only manuscript surviving from the Pentadrica, Capelin's account of the second decade of the fifth century, I maintain that Insects truly existed and were not the symbolic creatures that recently fashionable theories would have us believe. Moreover, they must have been rather larger than the ants of our island. My esteemed colleague Vadigo of Salmagundi has on numerous occasions criticised my belief in Insects. However, my research draws heavily on the precious Capelin manuscript housed in the Amarot library with which, perhaps as it is such a distance from Salmagundi, my colleague does not trouble himself.

The Queen of Pentadrica, Alyss, travelled with her court – a rudimentary senate – from her liberal and enlightened country known as the jewel of the Fivelands, to satisfy her curiosity about reports of the problematic Insects. Capelin, a scrivener at the Pentadrican court, relates that five Insects had appeared suddenly in the vale of north-east Awia and were the subject of much curiosity. Apparently of their own volition the Insects confined themselves in a small area behind a wall. The nearby Awians were observing and throwing logs into the enclosure when hundreds more manifested so suddenly they had to flee for their lives. When Alyss drew close to the boundary the creatures burst out, devouring the Queen and her entire entourage. Insects laid the fields waste, eating the crops and building as vigorously as our own ants. Capelin recorded that more Insects emerged than could ever have fitted inside, but this may be an understandable exaggeration or poetic flourish.

An envoy brought the news of Alyss' death to her palace and to the King of Morenzia in Litanee. Various of the Morenzian nobility immediately laid claim to the leadership of Pentadrica – that is, the throne.

The crude southern horsemen, the Plainslanders, realised that they could also gain land. We do not know, unfortunately, what a horseman would look like. The Morenzian humans and the horsemen fought over Pentadrican land and many of the Morenzian nobility were killed. One suspects the Pentadricans defending their towns and hamlets could do little against forays from the barbarians beyond their southern borders. Capelin's harrowing description of the destruction of Strip Linchit village forms the appendix to this book.

The kingdom of Awia tried to organise resistance to the Insects – presumably gathering young men whose hunting parties were now asked to net the maneaters. We know for certain that thousands of Awians were displaced southwards and determined to settle the north of Pentadrica. Historians following Vadigo have stated that from this point the story seems credible, but have given no criteria for their method of determining between reality and allegory.

Awians and Pentadricans both appealed to San for help. This mythological figure was supposed to have been given eternal life by god before it left the world; to advise the world on god's behalf. San seems to have been an itinerant sage who objectively advised all the courts of the five countries involved and was respected by them. Capelin assumes his reader knows the identity of San and gives no evidence to support immortality. It was probably a rumour arising around an extremely adroit and possibly aged wise man as it is not possible to credit the idea that he was wandering the world for four hundred years before the Insects appeared.

Some theoreticians postulate that San was god in a different guise; some hold that the appearance of Insects marked the return of god, or that god intended Insects to triumph over people and form the next phase of creation. The argument that there is a god at all is beyond the scope of this book.

It is self-evident that San realised the Insects were the greatest threat since he attempted to organise bands to hunt them. If Insects were some sort of metaphor for decadence and never intended to be understood literally as animals, how are we to explain the decision of San as recorded in Capelin's document? It is the best evidence available that Insects, whatever they were, were tangible. San blamed the Morenzian nobles for the civil war and, although some accompanied him into Awia, fighting continued in the Pentadrica. The Pentadrica collapsed completely in the year 415.

The intensity of the skirmishes seems far-fetched to our imagination, but it is important to remember that in and around the fifth century all the land was owned by individuals dependent upon it for their survival. The pre-Senate times were indeed difficult. A further reason why the settlers founded a senate was simple horror at the fact that all this confusion resulted from the death of one woman, the beautiful Alyss.

To bring peace, San divided up the Pentadrica. From being the centre of the Fivelands, its territories were distributed between Awia, the Plainslands and the new republic of Morenzia. Those three expanded countries were united and hostilities ceased. San proposed to lead volunteers from them against the Insects. In return, the several leaders met in Alyss' empty palace and agreed to bequeath the building to San and proclaim him Emperor.

Now we come to the most exciting part of Capelin's record. From all countries came a host of people who were appalled by the thought of one man, however wise, holding sway over the world. They met at the coast and numbered about one thousand. Awian refugees collaborated readily with men and women loyal to the Pentadrica who could not accept being subjected to the rule of savage horsemen and the greedy nobles who had so recently ravaged their land. They agreed to leave for an island well known to the Pentadricans. Under cover of the summer night, they escaped the mainland in a flotilla of galleys.

Today, if one strolls along the sandy bank of the Olio, it takes little imagination to envisage the travel-scarred galleys rowing upriver, their single square sails hanging stained and torn from the tribulations of the long crossing. Indeed, the site of their landing is numinous and sacrosanct, as if after their long voyage the ghosts of those tired but eager fugitives still frequent the beach.

Their outstanding achievements in founding the Senate and the colony of Capharnaum brought us to where we are today. Under the wisdom of a senatorial government, the colony thrived. Capharnaum grew rapidly and in the following century was embellished to its present radiance which, with the particulars of the naissance of Farrago community, will be the subject of my next chapter.

I turned the page, and almost dropped the book in astonishment. There was a portrait of the Emperor San. I recognised him instantly in the full-page illustration, although he was not in the Throne Room, seated on his dais in front of the electrum sunburst. He was sitting on a rock, and he wore breeches. A black and white cloak around his shoulders was secured with annular brooches. Across his knees, his ridged and wiry hands held a boar spear. The backdrop was a verdant plain of fields and, dotted into the distance, towns that were tiny collections of beautiful domes and stepped-gable houses. They reminded me of the broken domes of old Awia that project from the Paperlands; Awia has not built domes for nearly two thousand years. When Insects forced their country southwards, Awians deliberately changed the style of their architecture to symbolise a new start and express their defiance.

San did not look stern and forbidding. He was smiling. He looked like a fyrd captain; he looked like one of us. The caption read: *San, from Haclyth village, proclaimed Emperor in 415 on the dissolution of the Pentadrica.*

I thought, this is what San looked like when he was the only immortal man; counsellor turned warrior when, in another world, Insect eggs hatched, imagos amassed, and the swarm broke through into peaceful Awia. One would gain great wisdom by living through such times, witnessing incredible events – Litanee raiders sucked into the space Alyss left, riding at each other through standing crops and the smoke of burning thatch. Maybe the nomadic Plainslanders settled down somewhat once they'd gained Pentadrican farmland. So that, some sixteen centuries later, the Plainslands sprawls with twice the range, merchant families rule Morenzia and, in the city of San's birth, waterwheels spin in industry.

Some of Sillago's story fitted with what I already knew. I was keen to show Lightning my translation, because he had told me that his manor was created from land that was originally Pentadrican, where they prospered from the Donaise hills vineyards. In 549 wealth gained from the Gilt River gold rush brought his family to the throne. The Murrelet dynasty ended, and Esmerillion Micawater made her town the capital of Awia.

San has kept his position as Emperor for sixteen centuries, I thought. The current Circle is only his most recent system. If he had not founded the Circle, he may not still be Emperor. He must have come very close to being deposed in 619 when the First Circle was defeated. Our immortality seemed dangerously transient and unstable compared to San's long life. If he found a better system and no longer needed us, I wondered what would happen.

I stopped transcribing and simply read until my eyes ached. Candle-light shadowed the texture of the page. Sillago's prose tested my comprehension of old Morenzian but I read on, absorbed. In the Amarot library this was just a flawed textbook, but to the Fourlands it was a priceless artefact.

As I came down from my high, for the first time I felt the waves' motion as lulling rather than threatening. Outside, the whistle blew for the three a.m. watch. With a warm feeling of achievement I nodded asleep, curled protectively over the book, the pages kept open with one loving hand.

I woke with a quick intake of breath. I lay listening, afraid to look round, feeling that something was standing over me. I was used to the wide sky and the enduring size of the Castle – the *Melowne* was a claustrophobic floating wooden box. I forced myself to ease the cabin door open and look out at the empty night. I thought: shit, someone's stolen half the moon. But it was only clouds, I think. I must be more careful what I drink. Thin purple cirrus whipped past under the stars. There was no one about. Just a bad dream, I told myself. Go out and have a breath of fresh air.

I climbed down to the gallery and looked at the water. The open ocean was a wasteland. From edge to edge of its black expanse there was no visible life. But its endless sound and movement made the ocean itself seem like an animal. The whole febrile sea was horribly alive in a way that the static mountains could never be. A cold feeling lapped over me again. Something was wrong. What *was* that? Running alongside *Melowne*, about ten metres out from the hull, was a hollow in the inky water, silvery with the reflection of *Melowne*'s lamps. Is the hollow real? It must be, a trick of the light wouldn't persist for so long. I thought I knew all the sea phenomena by now. I shrank back; was something sentient there? I glanced up to the lookout in the crow's-nest but he stared straight out ahead. Either he hadn't noticed, or he thought nothing wrong. The wind was directly behind us. The indentation in the water was pointed at the front and rounded inside. I could see the far side of the wall of water inside, about two metres deep. The waves broke around it but didn't fall into the hole. It was as if something pressed down on the brine, like it was being displaced by the hull of a non-existent ship.

The indentation overtook us and veered away, gradually dissipating as it went. The hollow filled, leaving the surface smooth. I stared at the sea for a few minutes. Had I imagined it? Then a fin broke surface. I struggled with the perspective as the black triangle rose. Its wet tip came up to *Melowne*'s gallery, then passed it to the height of the deck. I could have touched it. It was fully five metres high. At its base, the rough back of a shark emerged, a thinner, more elongated shape than the ship. Way behind our stern, the tips of its tail flukes projected like a second dorsal fin, moving back and forth in the water. I froze. The shark was the same length as *Melowne*. It was fifty metres long. There *were* monsters out there. A flick of its tail would turn us to floating splinters.

The shark swam alongside. I suddenly wondered why the lookout hadn't seen it. I leaned over the gallery. 'Tarragon?' I called. 'Tarragon? Tarragon!' The dorsal fin rolled away from the ship, bringing the pectoral fin to the surface. The shark's silver fish eye, as big as a buckler, stared straight up at me for a second. Water washed through open gill slits like loose metre-long wounds. It rolled back. Water rose up around the wave-cutting dorsal fin as its body sank to the level of our keel.

'Tarragon . . . ?' The shark gave a slow wriggle, left–right along its length. Its immense power sped the fin past me, then its long arched back, the vertical tail flukes. It was gone, deep under the ship.

I became aware of panic on the main deck above. Pale, frightened faces appeared at the rails. Shouts in three languages stopped abruptly when Fulmer's voice bellowed something.

Tarragon said she would watch over us. Was it her down there? I thought she was a cute fish; I expected her to be girl-sized. I didn't know she was a hundred-ton leviathan.

Fulmer slid down the ladder and confronted me with an intent look. 'Are you awake, Jant? There's nothing there.'

'Whatever it was,' I whispered, 'she's gone.'

For the sake of my reality, I was relieved I couldn't see where Tarragon had gone, or what she could see underwater with her cold, filmed eyes.

## Wrenn's Diary

*1 June 2020*

Today Mist and Fulmer had a blazing row and one of the sailors was put to death. He had been caught stealing a gold boot-scraper from a chest in the *Melowne*'s forecastle. He was one of the sailors who didn't go ashore because we left before it was his turn. The men who missed their chance to see Capharnaum are very restless. Fulmer insisted discipline had to be kept, and for stealing cargo while under way the sentence is death. All seagoing vessels operate under Morenzian law. It is harsher than Awian justice; I think because Awia is in more danger of being wiped out by the Insects, we know better than to harm our own people. But Fulmer says that ruthlessness is needed at sea to stop mutinies happening.

This ship in Fulmer's charge is worth a dynasty's fortune. It's so crammed that I have to sleep sitting upright between sacks of allspice. Fulmer said that if the men before the mast can thieve as they wish there'll be nothing left by the time he reaches Tanager.

Mist Ata yelled, 'I forbid you! After all the losses to the Insect I'm not losing another crewman. Just put him in the hold and lock the hatch. Take your "I must make an example" and stuff it!'

Fulmer yelled, 'I'm sick of interfering Eszai! You're no better than anyone else just because you can handle a tiller or sword!'

I learned that at sea a captain is like a governor; on a matter of law Eszai can only advise him, not overrule. Fulmer was adamant and he had the law on his side.

Mist piled extra sail on the *Petrel* and swept ahead as if she was abandoning us. Fulmer said, 'Never trust a woman who has a point to prove. Yes? All hands to witness punishment!'

Jant refused to attend; he said it was stupid and brutal. He said that only Zascai exercise power so crudely and severely, but then only Zascai need to. He's been acting even more weirdly than usual; he keeps saying how vulnerable our cobbled-together hollow ships would be, should any sea monsters actually exist.

The thief was bound, wrists and ankles. He begged and struggled all the time. He was thin as a lath, a weather-beaten man from Addald Island off the Ghallain Cape. I was sorry his life had to end this way when he had seen so much, navigated the storms of Cape

Brattice on the southern tip of Morenzia, Tombolo and Teron Islands off Awia, the reef of Grass Isle, and the wild seas around the empty coast of the Neither Bight. He was brave enough even to have anchored in the rending whirlpools of the Awndyn Corriwreckan.

Two of Fulmer's sailors passed a rope across the bow and paid out line until the loop dragged in the water. They each held it at their waists and walked the loop down under the ship to the main deck.

One end was made into a noose and the man's ankles fitted through it. He kicked, both legs together, and screamed for mercy so horribly every man on the *Melowne* was chilled to the bone.

They picked him up and threw him over the side like a parcel. He splashed in, curled foetally; the loose rope snaked about him in the water. He bobbed to the surface, waggling his head and gasped, screamed.

Fulmer gave the order and a team pulled the other end of the rope that ran under the hull. The Plainslander's yells cut short as it tightened and he sank under. His body was drawn down a long way, still thrashing and bubbles rising all around. He disappeared from view.

I heard knocks as his body scraped over the rough, barnacled hull. Blood swirled up; it looked black. I hoped that he had exhaled the air from his lungs and breathed brine in before the scraping started.

The wet rope coiled onto the deck, water ran from the hands of the men pulling it in. Behind them a team of men paid the dry rope out. Halfway through, Fulmer wanted to stop the teams and offer each man a tot of rum, leaving the body under the boat while they drank Queen Eleonora's health. But the rope snapped. It went slack. Fulmer said, 'Lads, reel him in, yes?'

The men pulled the rope up fast, hand over hand. They dragged a pale pink and shredded mass to the surface. The cable hadn't broken, his body had. His arms were worn through, nothing was left of them. The noose had protected his ankles and feet but his legs were bare to the bone. Tiny waterlogged pieces of muscle tissue floated off, into the depths as fish food.

I saw his face had gone, just eyeballs in a fleshy cranium. Tufts of grey hair still clung to it. His back teeth showed in the gums. Tufts of wet grey hair still stuck to the skull. His back was flayed.

This wet skull on a spinal column dropped to the deck. Fulmer made sure every man of his crew saw it before they washed it overboard.

Mist is still furious, and rightly so. I hope I live till god-comes-back, but if I die, I swear it will be by steel or chitin, and not by Morenzian law.

I was in my cabin, putting the finishing touches to *A History of Tris*, when the *Petrel* raised a series of flags. Mist was asking Wrenn and I to come across for a meeting. I found Wrenn talking uneasily to Fulmer. We were all three thinking of the mess she had made of diplomacy with Tris, although only I had witnessed the worst of it. Fulmer said, subdued, 'She's making preparations for landing. We want to avoid pirate vessels as we cross the trade routes, yes?'

I flew and reached the *Petrel* long before Wrenn's boat rowed over the gently purling water. 'It's July the tenth,' Mist said. 'I'm confident that sometime today we'll have sight of the Fourlands. Watch for the coast, it's heart-warming to see it appearing. It feels like the first time a newborn babe is placed in your arms.'

I sipped water that was faintly brackish, owing to the habit of refilling seawater ballast casks with drinking water. Mist watched the big, gimballed compass in the binnacle dipping as if it was dowsing for land. The morning sky was a slightly powdery pale blue that meant it was going to be a hot day. The haze had burnt off by mid-morning and the temperature was so intolerable that I climbed the rigging and clung there, a black-clad starfish in a giant net, with my wings spread as a shade. When I opened my eyes the bright world was tainted blue.

Thick white salt dried on the stern carvings, encrusting them like the lumps of salt that fyrd throw into trapping ponds to immobilise Insects. It smelt as dirty as flotsam; I could practically hear it crystallising.

Whale fins gnomoned all over the ocean. Seagulls trapezed in the sky. We came in slow. The lookout in the *Petrel*'s crow's-nest used his own feather as a plectrum to strum his guitar. He gave a false shout of 'Land!' twice and Mist snarled that if he did it again she would slice his tongue out and fly it as a pennant. There were tiny glossy plaques of severe suntan on her shoulders. A sweat sheen covered the golden-brown skin above her breasts, startling with her cream clothes. She had cut her platinum hair short and ruffled like dandelion fluff. She squinted at the sun-glare and when she relaxed the folds at the edges of her eyes showed white.

Evening set in, and dry, porous ship's biscuits were dealt out among the crew. Heat was radiating back out of my sunburnt skin to fill the cool air. A thin black line began to rise on the horizon, becoming a part of the night sky where there were no stars, but nobody dared say anything until Wrenn strolled over and said, 'I might have heatstroke, or is that land?'

'Aye, that is land.' Mist admitted, tiredly. She raised her voice. 'Land, ho! We're home, boys! Send a signal to Master Fulmer.'

The *Melowne*'s sailors read the series of flags. They took up the shout and jubilation broke out all over the ship, in the topgallants and below in the galley. From the *Petrel*'s half-deck I heard them shouting and cheering Mist. We had been on our own so far from anywhere that sighting the Cobalt coast was like seeing an old friend. We surveyed it with unbridled joy but, because we had been self-sufficient for three months, with slight trepidation.

'Drinks all round,' I said.

'Order!' Mist snapped. 'We return as we left. Clear the decks shipshape and Sute fashion. Wait till you have your feet on dry land before howling with your hounds' tongues, or by god I'll separate them from you now.'

I was obsessively trying to judge the distance to the coast – the moment that I could safely fly back. I wanted to travel under my own power, at last! More importantly, I had to catch up on six months' worth of news. I was desperate to know the latest, and even more keen – as a Messenger should be – to give San my report of Tris. I was also determined to face Tern and demand the truth from her about Tornado.

Mist observed me hopping from foot to foot at the prow. She collapsed her telescope back into its casing with a snap. 'You want to fly?' she asked.

'I need to know the news.'

'Please don't leave us. I need you to deliver my account of Tris to San. I've just finished writing it.'

'I intend to give my own; it's Comet's duty.'

Mist scratched her fluffy head. 'Since when were you objective, Shira? You and your stupid eyeshadow.'

'It's not eyeshadow it's late nights. Look, Ata, I'll come straight back. I only want to buy a newspaper.'

She looked at me closely. 'If you go to land, promise not to breathe a word about what happened on Tris. Aye, god knows I can't stop you, but I'm trying to contain this discovery and you can see how important it is not to blab.'

'I'll just bring you the news, I promise.'

'Then off you go. And buy me a couple of bars of chocolate, as well.'

*

I landed on the dark strand, and jogged up the beach from the hard wet sand to the dry sand, then climbed some steps to the promenade. I looked back and laughed to see my footprints appear from nowhere at the point where I touched down. The days were already getting shorter; I somehow felt cheated. It was ten p.m. and the Artists' Quarter, that reputedly never sleeps, was just beginning to wake up. One seafront kiosk was open. A grey, hircine old man chortled when he saw me. I asked why, and he pointed to the headlines.

I said, 'Oh, fuck,' and bought a copy of every newspaper he had. I jammed them into my satchel. I gave the man a handful of pound coins and for my fifty-pence change he used a pair of clippers to cut the last one along the line stamped on it. He returned half the coin.

As instructed, I also picked up some chocolate but I had eaten most of it by the time I reached the *Stormy Petrel*. I called Mist, Lightning and Serein to Mist's office and spread the newspapers on her table:

### REBELLION POISED TO STRIKE THE CASTLE

Troops raised by Gio Ami are proceeding towards the Castle itself. Lady Governor Eske has, of her own accord, given over the first four divisions of General infantry and more than thirty Select Fyrd to his cause.

Gio Ami has also commandeered Insect-wall-breaking machines from Eske. They include two battering rams and seven catapults, probably mid-sized trebuchets although it is difficult to specify the exact type. At the time of going to press, the engines are en route along the Eske Road.

Gio Ami's volunteer force and non-combatant supporters are extremely varied in background and opinion but are strongly united by their discontent at the Castle's role in the slow recovery of the Empire from Insect damage. Gio Ami will address them in his second meeting, to be held at midnight on Thursday at the Ghallain Fencing Academy in Eske.

In response, the Castle has received command of four thousand General, one thousand Select Fyrd from Fescue and Shivel, placed under the control of Tornado and Hayl. The internal guard of the Castle, the Imperial Select, are on alert.

Sporadic clashes occurred today on the Dogvane Road from Ghallain between demobilised soldiers loyal to the Castle and rebels attempting to join Gio.

Kestrel Altergate
10.07.20

'How can Gio dare?' Wrenn said. 'This is all on its head! We're their guardians!'

'Many things are happening recently that have never occurred before,' Lightning said quietly, as if adrift.

'There's an embargo on ships,' I read.

Mist pressed her hand on her belly, growled, 'What kind of stupidity? Where does it say that?'

'Look, here. It says Gio's men have occupied Awndyn and nothing can enter or leave the harbour, including your caravels.'

'Oh, for god's sake. If I'd been here things would never have gone this far.'

I translated the Plainslands article aloud to make it easier for Lightning, and then I picked up the broadsheet he had been reading. He pointed out an editorial at the bottom of the page. 'The Grand Tour just got longer,' he said.

### RACE IS ON TO THE ISLAND OF DELIGHT

As Gio Ami's uprising confounds the Plainslands, news spreads about the Island of Tris. It has caused a stir in Lakeland Awia. Our correspondent at the court writes that Queen Eleonora Tanager yesterday summoned to Rachiswater Palace one of the mariners of the 2019 expedition. The Court was entertained to hear, at first hand, the bizarre travellers' tales currently filling the penny dreadfuls.

The *Wrought Standard* remains sceptical of the details, yet accepts that an island has been discovered since the flagship *Stormy Petrel* departed on another journey not one month after returning from the first. Mist's statement that she returned empty-handed is now regarded as a half-truth at best. The Castle must have planned her venture because *Stormy Petrel* was careened and resupplied within a month; the Castle is invited to reply to allegations that it has been economical with the truth.

No place is perfect, but Tris comes close. The islanders are both winged and wingless people. The climate is good, and the soil on the slopes of the central mountain is as fertile as Plow's black earth wheat fields. The sailor said their food was succulent fruit he had never seen before, and fish with sweet, rich flesh. The culture seems sophisticated, but sailors' tales are not wholly to be trusted. They also tell of having seen men with paddles for hands and mountains that emit smoke like chimneys.

The island is mostly in a wild and natural state. There are no settlements in the interior; the islanders travel around their rocky coast by canoe.

Queen Eleonora has expressed interest in mounting her own expedition, as has Lord Governor Brandoch. Tris offers opportunities to trade, and a place of settlement that can be offered to our displaced countrymen sadly suffering the lot of refugees. The race is on to construct or engage craft worthy of making this long sea voyage.

I was interrupted by a cry from Wrenn, who had turned straight to the sports pages. He pointed out a paragraph:

Gio Ami's admirable life's work was shattered in one flukish move by Wrenn, all reporters present at that immortal duel agreed. Wrenn proved that there are no universal laws in the Art; now, characteristically, the master of the Ghallain School seems determined to take unpredictability to extremes. His rebellion could not be foreseen by those of us who knew his cool fencing style. His aggression in the game used to be well controlled, he always kept some tricks back. Now he gains followers like swarms of Insects, determined to deal the Circle a mortal blow.

As Gio Ami told us, 'Serein Wrenn is away, maybe lost at sea. If Eszai can't give one hundred percent for the Empire, they should not be Eszai at all.'

D. Tir, Editor, *Secret Cut Fencing Times*

'So,' said Mist. 'Gio Ami doesn't know when to leave.' We were all silent, thinking of the man's gall.

Lightning said, 'There must be some mistake. It's unthinkable! What does he imagine he can achieve?'

Wrenn tore the paper up and cast the shreds on the floor. 'I'll meet him for you.' He glared round at us. 'I'll take him back to the amphitheatre and run him through!'

'It's his followers I worry about,' said Lightning.

'They won't stay with him,' I conjectured.

Mist slammed her hand on the table. 'Gentlemen, a council to decide our course because we don't know what we'll find.'

'We should hasten to the Castle as quickly as possible,' Lightning said simply.

'Aye, but I won't put in to Awndyn and risk a clash with any of Gio's followers.'

Lightning said, 'I will answer for Swallow Awndyn.'

'No, no, don't be so unwise. We can't trust any Zascai. Especially the allegiance of Swallow, whom San won't allow into the Circle. I will not chance the safety of my ships. I'll hide *Stormy Petrel* and leave an armed guard on her. You know in the past the most precarious times for the Castle are those when we've managed to beat back the Insects.'

Lightning nodded and said, 'Well, Serein wanted a chance to prove himself.'

The next day the mainland was nearer. At first it was a pale grey silhouette, and at ten kilometres out I saw the exact instant when it became green. Colours on the coastline differentiated as we sailed nearer. The water had a blindingly bright mirror glare, as moving ripples reflected the sun. It was so calm it looked solid, almost as if I could walk on it.

At five kilometres out the sea was busy with traffic of various vessels coming and going, small sails in the distance. Ships turned left on sight, out of each other's way; they hailed each other when gathering to approach the port. We were at the depth and bearings of the main north–south route along the coast, which the sailors called Carrack Roads. We anchored and all the *Petrel*'s crates of precious cargo were transported to the *Melowne*.

The *Melowne* sat lower in the water, a target for corsairs, so Mist ordered all her Castle pennants to be furled one by one until she only flew Tanager's ensign. The *Melowne* then parted from us and Fulmer steered her northwards, heading for Tanager harbour, where he and Mist had decided that the precious cargo would be most secure.

Grey dolphins packed our bow wave, jumping and snorting; their hard bodies slicked through the water. They rolled, breaking the surface and half-somersaulting as if they were spinning on a wheel. I wondered what Tarragon thought of them – snack food, probably.

'We'll anchor in a sheltered bay I know well,' Mist said. But we headed for a blank chalk cliff with none of the cleavages where harbours lie. I didn't much like it, so I climbed on the back railing, spread my wings and let the ship slip out from under me. I sailed up on a current, seeing the white chalk and lines of black flint speed past, till I was above the cliff. I looked down on the grassy top and realised that what I had thought was a continuous wall was an enormous flat, rugged stack hiding the narrow mouth of a cove. I soared along the cliff edge, hanging suspended in the wind which blew in from the sea and was driven vertically up its face.

*Stormy Petrel* tacked once, so close to the rock that the gallery at her waist scraped it. Mist and her bosun spun the wheel between them, and *Petrel* slipped through the passage behind the stack with only a couple of metres on either side. I turned again into the wind and glided back along the cliff top towards the inlet.

*Stormy Petrel* anchored herself fore and aft. She was hidden, but only from the sea. Anyone on the grass could look down two hundred metres to see the ship calmly bobbing in the dark quiet water crosshatched with ripples. Every wavelet made her dance; there was nothing in her hold but ballast and bilge water. The walls of the deep circular pool were sheer but there was a floating jetty constructed from barrels. From this landing stage a series of uneven steps hacked into the chalk led up to a cave entrance above the high-water line – a smugglers' hideout. Though since Mist knew about it their contraband would be long gone.

*Petrel* lowered her landing craft and spewed out a procession of tattered sailors who climbed the steps into the cave, where they vanished, and more men behind them tramped into the grotto that surely couldn't hold such numbers. It was like a conjuring trick. Half an hour later, the first man emerged onto the cliff top through a pothole I had not previously noticed. Another head–torso–legs followed, until all the sailors were sitting on the grass, scraping chalk sludge off their boots. Lightning and Wrenn climbed out last, absorbed in an intense conversation, but I couldn't hear what they were talking about. I was having too much trouble defending myself from fluttering little songbirds. My big cross-shaped silhouette pinned in the sky on motionless wings reminded them of an eagle. They could out-fly me; they orbited and dived on my head. I tried batting them away, but their tiny beaks were very sharp.

Mist paid her crew and told them when to muster at the Puff Inn in Awndyn-on-the-Strand to gain a cut of the profit from the spice ship. She briefed them to hold their tongues about Tris with a promise of future employment, and dismissed them.

I flew into Awndyn feeling that the atmosphere had changed; people were looking up at me suspiciously. I visited the offices of the Black Coach, the postal system of stagecoaches that uses the stables and hostels of coaching inns. It was set up by my predecessors who were reliant on horses. Its mail network was nominally answerable to me as Comet, and despite their palpable disquiet the Awndyn branch seemed to be coping just as well as the last time I visited six years ago. I procured horses from their yard for Mist, Lightning and the Swordsman, and had to sign in triplicate for a carriage-and-pair for our luggage. I joined the others on the main road and directed them to the Remige Road in the direction of Eske manor and the Castle.

The sensation of the waves' movement still lasted from the ship. I felt as if I was rising and falling although I had both feet on dry land. It was a pleasant feeling that lulled and confused my senses; coupled with the warmth of scolopendium it sent me into a condition of bliss.

## CHAPTER 13

The Remige Road was one of the main routes built by the Castle for the movement of fyrd to and from the Front. It was wide, for two wagons abreast, and it had worn a deep cutting into the chalk on the downs west of Awndyn where it had not been cobbled. Lightning, Mist and Serein led the coach-and-pair inland across a broom and gorse heath, under a sky of the vivid blue that is the field of the Awian flag. They rode alongside an oak plantation belonging to Mist, then an orchard. Sunlight shone on the horses' well-groomed flanks. Light reflected from the metal panels on my boots and darted bright patches on the path.

Flying is the most selfish pastime in the world. It's all I ever want to do. Flying is being alone but not lonely, swept up on the exhaust of the world; my wings and the ground two magnets pushing each other apart. The sky is more gentle than the touch of any lover, and gliding on a hot day is as effortless as sleep. I hold out my wings, supported on rounded air, and change direction with a tiny movement. I travelled at an altitude too great to be seen from the patchwork farmland and toy cottages. I urged myself higher, trying to cram more miniature moated granges and dwindling trees into my field of vision. I sang, 'Oh, we met in the Frozen Hound hotel, down on Turbary Road.'

Lightning and Mist seemed to be arguing. I dropped height and circled above them, my backswept sickle wings beating quickly with the wrist joint bent gracefully as a falcon's. I risked spooking the horses but I wanted to hear the Archer.

'This is far worse than the year fifteen-oh-nine,' he rebuked Mist angrily. 'Gio Ami is much more desperate than Eske was then.'

Mist said, 'Well, I agree, but the Castle will weather another such revolution, especially when you and I can negotiate.'

'Let us send Comet ahead.'

'No. I want to be present when he gives his report.'

'What was the year fifteen-oh-nine, anyway?' asked Wrenn.

'Oh, don't get Lightning started or he won't shut up till nightfall.'

'Your charm never falters. Wrenn, I'll tell you. Five hundred years ago we pushed the Insects further out of Lowespass than their Wall had been for centuries. The Insects were less of a threat, so the southern manors decided they were safe. They thought they no longer needed the Castle, so they refused to pay our dues. The governor of Eske manor led the way, and the whole Plainslands followed within the year.'

Mist sniggered. 'When the taxes dried up, many Eszai thought their power was being eroded and they panicked; it split the Circle half and half. The Sailor – my predecessor – led those who wanted to use violence, and San nearly expelled him from the Castle. But Lightning's diplomacy won, as it will again.'

'Oh, yes,' said Wrenn admiringly. He drew nearer to Mist.

Lightning continued: 'The wisdom of our Emperor resolved the situation. We're only his servants, whatever Ata may say. You see, San offered Eske's only son a place in the Circle. He was a damn good horseman and deserved to be Hayl. Lord Governor Eske died of old age fifteen years later, taxes unpaid. His immortal son inherited the manor and the uprising simply collapsed.'

They reached the edge of the escarpment and looked down; the land fell away like the inside of a bowl, to the flat – or at most gently undulating – Plainslands. From the curved grassy ridge that formed Awndyn's border they could see to the serrated horizon of Eske forest.

The square fields on the hillside were white with chalk soil; they looked like they were covered in snow. Yellow patches of barley with straggly orange poppies between them contrasted with the sky and hallucinogenic-green grass of the downs. Awndyn was a beautiful manorship.

Eske and Awndyn were the only two Plainslands manors owned by families who originated, centuries ago, in Awia. The Plainslands manors might seem weak and old-fashioned, incessantly bickering over their boundaries, but because the land was decentralised, its cultures were stable, tolerant and as varied as the Plainslands landscapes – peoples of forests, heath, Brandoch marsh and Ghallain pampas.

At the foot of the hill the coach and riders forded the pure water of a trout stream. Dust clouds and chaff blew across the road from a tariff barn where schoolchildren, who holiday at harvest-time, were brushing the paved floor in readiness to store next month's crop. They peered out from under the barn's thatched fringe. The older ones bowed their heads when they saw our sunburst insignia – while the teenage girls turned to each other and shrieked with passion.

I descended and said to Lightning, 'There are fewer farmers here than usual. If they've gone to Gio, more people are involved than I thought.'

'Great. With a shortage of labour and food the last thing we need is the farmers joining a rebellion.'

The air brushing the pits of my wings and the paler silky feathers under them was so erotic I started thinking of Tern again. How she giggled when I pushed my cold face down her bodice lacings. How her touch was so gentle I screamed but she kept stroking. I remembered Tern walking slowly in the snow, a parasol over her shoulder. My flitting footsteps crunch as I sprint round the corner of the black manor house. My body collides with hers. 'Caught you!' We fall embraced into the snow, laughing and kissing. She would bend my flight feathers to give me a sensation of speed, and I would encircle her whole body with them. Her wondering face looked up at my smile. And all the time she carried on her affair in secret. I snarled and spat down into a corn field.

I borrowed the horses just over ten hours ago. It had been one hour since we descended from Awndyn heath and entered the arable land. It should take another thirty hours' travel to reach the Castle. In five hours it will be sunset. One hour after that we will reach the Cygnet Ring Coach Inn in the dense part of the forest. In eight hours I would need another fix.

It was four p.m. when we entered the forest. The road cut through it cleanly; the spaces were open and bright sunlight permeated between the trees and threw moving highlights on the ground. Bracken and angelica sprouted among piles of bleached-white timber. In the tussocky clearings luscious purple foxgloves stood like racks of lingerie. I saw the road clearly from the air – two tracks from the wagon wheels with a grassy strip between them.

The air above the road shimmered; it looked wet and glassy. In every hollow of the dry track there was a mirage of a silver puddle that peeled away as we got nearer, and repeated further up the road in the hot air rising from it.

We passed a cleared area beside the road intended for a fyrd division muster point. About every forty kilometres we passed a coach inn. These pubs and stables were semi-fortified with high walls. Travellers, hunters and workers of the surrounding farms could seek refuge there if Insects set upon them. Luckily, there had been no attacks this far south for twelve months. I considered the forest to be free from Insects; we had spent the last five years hunting them down.

Wrenn dozed on the back of his palfrey. The Swordsman had no horsemanship whatsoever and sat like a sack of spuds, his chin on his chest, nodding forwards and jerking awake so I thought he was going to fall under the hooves of Ata's mare. Ata reclined in thought, under a denim cap. Her legs braced in the stirrups pulled her leather trousers tight over well-defined muscles. She stared at the backside of Lightning's stallion.

Lightning knew the forest well, and he loved it. He rested his bow horizontally on his knee and an arrow across it, nocked to the string. Holding a weapon changes your perception of the surrounding world. The very act of carrying a bow tunes your awareness to find the quarry. Lightning listened to every rustle in the undergrowth, or breaking twigs in the canopy. He noticed the 'coc-coc' of pheasants, the sound of grasshoppers switched on by the heat. He noticed the subtle odour of deer and differentiated it from the stink of the horses, wild garlic and ditch water. His senses were heightened – in the country, after an hour smell and hearing became as important as sight. A less experienced hunter would jump at any play of shadows and snatch up his arrows, but Lightning was confident. He knew that you always have more time to draw and loose a bow than you think.

I noticed a commotion further along the road. The highway ascended a slight hill; near the top it was blocked completely with people. At this distance I could only see splodges of colour, brown or black clothing, some pikes or flagpoles moving about, and an occasional bright flash in the centre of the milling crowd that was either a mirror or polished steel. I narrowed my eyes. This could be Gio's work.

I wheeled over my colleagues and called, 'Lightning?'

'Yes?'

'There's something strange ahead. I want to find out what it is.'

'A den for you to sleep in, perhaps.'

I clacked my wings together impatiently. 'It looks unusual . . . Just because I'm hooked doesn't mean I can't function,' I added, muttering. I pulled on the air and surged up. I was only between one and two on the room-spinning scale. I should be treated the same as when I'm clean, especially if I have a good supply; it takes very careful examination to tell the difference.

A company of about one hundred men was walking slowly up the hill behind a double ox team that pulled . . . At first it looked like a massive farm dray, but with an enormous wooden beam across it. At the front the square-sectioned beam was attached to a horizontal capstan whose great spiked handles projected like an unfinished cart wheel. A hawser made of twisted sinew joined a leather sling half a metre wide. It was a trebuchet, a thing of horrible potential.

The tops of heads, like dots, became pink as men turned their faces up to see me. The drover slapped the oxen's snouts, and when the trebuchet team ground to a halt he slipped wooden wedges under its solid wheels.

On the hilltop was another circular, grassed-over clearing maintained for a fyrd camp. Tents packed the earth, some small triangular shelters around a spacious cream canvas pavilion. Most were threadbare, stained with dirt, grease and wine, but some were from brand-new supplies. There were awnings and lean-tos, but I had no time to take it in because people on the ground spotted me and started shouting. Men dashed from all over the encampment to the centre where a huge bonfire smouldered. They stoked it, poked it, and threw on new logs and green boughs.

A thick column of dark grey smoke rose up. I saw it coming and a second later I was completely enveloped. Smoke burnt my eyes and nose. I breathed in a lungful and started coughing violently. Acrid smoke seared my throat. My sinuses were full of it; my inflamed eyes ran with tears.

Black flecks and sparks swirled past me. Leaves and lichen burning round the edges stuck to my shirt. I beat my palms on my stomach. I tumbled out of the billowing smoke, blinded and disorientated. I started to fall. Air whipped past me. Treetops hurtled up from where the sky was supposed to be. The sky was underneath me. I rubbed my face vigorously, tore out of my spin. I found myself above the road again, very low.

The hard-faced men by the ox team drew their longbows with disorganised timing and loosed. A hundred arrows flew straight up; I banked away hard. Long shafts passed in the air on my right. Flights whistled as they reached their zenith, turned round and plunged back. A breeze brushed my face from the nearest one. Spent arrows thumped on the upper surface of my wings. Shafts slipped between my fingered feathers. I straightened my flight path and beat madly away over the forest.

This could not be a case of mistaken identity.

Hot with panic I yelped, 'In San's name, stop!' Arrows poured around me like solid raindrops. 'In the name of . . . San Emperor, for the will of god . . .' But I was coughing too much.

I flew out of range but they kept shooting for five seconds to make their point. The arrows' broad heads crackled down behind me onto the topmost branches.

I winged back to the coach, furious. What's it like to be hit? To have a solid wooden rod impaled through my whole body – would I be able to feel it with my insides?

I landed next to Lightning and Mist. 'Did you see that?'

'Yes,' said Lightning.

'They aimed straight at me. Me! The Emperor's Messenger!' My clothes stank of smoke. I blew my nose and flicked mucus off my fingers. 'Bastards! Bastards! It's a wonder they didn't hit. If it wasn't for my agility . . . They wouldn't even stop for "the will of god and the protection of the Circle"!'

'Aye,' said Mist. 'You shouldn't have gone ahead. Now they know we're here, and soon they'll tell Gio.'

'Me! An Eszai!' I was smart enough to know I am not universally loved, but I never thought I was hated.

Mist said, 'There must be something in that camp they don't want us to see.'

'Probably another bloody big trebuchet like the one they're dragging up the hill! I didn't see its serial number.'

I described the ox team and Mist listened with a faint smile, either admiring Gio's ingenuity or passionate for a good chase. She said, 'Why's the trebuchet this side of Eske, if he's taking it to the Castle? Has Swallow given it to him? Or has he stolen it? There, Lightning; you see that Awndyn's as treacherous as the other Plainslands manors.'

Wrenn's eyes were wide in disbelief. He ventured, 'Stop here and see if they come down to us.'

'In range of the trebuchet? Why not carry a target and make it their sport? We could offer foreign gold as prizes!' Lightning had a clearer idea of Gio's character.

'They must be very confident,' said Mist.

'They shot at me!' I said.

'Jant, quit wringing your hands and tell us – you know these roads – how can we reach the Castle without pushing past them?'

I said, 'We're about halfway to Eske. This is the only coach route, unless we go back into Awndyn and join Shivel Road. It'll take a couple more days because it'd put us two hundred kilometres out of our way. And it's probably packed with mangonels.'

Mist took off her cap and ruffled her hair, which was damp with sweat. Her face betrayed the stress she was under, some puffiness around her disturbing indigo eyes. 'Into the woods and outflank them, then. I'm carrying important information that I don't want them to capture.'

Wrenn found this ignominious. 'We can fight if necessary!'

'Unfortunately, Serein, I think they'd shoot you, too.'

I ordered my driver to take the carriage back to the last coach inn, the Culver Inn, and wait there for instructions. If he received none after three days, I told him, he should return to Awndyn. I didn't want to lose my possessions. Lightning, Mist and Serein dismounted and led their horses off the road into the forest undergrowth. At first the going was hard; brambles hooked in my trousers and tore them. The pungent smell of bracken was up round our noses. Further from the track, less light penetrated the canopy and fewer plants grew between the trunks. The forest floor was covered in tinder-dry oak and beech leaf litter that crunched under our feet and the hooves. 'I hope Gio's rebels don't torch this,' I said.

Mist said, 'God, now he thinks of it! Scout ahead and tell us how far we have to walk before we can rejoin the road.'

I shrugged off my water bottle that glugged at every step, and hung it on Wrenn's saddle. I dashed away. It was impossible to move without sound in the forest; stories that tell of my predecessors doing so are just flattering lies. But I have lively reactions and I can run so swiftly through the tangle that no one registers the sound as human. I ducked under branches, leapt over fallen brushwood and sprinted with long strides. I sped up the rise and doubled back to the road. It seemed clear beyond the camp. I hid behind a tree, peered out and withdrew immediately. Another band of men strutted past with their pikes on their shoulders.

I ran on again, enjoying myself, but every kilometre I spotted more groups, so I returned to my friends, nimbly through the spaces between snarled undergrowth. Hot saliva was gushing into my mouth; I felt real once more. 'This isn't good – they're all along the road! We . . .' I lowered my voice. 'We could walk in the forest all the way to Eske but there's a hundred and twenty kilometres to go, so it would take you days. I say we keep going until nightfall and then try to rejoin the road further on, when the rebels should be encamped or indoors. I'll scout ahead.'

Mist said, 'Lead on then, smoky creature.'

'Somewhere around here is the Cygnet Ring Inn ratskeller. Foresters drink there so we should pick up a track eventually.'

'Damn, you move so fast I can't even see your footholds,' Wrenn grumbled. 'There's no path here.'

'Then we make a path.'

We walked, leading the horses, over the copper-coloured floor, under the stippled green ceiling for the next few hours, some distance from the road so we wouldn't be heard. The light began to fade and the dusk became darker by degrees. The ground could not be seen clearly; tree-boles seemed to float towards us, distanceless. I felt as if something sentient and silent was watching us. I couldn't decide whether it was large and invincible, or small and instinctive.

On the road with their mounts, the others had been slow, but now negotiating trees and bramble thickets they slowed still further until they didn't seem to make any headway at all. I burned with frustration. I kept urging them on until Mist lashed out, 'I'm going as fast as I can! I can hardly see. I keep stumbling over things and so does this stupid nag. I *hate* this; we're in the middle of nowhere and the Empire's suddenly crawling with people who despise us.'

Lightning intervened. 'Look, Jant, let's rest here, have a few hours' sleep and then check if the road is safe. The newspapers said Eske is full of unrest and I don't want to be exhausted when I travel through town.'

'You're all so unbelievably tardy,' I said, but I flopped down immediately and made myself comfortable on the leaf litter. The others, who were not as practised at bivouacking or as careless as a Rhydanne, looked about for a patch of grass or a landmark to camp next to.

Wrenn threw his pack on the ground and sat on a stump that was so rotten he bounced off it and it fell to pieces. He brushed moss from his arse and began to unlace his boots.

Lightning paced about. 'I think that the town will be safe without Gio to stir up the Zascai. The ingrates don't understand how hard we have been working for them all this time . . .' He tripped over a tree root and kicked it angrily. 'Creeping about in the dark like highway-men!'

The post-coach jumps the news from manor to manor. I imagined every governor realising that the Castle is only protected by tradition and their own beliefs. I almost heard them thinking: what could be in this for us? 'Half the Plainslands has supported Gio for six months. We don't know what we're heading into.'

Mist said, 'I only know we must make haste to reach San.' She made a small hearth, unrolled her blanket and shared out some Trisian *pan forte* and a flask of red wine. 'I think Gio wants to cause us as much pain as possible before we inevitably catch him. I can tell he must have little hope because his methods are so desperate . . .' She fell into a reverie and did not speak again. We heard people passing by at the road's nearest approach. I felt satisfied that I could lie hidden and observe them, and they wouldn't know I was listening.

Lightning took out one of his books. He was writing his three-hundredth romantic novel, which would probably be much the same as the other two hundred and ninety-nine, but maybe this time with a nautical theme. Their popularity was a constant source of wonder to me. He usually pays me to translate his unimaginative but ardent scribblings, but he always has my translations checked. Lightning looked wistful, a powerful emotion he had practised over centuries, which he now fell into easily. He had adopted it when it was fashionable, although it didn't suit him. 'Swallow is never here when I love her,' he said. 'I wish I could speak to her. In times of trouble, she finds an inner strength. Maybe it's because she lives in pain and is hardened to it.' He sighed, and went back to writing, with the practicality of a lover who has sought the same character in different women over fifteen hundred years.

For the past hour I had thought of nothing but scolopendium. My mouth watered for it and my joints ached. I couldn't hold out much longer before my need began to show. It's just a weakness of my body, I thought; it isn't really *me*. I opened a knotwork painted tobacco tin containing my stash and a syringe. I acted casually to protect me from the others; underneath I bubbled with excitement and blame. 'Don't mind if I hook up?'

'Oh, go ahead.' Mist shook her head in disgust, though I could tell she was taking notes.

'Thanks. You don't know how much I . . .'

'I'm beginning to guess,' said Wrenn.

'So one day it'll kill me. Want some?'

'Certainly not!' he said contemptuously. He walked to the edge of the clearing and stood with his back to us to have a piss. Then he returned and lay down on his coat with his rapier to hand. He watched me covertly, pretending to be asleep.

I hunched over and mantled wings round a candle stub. I licked my needle more or less clean, ran it through the flame and filled it from a skylark phial. I tied a tourniquet around my upper arm, and made the injection. I flushed the syringe out with my own blood and pulled the spike from my arm. Then I keeled over, into the leaves. An aching nausea filled my empty stomach and dispersed as my rush came on. Gradually and gratefully I gave up on thinking about anything at all.

The tops of the oak trees were pushed by a wind that didn't touch us below. Each gust churned the topmost boughs in the distance, then shook the branches above us as it passed.

A crunch sounded somewhere deep in the forest. Lightning glanced up from his book and stood up silently. He bent his longbow against his boot and strung it. He kicked the fire out, then hauled me to my feet by the scruff of my neck and simultaneously gave Wrenn a hefty kick on the bum. The Swordsman woke with a start and Lightning raised a finger to his lips. 'Footsteps,' he whispered.

'Insects?' Wrenn's eyes widened.

Lightning shook his head. After the first few trees the ground was obscure. I listened. The footfalls extended deep into the woods from our left to right. As they came closer, we could tell they were made by men. There were at least five directly ahead of us, but the noise seemed to stretch out far on both sides.

'How many?' Ata mouthed.

Lightning held up his free hand with the fingers extended, clenched his fist, then opened the fingers again.

Wrenn sprang to his feet, crossed his arms over his waist and drew his rapier and dagger at the same time. Mist pawed uneasily for the 1851 Wrought sword that she carried buckled to her pack.

The footsteps resolved; the people making them walked about three metres apart. I peered into the gnarly gloom but I couldn't glimpse anybody. We should be able to see them by now. I smelt hot oil. The crunching continued; they were almost on us. They stopped. There was silence.

Wrenn went into guard.

A yellow glare turned our camp bright as day. Black jumped to colours, disorientating us. They had been carrying covered lanterns and with one accord they raised their shutters.

I was less blinded than the others. I turned as a man jumped from the forest behind us. Dagger in hand, he ran past Lightning and cut the bowstring with a neat slice. Lightning's powerful longbow sprang back straight.

It gave a sickening, quick dry crack. Splits opened along the bow's limbs from the tips to the grip. It snapped its eighty-kilo draw weight back into his arm. Lightning jerked away so the string didn't gash his face. The shivered wood creaked. He dropped it and the arrow, and grabbed his left arm. 'Damn you, Gio Ami! Traitor and sneak!' He drew his sword with an efficient gesture but his wrenched arm seemed awkward.

The horses neighed and reared, frightened. They pulled out their tether pegs and scattered.

I can't take off. The branches are too dense for me to push up between them. I'd be scratched to bits and never break through into the clear air. Fuck it, there isn't even enough room between the trees for me to open my wings, let alone run with them spread.

Gio sauntered towards Wrenn, gazing fixedly at him.

'Revenge isn't worth it,' I said quietly.

'Comet, aren't you fast?' Gio sneered. 'Is fame worth it? I walked through Wrenn's party and no one spoke to me. When I entered the hall, the Eszai all fell quiet and turned their backs. *You* didn't even *notice* me!'

He pointed his rapier at Wrenn. Gio still wore the blue frock coat, open to his naked chest. His dusty trousers were the same, tucked into scuffed boots with stirrup guards. He had probably been riding between manors, raising his rabble, for weeks. His fair hair was dirty; strands escaped his ponytail and hung round his face. His lip raised in loathing, hatred contorted his features; it burned in his eyes as he stared at Lightning. I thought: This is not the Gio I once knew. I must be careful until I know what he's become. I said, 'What do you really want?'

'I want to fight the *novice*.'

Wrenn's whole body language was a swagger. He spun his poniard like a drumstick. 'I'm Serein. I get to live till god comes back. What's it like to be older, Gio?'

Gio kept his rapier levelled at Wrenn. He motioned with his dagger and the twenty or so men behind him placed their lamps on the ground and advanced.

Lightning stepped across in front of Mist. His gallantry annoyed Gio so much that he turned from Wrenn and made a thrust low under Lightning's sword. Lightning evaded it expertly. Gio's rapier was blacked with boot polish; the point was difficult to see. He stabbed in again. Up went his other hand to ward off an overhead blow from Wrenn.

'Oh, shit,' said Mist. She slid her Wrought sword from its scabbard.

'Keep a clear head!' I shouted to her. 'They're nothing but Insects – defend yourself!'

My old gangland fury seeped through my high. If these guys are attacking me it's their funeral! A man squared up to me, tall and very broad. Everything was dark and indistinct but I glimpsed the purple ribbon of Ghallain Fencing School wound round his swept hilt. Bugger. There's no way I can stand against one of Gio's fencing instructors. The man smiled, his teeth incandescent white in his shadowed face. He watched me like a cat with a mouse many times its size. He strutted and said, 'Comet?'

A fencing master wouldn't use such bluster, only a poser apprentice. To bolster their own self-esteem town-boys have to believe they can fight. Heat rose into my head. I yelled, 'What?'

I ducked under his blade, came up well in distance, kneed him in the balls and as he fell sank my ice axe in his throat. The pick emerged from the back of his neck, shining, covered in blood.

I didn't see Gio's next moves because I pounced onto the man's body, both feet on his chest, to pull my pick free. I rolled and slammed it through the nearest foot with so much force that I fastened it to the earth. The foot belonged to the man Mist was fighting. He howled. He jerked his leg, tripped over the handle, which jolted the pick from his shoe. He reeled away.

It seemed that Gio was now the one prepared to die in the struggle for immortality. Wrenn stamped the ground and thrust at Gio. He blocked it halfway. His rapier and dagger moved fast as an Insect's feelers, keeping Wrenn at bay. Wrenn failed to engage his blade and Gio reached right to cut at Lightning.

None of the Zascai were prepared to help Gio take on Lightning or Serein. They concentrated on me instead, stepping forward warily, trying to time their attack together. I backed against a tree and motioned for Mist to do the same. She never stopped swearing as she raised her katana with both hands. A gleam ran along its perfect edge, daunting the rebels.

Gio circled Lightning's short sword with his rapier blade and then hit it hard under the forte. He flowed the move on with grace, beat away the straight thrust Wrenn made at his chest. He kicked a foot at Wrenn's hips, shoving him off balance. Wrenn bounded back, spread his wings.

The man fighting me turned and ran. I looked to Mist; she was shaking, white hands wrapped around her hilt and an expression of disbelief on her face. Blood peeled off the blade's razor edge. Her adversary lay on the ground in two pieces. For one beat, blood pumped out slickly around his solid guts. His lips moved, then set.

'Shit,' I said. 'It went straight through him!' I hadn't seen before what a blade designed for cleaving Insects could do to a human.

Mist said nothing, trying to think her way out of the horror.

Gio spun on the ball of his foot and lunged at Lightning. Lightning missed his parry but instinctively turned away from the point. It ripped through the left side of his shirt at the waist and into his back.

Gio whipped out the black blade, thirty centimetres slick with blood.

Lightning fell to his knees, heavily. Gio turned to Wrenn.

The Zascai stopped and looked at Lightning. He lay on his side with his body arched, knees bent, his wounded side raised from the ground. His eyes clenched shut with agony; he drew deep breaths through his open mouth.

The thugs shrank back, their broadswords loose in their hands. Gio's charisma had worn off and they were themselves again, every terrified individual. I shouted, 'See what you've done? Killed the Archer!' I made no attempt to hide the panic in my voice. '*Lord* Micawater. The oldest man in the world after the Emperor himself! Put your weapons *down*!'

Their blades dropped to the earth. They turned tail and fled, in ones and twos, every direction into the forest. I yelled after them, 'San will bring you to justice! I'll see you all hang!'

Gio and Wrenn were still duelling to kill fifty metres away. Gio forced Wrenn to retreat against a broad oak trunk; he was in danger of tripping over its roots. The last of Gio's allies raced past. A look passed between them – the terrified man urged Gio to run. Gio glanced back, realised his friends had split and his chance had gone. He jumped out of Wrenn's reach, shouted something I couldn't catch, then disappeared between the trees.

'What did he say?' said Wrenn. 'Jant, chase him!'

'No such thing – look at Lightning!'

'Hurry!' Mist snapped. 'Help me with Saker! Saker, you're going to be all right.'

Lightning's square face was pallid as clay; sweat broke out on his forehead. His body was rigid. 'Leave me alone,' he said faintly. He tried to fend me off and pull himself into a sitting position, so Wrenn and I supported him, me on the left and Wrenn on the right, and eased him against a tree trunk. We propped him upright and I rucked up his shirt to see the damage.

The rapier had passed through the forearm of his left wing, between its two long bones; radius and ulna, and then out and through the wing's bicep before gouging deep into his side. So his folded wing had been stuck through twice, leaving two entrance holes and two exit holes, but it had protected his side from receiving the length of the blade.

Lightning tried to spread his wing but couldn't. 'It's only a scratch,' he said, vaguely and inaccurately. I took its wrist, held together its three elongated fingers and pulled it open with a grating sound deep within the lacerated gristle. Blood flowed in strong pulses from the upper limb and soaked it. Normally broad with splayed feathers like a hawk, it looked thin with the wet golden plumage plastered down to the skin.

'Water. Hot water.' I rounded on Wrenn. 'You can do that, can't you?'

Wrenn fetched a canteen from the fire Ata had built and began to pour water through Lightning's wing. I whispered, 'He can live without a pinion. The stab in his side's more serious. Here, cut away the shirt.'

Lightning tried to tug his wing out of my hand. He would rather die of blood loss than be in such an improper position. 'I'm sorry, Saker,' I said aloud. 'We have to treat it.'

We mopped away the blood on his back, leaving a red-brown map of his skin's tiny pores and lines. The skin around the puncture hole was spongy and inflamed. Lightning was growing too confused to be rid of our administrations. 'Better luck next time,' he said to Wrenn, then rested his head on his knees. 'Ah . . . it *bloody* . . . hurts.'

I applied my tourniquet to his wing for a minute while I cut strips from his shirt to make a field dressing. It was impossible to tell how deep the wound was. I saw that it was more than four centimetres, but I had been taught not to probe them. I couldn't do anything about internal bleeding. I couldn't prevent infection; I didn't have sutures, nothing even as basic as a mould plaster or a clean bandage. Lightning looked so weak that all I felt was shame. I had never seen him like this before, and I should never have to. It wasn't the right way round: as at Slake Cross, I should be the injured one and Lightning should be helping me. He's the second-oldest Eszai, the richest immortal. He is the centre of Awia; he taught me its language, etiquette, martial arts. His money drip-feeds Wrought. What will happen without him? 'My god, what are we going to do?'

Mist said, 'Finish the job.'

Wrenn said meekly, 'How can I help?'

I yelled, 'Look after your own sorry hide! Gio had a system for fighting two men that you didn't know!'

Mist spat, 'Shira, keep working. Wrenn, go and fetch the horses.'

Wrenn plunged about in the forest, falling over, cracking branches and making an awful noise. When he returned holding the reins of our three mounts Mist took two from him and left him with his palfrey. 'Ride back to the Culver Inn, find our coach and summon the driver. I'll build the fire up so you can see where we are.'

The Swordsman was only capable of a canter rather than a gallop;

he led his horse to the road and we heard its hooves resound loud in the night then steadily fade. Mist said, 'I wish you weren't tripping so hard.'

'Ha! I saved you.'

She looked surprised. 'Well, a second later I saved *you*! That man I cut apart, he . . . Oh, forget it . . .'

A quick fix would steady me and help me think clearly. Or I could take my whole supply; unconsciousness was very appealing. I pushed the inappropriate thought away and said, 'He can't reach the Castle. In fact, I don't want him to lie in a coach even as far as Eske.'

Lightning forced himself to recover a little. Calmly but muzzily he said, 'San needs us. I'll be there. Gio broke my bow . . . Pass me my bow; I want it.' He was blanking out the pain, which I admired because I have tried to do that more than once and failed. 'I *hate* rapiers. A *murderer's* sword. This is worse than . . .'

'You haven't been hurt before in my memory,' said Mist.

'Long ago,' Lightning sighed.

'There's something I can give you,' I offered, gesturing for Mist to fetch the splintered longbow and my pack. 'Everything will look a little strange for a while but you'll be too relaxed to care. Don't worry and let yourself—'

Lightning seized my hand and clenched it so tightly I winced. 'No drugs. Promise?'

He spoke with such certainty that I nodded. 'I promise.'

He huffed in great breaths, chest heaving like the sides of a tent in a gale. Then he lay down carefully and in a couple of gasps was unconscious. Mist dragged across his opulent gold and pale yellow coat, its grey fur lining collecting beechmast and broken twigs. We draped it over him.

Then I sat down beside him on a tree root. I ignored the blood soaking through my trousers and tried to sense the Circle. The Doctor once told me how, but she had more practice than me. She had taught herself to feel when the threads of our lifelines are strained. She can sense if someone is close to death because they pull on the Circle and it tries to hold them. Like a spider with her fingers on invisible filaments, it's possible that she already knows Lightning is injured. The Emperor would feel it; after all, he makes the links, sharing our time and preventing us from dying.

I watched the rise and fall of Lightning's shallow, in-shock breathing. If it stopped, I wanted to be prepared for the terrible sensation, the very moment when he rips through the Circle. No, I mustn't think that.

Mist stalked up to the fire and turned to me, her expression livid. 'Zascai shouldn't be *able* to murder Eszai. Immortals can't be struck down this way! Saker *can't* die. He'll wake up. I'll kill Gio Ami. I will – the bastard – how could he dare?'

'Ata—'

Her white hair tousled as she beat her fists on her thighs. 'Gio Ami. When I've finished with him there won't be enough left for a dog to roll in!'

'Look,' I said loudly. 'The thrust hit his wing and didn't go deep in his back. If dust doesn't infect it, the wound may not be fatal. But if we stay here, I won't bet on it. Return to Awndyn, and his so-called lover can nurse him.'

Mist's eyes glittered; their shine in the darkness looked halfway insane. 'No – on to the Castle.'

'You landed us here. For once plan for someone other than yourself.'

'I can't believe a Rhydanne has the gall to say that!'

'Only half—'

She interrupted, 'If we retreat we give Gio the advantage.'

'As if we have the advantage now!' I glared at her. 'Wrenn's illegal vendetta against Gio is bad enough without you joining in. He'll duel with Gio's followers all together or one at a time. Now *you* are trying hatred on for size.'

'You're right,' she said softly.

'Eszai are supposed to work together; let's earn our immortality. Damn it, Mist, god will show up, coffee mug in hand, before you bother cooperating. Go back to Awndyn, where I'll bring you San's directions as I should have done in the first place.'

Hours passed and Wrenn did not return. I watched over the Archer, straining to see by the insipid moonlight. Mist said little but glowered more and more until sometime in the early hours she burst out, 'I should have gone instead!'

'Serein is a poor rider but the best Swordsman,' I said shortly.

'Well, where has he got to? Has he been captured?'

'I hope not. Lightning's condition is deteriorating, thankfully slowly because he's strong. It's imperative we get him out of this wilderness.'

Mist stomped around the clearing, cracking twigs underfoot and kicking dry leaves onto the hearth. I hissed, 'Keep quiet! And keep listening; Gio might return. You islanders don't realise how far your noise carries.'

Lightning woke up but only stayed conscious, unmoving, for a few minutes. I tried everything except scolopendium but I couldn't bring him back.

I sighed. 'Gio's wrecked his chances of regaining the Circle, that's for sure. He could have – one of my predecessors was displaced then rejoined it.'

Ata shook her head. 'There was such a fast turnover of Messengers that they had a good attitude; they saw it as a temporary prize and a few more years of life. I remember one man, three or four Messengers back, who when he lost his Challenge joined the Imperial Fyrd. We saw him grow old. But most people who leave the Circle are too broken to try again.'

If I was displaced from the Castle as a Messenger, I would try to convince San to make me a new place in the Circle – an Eszai for reconnaissance. Somebody might one day be able to outpace me, but they would never manage a bird's-eye view. It is theoretically possible for someone to hold two titles in the Circle but it has never happened because it's so difficult to keep hold of even one title. Anyway, seeing as every Eszai has to be beaten on his own terms, I would change the requirements of my Challenge to favour my strengths no matter who I'm up against.

All I really fear is the advent of another hybrid like me who has taught himself to fly and appears out of the blue with a Challenge. As far as I know I am unique and I'm careful not to have any children. In mortal living memory, relations between the countries of Darkling and Awia have become appalling; Rhydanne and Awians are active enemies, at least in the Carniss area. I only know of one marriage between them, when Jay 'Dara', a fyrd captain from Rachiswater and man of rare tastes, climbed to Scree to find himself a wife.

Jay was my best soldier and after Pasquin's Tower Battle nearly thirty years ago, when the governor of Lowespass was killed, I placed Jay and his wife Genya as governors in Lowespass fortress. I knew that I could check on them there, and especially on any of their offspring that might have both a sprinter's speed and long wings. But unfortunately for Jay running Lowespass fortress is a hazardous job, and twenty-one years later he died childless when Insects ambushed him by the Wall.

Gradually the sky paled; the darkness shrank away into the long shadows of the trees across the whole forest. The dawn chorus broke out; roosting birds roused and called from the branches above us. Mist listened to them with extreme suspicion as she chewed the last of the *pan forte.*

She paused, hearing the clop of hooves and the heavy whirring of iron-bound coach wheels from the direction of the road. Between the trees a light glowed, faded. The din ceased. Wrenn's voice called, 'Comet? Hey!'

I raised my voice: 'Hey, Serein! Over here!'

'Good morning. I'm sorry I took ages. It was a long way and there were rebels everywhere.' The young man's voice swung towards us, obscured by the sound of hacking as he cut his way through dewy briars. He emerged from a thicket, grinned and pointed his rapier at the road. 'But they've all passed by now.'

I motioned for Wrenn to help me lift the Archer. He said, 'I feel as if I shouldn't touch Lightning.'

'I understand. You heard tales of his exploits in history when you were a boy, right? Well, you take his legs and I'll lift his arms.'

We struggled to carry Lightning out of the forest, over the uneven ground. He seemed even bigger limp and lifeless, and was a dead weight, although his bones were hollow. Wrenn climbed into the coach, reached down to grasp him under the arms and pull him up.

'It's not as elegant a carriage as he might have wished,' Mist remarked dryly, but with obvious relief.

I laid Lightning on his side, on the floor because the seats were occupied by our sea chests. The wound in his back started bleeding again, dark and clotted blood. Mist staunched its sluggish flow with the last of the cloth. 'What am I supposed to do?' she snapped. 'I don't have the faintest idea how to care for casualties. Jant, come with us to Awndyn. Tris is three thousand kilometres away, and at the moment your report is hardly San's vital priority!'

'But I have to help San muster fyrd against Gio.'

Wrenn said, 'You can't stop Gio; you're just a messenger . . . Shit, I'm sorry, Jant.'

I said, 'Don't you *dare* go after Gio! Sit up there with the driver.' Wrenn hopped onto the bench with the nervous obedience of a captain receiving direct orders. I took the opportunity to whisper, 'I'll accompany you to Awndyn and we won't stop en route. But when I leave you, don't trust Mist. She doesn't fancy you, Wrenn; it's all bluff. Ignore her seductive words and low-cut tops if you know what's best. Without Lightning, you and I have little protection from her schemes. And – I never thought I'd say this, but – beware of Zascai. Too many are Gio's devotees.'

'Jant, this is overcautious.'

'No. Do as I say. When I return with San's orders I want to find you alive.' I climbed into the coach and thumped the ceiling. The driver cracked his reins, and we gathered speed down the straight road. The forest formed a block on both sides, a palisade of trees. The Remige Road was so silent that I found it hard to believe our desperate fight had actually occurred.

We reached the manor house after five hours and I ransacked it for medicines. I explained everything to Swallow Awndyn, who made sure that the Archer was given a clean bed. The manor's resident sawbones was a sensible man, but seemed to be completely out of his depth.

I wrote a letter for Swallow's courier to deliver post-haste to the Doctor at Hacilith University: 'For the hand of Ella Rayne only. Follow the bearer to Awndyn manor where Lightning lies in a serious condition from rapier wounds. A single thrust pierced his wing twice and made a puncture lesion in his back near the kidneys which pours blood at the slightest provocation. Rapid pulse and dyspnoea; the rapier blade was dirty. C.J.S.'

I caught a few hours of sleep but it was late on Monday evening, a full twenty-four hours after we were ambushed, when I felt able to leave Lightning and set out for the Castle.

I flew in a strikingly clear sky. A full moon gibbered over the forest. Above me, stars between stars; the familiar constellations could scarcely be distinguished among the litter of faint points of light. The immensity of what had happened began to weigh on me. 'Saker,' I said aloud. Lightning was hurt. But why now? He had survived so long. I had never known him injured by Insects; he could only be hurt by people, now that the Empire was turning on itself. I flew, chilled by extreme loneliness. Tern has abandoned me and now Lightning was gone. I need to take a bit more scolopendium, I thought, and was suddenly terrified that I might. I was vastly more afraid of scolopendium now that I was alone.

Strange. I beat my wings, finding their strength reassuring. I can rely on no one. Whatever I am going to do is up to me now and I have to stay alert. We must trust the Emperor. My wingtips brushed the forest canopy as I flew low, throughout the night, back to the Castle.

# CHAPTER 14

I followed the Eske Road in, a grey line ruled through the woods. If I had to rely on my compass, then the crosswind, gentle as it was, would have pushed me northwards kilometres off course.

By dawn, the Castle was a dark smudge on the horizon. Even at this distance I could sense the tension: something was wrong. Dozens of tiny fires were scattered just inside the forest's fringe where it ended at the clear grass of the demesne surrounding the Castle.

Hundreds of specks fanned out from under the trees – running men who purposefully converged on a few sites and set to work. I approached watching timber being felled, ranks formed out of thronging mobs. They abandoned carts to choke the final approach of the road, and at the forest's edge they were winding back the huge wooden arms of trebuchets. I counted six machines of the largest class. Men with shovels were rapidly topping up their counterweight boxes with earth, while another team systematically dismantled the last watchtower on the Eske Road, carting blocks back and distributing them, stacking a pile beside each catapult.

Just forward of the trebuchet line, Gio's rebels drew up into a long ragged crescent in front of the Castle's east wall, centred on the Dace Gate. Facing them across the open ground, with their backs to the Castle and the outer moat, was a much smaller formation, the Castle's defence.

They were framed between the Northeast and Southeast towers: Fescue Select, Shivel Select in front of Fescue General, Shivel General – the full fyrd of two Plainslands manors, but only two. Either the rebellion was very widespread or the manors could not marshal men in time. Their banners cracked in the breeze, a sound that always filled me with dread. The centre was a solid block of heavily armoured hastai – veteran Select infantry – and a figure so huge that as I angled over them I easily recognised Tornado. To either side ranked pikemen raised a forest of jostling pikes. Cavalry pawed restlessly at the flanks, Hayl's white horse pennant above the larger group. All the loyal fyrd were unusually well equipped and their armour shone – they were offering a deliberate contrast to the ragged rebels.

Hundreds of helmets glinted as they looked up to see me flying over. I waved my arms in acknowledgement. Don't look at me, I thought; watch the rebels! I passed above the curtain wall, reassured by its bulk. Along the east wall, longbowmen of the Imperial Fyrd were stationed between the crenellations – I suddenly realised that the toothed tops of the towers were not just for decoration; the defenders on the parapet could shelter from missiles behind each merlon tooth. But the Castle was the only fortress to have crenellations – the Insect forts, like Lowespass, didn't have or need them. The Castle was a fortress designed for protection against people as well as against Insects. 'Shit,' I said aloud in astonishment. 'How long ago had San anticipated this?'

The two forces faced each other, hearing the clacking as six trebuchet arms wound tight and still tighter. Each side waited for the other to move first. I banked around the Southeast Tower thinking that I couldn't tell Tawny anything that he couldn't see from the ground, so I circled up a couple of hundred metres in the dawn air, wary of more arrows.

Archers detached from the main crescent of rebels and advanced slowly, their line like a loose screen. Tornado's infantry responded by locking their hooked square shields together into an unbroken wall. A second later the ranks raised their shields over their heads, forming a makeshift roof against the arrows. The odd formation was unlike anything I had seen before, but I admired Tawny's ingenuity.

With a crash of counterweights, the arms of all six trebuchets jerked up. I was far above them and saw, in plan, six stones arc out. One smashed down just in front of the machine – the stone had been too light; the middle two fell short, ripping up swathes of turf; a fourth crunched through the canopy of the furthest plane tree in the paddock and dropped into the moat in a white water spout. Two rocks seemed to grow in size as they came up under me, shrank on their descending trajectories and struck the crenellations. Bowmen dived out of the way as chips flew off the facing stone.

A distant roar of exultation burst from the woods, tinged with fear at their own audacity. Teams of men hauled on the capstans to rack the trebuchet arms down; then others staggered forward and rolled a stone into each sling.

Appalled, I thought, isn't Tawny going to *do* anything? People are actually damaging the Castle itself. Zascai are really attacking *us*. What have we done to make them hate us so much they want us dead? Do they want to harm the Emperor and annihilate the Circle? If Gio gets inside he knows the way to the Throne Room. My mind whirled at what would happen if every Eszai at once found himself suddenly returned to mortality.

In less than a minute the trebuchets were ready to launch again – their crews were obviously Eske's trained fyrd. Their accuracy improved: only one block fell short, in front of the Yett Gate on the southeast wall. One went wide and bounced along the paddock fence, smashing it into matchwood; the remaining four thudded into the curtain wall. The Castle bled more rubble into its inner moat. I noticed that the wooden bridge to the Dace Gate had been removed.

Now the rebel archers started to send volleys of arrows towards the loyal fyrd. They stuck in the shell of shields protecting the infantry. They found their marks in horseflesh spreading disorder and agitation throughout the cavalry.

Hayl Rosinante had had enough. He waved his horsemen forward, and they surged and gathered speed, spreading into a thin line, raising their lances. The archers immediately turned and raced back towards the safety of their own spearmen. From my vantage point I saw they wouldn't make it. Swift as Insects, Hayl's men ran them down. Ridged lance points devised to crack shell drove straight through the soft bodies of Awians and humans. Half the riders abandoned their lances in their impaled victims and drew swords, continuing their charge towards the rebel line.

I was . . . I had never expected to see mortals fighting immortals, and here of all places. In front of the Castle with Eszai leading troops against the Zascai we were sworn to protect! I wheeled round, sick with disgust, and sped towards the Throne Room.

As the breeze propelled me sideways, I kicked away from the pinnacle tops and lead sheet roofs coming up under my feet. Another horrible crash sounded from the direction of the Dace Gate.

The Throne Room spire sprang like a frozen fountain three hundred metres into the air. Its shadow swept round an enormous sundial on the berm lawns. The spire was built on Pentadrica Palace, which settled to accept it, ninety centimetres into the ground. The pressure caused little splits in the beams, cracks in the plaster. Its base was a harder stone, to stop the spire's weight crushing the blocks.

The end of the Throne Room was pierced by stained-glass windows in primary colours. The rose window crowned it, twenty metres across. One of its multifoil panes was propped open. I could fit through there. I pulled my wings to my body and folded them up as I felt the feathers brush the mullions. The arcuate sill passed below me; I slipped through.

The dim, silent hall was five hundred metres long, its cross-vaulted ceiling thirty metres high. At the far end was the black screen; way below me was the tiled floor with its scarlet carpet. People no taller than a centimetre looked up as I appeared in front of the rose window, my wings stretched in silhouette against its red and blue light.

I flew at the height of the diaphanous gallery adorned with different colours of marble. Above me were smaller lancet windows, the great bays divided by pointed arches below. Every window gave a fragmentary view of another part of the Castle.

My body rose and fell with wing-beats. With every beat I passed an arch – with columns like bundles of thin tubes, supporting ribs interlacing the ceiling. I was in perfect rhythm with the arcades' march down the Throne Room. They met at the vanishing point, where the Emperor sits.

The capstone bosses were larger than life – a double-headed axe, oak leaves, turtles, cascading cornucopias, flowers complex as chrysanthemums. The walls were bright with daylight. The sun shone on the east side and cast the shadow of the pointed windows all the way down the west vault. San watches these shadows tilt, shorten and reappear on the east vault every day. Above him, the ceiling vanishes up into the octagonal spire; behind him shines the sunburst.

The scent of incense thickened. The marksmen on the balcony looked distressed; then the carved ebony screen filled my vision. I swung my legs down, alighted gently on the carpet before it, and trotted through the portal, pulling my wings in and folding them. I knelt fluidly before the dais.

'My lord Emperor, I have returned from Tris and await your command.'

A crash, scarcely muted by the pierced walls, echoed through the hall. I winced. 'What's happening out there? How can I help?'

San said, 'The guards will inform me of the situation outside. Am I right that you can add little news about the rebellion?'

'Lightning is wounded. I left him at Awndyn manor.' I outlined the ambush, the spice ship, and *Stormy Petrel* hidden in a fissure. I paused at every clash or an outburst of shouting, wondering if they were coming nearer. I could only hear the loudest shouts, chaotic and disjointed. I fretted – why didn't San send me outside to watch them? The rocks were smashing the outside wall and destroying the buildings in the gap. Can they reach as far as the Palace? If Tornado doesn't keep them out of range Gio will aim for the spire.

The Emperor listened impassively and at length said, 'Be calm, Comet. The Archer's injuries are to be regretted, yes, but he is not the whole Circle. There are other ways to defeat Gio. Tell me about Tris – everything concerning the island.'

'I have Mist's written account.' I took the scuffed stack of papers from my satchel, climbed the four steps to the rostrum and passed it to San. His pinched, wolfish face watched me keenly. Under his ivory cloak, his sleeves were loose to the elbow. His fine white hair hung down to curl on narrow shoulders.

A breathless guard ran past the screen then prostrated himself on the floor, his sense of etiquette battling with the need for urgency. 'My lord,' he panted, 'Hayl's cavalry have been turned back by the rebel pikemen but casualties are light. Tornado says he must break the rebel lines in a melee if he's to stop the trebuchets.'

San nodded. 'Tell Tornado I have full trust in his judgement. However, remind him that there must be no pursuit once he has broken the resistance.'

The guard stumbled to his feet, bowed, and left.

'My lord,' I said. 'Perhaps I should go and help the Strongman. We're heavily outnumbered.'

The Emperor gave a grim smile. 'This situation is not unforeseen. Last month Queen Eleonora offered half her fyrd to guard the walls. I declined as the involvement of Awia in any such engagement would increase discord. Instead the Plainslands manors have shown their loyalty, and the weakness of Gio's support.'

Two more crashes, only a second apart; falling slates then silence. I looked tentatively at San, unable to hide my doubt.

'Comet, remember that the Circle is composed of the unsurpassed. The strongest warrior and finest horseman in the world defend us. These walls were built by a succession of the world's most preeminent architects. Gio Ami may be the *second*-greatest swordsman ever but he cannot be everywhere. His followers have disloyal natures or they would not have joined him, and once the battle turns against them he will be unable to hold them for long.'

'My lord.'

'Now, report on Tris.'

I began to describe everything that had happened on our voyage, in chronological order. I took pleasure in doing my job well. San listened to me talk, and act, as I paced back and forth on the carpet before the dais, in a red patch of light cast by the stained glass windows.

Another crash resounded, and the noise of shattering glass – the telescopes and sundials in the Starglass Quadrangle. The Emperor frowned and sent a guard to check on the damage. The Starglass Quadrangle was full of accurate instruments that set the time for the entire Fourlands. In fact, the Fourlands' prime meridian runs through it; the north axis that crosses the east axis at zero degrees through the Emperor's throne.

Another soldier sped in. I stepped aside while he flung himself on his knees in front of the throne and spieled out the latest news seen from his vantage point on the Skein Gate tower. 'The Select Fyrds have engaged the rebel centre. The cavalry are regrouping on the flanks.'

'Very well, return to your post.'

I thought of the picture of San in *Tris Istorio*. He was acting like a fyrd captain once more. I resumed speaking but was interrupted every fifteen minutes by news of the battle. There were longer waits between the trebuchet impacts now and the shouts were further away. Tornado and Hayl are driving the rebels back, I thought with relief.

I spoke for so long that we had to break the court session to give me a meal. The four hundred kilometres I had just covered were taking their toll. By the time I finished it was early evening, and the bombardment had ceased some time ago. Nervous servants came in to light the torchères and wind lamps down on chains from the ceiling to fill them. I was exhausted from sleep deprivation and practically flayed by San's questions.

I stared at the four gemstone columns in the niche behind the throne: blue azurite for Awia, purple porphyry for Morenzia, green jade for the Plainslands, silver-grey haematite for Darkling. For the first time I noticed that although there was equal distance between them, the four columns did not span the apse symmetrically. There was room for another pillar on the far right, just by where some small steps descended to an arched and iron-studded door that led to the Emperor's private rooms. There was a gap where a column used to be – for the Pentadrica.

An Imperial Fyrd guardsman entered, bowing to give his final message without meeting the Emperor's eyes. 'Tornado reports that the rebels have been routed. Gio Ami didn't dare face him in combat and his body is not among the fallen.'

'Very well. Tell Tornado and Hayl to bring their reports as soon as they are able.'

The guard left and San returned his gaze to me. 'So you even left the Insect running loose?'

I picked at the unravelling seam of a fingerless glove. At this very minute the Insect was probably dining on the Capharnai. 'Yes, my lord. We respected the Trisians' wishes. It'll be difficult enough to deal with them in future; we didn't want to exacerbate the crisis still further. Vendace found it easy to reject Mist's offer, because to the Senate immortality is just a nebulous concept. Half of them don't believe in it.'

'I see. You failed to convince them. In fact you have given them one more reason to mistrust us. The situation must be healed, and quickly. Comet, you have worked hard so far. Can you do better?'

I bowed. During my meal in the empty guardroom San had written a missive that now lay on the marble arm of his throne, neatly sealed with the crimson sunburst. He regarded me carefully, as if he could read all my private thoughts from my face. He resumed: 'Gio's followers hold up our stagecoaches at every point between here and Cobalt. Gio himself is not easily found, except when he wants to be, it seems. This letter' – he picked up the small envelope – 'must be delivered to Mist urgently. Do you have someone you can trust to do it?'

That was a poor precedent: a mortal asked to do my work. I said, 'Messages are only truly secure if delivered by my hand.'

San's pale thin lips turned up slightly at the edges. 'I don't doubt it, Comet. But I have other work for you. Following his defeat, Gio Ami will attempt to regroup. I know that he will be holding a meeting in two days' time in Eske, in a *salle d'armes* hall that is a branch of his school.'

'Yes,' I said. 'I've been there often.'

'I want you to go and listen to what he has to say, and then come back and inform me.'

'Your wish.' Obviously I wouldn't be able to walk straight in, but I would relish finding a way to spy on Gio. He had once given me fencing lessons and I knew he was an excellent teacher; when in front of an audience he was a born performer. I said, 'I'll send the letter with a fast, dependable rider who should be able to slip past Gio. Mist should receive it late on Wednesday night.'

'Very well. In the meantime, if Tornado needs your assistance as a lookout or envoy do as he asks.'

Help the man who was fucking my beautiful wife? But San gave me no time for introspection: 'Comet, what do *you* think of Tris?'

Danio was immediately brought to mind; I shied away from the memory of her drumming feet, and recollected the Amarot library. 'The islanders love debate and casuistry that's misguided compared to

181

our practicality. It's great that Tris now knows of the Fourlands. If we can make allies with them, if they become willing to communicate with us, their theories added to the Empire's will increase our inventiveness a hundredfold.'

'What is your opinion of the riches of Tris?'

'My lord, I think they're very dangerous. They'll cause avarice, not to mention inflation.'

'And the people?'

I sighed. 'On Tris, everything works, but that's because it's a tiny island. I think they have sorted out their problems – a very long time ago, perhaps – and they've not changed since. On Tris, a thief can become a honest governor . . .' In our case, it's usually the other way round. 'But I find it strange that the citizens of Capharnaum don't want to cooperate with the Empire, like Rhydanne, and they hide themselves away when they clearly do care about the world and want to improve it, like Awians . . . It'll probably do Tris good to learn of the real world. Maybe they're in shock. I hope that when they understand us the whole Empire will benefit.'

San watched me carefully, sitting straight in the throne without stirring. He was satisfied that I was telling the truth. 'Make sure that letter is sent to Mist swiftly and with the highest security,' he said.

'Yes, my lord.'

'Go now and rest, but return on Friday and tell me exactly what Gio says in Eske.'

San gave me the Top Secret sealed letter. I made obeisance, taking a few steps back before turning and passing the screen. As I left the Throne Room I called, 'Immortals and fyrd, bring any letters for Eske to my room before midnight. Any questions about Tris, keep them.'

Walking down the corridor I caught sight of a flicker of movement on the opposite wall and went back to investigate. It was my reflection, pickled in a tall mirror speckled with tarnish. An expression of horror crossed its face – even in the half-light I don't look as good as I did this time last year. Still the same age of course, but my eyes were ringed with deep shadow; my cut-off T-shirt was the grey texture of clothes washed hundreds of times.

I called at the stables and watched my courier race away with San's letter. Enormous plane trees grew in the wrecked paddock outside. I walked past the one that I had sheltered underneath, two hundred years ago. Suddenly I saw a vivid image of my tattered self back then, leaning against the tree trunk. If I had known that any Challenger was welcome to walk into the Castle at any time, I would not have spent three days sitting under this very tree, wondering how to present myself. On our way from Hacilith, highwaymen had murdered my girlfriend and stolen the money I'd gained by blackmailing the city's governor. I owned nothing but my crossbow and a switchblade.

On the third day under the plane tree I felt a presence watching me – a man, all his colours subdued and outline unfocused as if seen through gauze. I felt a chill and didn't dare move. I stared at him and he looked back, so strange, full of confidence and concerns larger and more frightening than I could comprehend. An adult world, seen by a young man terrified for an instant by the inkling that he will join it and have heavy responsibilities every day.

I didn't know in eighteen-eighteen that I was looking through thinned layers of time, at myself. But now I realised that I was the ghost that my younger self saw. I wanted to tell him that everything would work out fine, that he would win his Challenge and two hundred years later he would still be twenty-three. I couldn't speak to him, but I smiled – and I remember receiving that warm compassion, because when I sat with my back against the plane tree's bark, I wondered at the manifestation but felt heartened and at ease.

Two centuries ago, what happened next was that at nightfall some immortals returned from the Front. I rushed to hold the reins of a horse carrying a well-built man with stripy grey and white hair, and the Castle's sunburst on a big round shield. The withers of his horse were smeared with yellow blood.

I don't know why I expected Eszai to look different. A sparkle of the Circle about him was simply my excited imagination. He said, 'You're no groom.'

'I want to be Eszai.'

He must have wondered at what in the Empire I could possibly excel. 'Then come in, waif.' He kicked the horse's ribs and it cantered forward. Its hooves boomed over the wooden bridge and echoed between the weighty towers of the massive barbican.

I picked up some more steak sandwiches; I expend so much energy flying that I have to eat vast amounts. I walked from the kitchens through the ground-floor corridor of the Mare's Run, the inner west wing, past Hayl's apartments. I passed the Southwest Tower, where Tawny's well-lit room was located, full of indiscriminately chosen prizes: Insect legs, bear pelts and jousters' helmets. Then I climbed the three hundred and thirty steps of my tower, leaning on the wall all the way up, past the myrtle-green storeroom and the bathroom on its first floor that smelt as musty as hessian. I could lie on the bed for a while and fantasise about Tern – although I am more in a mood for a Rhydanne. Or I could, and I know I will, be distracted by the obvious alternative.

Wind-thrown rain began to scour the shutters. Tern had not been in for months; my room was dark and bundles of letters overflowed the shelves, piled everywhere. My valuable pendulum clock had stopped; I wound and set it to the right time and date. Masquerade masks hung around the mirror, beside a hookah as tall as I am, its fuzzy orange tube coiled around its brass pipe like a python. I spun the oval mirror around on its stand, face to the wall.

Faded posters taped to the round ceiling advertised music festivals, marathons, and Challenges when I wiped the floor with the mortals who wanted to contest me. I'm usually Challenged in winter when conditions for flying are at their worst, and I set the same test that won me my immortality – a race from the Emperor's Throne Room to the throne room of Rachiswater and back.

There was a vase of dried flowers, the only plants that withstand Tern's immortal forgetfulness. There were a few neglected old projects: my guitar, tennis racquets and a crossbow, all equally broken. There was my bike on which I lavish much attention, wrapped in its red rope that I use to lower it out of the window. Hanging on the wall above it was a series of obsessively concentrated little pen-and-ink sketches by Frost of jousting tournaments. The mantelpiece was cluttered with some wax seals in their skippet boxes; a souvenir from Hacilith – a spider's web preserved between two sheets of glass; and a lump of solidified Insect paper with a coin pressed into it. By the window stood 'Butterfly' my Insect trophy wearing a sailor costume, and my suit of armour stuck fast to the wall with decades of rust. An array of kettles, toast forks and dirty plates filled the hearth. On the dusty table beside my still's retorts and condenser was a note covered in Tern's dying-spider handwriting. I screwed it up and threw it in the cold fireplace. Looks as if the temptation of Tornado was more than the pretty lady could stand, I thought, fishing in my satchel for my syringe.

Once I start to feel the need I can go downhill very rapidly, and the room seemed suddenly very warm. I have to shoot some, I found myself thinking. No, I don't need it. Oh, yes, I bloody do; I don't want to be sick. Maybe when Tern sees how badly her adultery affects me she'll come back. The trouble is that we spend so long apart that when we do meet we are still self-sufficient, which is a barrier to becoming really close.

I sat down at my desk, reached behind me to pull down one wing, unfolded it in front and held it between my knees. I preened fingers through feathers like a harp, hearing them rasp, and felt the thin skin ridged over my quills. Here are veins I haven't used and they looked tempting. But if I made a slip and something went wrong, or if I damaged it and was paralysed, that would be the end of me. I have only shot up in a wing once before when I was desperate. This was sacred. Sighing but pleased at some show of will power at least, I untied the pendant thong from round my neck, looped it over my right arm and licked the ends up between my teeth. I flexed my fingers, impatiently tried to raise a vein. Don't poison yourself, Jant. Meditate your way to Epsilon. Yeah, right. Why did Tarragon think I wanted to go to Epsilon? The Shift was an unwanted side-effect when I only needed the drug to make me forget my pain. Why walk through worlds if you're immigrant in each?

I sat with the needle poised, feeling a last blast of guilty defiance, then pushed it in neatly. In the space of a heartbeat it hit like a coach-and-four. Feeling like a god, if a rather incapable one, I located the chaise longue under my maps and lay down. This was like flying into a wall.

My thoughts played out in the air above me, but they were rudely curtailed by the door unlatching. A graceful and chic figure entered, and seemed to flow over to me. Tern looked at me closely. Her body was a fair; there were dances there. Her spine a snake, voice like icing on cakes—

'Oh, typical,' she said crossly. She touched up her lipstick in a mirror above my head.

'Where have you been?' I asked suspiciously.

Tern glanced down and must have realised from my expression that subterfuge was pointless. 'At Tawny's apartment . . . I had a good time.'

'What, all of it?'

'Tornado single-handedly held Gio off from attacking our home. He said if Gio came nearer I should run to the Throne Room. I have been encouraging him . . . Is it OK for you to enjoy yourself but not me? I've heard that Tris is a perfect land. You sailed off and left me here.' Tern slipped out of her dress and searched around for her silk dressing gown, clad only in a white bra and underskirt. I was too stoned to be angry. I found it hard to care about anything, not even if the strongest man in the world came in and bent her over in front of me. I gave her my orphan look: please take me home and put me in your bed.

'Wipe that off,' she said. 'Are you going to lie there all night with your hand dangling? We had a pact, Jant. You're not being sophisticated, just sedated.'

Yes, we had a pact, which we began after the span of a mortal lifetime had lapsed. We promised that it is acceptable to have affairs because we will still love each other the most, and we will always return to each other. Actually, sleeping around should be refreshing because we have to spend the rest of eternity together without becoming bored.

I propped myself up on the velvet cushions. 'Tern, why Tornado? *Amre*, he's stupid; *demre*, he can't converse worth shit; *shanre*, he's bald; *larore*, he's ugly; *keem* he's poor! Is that the kind of man you really like, so you don't love me any more? Was your pride among the possessions you lost in the fire? *Keemam*, is he better in bed than me or, *keemdem*, are you so worried that I might be beaten in a Challenge that you're prepared to shag the whole Circle?'

Tern said, 'Why did you steal my money? Can I have it back, please, or have you mainlined it all?'

I ignored this transparent attempt to change the subject. I kept pleading: 'Remember when I proposed, how I brought you the filigree spider? We could go down to the Hall and dance without music, the way we did back in 'ninety-five. Come on! Wear your brooch – it can be our seventh honeymoon.'

'Ten minutes and you'll simply collapse.'

'Come to bed then.'

'That's not the point! Shira, you're never here yourself!'

'I'm the Messenger! The point of my existence is to bugger off and bring back news! It's my job!'

Tern drew the curtain across our room. I lay and watched the details of its velvet folds; they looked like letters of the alphabet.

Tern wiped her eyes and said quietly, 'All your holidays are spent in Scree. Fighting Insects nearly burnt you out – so off you go to the mountains. Do you have any women there? Even when you're here, you're unconscious! I knew your cycle would come round again. You can't stay off cat – you can't stand to be sober for more than five years. You're not thinking about us; you are thinking about that *fucking* drug.'

Tern knew how to hurt me. She had observed it well over the last century and her infidelity had pushed me into addiction before. If she was not adulterous I would not be a junkie. 'I took cat because I'm scared of the ships,' I said. 'Everybody knows that but Ata still forced me to sail. Besides, I would rather not use cat at all than bother you with it. It's under control.'

'That's not always apparent.'

Well, it wasn't always true.

Tern kept going. 'Oh, for god's sake! If I upset you, you suddenly start to notice – but you don't think how your actions affect anyone else! I should never have married a Rhydanne.'

'Where did *that* come from?' I blinked.

'I don't mean your appearance! Some things you just can't grasp, no matter how hard you try. It doesn't occur to you to think of anybody else, like you're still living alone in a hovel in the mountains. When you're away on errands do you ever think of me?'

'Yes. Yes, all the time! That whole Rhydanne thing is just bullshit. Don't lay it on me as well now.'

'The pact—'

'Sod the pact! It's all right in theory but neither of us can actually stand it!' In a lull between the waves of chemical pleasure I sprang to my feet and stalked around the room. I ran my hands down the embossed spines of the books on the shelves. I ended up leaning on the stone mantelpiece looking at outdated invitations to dances. Our marriage rings were smoke rings and they soon dispersed. 'I'm still Eszai,' I said.

'Shira . . .' said she, and then fell quiet as she remembered what my name meant.

I kicked a neat hole in the bottom of the wardrobe door, then sat down cross-legged on the bearskin rug. 'Yes! See how important fidelity is to Rhydanne. If you're going to make all these unfair comparisons! I'm mostly Awian anyway!'

Tern said nothing; she had not seen me this angry for years. I stared at the ceiling, the only part of the room that didn't spin. I understood affairs; Tern wanted the same intensity of feeling now that she had when she was young. We might have young bodies, but we have had so much experience that we can't be young again. Tern should face it: she's one hundred and twenty-one. She would be dead by now if it wasn't for me, the ungrateful bitch.

'Do you drop your underwear on Tornado's floor as well?'

'At least I don't vomit on the floor!'

'Where do you think I've been? Tris and back! This is the first rest I've had in months; I'm serving the whole Fourlands, not just Wrought! You can't see further than your own nose! Having been through all that – *ocean* – don't I deserve some affection from my wife? Well, I can speak a patois that Tornado will understand. I will challenge him to a duel.'

Tern laughed. 'Don't be ridiculous.'

'I'll throw down the gauntlet and fight him. When I have a clear year to recover from being hospitalised. Of course he'll rip my wings off but it's worth it to get through to him.'

'You mad bastard,' Tern said, with something of her original admiration.

'Yes, I am. And remember, none of the mortals were. Not Sutler Laysan—'

'I didn't—'

'Or Aster—'

'That—'

'Or Sacret Aver—'

'No!'

It was the fact that her latest affair was with an Eszai, not a mortal, that angered me so much. I would outlive the mortals and my talent reassured me; I knew that Tern would always come back. Now for the first time she had a choice. 'Are you going to divorce me and marry the Strongman?'

'Jant, don't ask such questions . . . I'm going now. I'll come back when you've straightened out. When you can return the money you stole.'

'Money has nothing to do with this!'

'It does. Oh, it does indeed.' Her pure, sparkling voice instantly froze. She picked up the most expensive beaker from the still, turned it over and put it down thoughtfully. 'I can't keep up repayments on Wrought's debts. I can't afford to rebuild the foundries. With no workers in the colliery or armouries, my manor is sunk.'

But I knew all that; I had always tried to help Tern. I was suddenly uncertain how to answer because I had been listening more to her voice than her words. 'What are you saying?'

'Wrought will have to be leased. I considered selling but I don't want to lose my title, so I have managed to find a tenant. A coal-quarrying, canal-building nouveau-riche Hacilith businessman. I have no idea what Lightning will think of that. But who cares? Micawater itself is not in a position to help us financially any more.'

'But that's terrible! How will we live?'

'Soberly. The rent will pay my creditors – thankfully credit rates for immortals are good – but there will be little left over, and I will have to live *here*. The man from Hacilith and his family will help me reconstruct the manor house. Until my fortune improves, he'll reside there and also take the revenue from the armouries. He's keen to work with Eszai.'

'I bet he is. I'm sorry. I do love you, Tern.'

Tern came and placed manicured hands around my cheeks. 'You look awful,' she observed, and laughed red-wine fumes into my face. She lightly kissed my cheek and I smelt her powdered skin; the scent went straight to my groin. I swept one wing across my body to hide an erection that swelled so large I thought it was trying to climb into my belly button. I might get some sex tonight, after all. 'What would you say to a quick fuck?'

'Don't push your luck, quick fuck.' And she left, bound for Tawny's rooms.

I yelled after her, 'Don't ever come back! You're not that important to me anyway!' I picked my needle off the floor and threw it at the dressing table. 'Cat makes me feel better than you ever did!'

I felt as if I had a hole in the middle of my chest, and everything I am and everything I had been was draining through it until there was nothing left. I was hollowed out, utterly emptied. No smile or kindly deed I will ever perform will be rooted in myself; it will be carried out from duty rather than love. The world's conflicts carry on, oblivious, elsewhere and unreal; from now on there was no way to connect with them. I was animated only by that sick sense of duty, because all the love had been washed away.

I retrieved my needle and staggered up the steps to the four-poster bed with a feeling of desolation and a strange desire to get down and walk on all fours like a dog.

I drew the curtains; the dark brocade bed became a ship spinning on a whirlpool's rim. Its sails would not fill. Cold fish push up under my feet, fall flapping from beneath the bolsters of this bed and everywhere I'll ever sleep. In the tiny phial eels seethe and bite. I wanted to sink out of the world. I tapped up a vein running over my biceps and slid the needle in deep with a practised hand. Then I huddled against the ivy-covered headboard, sighed, and bubbles rose around me. Scolopendium pulsed through me, so good, to my toes and fingertips. A solid blow hit my heart and I squeezed a fistful of shirt tightly. I can ride the rush. But there's nothing to hold on to on this ride, because the ride's yourself. I gasped ice water into my lungs and then was nothing. It kicked me heavily out of my body and into the Shift.

Into Epsilon, the place you find when you take a wrong turning and decide to keep going. There is no easy way in.

I walked down the street. It's a one-way street; from the other end it looks like a mirror. Litter blew past, in the opposite direction to the breeze. Some of the Constant Shoppers were already arranging their wares, buying from each other with a muted morning energy. Tine made their stalls of smooth, living bone. They shaped a grainy bone gel with their hands and it set in sculptural sweeps. They exhibited framed emotigraphs, pictures faint with age or new and piquant, that recorded the subject's emotion and emanated it for the viewer to experience. A wedding picture radiated every feeling from rapture to secret jealousy. A picture of an autumn forest evoked nibbling nostalgia: lighting up a stolen cigarette, smell of leaf litter and first-night stand sweat.

Traders at a pet stall were herding some pygmy house-mammoths, the size of dogs, into an enclosure. An indigo-feathered archaeopteryx on a perch rattled its scaly plumage and twisted its head down to bite at its toes. The strawberries on a nearby fruit stall chatted between themselves of whatever strawberries talk about.

I walked to the edge of Epsilon city, along the bank of the river that runs mazily in right angles and often uphill. The market clustered round, infesting both banks. It seeped out of the town's perimeter, down to the estuary and towards the open plain, a lush grassland dotted with tiny isolated hermite mounds.

Out on the savannah, in the distance the skeletal white city of Vista Marchan tilted in the air, hanging like an enormous moon in daylight. Flocks of birds flew through its insubstantial mirage towers. Single-humped dromedaries grazed the long grass. They wandered, complaining, without even glancing at the ghostly streets around them. An Insect bridge arched up from the green plain, became transparent at its apex, then descended into the centre of Vista Marchan. The bridge was so old that cracks showed in its silver-grey patina like weathered teak.

Vista Marchan is a city that crashed through in the wake of an Insect invasion. The entire world of Vista was undermined by the Insects and collapsed into the Shift, where it is now visible from Epsilon. Its sandy wasteland seemed to emerge from the ground and extended at an incline to high in the sky. The dead towers of its capital city leant at forty-five degrees through the Epsilon plain, listing so that their tops hung over the Insect bridge. Their basements looked to be embedded in the ground, but actually they neither entered nor overlaid it, and they shimmered slightly in a heat that the savannah did not feel.

Nothing survived the Insects in Vista Marchan, but since they destroyed the boundary between the worlds so completely, people could walk there now, over their bridge.

One Insect tunnel bored into Vista's deep sea abyss, causing a kilometre-high waterspout in another world, through which the entire ocean drained away. No good came of this apart from the fact that it killed god knows how many millions of Insects, and there is now a peaceful saltwater sea in downtown Somatopolis.

I wondered if the Insects would eventually reach Tris of their own accord; some time millennia from now the Trisians might truly need Eszai to defend them. I wondered if the Insects burrowing down and piercing through the worlds would in the far future infest them all – the last worlds forming the outer layers of their teeming nest. Were they imperceptibly surrounding the Fourlands on all sides? Were we at the centre, near the Insects' long-overrun world of origin, or were we on the outer reaches, one of the last to fall?

Tarragon said she wanted to view the ocean's sphere from the outside. I wanted to strip away the worlds and look at the complex extensions, apertures and twisted continuous shapes of the Insects' domain.

Lost in contemplation I wandered through the market's fresh clothing region and the designer food district, to the edge where the Constant Shoppers' rickety shacks were dotted around between the stalls. The poorest Shoppers had to walk hours to reach the Squantum Plaza, heart of the market. They are a collection of all species but habitually a breed apart. They are either creatures of Epsilon, or Shift tourists like myself, so overwhelmed by Epsilon's bazaar they never escape.

'They buy things all the time,' Tarragon had said. 'Compulsively. I mean, that's their only pastime. They trade morning to night, and then all night in the southern souks. It's fashionable to spend money. Some of them are terminally addicted, which is as terrible as your habit.'

'These Constant Shoppers, what do they do when they run out of funds?'

'They set up their portable stalls on the other side of the Plaza and sell everything they've bought. Then, with that money, they start shopping again.'

I explored towards the river mouth. The market did not end at the waterline; the rows of stalls kept going, unbroken, straight into the estuary and along the sea floor.

Out here in the periphery Epsilon market extended into the air as well. Tall metal struts supported stalls on platforms thirty metres high. Creatures on top flitted, squawked and chirruped, eager to buy and sell. Marsh gibbons swung hand over hand along ropes strung between the poles; vertebrate spiders with metre-long fangs spun webs across them to catch flying machines.

Seldom ripples came in on the limp Epsilon sea. The water was as clear as air. At first half-submerged, the market continued down to great depths, where it faded from view in the poor light. Jellyfish hung motionless above it. Things with long, intricate shell legs waded between the stalls and reached down to select bargains. In comparison with the aerial stalls, the underwater market moved slowly and gracefully; columns of kelp swayed like trees. Temblador eels glowing eerie white swam at a sedate pace in shoals through the passageways. Nicors with ivory tusks and whiskery faces flapped along with lazy fins. Saurians snacked on pre-Cambrian sushi, tasty bundles of seaweed and writhing worm junk food. They haggled over jewels – green glass beads on silver rings. Anorkas clustered with geeky excitement round a shell stall and frales – very small whales – cruised picking up crumbs just as dogs, rats and trice do on land.

There were red octopi with pale undersides and eight shopping baskets. Rays with sinister ripped-off goods under their cloaks avoided the pikemen patrolling the aisles.

The market surrounded a large, translucent hall that the stinguish had constructed out of solidified water. Their building materials were monumental, colourless pyramids of spring water atop black water slabs from the lightless abyss, and grey speckled blocks from the deep silt where soft carcasses degrade to their elements. Their edifice was decorated with bricks coloured bright blue from the brine captured in sea caves, and rare aquamarine from the surface water that flares green when the last ray of the setting sun flashes through it.

A mirth of female stinguish looked up from the forecourt of their hall, through the surface tension. I waved to them; they turned to each other and giggled, long silver fingers over their lipless mouths in girly gestures.

Stinguish are a light-hearted people who live in groups called mirths. They communicate by laughter that carries underwater for thousands of kilometres, so any two individuals can chatter to each other through a network of mirths, anywhere in the vast ocean. According to Tarragon, chatter is exactly what they do; their flaky airhead nonsense pervades every cubic metre of the sea. Stinguish mirths migrate fifteen hundred kilometres twice a year, dive two thousand metres down to chasms, or lounge on the beaches in the tidal zone and breathe air. No stinguish was ever solitary. They had even more camaraderie than Plainslanders did. If you kicked a football along the streets of Rachiswater, an Awian would either tell you to keep the noise down, or point at the KEEP OFF THE GRASS signs. If you kicked a football about in the wrong side of Hacilith, someone would knife you and steal it. In Eske, Plainslanders start fifty-a-side matches that last for a week. But stinguish never stopped playing. How they managed to swim vast distances and remain cheerful is one of the great mysteries of nature.

My boots crunched on the pebbles. I passed a refreshment stall under which crouched a pair of brown, scaly tea dragons. Their innocent yellow eyes tracked me. Tea dragons breathe streams of hot, black tea. They were being used as caddies; I approached carefully because I didn't want to be sprayed with it. The stall holder was a polyp, a teacup held in each tentacle and its wet skin shining in the sun. 'What's it like being a polyp?' I asked.

'It's awful. Bits of me keep budding off and becoming accountants.'

The polyp sold tea to a flabberghast who bought a whole armful of ghostly doughnuts. I didn't see the flabberghast in time and accidentally walked straight through his corpulent, overhanging belly.

'Hey!' he exclaimed. 'Look where you're going, skinny boy!'

'Sorry, sorry.' I backed down to the water's edge, my hands raised.

Immediately a stinguish girl shot out of the wavelets. She grabbed my ankle with fingers as bony as a bird's feet.

I shook my leg. 'Get off! What are you doing?'

'Can you spare some change, please?'

The stinguish was young, with circular silver eyes, not much of a nose at all, and an ample mouth side-to-side of her round smooth head. Her mouth turned up at the corners like a dolphin's and was full of small pointed teeth. Her thin arms grew down into long, bony claws, her chest was flat and lacking nipples, and her body ended in a broad tail like an eel's – thick in the middle, edged with a fringe of fin that came to a point. She coughed up some water, shuddered and quailed as she took a lungful of air, as if she didn't like it at all. Water drained out of the gills that lay shaped over her ribs. The stinguish's smooth silver skin was extraordinary; every imaginable pastel colour shone on her iridescent metallic hide. I could see the herringbone arrangement of muscle in her tail. Her ribs were like ripples in platinum sand; she looked malnourished.

Oddly, she was alone and she hadn't laughed once. She was not behaving like a stinguish at all. She waved her tapering tail exhaustedly and pleaded with her big lidless eyes. 'Please. I need to buy things.'

I crouched down and peeled her pointed, nail-less fingers from around my ankle. 'Hello, little urchin,' I said.

'I'm not an urchin. Urchins are prickly.'

'No, they're not all bad-tempered. I was one once.'

The stinguish shook her head and an expression of confusion appeared in her medallion eyes. 'What are you going on about? Can you spare any change, or not?'

I wondered what a cheerful, giggling, stupid stinguish wanted with money. 'Why aren't you with your mirth?'

'I don't have the time for this. I have to go and buy more things. Look at it all,' she said, distraught. She turned her face left and right taking in the vast market. She was desperate to be out there, beachcombing among the stalls.

'Listen. There's a stinguish representative in Epsilon's court. I can introduce you to her if you're lost. She's called Far-Distant. I'll—'

'I'm not called that any more. My name is Summer-Sale.'

'Far-Distant? Is it you? You've grown very thin! Don't you remember me?'

She bubbled distractedly. 'All the things on the stalls look really pretty and exotic when they're arranged together, but if I buy one and take it away, it's not the same. It seems to turn into tacky crap. I just want them all. I spent all my money on clothes, slime and jewellery, and now I've no money left. Please . . . I'm missing the music and the lights, and the stall holders talk so friendly.'

Far-Distant had evidently become a Constant Shopper. 'No, my sister. I won't give you anything. No one you meet in the market will be as friendly as your mirth. I think you should go back to them.'

The stinguish started wailing. I understood why, because I know the torment of addiction, and the effects of all addictions feel similar. Far-Distant would have to do withdrawal from shopping, and whatever world she must return to will seem very cold and unforgiving. I stroked her head but hundreds of tiny circular transparent scales rubbed off and stuck to my hand. Her mackerel skin shone.

She tried to shake me by my ankle. 'I need money; I'm so unhappy.'

'There's much to be happy about. If it had seasons, the ocean would be beautiful at this time of year.'

She looked for a way to escape me. 'I'd rather go hungry than trouble you further . . .'

'No! Come back! OK, I'll give you some cash,' I said soothingly. 'You're just a bit lost. Why not call for your mirth, they'll help you.'

'You don't understand,' she said bitterly. 'All stinguish are lost and

194

they always have been. All of us! We don't belong here. Insects keep destroying our homes.'

'You mean Epsilon isn't your home?'

'No. Up there.' Far-Distant dragged her arm out of the water and pointed vaguely away from the sea, across the open grassland.

'In the sky?'

'No, silly. Vista.'

Vista's pale wasteland seemed to focus as I stared at it. For all its immense size, it looked weightless, part of the air. 'I know that the Insects bored through from Vista to Epsilon so thoroughly that Vista slipped down the path they made.'

'All the sea fell into the Somatopolis,' said Far-Distant. 'And the water carried us through, too. Ha! Not us exactly; our ancestors – it happened a million tides ago. But Insects ate the Somatopolis so we swam on again, and we ended up here. We're very lucky to survive; the sea kraits and so on all became extinct. Everyone who was too big to fit down the waterspout died, left high and dry. The bad old snakes squirmed around in the ooze, too heavy to support their own weight in the air, and they were crushed. The ones trapped in pools starved when the food ran out. All of us stinguish rejoiced. The kraits used to eat us, but we escaped and they didn't, ha ha. But that's why stinguish are very lost. No wonder I feel lonely and have to go shopping to cheer myself up . . . Now can I have some change?'

'Well, all right.' I dug in my pocket for coins. 'But tell me first; it's just a myth, isn't it, that stinguish can chat underwater?'

'We can! For two thousand kilometres.'

I shook my head. 'I hardly believe it. I'm a messenger and if it was possible to shout that far I'd be redundant. But I'm not worried by those tales; I know water's thicker than air and probably just muffles the sound.'

'It's true!' she said indignantly.

I shrugged.

'Look! It's true! Watch!' She ducked under and gave out her signature laugh. Bubbles rose from her gaping mouth and burst, releasing her wonderful inflective giggles. 'Ha ha ha ha!' the bubbles chuckled. 'Ha! ha!'

She listened for a second, then surfaced, blowing out spray. 'I called "Hi." The littoral mirth is passing it on.'

Stinguish began to swim in from all directions. They all looked the same but different sizes. Naked and grinning they wriggled between the market stalls or glided effortlessly above them. Their tadpole-like tails waved in sinuous ripples, their long arms trailed, heads raised, watching the surface tension. Their swimming reminded me of flying; the grace of both belies the strength it takes. I appreciated their sturdiness, but I didn't envy them the cold water.

The first stinguish thrust his hands against the estuary bed and burst upwards, in a shower of spray. He gave a smile so wide I thought he would drink the ocean. 'Far-Distant! I haven't seen you for tides and tides.'

'Way-Farer!' shouted Far-Distant.

He batted her with his tail. 'Have you recovered from your latest spending spree?'

'I think so,' she said uncertainly.

'Ho ho! So come back to us! We won't lose you again, Far-Distant. We'll surf the warm current over the reefs while fish shoals scatter before us. We'll echo the sonar laughter rising from the benthic mirth five hundred fathoms down!'

Her mirth all broke surface at once; a hundred rounded backs rolled on the wave. The sea was silver with their bodies; chuckles and gasps wet the air. They surrounded Far-Distant, guffawing and tittering. Their round heads bobbed up, some leapt from the water and somersaulted back, flicking their gleaming tails. The nearest ones beached themselves on the pebbles, propped up on their spindly arms. They pointed at me in my 'Club 18–∞' T-shirt and black wings, and collapsed in helpless belly laughter.

Far-Distant looked up at me. 'It's my mirth. Mine! They want me back. Thanks for your help; I'll always remember. Um? Bye!'

'Wait!' I called. 'I want to know about the sea kraits. If they're extinct, how can Tarragon save them?'

'Tarragon?' Cried Way-Farer. 'Where? A shark! A shark!' He submersed and laughed an alarm call through the water.

'A shark?'

'Worse – a megalodon! Swim for your lives!'

Their heads bobbed down and their fleshy tails fluked up. Bubbles trickled between them. They whipped the sea into froth which the next wave brought ashore. The tight crowd of stinguish glided towards deep water, vanishing into the gloom. I shouted, 'Far-Distant! Come back, you annoying amphibian!' But her mirth had gone, leaving just the occasional giggle swept back on the wind.

I felt the unusual warm glow of having done something right. I lingered and observed the aquatic commerce in the soaked souk. Far-Distant was an addict, and I managed to help her; maybe there was some hope for me. I couldn't tell if her cure was temporary, or what strains drove a carefree stinguish to class-A shopping. For me, it was my past, and now Tern's infidelity was eating me alive. But every Shift I start to die, and that's the trip. I wished that someone in the Fourlands would save me the way I have saved Far-Distant. I needed someone strong and forthright to barge in and force me to stop.

The attraction to my body began to drag me back. I concentrated and redoubled the rate at which the vivid marketplace faded to grey. To black.

To black. t o  b l a c k  t o b l a c k  o b l a c  o b l a  b l a  l a  a  w a s  e was f g e  was fu l i n g e  was f u l i n g e  was f u l l  r i n g e  was full y r i n g e  was full s y r i n g e  was full syringe  was full of blood. The syringe was full of blood.

Blood was trickling out of the back of the barrel. It had soaked into the sheet and mattress in a patch around my elbow. The syringe looked like a red glass feather growing out of place on my arm. Fuck it. I sat up and wiped at a warm trickle that had been running out of my nose and horizontally across my cheek. I stared at my hand – it was smeared with red.

Shit, I thought; what time is it? I glanced at the clock – six p.m.! And it's Thursday! How could I have slept for two days? Oh, by god – Gio's meeting! I'm late! I pulled myself out of bed, feeling weak and sick, viscid with self-recrimination and resentment. Shira, you stupid bastard; you really can't leave it alone, you can't control it. Ninety years in and out of scolopendium; you should have learned by now. I snarled, 'You don't fucking deserve to be an Eszai at all!'

Evening was now invisible through storm clouds clustered over the Castle. The rally starts in three hours; at full speed I might be able to make it in time. Torrential rain had seeped in through a broken shutter and my satchel was lying in a shallow pool. I couldn't stand the thought of putting my hand in cold water, so I kicked it to a less saturated part of the floor.

I looked for any sign of Tern, but she had spent the day away. Catching myself shaking, I suddenly flooded with anger. Nothing rules me; what the fuck have I *become*? My syringe lay on the floor under the bed and just the sight of it overwhelmed me with lust and despair. I picked it up and, holding it like a dagger, I smashed it down onto the slate top of our dressing table until fury deserted me in a wave and I was left looking rather cynically at the bent object. You are really going to regret doing that in a few days, Shira.

Can't waste the rest, anyhow, I vindicated. I stalked down to the lower room, where I diluted my last phial of cat and decanted the preparation into a little hip flask so I could take sips while travelling. A drift of letters had piled up against my door and when I opened it they fell into the room. I ignored them and pinned up a withered note that read, 'I'm not in but you needed the exercise.' I spread my wings, wriggled through a slit window and jumped off bound for Eske.

# CHAPTER 15

My wings skirred in the wet air. I flew fast, but the faint trace of Tern's perfume on my clothes kept distracting me. I pulled the neck of my T-shirt over my nose and sniffed her rich and peppery scent. She smelt the same as she did the first time I saw her. I met Tern when, on a Messenger's errand, Lightning gave me a missive to deliver to his neighbour, the Governor of Wrought. The letter was a blank piece of paper and Lightning is an accomplished matchmaker, but I didn't discover that till decades later. I think that Lightning, being a connoisseur of exquisite things, appreciated Tern's beauty and hoped that I would preserve it forever in the Circle. I sought an audience with Tern in her stateroom. She was untouchable, as self-contained as a cushion cat, small and dark-haired, infinitely more refined than a Rhydanne. Her white dress clung to her body all the way down to the floor. I adored her voice the instant she spoke; it was like being dipped in warm caramel. I wanted to offer her books to read aloud.

In the following year, 1892, Tern decided to marry. She put out word that she would welcome challengers for her hand and organised a series of formal balls and dinners for her suitors, who arrived in droves and began to decant gold into the vaults of Wrought. The competition was much tougher than I had imagined; they all had titles and most of them had manors. I had nothing to offer her except my kiss, which bestowed immortality, but I thought she could not possibly want someone like me.

I had lost my virginity with three girls together in Wellbelove's *petite maison* – a whorehouse in Hacilith that I had rented one night for my own use, and I was a drug dealer so I could afford it. I knew never to pick a skinny whore: Rosie Brosia, Titmouse Slow and a girl called Anything Once threw themselves on me and taught me well and good.

When I first visited Awia I was just as wild; I swept through the country like a swarm. In Peregrine and Tambrine I partied till four of the morning. I frequented the theatre each night in Micawater and strayed from pavement cafés to bars, meeting artists and dollymops in the narrow streets of that pristine town. In Rachiswater I took advantage of the local girls and long walks by the lakeside. In Sheldrake I stayed, finding the sea air analeptic, and at Sarcelle's palace they set fifteen tables of feast for us each night.

From there I rode the Black Coach to Tanager, and dropped meringue and absinthe on the patched bedspreads of the Corogon School Whorehouse. Enclosed by bowers and founded by schoolgirls, its roof garden was rampant if the weather was fine. It slouched across the adjoining roofs of a whole street, warmed by the hot, stale shops below. I fucked the girls and drank their homebrew while cries drifted out from the inmates in the lunatic asylum; the girls knew them all by name.

I never believed that love existed. I wanted to smash it all up into shards and cut myself with the sharpest. But Shira Dellin changed me. Then came Tern, who transformed me a little more. I loved her, the colour of her skin, shapely legs and plumage; I wanted to fill my senses with her.

Tern's unattainable demeanour was an aphrodisiac and a barrier. I didn't want to join her noble class but I dreaded that her chocolate voice would laugh and reject me. Her suitors sensed my insecurity and uttered barbed comments to convince me; she wouldn't want to marry a freak. When I met Shira Dellin I had been surprised to discover that I found Rhydanne girls captivating, but she had turned me down spectacularly. I flew to see Lightning, who instantly understood the cause of my haggard, insomniac appearance. I desperately begged him for advice. After all, he was the expert and I was so bewildered I was prepared to follow any instruction. He suggested, 'Lady Wrought would love to receive gifts.'

I gave her a live kestrel that I caught in the air, its wings bound to its body with embroidery thread. 'Comet,' she said, 'what am I going to do with this?'

Next day I stole in, offering her edelweiss from a mountain that no one can climb. 'Get out!' she said. 'I'll only see you at dinner with the rest of the suitors!' I backed off, stepped up to the velvet window seat and, horrendously, found that my boots were still filthy from the stables. She pointed sternly at the casement through which she had released the kestrel. 'Your turn to fly away!'

In despair and fatigue, I started to use scolopendium. One night, because I was unaccustomed to it, I overdosed and discovered the Shift. I slowly had a palace built there, Sliverkey, in order to give me confidence to court Tern, but in my homeland I owned nothing, no lineage, barely a pot to piss in.

'No, no!' Lightning admonished, amused. 'It's important to give her beautiful presents, ones that will last, to remind her of you when you're absent. You must make her feel wanted and special – I suppose you could always offer her stories. Ladies love tales and you seem to have an inexhaustible supply.'

I flew from the Castle to see Tern when my duties were done. I perched by the bedroom window and told her stories. She was very eager to know about the Castle; she urged me to tell the things I took for granted – what's behind the Throne Room screen? What does the Emperor look like? How does one talk with him? Few of my exploits genuinely held Tern's wandering attention, but she liked me to describe a ruined ancient Awian citadel far north in the Paperlands.

The unreachable chateau had interested me since the first time I saw it, from the sickle summit of Bhachnadich. The Paperlands surrounded northern Darkling like an ocean, an unbroken surface of grey Insect constructions that lapped into points and fell away into shallow valleys. In perfect conditions, a ruin was seen on the horizon, rising through the paper crust. It appeared to be a massive square edifice topped by a stone dome. Sunlight flickered on its peeling leaves of gilt as they fluttered in the wind.

Tern's interest spurred me to the idea that if I dared travel to the ruins I might touch down on the dome and return alive. I trialled a distance flight without landing once, I then climbed Bhachnadich and launched myself from its thousand-metre rock face. I picked up the katabatic Ressond gale and sped over the Insects' territory.

A long lion-gold winter light lay across the Paperlands. Far below among the rigid cells I saw Insects scurrying, going about their instinctive lives. If I crashed, thousands would dart out of their tunnels and tear me apart. If I don't crash, Tern will love this story.

I glided to rest and then flew on. After hours of alternately gliding and flapping I became exhausted. Burning and stiffening in my wings and back distracted me from Tern and punished me for being so stupid as to fall in love. When it became too much to bear I took tiny sips of the wonderful panacea painkiller I had bought; the agony melted away.

As evening advanced the Ressond wind declined in strength. I shed all unnecessary weight in mid-air; unlaced and dropped my boots and bits of clothing until I was just wearing a shirt and shorts. After sunset I flew by a hunter's moon and as I drew closer to the derelict building I realised how truly gigantic it was. The Paperlands broke around it.

Ridges of paper adhered to it like buttresses and thinner web-strands reached up and anchored to the base of the dome.

The tops of adjoining walls were still visible, kept upright by Insect cells, but the roofs had fallen away. Insects had eaten the timber rafters and the entire structure was unstable.

The broken dome loomed beneath me, rounded and silvered with moonlight. I landed on its cold stone apex and looked back towards the jagged Darkling peaks, while I ate some honey sandwiches and glugged the last drop of water, then threw my pack away. I was utterly exhausted and my wings ached so much I couldn't close them. The landscape was dead; no birdsong, the silence pressed me like deep water. For hundreds of kilometres, nothing was alive but Insects. I was the alien here.

I dozed until I felt some energy returning, but all the time I listened for Insects. I lay on the dome and looked through the lightless hole. I couldn't hear any beneath me so I dropped through, landing awkwardly on a slope of rubble and roof blocks that had collapsed onto a travertine-tiled floor. I only had seconds before the Insects smelt me – some new food in the Paperlands they had chewed bare – and they would amass around the building, race up the echoing steps.

Moonlight lit the angular corners of fallen masonry blue-grey. I could see just a small part of the circular room but it was empty. Insect mandibles had scoured the fabric off the walls leaving grooves like chisel marks.

Perhaps it was a municipal edifice rather than a royal residence after all. I curled my toes around a carved cornice block. I dared not leave the circle of moonlight directly under the hole; the room was in shadow. As my eyes became accustomed to the dark, I saw a dull shine among the furthest blocks. I picked my way over them and reached down. It was a bronze castor from a table leg, and three more were scattered nearby. Presumably they were left by the Insects when they ate a wooden table. Anything inorganic left on the table would still be buried. I hefted a couple of the smaller bricks aside – and uncovered the lair of a spider as big as my hand.

I fled to the top of the cone of debris, glanced back. The spider did not move. Its ovoid abdomen glittered darkly. I approached with great caution and prodded it; it skidded over the stone dust with a tinkling sound. I lifted it carefully. It was a brooch made from two flawless emeralds fixed in peculiar curlicues of silver wire, a reticulate casing ingeniously twisted into eight jointed legs. I pinned the spider to my shirt and was about to dig around between the blocks in the hope of uncovering more jewels when there was a clattering noise outside.

My pulse soared so fast blood rushed in my ears. Feelers waved in the doorway and an Insect charged into the room. I scrabbled up the rubble. I jumped, grabbed the edge of the roof and pulled myself onto the dome. Claws thrust out of the hole and snatched at the air. The open ground around the building bristled and seethed with Insects. I watched them erupt from the tunnels, like red-brown droplets racing towards a simmering sea.

The ache of flight and the anxiety of proposing to Tern are all too easy to remember now I am speeding towards Gio's meeting in Eske. I recall that it took me a fortnight to recover my strength, muster my courage and present myself decorously at Wrought manor. I dropped the filigree spider, the priceless gem of old Awia, into Tern's comely hand and her sloe-eyes lit with admiration.

I said softly, 'A talented jeweller must have crafted it before the Insects invaded. It held some wonderful meaning for a lady in antiquity, maybe one of your ancestors.' I looked down. 'I want you to wear the spider when you kiss the Emperor's hand.'

'You mad bastard,' Tern pronounced. 'You could have got killed.'

'The aim is to give *you* eternal life.'

She examined the emerald spider that sparkled in the light from twenty candelabra. 'You mad, crafty bastard.'

I had turned away, wondering if this was a compliment or slight. She poked a finger under my chin and lifted it. She kissed me; we kissed for hours.

Tern dismissed her suitors from the mezzanine where they queued with their plumed hats in their hands. A gust of wind through the tall sash windows swirled out white gossamer curtains and the dust covers on the furniture in her nearly empty bedroom. Outside, snow clouds passed over a crescent moon. Wrought's twisted river roared in spate through sparse black woodland. Beyond the doorway three cats postured in the long hall where the shadows of spindly trees moved on the polished floorboards.

She undressed me and dropped my clothes to the floor one by one. Her small hands fumbled the front of my trousers, pushed them down and unhooked my pants from my hard cock. Her fingers traced the grooves on my hips that lead down to it; she took a good look. She touched the tip; it swelled under her fingers. I moaned and she said, 'Hush. You chanced your life to impress me, Eszai. Don't you want me?'

She walked to the four-poster bed and sat on the counterpane. The spider brooch squatted on the pillow. I approached her slowly; she was five years older than my physical age and confident in her extreme beauty. I did not know how to have loving sex; I had only ever fucked whores and the ambitious. I had a horrible feeling that I was being tested but all I could do was surrender and follow Tern's lead. She stroked my wing and encouraged me to slip under the covers.

She undressed elegantly, leaving her stiffened silk bodice, with white suspender straps to her stocking tops. The bodice covered her breasts to her belly; her panties had somehow gone with the dress. She lay on her side as Awian ladies do, but unlike the others I'd slept with, she did not avert her gaze. She was uninhibited, too proud to follow fashionable repression. I lay behind her on my left, my body fitted close to her. The smooth hollow between her shoulder blades was snug against my chest, my scarred shoulder high above her. Her warm wings were tight between us, tucked up in the small of her back. Her satin feathers rustled and rubbed, driving me mad with lust. She trapped my hard cock between her thighs. I moved my hips, pulling it over her silk stockings. I was not sure what to do. She made no move to help me so I pressed and only felt soft flesh. She leant her whole body backwards and opened her legs slightly. I pushed upwards carefully and felt flesh part. She enveloped the tip of my cock.

She opened her eyes and looked back over her shoulder. 'Oh, please . . .'

'My lady.' I propped myself on my left elbow and made quick flicks but not very deep. I couldn't penetrate far, the angle was wrong. Just the head of my cock rubbed slickly in and out of her. I felt her cunt yield and stretch, hot and wet.

'Keep going,' she ordered quietly. 'Harder. Fuck me harder.' She began to whisper filth. I was shocked to hear her murmur, calling up wisps and bodies in twos and threesomes that populated the dark room with ethereal fucking. She was not delicate; she kept straining to see my chest. She raised a knee, backed into me trying to impale herself deeper. Her thighs were becoming very wet. I wiped a hand over her outline, pausing in the softer reprieve between ribs and hips. I wriggled my left arm under her waist to angle her higher, all the while hoping that my best performance was good enough.

'You'll do,' she said with wonder. 'You'll do . . . you'll do, you'll do, you'll do. *Don't* scratch.'

She firmly pushed my hand between her bodice lacings and flattened it against a small breast, encouraging me to rub it in circles. No other girl I've slept with has ever done that. Her brown nipple was hard against my palm. Her locks coiled on the pillow. A braid hung down from my hair and brushed her neck.

I pumped and struggled. I changed my stroke, long and slow. I could see my cock going in and out of her. Amazed, I thought: It's actually happening. This is really happening to me. Her small rounded buttocks pushed me back every time she rolled against me. I bent my arm that was underneath her and easily lifted her body up. I rubbed my stomach on her black glossy wings and felt the tips of her flight feathers bristle into my crotch.

I brushed my hand down to her front and wiry pubic hairs. I found her left hand already working away there; her fingertips traced wet circles. She took shallow breaths through parted lips. She pushed my hand away. Low, under the skin of her back, her wing joints moved as if she wanted to flex them.

'Open them around me.'

She spread, either side of my waist. Her black wings shuddered with every thrust I gave her, and brushed my skin. I almost came helplessly into her. I paused, held myself still.

'Look at me,' she said.

I was right on the edge. Another thrust and I'd come. I paused to gain control; Tern moaned her displeasure. She shook her body on my cock.

'I can't,' I gasped. 'I have to wait.'

She looked into my eyes and came. Her body thrashed and whiplashed. Her uppermost wing fluttered. She breathed deeply and cried out, 'Now harder!' She almost slid off me but I gripped her hips and laid into her, thrusting as hard as I could. I leaned over, twisting her top half down, breasts to the sheet, my chest pushing above her back. My hips slapped against her bottom. I forgot her status. I pumped as hard and selfishly as with a whore. I felt the flutter in my groin. Her cunt pulsed, squeezed like a fist and drew my come out of me in quick hot spurts. I thrust slower and stopped, panting.

I couldn't tell if she was giggling or crying. She pulled my arms around to hug her. Relief filled me; I had done well. 'Stay here tonight, Jant "long-nails",' she said warmly. 'My legs are tingling.'

We cuddled close and listened to the river. I wondered how many other men she had slept with before me and I hated them. The stiff sheets crackled under the white brocade coverlet; a draught stirred lace hangings on the heavy four-poster bed. After a while Tern murmured, 'Mmm . . . I want chocolate . . .' Then she fell asleep.

I held her for months and years and decades. I took her like poison through the skin. I knew her salt taste like sea bruises, stretched nets of sinews in her neck and waves of ribs. I loved her body as she twisted like a hooked fish, kicked like prey. I was dog to her: I laid my open mouth over her throat.

I thought of the many times when I have been asleep or drugged and gradually wakened to find her touching me, my cock already hard under her hand. I wanted Tern. It took a trial as harsh as a sea voyage for me to feel the first pangs of loneliness and realise how much I need her. I was wrong to neglect her. I must apologise. I'll win her back.

# CHAPTER 16

After midnight, people were gathering at the fencing school in Eske. I landed on the tiled roof, well-concealed by a chimney stack, looking down at the wet streets. Below the dripping thatch of the last houses in the town, I could see dark coats underneath bobbing umbrellas. Men carried lanterns hung from hooks on their shields. Some drunken kids on tired nags clattered past on the Hamulus Road from the direction of Hacilith, slowing and relaxing as they travelled the opposite way from the city's magnetic pull. I perched on the roof, out of sight and watched through the rain.

A cold front was coming in. The clouds scudded across to merge in one mass in the eastern half of the sky. Lightning flickered in the fingers of the bare forest. The rain fell with more intensity and the pitch of its noise increased. I really didn't think it could rain any harder. The constant hiss of the wind in the trees was indistinguishable from the rain hissing on the roof. Drops pattered on the sagging willow leaves along the river bank.

Dace River wound through the south side of town close to Gio's hall. I could still see the river but the surrounding countryside was too dark to make out detail. Silver snakes slithered over the river's surface. I watched them resignedly; Tern had put me in a melancholy mood. I had run out of people to shout at, and was rather regretting storming off in disgust with the world because it was evident by now that the world had no intention of going away and leaving me alone.

Some of the snakes are actually part of the river. Fascinating. I tried to disentangle the snakes' silver bodies and the reflection on stirred water, before I realised that the whole thing was simply a hallucination. Only take me a couple of weeks to quit. Shouldn't be any problem. Theoretically. I shrugged, sending all the water that had gathered on my broad-brimmed hat down my back. I swore silently, taking my hat off and wringing out the rain.

I don't even know if fucking her will be the same now Tawny's had his big cock in her. I pulled the hip flask out of the top of my thigh boot and took a satisfying swig. It tasted green, like cut-grass smells. I felt lighter and tighter every second. Under my long coat, my wings were warm. To cope with the gusts I had had to fly constantly flexing them open and closed at the elbow, and now they were aching.

The fencing school's steep roof was a sheen of water reflecting the lanterns of people arriving. Rainwater was running in wide rivulets over the tiles, dripping off the guttering. Yellow lamplight beamed out of a high square window just below me. At the far corner of the whitewashed hall Gio's watchman swung a lantern, illuminating the empty road. He saw there was no one else to come and banged the iron-studded door closed. I flicked my wings out from the slits in my coat and bounced along the ridge. A couple of slates gave way. I scrabbled madly, slid with them down the roof. I hit the gutter, heels in the trough, my pointed toes over the edge. The tiles shot off, fell and broke on the road ten metres below. I lay with my back against the slope and listened. There was no response from the hall.

I grasped the lead gutter, swung myself over in a controlled drop onto the window ledge. I pressed against the frame, pulled myself into the smallest area possible, inhabiting space slyly as if stealing it, with the concentrated acrobat grace of a Rhydanne. I peered through the window.

Gio's fencing academy was packed. About eight hundred people were taking off their coats and settling down on the folding chairs. Some were seated on the floor; between them on the floorboards I saw white diagrams painted to teach fencing exercises.

A small stage directly below me was decorated with the coats of arms of Gio's past pupils from the nobility. The walls were hung with charts and geometrical figures, the rear wall was covered with a mirror. Padded gloves and chain mail gauntlets hung on racks, with rapiers and their corresponding diamond-sectioned daggers, round leather target shields and lead-soled shoes – which Gio used for training lightness of foot. A pendulum clock with a large, clear ceramic dial had run down and stopped, showing the wrong time. Beside it in a polished glass case awards were displayed in tiers – engraved silver cups and plates, tiny posed figurines of swordsmen on black plinths, and hundreds and hundreds of satin rosettes.

Gio stood by the stage, looking at his audience. He was as relaxed and confident as always, perhaps more so now that the anger of being dropped from the Circle had caused him to lose his respect for people.

Veteran Awian soldiers grouped at the back of the hall, probably fresh from fighting Tornado. They carried their reflex longbows in waxed cotton bags on their shoulders, arrows in lidded quivers. The edges of their dark blue cloaks were cut to look like feathers, drawn across each man's body and pinned at the shoulder with enamelled or billon badges. The shell-edged armour on their legs was damp with condensation. Their worn, damp lorica had some chrome scales missing. Their expressions were as grim as the weather; they only spoke amongst themselves. I guessed they were men disbanded from the General Fyrd who, upon finding their homes and crops destroyed by the Insects, had a very valid reason to harbour grievance against the Castle.

The same was not true for the excited, fractious Hacilith kids, in tooled leather jackets, loose jeans and chain-link belts. Some seamen in ox-blood check or orange shirts laced at the neck tucked their wet oilskins under the chairs. Unshaven highwaymen brushed down the arms of their greatcoats that were silvered with rain. They undid the spurs on their side-laced boots and let them hang loose. Gio had no coherent force. He had gathered deserters, poachers, outlaws, smugglers and fugitives.

Twenty fencing masters leant against the walls, with wryly amused expressions at the defiant party taking place within their hall. They were Gio's accomplices now, not potential Challengers. They had the swagger of swordsmen who knew the brilliance of their skill.

The cold Insect-wing window was steamed up inside and droplets ran down, channelled along by the black veins. No one could see me at this angle and the hubbub was so loud I was quite safe. I was so intrigued, I became unaware of the chill seeping into my body from the stone. I seized up, wedged into position in the corner of the window with my legs out along the ledge.

A limber young man wearing a beautiful rapier tiptoed to the stage and held up his hands for silence. He was shaking so hard he practically blurred. The crowd fell quiet in patches, and Gio picked out one or two individuals at the back to stare at until the hall was completely silent. I strained to hear the young man introduce his master: 'Gio Ami, rightfully Serein.'

Gio nodded, stepped forward, and immediately a hundred voices vied with each other, shouting out questions. A frown line appeared between his eyebrows. He walked beneath my window, so I could no longer see his expression. He still wore the same coat, still open to a bare chest, but he wore the light purple Ghallain armiger ribbon in his buttonhole as if it was a manorship badge. His lank hair was pulled into a little ponytail.

Gio looked at the stage floor as if thinking the elevated position didn't suit him. He sat down on the edge, with his legs dangling over. He began to talk to the crowd rather than at them. He was a teacher and he knew how to make his voice carry.

'Put up, put up,' he said loudly and then, 'All right, I will answer one or two questions. What is it, Cinna?'

A very fat man seated at the front wallowed to his feet. I was astonished to see it was Cinna Bawtere. His cheeks wobbled as he shouted, 'You *never* said we would attack the Castle! You *said* we would speak to the Emperor. Why is there fighting between the fencing masters and the Circle itself? It's a simple matter for San to send Tornado to Crush Us All!'

Gio took a deep breath, 'I have no argument with the Emperor. I think San knows that—'

'Or we'd be behind bars already!' Cinna's riposte raised a susurration of agreement from the crowd. They seemed to be thinking in similar fashion – they had trusted Gio to air their grievances with the Emperor, and he had lead them into conflict instead, with the Eszai who had always been their protectors. For an instant I thought that the crowd might turn on him.

'The problem lies not with Emperor San but with his deputies, the Eszai, who are corrupt and mislead him. You all know the Emperor doesn't leave the Castle. To understand and rule the world fairly he needs his immortals, but their own interests are embroiled in what they tell him.'

The crowd fell silent; this was what they wanted to hear. A chill wind stuck my soaked clothes to my skin; the gale whined, high-pitched, through the eaves. I pressed my ear to the pane to hear Gio's words.

'There is no present like time. San gives the immortals lifetime in return for their service, but few of them deserve such a priceless gift.

'We are lucky to be alive at this point in time. Times are hard for us all, I grant you, but the opportunities are better than any period I have lived through in the last four hundred years. I truly remember the past, and I know that the only cure for despair is action.

'Since I left the Circle I have realised how little the immoral immortals understand us Zascai. They're all too slow and spoilt by luxury to see the advantage of this great opportunity we have: Tris. It's up to us to make the most of it.

'None of you worthy people will be able to join the Circle. Cinna, although you're a good sailor; Mauvein, although you're an excellent jeweller, the Circle's too corrupt for either of you to enter in an honest Challenge. And I, the greatest swordsman of all time, am forced to give way to a newcomer because I speak too much truth. The prospect of immortality they hold up is nothing but an illusion to lull you. The Circle would never accept a man who really recognises the need for change.

'Awia can't feed itself – they tell us – so they ask us to send our money to what is the richest country in the world. The shortage of workers is caused by bad management. Five hundred men are employed just to clean the Castle, to scrape lichen off its walls and polish its sumptuous treasure when every last drop's squeezed out of the Plainslands to nurse Awia. Food is short all over the Fourlands except in the Castle because immortals must have their strength. Isn't that so?'

He looked to the winged soldiers at the back of the hall. 'Awians are angry because you feel you're making the most effort against Insects. It's your kingdom that disappears under the Paperlands each time they advance. You feel threatened. I can understand why you think that help from Morenzia is not forthcoming. You're right, but for the wrong reasons.'

Gio glanced at Cinna and the city ruffians on the rows of chairs. 'Morenzians and Plainslanders are angry because you're overtaxed and fed up to the back teeth with money being sucked out of Hacilith. You're right to feel discontented, but for the wrong reasons. Last time the Insects attacked, the Castle just followed the downright craven policy of the Awian king and it failed to control them. They fed so well on the plenty of Awia that they almost reached the banks of the Moren.

'I have lived in the Castle and been part of the Circle. I have felt San hold time still for me. If I were yet Eszai at least my voice would be heard. I could try to make things better. San is keen to hear us – if Tornado was not bloodthirstily blocking the way we would be standing in the Throne Room now. San would open the Castle's treasury to aid us. But in respect of your fears I have called my men to retreat. Now I'm mortal again, same as you, I'm free to tell you how the Circle is a web of deceit. San would benefit greatly to be free of the lies of his ministers.'

The crowd sensed his conviction and gave their faith to his terrible mendacity. By god, I thought; he's not acting, he believes it.

Gio stood and stretched then sat down again, swinging his legs to tap the folded-down bucket tops of his boots against the planks. He swept a hand over his hair, which slipped out of its ponytail and hung around his shoulders. The crowd watched, some uncomfortably, although I imagined Cinna alert for the promise of scandal. Gio did the public speaking equivalent of swapping hands in a fencing match: 'Your suffering is the fault of the duplicitous Eszai. Mist Ata Dei's one of the worst. Ask yourselves how she could be allowed to be immortal at all.'

Gio paced across the stage, around the lowered wrought iron candelabrum and back, his coat tails flowing out behind him. He wore the 1969 Sword, a faultless rapier custom-made for him, and the jewels on its scabbard scattered lamplight as only diamonds can. Their adamantine lustre threw moving spectra on the walls.

'Zascai don't know half of what this monster has done, because of course the confessions of new Eszai are customarily kept secret. You already know that Mist once razed your harbours, raided the coast and sank the fleet – out and out piracy from which the coast has hardly recovered! Would we be in such a poor state now if this arch-bitch hadn't wreaked carnage? How many lives were lost? Well, we don't know because Comet never told us.'

I tensed at the mention of my name. How was I supposed to know? I had other pressing matters to attend to back then, like Insects besieging Lowespass. But the mortals followed Gio's every word.

'Ata was a wife who brought her husband down. The Emperor let her Challenge stand legitimately. Why did he make the decision to let her run riot at such a vital time? Was Comet informing San properly? What was going on between the Sailor and the Messenger that that layabout ladykiller should support Ata so much?

'And while Comet misleads the Emperor – either deliberately or through laziness – his wife spends her time living lavishly. Every other governor leads their fyrd. How many parties and fashion shows have been thrown by Tern while Wrought is still smoking rubble?

'And while we consider the misgovernance of manors by those Eszai lucky enough to own land, consider the most corrupt of the Circle whom you may have thought of as the most capable because you are accustomed to lies. Lightning Micawater is the best Archer ever. Nobody can deny that. Of course he is – his family could afford the best tutors in the distant past when he was a student, and he makes sure the skill of archery hasn't changed since then. What an unfortunate mishap that he chanced to inherit the manor on the glittering river. Lightning embellishes his palace even as your farms and towns lie in ruins. What happened to Awian artisans anyway – those of you who aren't here?'

A chuckle went round the hall.

'They're all competing for work in other countries. Lightning the romantic archaist does not spend his money rightly but spends his time having affairs with married women – how chivalrous can you get? He was involved in the destruction of the harbours with his lover, Ata, and when the greedy blue-blood bagged Peregrine manorship in the spoils of war he gave it to his illegitimate daughter!

'The newfound Island of Tris is part of Lightning's kingdom too, now he's just returned from playing at explorers with his pirate queen and their drunken lackey.'

Drunken lackey? Who's that? I puzzled. Oh, no, he means me, doesn't he?

'Lightning is not venerable but obsolete. He was young in spirit when the world was young but times have moved on. He's a thing of the past; he holds us back. It's time we took control and it's an exciting moment for Awians to make their own decisions and live without him.

'Frost and her River Works Company profiteer from the rebuilding process. Hayl and his immortal husband are both reckless men. Only yesterday, they attacked us without provocation and Tornado joined them soon after with a division of your own brothers in the fyrd. Now I believe that too many people are being drafted. Since Tornado lost his girlfriend five years ago, he's taken his fury out on the Insects and the draft continues while fields lie unplanted. The Circle should preserve lives but the Messenger flies in to the Plainslands to tear families apart.

'Comet is fond of the bottle. The truth isn't widely known because he really indulges in the Castle – out of the public eye. I've seen him staggering drunk in the Great Hall. He often isn't spotted for days at a stretch – during which time it's known he hasn't left his room. Why does the Emperor keep him when I felt the Circle twitch every time he binges? I don't know if the alcohol affects his *reliability* – but is it any wonder there are rumours that his wife sleeps with another man?'

Gio waved his hand against the crowd's torrent of wicked laughter.

'No, no,' he said. 'I go back on that. Far be it from me to slander anyone. Tern manages it very well herself. The rumours are unsupported – just like her!'

How dare he call me a filthy drunk! I nearly flew down and told him – scolopendium is a much better type of substance abuse. And I'm good at it; I have it under control! But at least alcohol is legal. The crowd believed Gio because it matched their caricature of a Rhydanne, and that hurt even more.

I ground my teeth and the blood rushed, red hot, to my face. Oh,

Tern, why did you do this to me? In private it's bad enough, when my prowess in bed is the only reputation I have – but I don't think I can stand being the capricious and irresistible Messenger cuckolded in front of the world.

Gio strode up and down, his hand resting on his sword hilt. He mused, 'The worst thing about these corrupt members of the Circle is that they'll never die.

'I can offer you a way to live outside their rule. Better still, it comes with riches, a chance to shape your future free of kings, governors and fyrd captains too. Anyone who follows me will be set up for life. I can give you Tris.'

The crowd was silent. Gio saw this and didn't pause for long. 'I've spoken to some of the mariners who saw Capharnaum. They say the tiles on the roofs of the houses are embedded with turquoise and tourmaline. Even Trisian infants wear crowns. They esteem gold because of its beauty, not because of its rarity – they think less of it than we do of spelter or brass. They use it for household objects: mangles, boot scrapes and – you'll love this – chamber pots.'

Gio scanned the aisles of sceptical faces. 'You clearly don't believe me. Well, look; I have one here.' As he spoke, he trotted to the back of the stage and unpacked several items from a canvas bag. He held up the very chamber pot that Danio had given to Wrenn. He had polished it to a brilliance and it dazzled.

Everybody in the hall began to laugh, and Gio smiled too. He was scarcely audible over the tumult. 'Mauvein is a practically Eszai-good jeweller. Verify this for me.' He slipped down off the stage and gave the pot to a portly man whom I recognised as one of Ata's sons – although by now he was much older than his mother.

The gleaming chamber pot was turned round under his big fingers and then he nodded. 'It's enough bullion for a manorship to buy out of providing fyrd for two years. I could find better things to do with this than piss in it.'

'Well, you can't have it . . . yet.' Gio flourished it. 'You see that Trisians have so much wealth the meanest utensils are solid gold. Yet Mist's clique are determined to keep it for themselves. I have bought the caravel *Pavonine*. At this very moment my allies in Awndyn are stocking her, and other ships. From Hacilith University I've found it easy to hire a pair of crusty scholars well versed in Old Morenzian inscriptions. They are optimistic of being able to interpret the basics of Trisian for us. The journey will be a challenge, I grant you, but not so difficult now a trail is blazed. There's safety in a convoy – if you want to commandeer berths in other caravels who'll stop you?

'I earned wealth enough from the Ghallain School to pay the crews and create an ideal life in Capharnaum without being constantly tested by the Circle. Who knows, in a couple of years, consolidated and stronger, we might return.'

A swordsman called something I couldn't hear.

'Ah, Tirrick. I'm just skating all over the floor on those pearls of wisdom,' Gio answered sarcastically. He put the chamber pot down, fished in his inside coat pocket and held up a thick notebook that I recognised immediately. 'This is Mist's own rutter. My agents stole it when they took the chamber pot. Here are the coordinates of the island, and a comprehensive description of the route. "Twenty-nine degrees south, one hundred and twenty-nine degrees east",' he read in a respectful tone. 'Nearly on line with the Awndyn northing, I'm given to understand. So, how many of you will join me?'

Two or three hundred hands went up immediately; these men had nothing to lose. Gio pushed the priceless piss-pot with his toe. The Awian soldiers conferred among themselves, weighing the risks of the voyage against the rewards. Having fought in Lowespass, they were accustomed to frontiers. They raised their hands.

In fencing, it is very important to be able to change the direction of your thrust the instant you see that it's going to miss its target. Gio knew now that he could never be strong enough to destroy the Castle, so he turned the thrust to Tris. He was prepared to exile himself to survive.

My lamp-lit window was the only source of light and sound in the whole pitch-black landscape. Everything that existed was in this hall – Eske Forest was a void. Gio raised his voice above the roar as again the rain swelled to a cloudburst. Drops bounced off the brim of my leather hat. Forked lightning bit colour into the forest for an instant. Gio paused as a ten-second-long thunder crash rolled around the hollow of the little town. It hypnotised everyone in the hall. Gio stood right foot forward, held the rapier scabbard and drew the 1969 Sword with his right hand. He swung it casually, feeling its balance.

'We start for Awndyn tomorrow morning. By Sunday I'll be in the harbourmaster's house to meet you adventurers. We will sail next week.' He held the rapier up above the crowd ostentatiously. 'The Eszai have outlived morality. I won't lie back and think of the Fourlands while the Castle screws us, time and again. Come with me!' he exclaimed. 'To seek this new world – for gold and brandy!'

Gio ended, and the crowd began to applaud. They stood up, clapped and cheered him. The ovation went on and on. Gio glanced up at the windows; I turned my white face away and shrank back against the frame. Gio bounded off the stage and his friends shook his hand and slapped him on the back all the way down the hall. His eyes were hectic bright and his cheeks were flushed. The doors were thrown wide – light and people spilled out. I looked with hatred. Kill him, god, if I only had my crossbow! Kill him, I'll jump straight on his head! If he wasn't surrounded by swordsmen.

Gio's voice was too low for me to hear as his knot of well-wishers bustled him out of town along the woodland path. Some men fetched their horses, others dawdled in the doorway fiddling with their lanterns.

Autumn, dead cold, howled in under the strength of its gales and dampened rather than crispened the rotting countryside.

Gio is impugning my virility and I can do absolutely nothing about it. I banged the heel of my hand against my forehead. Be calm! There will be time for revenge later. I'm not very good at later; I wanted him to suffer *now*.

God, I was livid. I was going to take this out on someone, and since I couldn't beat Gio, Cinna Bawtere would have to do. I dived off the roof and flew in very turbulent air just under the low storm cloud's base. I risked being sucked up into it. A gull battled along underneath me, vivid white against the dark iron-grey. The hurricane tussled my hair and coat out behind me. My clothes were light even when waterlogged. My wings cleaved the gale, driving rainwater off their oiled surfaces, but the covert feathers were becoming damp and thinning; I was beating harder to stay up.

I followed Cinna out of Eske along the dark forest track, straining to see him. He was hidden beneath his black umbrella, sploshing towards the nearby Slaughterbridge village pub. Air roared over my wings as I slid down the sky. I struggled to slow my ground speed and manoeuvred directly above him. I folded my wings back with a jolt and fell on him.

I hit Cinna with the soles of both boots between his shoulder blades, bowling him over and over into a puddle. I absorbed the impact into my legs and landed in a crouch. Cinna rolled around on his back, knees pulled up, winded. I burst out laughing; falcons must feel this exhilarated when they hit prey. 'I take my hat off to you, Mister Bawtere! Never knew you had an acrobatic streak!' He kicked like a struck rabbit. A dagger appeared in his hand. He crawled out of the chalky, rain-pitted puddle and collapsed in a milk-white wet heap on the path. 'The gallows waits in Eske; it's a much shorter drop! I can take my pick of felonies in your catalogue of crimes. You're as good as dead!'

I did want to kill him. I wanted to feel the life go out of him under my hands. He saw my cruel expression – comprised of Tern's rejection, Gio's slander and six hours in a rainstorm – and he curled up, sobbing. Cinna's predictability was consoling – I had thought I was losing the ability to read people. They seemed to be becoming gradually more incomprehensible.

'Ah . . .' Cinna panted. 'Please don't hurt me. Please . . . I . . .'

'How did Gio acquire the logbook?'

'I don't know! . . . Ah . . . I swear! He's a clever man; he has many agents. Ah . . . I respect you, Comet. You're Eszai. You're a legend in Hacilith.'

'Put the dagger down, then.'

Cinna did no such thing. I kicked his hand and the knife flew out of it. '*Put it down*!'

Cinna huddled under the remnants of his broken umbrella.

'How did Gio know of Tris?'

'I informed him. I'm sorry! You never said it was a secret!'

I suddenly realised that I had told Cinna everything, six months ago, under the influence of a fingernail full of scolopendium. Shit. It began to dawn on me that this appalling turn of events could be all my fault – caused by my big, stupid mouth.

I bated forward with my wings spread, made as if to kick his jaw and he cowered. 'Are you sailing with Gio?'

'Yes . . . Yes, what of it? I am My Own Man.' He huffed in a breath. 'I'm to be captain of the *Pavonine*. Yes, Comet, I was a sailor by trade; had you forgotten? I'm returning to that trade now. It's legal!'

'I see.' I drew my sword from under my coat skirts. 'Do you believe all that bullshit Gio was spouting in there?'

Cinna knelt up, several acres of ghastly fawn brocade, and started prodding his saggy chest to check for broken ribs. His blond pin curls were plastered to his skull, his fat cheeks were ruddy. The pathetic specimen looked at me carefully through the pouring rain. 'No, of course not . . . Though there's a seed of truth in everything he said . . . He thinks you're an alcoholic.' A knowing, assertive look appeared in his eyes. 'I have a reliable source for decent cat, by the way.'

'Blackmail now, is it? That's just one more reason to kill you!' I snarled, though his words set my mouth watering.

'Come on, Comet. Just because you're illegitimate doesn't give you free licence to be a bastard. I haven't told Gio about your love of

217

scolopendium. Why should I? It'd bring me no benefit, and I'm a savvy businessman . . . Of course I don't believe that the island is full to bursting with precious metals for the natives to bestow on us. However, I do know that Gio's As Rich As Rachiswater. He's paying me five times a merchant captain's wage. He's packing coin, plate and banknotes – he has chests full of it! He wants to set himself up on Tris. I've just finished conveying it all to Awndyn myself. Look, I still have the letter he gave me. I'll show you, here.' Cinna fished inside his coat for a crumpled envelope with a broken seal, Ghallain manor's whale emblem. I took the letter from his gnawed fingertips and raised a wing to shelter it from the rain, whilst I read:

To: Sitella Grackle, First Bank of Hacilith
I hereby instruct you to immediately liquidate all my assets currently in your care and to dispatch the monies to myself at the harbourmaster's office, Awndyn. They are, to whit: i) the proceeds collected to date from the sale of my academies, ii) all ordinary stocks held in the Hacilith bourse, iii) gold and silver plate held in the bank's safe.
The bearer of this letter, Cinna Bawtere, holds my full confidence in this matter and is to be trusted as the guardian of the money.
Gio Ami

Money, lots of money, I deliberated while I refolded the letter. Cinna was smiling, showing textured teeth. 'Comet, are you envious? You know you'll never be free to escape to Tris yourself. You have to fly around the Fourlands until the inevitable happens – a goddamn Insect eviscerates you – and I don't mean like at Slake Cross, I mean fatally. You're cast off the Emperor's fist like a hawk, to spy, and he lures you back and tethers you with the promise of eternal life.'

I took a squelching step towards him. 'But, Bawtere, it's jail for you! Make haste! We'll see how far Gio sails without a captain.' I gestured with the sword and Cinna staggered to his feet, protesting and quaking. 'Into town, Cariama Eske's guard will look after you . . . They'll throw you in a freezing cell, lock you in fetters and you can fuck your mother for all I care.'

'She's dead.'

'Should make it easy for you, then. Hurry! I've a lot to do tonight. I'm busy because I have to find someone who will keep an eye on Gio and accurately report his plans to me when, for example, I land on the *Pavonine*'s gallery at dusk.'

Cinna had begun to snivel. 'OK,' he said, miserably; 'I'll do it.'

I said, 'Oh, good. Then the noose can wait; tell me a little more about Gio.

Cinna said: He knows that the Trisians distrust the Castle. He has a silver tongue, that man.

I said: Even if it was gold he couldn't Challenge me.

Cinna said: Gio's failed and he knows it. He might have got away with insurrection, but he tried to murder an Eszai. Oh yes, I heard from his own lips how he stabbed Lightning!

Me: He's running?

Cinna: Yes. He can't storm the Castle and skewer every Eszai much as he wants to. So he's making his mark – leaving his name on history is immortality of a sort, seeing as he can't have The Real Thing. If he holes up at Ghallain or hides out on Grass Isle it'd only be a matter of time before he's betrayed and captured. But on Tris . . .

Me: Never!

Cinna: He wants to win over the Trisians. And San would have to leave him there, the King of Tris, because the Castle's purpose is fighting the Insects. San could never fight people or invade islands.

Me: I'm glad you trust San.

Cinna: Yes, but I'm fed up of being kept in the dark. He keeps everyone hooded like falcons, whether callow Zascai or haggard old Eszai. You don't know what San's real quarry is, even though you're one of his spies, and you will just go back and tell him my every word.

Me: Um . . . Cinna said that, not me.

San: Yes.

I skipped a few pages in my report, and resumed: 'Then I said to Cinna, "If I fail to stop Gio setting sail, I will meet you again on the ship." I followed him to the tavern, stole – I mean, requisitioned – a fast horse and rode here directly, my lord. I sent a courier to lock every stable at every coaching inn between Eske and Awndyn. That'll slow the main part of their force down by a couple of hours, and as it takes five days to walk to Awndyn those without horses might miss the *Pavonine*.'

Drops of rain ran down the shafts of the wet feathers in my hair and dropped off their curled tips behind me onto the carpet. I shook my head, flicking water from the backward-pointing quills. I had ridden out of the storm; my skin was singing. I was covered in the stringy mud thrown from the horse's hooves. My svelte boots were sheathed in white liquid mud up to the thigh. I smelt of clouds and the thin air.

My heart beat hard; cat made me feel too fast and bracing, thermalling on a strange energy burst that I knew I was going to pay for later but really needed now.

# CHAPTER 17

San said, 'Good. The majority of Gio's followers deserted him during the battle. The only people prepared to flee with him are those who have no option and no dreams other than those he concocts. So his last act of defiance is to stop Tris joining the Empire . . .'

I knelt on the damp carpet. 'My lord, why should they listen to him?'

San continued as if he hadn't heard me. 'Whether Gio means to build his own stronghold or – more likely – take the Senate I cannot tell; but we must not let him impose any rule on Tris. Mist has sold swords to the Trisians, now Gio can train them. He is a teacher, is he not? He can perform several deeds to ingratiate himself with the Senate: he can hunt down the Insect that you so carelessly set free! Assuming a Trisian has not caught it already. And if a man has, he is more worthy of immortality than all of you!'

'My lord.' I closed my hot and bloodshot eyes for a second, ran my hands over the bangles on my left arm – my pointed nails in a variety of chipped colours. I squeezed water out of a handful of hair and managed to ask, 'What will you do?'

San began again in a brisk tone of voice: 'Before Gio became the Swordsman, that place in the Circle was for broadsword fighting, not fencing. But my current Swordsman has clearly demonstrated what everybody knows. Rapiers are ineffective against Insects, so immortals should not use them. From now on, Challenges for Serein's position must be with broadswords or Wrought swords or, taking future improvements into consideration, the most effective blade to kill Insects. Tell Serein that.'

'Yes, my lord.' With a single edict, the Emperor had put an end to the Ghallain School and all its flamboyant sparring. Few people would practise rapier combat if it was not a key to enter the Circle and if there were no successful Eszai to inspire mortals to take up the art. The Morenzian and Plainslands fashion for duelling and wearing rapiers would decline.

San stated, 'Now to deal with Gio himself. When he leaves harbour, the Sailor must pursue him. But if Gio arrives at Capharnaum, he will wreak havoc as he prepares for her.'

'I'll go and tell her.' I stood up, tucking strands of wet hair behind my ears. San must want Mist to catch Gio at sea and deal with him out of sight of land, where there would be no witnesses, he would have no reinforcements, and the sea would cover the remains.

'You will travel *with* her.'

'My lord . . .' The last thing I wanted was to be involved in a sea battle.

'The Castle protects the Fourlands against aggressors, Comet. Thankfully Tris is free from most of them, but Gio is certainly an aggressor, and one of our own making; our duty is to stop him. If he succeeds in reaching Tris you will deliver Capharnaum from both him and the Insect. I hope that if that eventuality occurs, the Senate will be inclined to communicate with us. You could tell them: "Our Emperor has sent us to protect you from Gio Ami and his criminals." And, only if the situation is right, tactfully restate my offer to join the Empire.'

San perceived the doubt in my eyes, and added, 'With the help of Mist and Lightning you will be able to do it, I am sure.'

'My lord, have you heard news or can you feel . . . Would you tell me how Lightning is doing?'

'He lives, Comet. Walk with me.' San rose from the throne that had been worn over time to the exact shape of his body. He paced down the dais steps; his stiff white satin cloak trailed over them.

Amazed, I followed slightly behind him. We walked between the piers of a tall ogive arch into the west vault, up some worn steps and through a side door that led to a long outside terrace five metres above the lawns. Next to us, the arched windows of the Throne Room triforium ran the length of the building. Last night's downpour had stopped, and a quite hot sun was sending all this travel-sick water skywards again.

I had never accompanied San outside the Throne Room before and had never seen him out on the terrace. I felt very awkward. I had some conception that I should kneel, but when I abased myself San just sighed and motioned for me to rise. So I stood next to him, looking towards the Dace Gate, and I felt like the most honoured immortal until I followed the Emperor's gaze and saw, for the first time in daylight, the destruction that Gio had wrought.

The Dace Gate was completely destroyed. Its tower was smashed open to the sky. Holes half a metre across shattered the top of the east curtain wall for fifty metres to our left, and chipped stone blocks lay all over the rutted lawns.

Northwards, in the gap between the Palace and the Castle's outer walls, the trebuchet stones had obliterated the Aigret Tower's top arches; their uprights remained like broken stalagmites. Cylindrical marble blocks lay among the statues in the monument square beneath and, peering through the skeletal tower, I saw that several of the Finials had fallen. Two whole trefoil arches on supporting pillars lay full length on the ground. I could see the signatures that covered them, like tiny cracks in eggshell. Gio had no right to attack the cenotaph, bring down the statues of mortals or wipe out the names of Eszai more ancient than him.

Tornado emerged from the Dace Gate barbican and ran heavily across the grass. He looked outsized even without any other men for comparison. He threw himself on his knees and looked up to our balcony, showing a round chin covered in stubble and enormous pectorals. His thick leather trousers and steel-toed boots were smeared with mud and I was satisfied to notice a bandage wound around his huge left shoulder, under a chain mail waistcoat that was mended with pieces of twisted wire. Hooked in his belt was a soup ladle, because whenever Tornado was not fighting, eating or drinking, he was cooking sumptuous meals. He smiled so hard his eyes disappeared. He boomed, 'My lord, the clean-up's going well; we're just dismantling the last trebuchet.'

San nodded. 'Good. Tornado, Gio will certainly not return. He is in the safe hands of the Sailor.'

The Strongman said, 'I can march the fyrd towards Eske to trawl for any stragglers but – like – I need outriders or we might get ambushed in the forest.'

Tornado was ten times smarter than people gave him credit for. He glanced at me; I glared back daggers and he looked a bit puzzled. He was easy-going and probably thought that Tern wasn't worth fighting over. It's a shame to break such a long friendship but he's doing the breaking, not me. I will fight him. I dropped my gaze only when I realised how closely the Emperor was studying us both.

'There is no need,' San said. 'Take your Select Fyrd to the Front where the governor of Lowespass is calling for help. Please take the dismantled trebuchets with you; you may well need them.'

Tawny ran a big hand over his shaved head and the thick corrugations of fat and muscle at the back of his neck. He stood, bowed in a gainly manner, and walked back into the ruins.

The Emperor said quietly, 'No one has attacked the Castle before. Whatever precedent it sets for the future, the governors are now abashed. They are already competing to demonstrate their loyalty by repairing this damage. They are sending their best architects, money and materials. A particularly generous quota is expected from Ghallain and Eske.'

'My lord, I can fly a circuit round the Plainslands and—'

San's voice was unexpectedly sympathetic and warm. 'I know you do not want to go back to Tris. You feel forsaken; you do not trust Tern and you want to be with her. But listen, your wife will not stay with Tornado.'

Then San stepped back into the Throne Room and was gone, leaving me on the balcony. The Emperor had mystified me again, this time with kindness. The warmth of his reassurance sank into my very core; I was overcome with gratitude. He touched me with a word and inflamed me with his energy. I felt like a great Eszai once more.

Long ago, Lightning told me how Tornado joined the Circle. In the year 885, Tornado strode into the Throne Room while court was in full session. The guards at the gate tried to stop him but Tornado just carried them along. Everybody fell silent as the giant stranger deposited two guardsmen in front of the throne. He leant on his axe and said loudly, 'I'm a Lowespass mercenary. I have no idea who to Challenge but I'll fight any one of you!'

The silence continued; everyone stared at the nameless fighter. The Circle members looked perturbed while the Emperor regarded them expectantly. 'I didn't answer him.' Lightning shrugged. 'I'm a bowman, not a brawler.'

The Emperor listened to the shuffling of feet before he broke the silence: 'Very well. Warrior, tell me about yourself.'

Tornado came from the area where Frass town is now, a ravaged landscape since strengthened by the chain of peel towers built by Pasquin, the previous Frost. He led a company of mercenaries who were paid by the farms in proximity to the Wall to protect them from Insects. Back then, the bounty was a pound per Insect head, and his troop made enough money to survive. Tornado loved his itinerant life until his wife died from food poisoning – a dodgy beef curry killed her when a thousand Insect battles couldn't.

The day after he arrived at the Castle, Tornado was taken to the amphitheatre and the Eszai loosed Insects against him. He chopped Insects into pieces all day until San, satisfied, created a new place in the Circle for the Strongman. Tornado remains the world's strongest man in eleven hundred and thirty-five years. He owns no lands nor houses, nothing but a shelf of Lightning's novels and seven-eighths of the Fescue Brewery – from which he takes his dividends in kind.

My buoyant mood stayed with me all day, as for fourteen hours I rode a convenient south-easterly to Awndyn. It was cold and rather damp, and the clouds gathered at nightfall, hindering my navigation. I gained altitude and flew above them.

The flat cloud cover ended above the last extremity of the land, precisely following the coastline. As I descended through the clear space in the cloud surface I felt as if I was diving to an underwater Awndyn far below. The full moon gave a much better illumination than the autumn evening daylight; the roads looked smooth as glass. I imagined the news of Gio's conspiracy flashing in along them from Eske and Sheldrake.

The promontory at the head of the strand was covered with grass the colour of rabbit fur and, with patches of bracken, it looked like aged velvet that was losing its nap. The beach was a peaceful collage; bottle-green waves soughed and sucked back through the sand. It could not be more different from yesterday's hurricane, which had spun windmill vanes around so rapidly that across the plains three hundred were still burning.

I landed and ran to the squat manor buildings, finding them dark and silent. The dewy grass around the annexe was criss-crossed with smudged footprints. Sometimes it could all just be one of my fever dreams. A glow radiated from one window on the ground floor. Cyan Peregrine was sitting on majolica-orange cushions on the window seat behind a pair of curtains that separated the window alcove from the rest of the room, to make a cosy den. Cyan's head was bowed; she was reading intently from a large book by lamplight. Her straggling blonde hair escaped its ribbons; the sleeves of her dress were puffed like cream cakes.

I tapped on the glass with a pound coin. Cyan jumped and looked all around, saw me beaming at her. She grinned and reached up to raise the latch and swing the window out. 'Jant!'

I gave her a hug but she pulled away from my cold skin. 'Sorry to scare you, little sister.'

'I'm not scared. Are you looking for Daddy?'

'Yes. Where is Lightning? Where is everyone?'

'They went out to the boat. Mist's red carnival. Caravel. She sailed it into the bay . . . I saw it. I wanted to go on it but Daddy wouldn't let me. He's ill.' Cyan sat back on her heels, hazel eyes wide.

'He's awake? How is he?'

'That old woman said he'd be OK. I don't remember her name.'

'Rayne?'

'Yeah.' Cyan reached for my feathers and I gave her a wing to stroke. She often pestered me to fly carrying her, although at twelve years old she was far too big. 'Governor Swallow told me about the battle at the Castle and there are loads of men coming into town who don't like Eszai . . .' Cyan made an effort to remember. She forgot the book of natural history that lay open on her knee but her finger still pointed, holding down a page with a grey watercolour of seals reclining on a shingle beach. 'Swallow said she . . . Um, she "couldn't guarantee their safety" so Mist took them aboard. Are you going to fly after them? You're not going to stay?' She sounded resigned.

'Where is Swallow?'

Cyan sighed. 'Governor Fatbottom is trying to get rid of the men who don't like Eszai. She wants them out of Awndyn. She says they're troublemakers. I was supposed to go to bed, but I didn't want to, so I hid.'

'Fatbottom?' I giggled.

There was a wicked gleam in Cyan's eyes. 'I keep thinking you're the same as the rest, but you aren't.'

'I can't be.'

Cyan complained, 'Swallow tries to teach me the harpsichello. The piccoloboe. Loads of instruments . . . I hate them. She says, "You think you're good because you're Saker's kid." I feel like I've always done something wrong. I don't belong here.'

That sounded like me at her age. 'You don't have to do what Swallow says! You'll be a governor when you're twenty-one.'

'When I grow up. Yeah, yeah.'

'It's not a long time to wait. Take it from me; I'm twenty-three.'

'Hmm. That's reallllly ooooold,' she said thoughtfully.

'Isn't it?' Cyan had everything she could possibly want, but her fortune was just a spacious cage, as Lightning had planned out her life. Swallow, her guardian, knew of nothing apart from music and she found the child an obstruction to her obsession. Swallow may well never succeed in joining the Circle but she was determined to spend her whole life trying. I thought that if the bitterness set in, she wouldn't stand a chance. 'Remember that you can do anything you want.'

'I want to grow wings – it's like having four arms. And to fly like you.'

'Within the bounds of possibility. Cyan, lots of people who live in

Awia don't have wings. The Emperor doesn't, either; it's not important that you take after your mother.'

She gave the concept serious consideration. 'I like it when Daddy teaches me archery. I wish he was here more, but he's very busy and now he's hurt. Everything's collapidated again. I like talking to him – he brings me presents – but he says I should do what Swallow tells me.'

I waved my hands emphatically. 'You don't have to believe anyone, no matter who they are – not Lord Daddy and not Diva Fatbottom. Think things through for yourself instead. Swallow isn't teaching you the right subjects, for a powerful governor-to-be, so you will have to observe and question. Remember, brother Jant is at your command; all the Eszai are. Governors don't seem to realise their power, and we need you to keep us in check with Zascai reality. That's what's been going wrong recently.'

She scowled, slightly resembling Lightning. Her tattered socks were rucked round her ankles and her shoes were scuffed with the grey-green mould found on tree trunks. She clenched her jaw to stop her teeth chattering; her breath hung in the cold night air.

'Goodbye, Cyan; look after yourself.'

'Are you going to fly? Why can't I fly?'

'Because you're normal.'

'Why can't I see this island?'

'Soon you will, sister. Soon everybody will.' I ran on the wet grass and took off, bound for the harbour.

Many humans envy wings. A few years ago, a serial killer murdered only Awians, chopped their wings off and wore them. But it doesn't matter whether one has wings or not when none of them can get off the ground. Cyan was more perspicacious; she envied flight. I worried about her as I remembered the Carniss saying: Wolves track lonely people.

When I was her age, in 1807, I was solitary too. No child wants to be left alone, but Rhydanne children grow up quickly. When they fall, they don't cry; when abandoned, they're independent.

My childhood in Darkling came to an abrupt end in my fifteenth year. Eilean insisted we remain every winter in our scanty summer dwellings in the high peaks. She said it was for my own protection that we did not go down to Scree pueblo with the other herders, although winter storms brewed and raged in the cirque every night.

Eilean Dara, my grandmother, was forty years old. She was a good runner; she had only ever let herself be caught by one man, who married her and treated her gently, but he died shortly after their daughter was born – my mother inherited a very fast speed indeed. I never understood how my rapist father could have caught her and Eilean wouldn't say.

My presence forced Eilean to change from her beloved hunting way of life to herding. She built our shieling herself, although it looked as if it had grown, part of the uncompromising mountains; an antlered hillock with moss on the roof that the goats ate in summer when the ice thawed. The shieling was a one-room box with bedding on the floor. Every wooden surface was covered in pokerwork designs, my grandmother's pastime in our desolate world. She burnt board games into the low table top – a chequered square for solitaire and trapper's luck, brown teeth for backgammon, and rectangular patches where packs of cards were placed for telling fortunes. When hunters visited they played games that were fast and simple compared to those I learned later at the Castle.

I discovered the rules of flight from trial-and-error; no child was ever as covered in cuts and bruises. Eilean made me look after our eight goats; I was good with a sling but I was never taught the bolas so when hunters came to poach them, I had to call her for help.

I left the goats tethered while I improved my gliding, soaring too far to hear their bleats and bells clacking. A pack of white wolves attacked the herd. The goats panicked, leapt high and strained at their ropes but the wolves devoured them in a leisurely fashion. When I landed hours later I found a pile of bones, tethers and bells. I hid from Eilean for days before she gave up trying to throttle me. She then steadily reverted to her previous life, chasing ibex and swigging whisky to forget the strain of my existence.

I sat cross-legged in front of the hearth and stared at the flames. After a while the door was nosed open and two massive tame wolves slipped through, padding solemnly. I relinquished my space on the mat for them; they lay down and sighed simultaneously. Compacted snow sticking to their pelts became translucent as it melted and dripped. Thunder tumbled down Darkling valley; there was a great sense of waiting in the air. Eilean Dara kicked the door back on its leather hinges and strode in. She hung up her bolas, reclined on the rugs, resting an elbow on the table, and looked around vaguely for me. 'Look at you, Jant; why are you still here? You should have left home by now. Have you no sense of shame whatsoever? I think you're determined to slow me down like powder snow. First, I can't even marry you off because how do I find someone who wants a deformed Shira as a husband? Second, you remind me of what those vile Awians did to the daughter I loved. Third, then you killed her, with your chunky body and wings trapped in her belly. We had to cut you out with an axe.'

I gathered her plate from the fireplace, pine nut crackers and meat stew cooked for so long it was a stringy paste. Eilean continued: 'A full seven-month pregnancy and you were still tiny. I fed you goat milk and raised you despite the fact that of course your birth wasn't timed and you arrived in the middle of the freeze season. So now you're grown, the way you show gratitude is by feeding my vicuna to the wolves.'

She reached out and I flinched. 'Have you caught anything?'

She carved a chunk off the stew, stuck her fingers in it and licked them. 'Nothing,' she taunted. 'Not faun not fowl not fuck.'

'Do I go bring them in?'

'Not green sludge in a dead deer's gut, not frozen milk in a dead girl's tit. There's no game this side of Chir Serac any more. I think we all starve.'

I peered at the whited-out valley. The temperature was plummeting and the sky was fantastically clear. There were more stars above the Darkling Mountains than anywhere else in the Fourlands, because they liked the clear air. Stars gathered there and fell as snow.

Two grouse were strung up on the shack's wall, their feathers harassed by the wind, purple in the impure light. A llama from Mhadaidh shieling still had a bolas wound round its legs, and a light covering of snow settled on the black antlers of a buck chamois. Its slack tongue was freezing to the ground; it looked at me with yellow teeth.

Eilean's fingers chased the last shreds of meat around her bowl. 'Oh, you are always under my feet. I need some space. Get out! Out!' She shoved a couple of thin skewers into the embers, knocking out sparks onto steamy wolf fur.

There was nowhere to go but the empty goat shed high on the rocks, built around the twisted trunk of a rowan tree that spidered up the cliff as if trying to creep away from me. I had believed Eilean's gibes that if I ran down to Scree the other Rhydanne would pull my wings off.

I wrapped a blanket around my shoulders and nestled in the bothy among the heather hay. Thick cornices hung over the vast black splintered cliffs, looming dark against the snow clouds. Eilean shouted, 'And don't come back in tonight!' She slammed the door, cutting off the firelight abruptly.

I listened, motionless, as from far up on Mhor Darkling, the highest spire of the range, an ominous creaking echoed down the valley. Tabular layers of snow began to slide.

My head was full of its white roar as I flared my wings and landed on the deck of the *Stormy Petrel*. I shook my head to silence the resounding smashes and splitting, buckling rock. For two centuries the avalanche has echoed in my ears.

I ducked into Mist's cabin and she immediately leapt up, dashed across and flattened a piece of paper against my chest. She yelled, 'What is the meaning of this? What's going on?'

'Huh?' I tried to pick at the note but her palm pressed it tightly to my shirt.

'What have you done, Jant?' she demanded, clapping the paper to emphasise every word. I recognised it as the Emperor's letter that I had sent to Awndyn with a loyal rider four days ago. My handwriting covered the back of the envelope.

'Hey, hey . . . Don't blame the Messenger. San sealed this, not me. I haven't read it.'

Mist threw up her hands in complete exasperation, 'Then read it!'

Deliver to the hand of Mist only
Gio Ami shows interest in Tris. Be informed that his spies will try to discover the coordinates and the means to reach the island. You will make it easy for them to learn this information. With discretion, leave your charts or records where they may be readily accessed. Comet will tell you my further orders.
San, Emperor of the Fourlands, 13 July 2020

I threw a cushion to the floor and sat down. Through the stern windows the panorama changed as *Stormy Petrel* turned on her anchor. The lamps of homes and pubs on the seafront, the lighthouse on the harbour wall, the notched tops of yew trees in Awndyn cemetery protruded above the land's dark profile. The ship swung back: yew trees, lighthouse, seafront.

'I don't know what this means,' I said weakly.

Serein Wrenn had his feet crossed on the table, honing his rapier's edge with a tiny silver whetstone and watching the barometer drop. He said, 'We hoped you would explain.'

I told him San's edict on rapier fighting and Mist listened intently as I described Gio's rally. I folded the letter and held it in a candle flame until it burnt completely back to my fingernails. I finished by saying,

'So, Wrenn, you have to relearn broadsword techniques quickly; and Mist, you gave Gio's spies that chamber pot and notebook.'

Mist tutted. 'Never! As ordered, I neglected to lock them in the safe, and they were stolen by a midshipman with confused allegiance. He thought he had performed a cunning heist . . . But it makes me scream with frustration; after all last year's secrecy.'

'Gio has a very strong force around the *Pavonine*,' Wrenn added. 'And he's got three other carracks. It's not going to be easy to stop him leaving.'

'Damn. That explains the lights I saw on the quay.' Wrenn threw me a packet of ginger biscuits and I started munching them. I said to Mist, 'San said you have to take care of the rebels offshore. Can we follow him?'

Mist gave me an incredulous look. 'You have no idea, Rhydanne. Ninety per cent of Awndyn supports him. He recruited most of my old crews and he's cleaning out the harbour stores. Gio's more ravening than Insects! May dogs shit on his grave. I need to send to Grass Isle to hire sailors loyal to me – mobilise some Awndyn Fyrd – call in old favours. He'll be long gone before we can raise the troops. So I must find food and . . . blood and foam! That's without counting recaulking, fumigation, repairs! It'll take at least a fortnight! San *knows* that!

'Tell him I'll certainly follow Gio – *Petrel* is faster than those Plainslands crates. We have stun sails, bilge keel; we're stable while they corkscrew, pitch and roll. I have tricks up my sleeve. If I catch them I'll sink them all right, but I might not gain more than a couple of days on their tail.'

She ruffled her hair vigorously. 'This is not like the Emperor. San knows very well it takes me two weeks to get this ship prepared. He doesn't make mistakes. Gio's Awndyn carracks are tough second-class merchantmen designed to round the cape. Ships Taken Up From Trade. In the right hands they could reach Tris. So now we're all STUFT.'

'I heard that Tornado already had the dissidents under control,' Wrenn said. 'San's given Gio a means of escape. Why in the Empire does he want to do that?'

Mist said, 'He usually asks a lot of me, but this . . .'

Wrenn slid a scabbard over the rapier lying across his knees. 'Perhaps San thinks Gio will sink, then he'll be rid of the little plucker and two whole boatloads of bastards.'

Mist said, 'He never leaves anything to chance. Sometimes I think even god coming back is just a story he invented to suckle us.'

Nausea rolled over low in my stomach. I wanted scolopendium and my hands were beginning to shake. 'San can't be allowing Gio to reach Tris. Tris is so peaceful. Gio intends to ruin it.'

'True, but if we save the island from Gio, it's more likely to become part of the Empire,' said Mist. 'What does Tris mean to San?'

'I don't know. It must be more important to him than Gio's rebellion is . . .' Then I figured it, and in a moment I saw time as San sees it. Its profound length funnelled out before me. I stared into a black well, as linkages and patterns suddenly lit up across centuries. Even Eszai can't see them; the Emperor plans them.

Of course I had no proof, but I was convinced that I was right. It was a feeling of falling as terrible as when the Circle breaks. One life was a second, a spark. No human can think back and forth over such an immense span. 'Oh, my god! I'm absolutely certain . . . Gio is acting as the Emperor's cat's paw.'

Mist gave Wrenn a smile. 'I know inspiration when I see it. Jant, what's the real meaning of San's command?'

'He's sending Gio to Tris!' I jumped to my feet and pointed at her. 'You didn't discover Tris *by chance*, did you?'

She blanched, but stood her ground. 'Comet, let's work tog—'

'*Did you*? How stupid I am! One little island – the vast ocean! What are the odds on that? *Petrel* should have sailed straight past on either side! You weren't just lucky; San gave you the location, didn't he? He *sent* you to find Tris. San must have wanted to find the Trisians ever since they left the Empire in the first place!'

'What?' said Wrenn.

Mist said, 'I don't understand. What do you mean, "in the first place"?'

'Ata, what were your orders? Why did you do it – to prove yourself? No wonder you even played the marriage card. San wants Tris back in the Empire at any cost.'

Mist admitted, 'Yes, Comet. All he gave me were the rough coordinates and I tacked east until I came upon Tris.'

'The *rough* coordinates? You must have itched to ask him how he knew!'

'Yes,' she said softly. 'But I can't question the Emperor, and I practise self-control.' Her eyes were expressionless.

'Everybody knew, back then,' I said, awestruck. 'Two thousand years ago, the whole Four – Fivelands knew there was an island in the eastern ocean. San wanted us to rediscover Tris.'

'But why give it to Gio?'

'Because every new problem is a solution to an old problem,' I ranted. 'San has sent Gio to invade the island instead of us!'

Mist said, 'Oh. Because he can't be seen to do it himself?'

'Yes. Listen; San ordered me to tell the Senate, "Our Emperor has sent us to protect you from Gio Ami." He makes Gio sound like a formidable enemy, so that he has an excuse to send us!'

'Gio *is* a formidable enemy,' Wrenn pointed out. 'I'm determined to prevent him and his scumbag highwaymen from destroying Capharnaum.'

My hand on the door handle. 'Well, at last San has the means to reach the Trisians, to catch up. Tris is a loose end that must have bothered him for two thousand years! He gave you money to rebuild the fleet after the last Insect swarm, didn't he, Mist? How does it feel to be one of his instruments? And Serein, what's it like to be his Swordsman executioner? No better than Gio, who thinks he's rebelling but he's just San's pawn. San wants the descendants of the fifth-century rebels returned to the fold; wouldn't you? Oh, I really need a fix.'

'Come back!' said Mist. 'Tell us how you know all this. Where are you getting it from?'

'*A History of Tris*. It's . . .' I faltered. 'I could do with some cat.' I ran to the hatch and down the ladder, heading for the sickbay.


The book I stole from the library recorded that a group of radicals left the Pentadrica to found Capharnaum. San must have known. I was sure that he wanted their reintroduction to the Empire, and Gio provided the means. I knew that we had to stop Gio. I also knew that I had just flown an awful, demanding itinerary all over the Plainslands and that being back on a caravel was not helping the fact I badly needed cat.

I ducked along under the low beams. Smells of gravy and hot flour rose from below. The ship creaked; the deck was gloomy. I paused and listened at the sickbay door lit by a single swinging lanthorn because a compassionate voice emanated from inside. It was the Doctor. I thought she was addressing Lightning, but no other voice answered or interrupted her. The old woman was talking to herself.

'Over time, Eszai are supposed t' get worn out and replaced. You're no' supposed t' live for ever, really.' I heard her bustling about. 'My dear, you like stories? Of course you do, you're a romantic. Hard t' believe once I was a lit'le girl with brown plaits and a patched skirt tha' spun ou' when I twirled. I was walking down the cobbled back streets in a Hacilith summer, and I heard music. That were before you were born, Saker, a long time ago. Such music! It were a shawm an' sackbut, though there could've bin a hundred of each, the way they wove t' most tempting tunes. T' music were coming from behind a high wall, with an arched green gate in it. I tried t' gate but i' were locked. I shouted to t' musicians, but nobody answered. I sat down on t' cobbles and began to cry.

'Then along the road there came this crowd of people, dressed in t' most beau'iful costumes, with plum-coloured feathers and foil masks. They caugh' me up in their masquerade, an' I slipped in behind them when the green gate opened t' le' them through. From then on, I were lost among t' drunken guests of an outlandish party, and I, only a lit'le girl with a calico skirt, became their amusement. They whirled tall and grotesque around me, an' I stared in fright. When I tired of t' constant noise and mysterious innuendo, I tried t' run away. I tried t' ge' out of t' ornate garden, but t' high wall trapped me in. Ladies and servants bat'ed me away, their sharp heels ripped my skirt. Eventually I crawled under a bush covered with these massive waxy flowers and I fell asleep. When I woke up I found myself out in the stree' again. I had been cleared up and put ou' with all the refuse from t' party.'

'Saker,' she said tiredly, 'I heard how men break wild horses; tie their back legs, and when they attemp' t' run, they fall. That's how i' was for me before the Circle. You saved me then and we've been friends since. I'm saving you now. I can't do withou' you. Simply, if you leave me, I shall be alone forever.'

The voice stopped and all was quiet behind the door. I pushed it and slipped inside. The Doctor was sitting beside Lightning, playing a game of solitaire with glass beads. She put her wrinkled finger to her lips.

Lightning lay on his side on a cot that was attached head and foot to the ceiling and swung slightly with the ship's motion. His wings were open, one thoroughly bandaged, the other spread to stop him moving on the mattress. The feathers had been cut down in accordance with Rayne's theory of cleanliness. He was asleep. The blanket rose and fell with uneven breathing but in the indistinct light he looked like a tombstone effigy.

Rayne followed my gaze to a half-empty brandy bottle on the floor. 'Tha's the strongest narco'ic I can get him t' drink,' she said. 'He's feverish and t' wound's infec'ed bu' he refuses t' take painkillers. He's afraid of them, I think, having seen what drugs have done t' his friend.'

I hugged her; her face only came up to my chest. Wrinkles beneath her eyes overlapped like an oyster shell. Her plain cotton frock smelt of wintergreen oil and steam. In the small cabin she stood tall whereas I had to stoop.

'How is he?'

'In a serious condition. T' wound won' close. I' will take a long time, stabs have t' heal from t' base up and this one's deep. He los' a lo' of blood. He's weak, but a' least he's eating. A blood transfusion is t' las' resor'. I told him, "Lie still or i' will trouble you for a century." I'm treating his sprained arm as well. What about you? You look like you're dependen' again.'

'Yes . . . I'm . . . I'm back on the needle. Is there any way I can help Lightning?'

She seized my wrist firmly and pushed my loose sleeve back. 'Shi', Jant. T' pet cat you're keeping has been scratching your arms again. What a mess. Thought you'd beaten i' las' time. More fool me.'

I crouched down against one of the ribs that supported the deck above. If you use drugs, in time you grow unusually familiar with the corners of rooms. My own predictability sickened me: 'Do you have any cat?'

'Yes. I had t' bring new supplies' cause *someone* made off with t' ship's complement of skylarks. No pity this time, Jant. You use your habi' t' bask in sympathy, soaking i' up like a sponge.' Rayne shuffled to prop her ample bottom on the work surface, obscuring her medicine case. 'T' chest stays locked. I can shou' for Wrenn. He's easy strong enough t' chuck you in the brig.'

'I'm not violent,' I said, aghast.

'I know. Bu' in a few hours you'll be desperate.'

I wanted to get away. 'Look, I don't want to take cat any more but I don't have the will power to stop. In the last week I've had three nights without sleep and small shots give me the energy to keep going. I am trying, Rayne.'

'You certainly are. Wha's your dosage?'

'Five grains every two days.'

'Shi'. A Zascai wouldn't live long a' tha' rate. I thought I felt t' Circle strain to hold you.'

Slumped against the hull and starting to shiver, I wretchedly submitted to her examination. She cleaned down my track marks and peered at my tongue and red-rimmed eyes. Macabre old woman. 'If you don't qui' soon ca' will kill you. You have one bugger of a problem.'

'What problem – Gio determined to ravage the Fourlands' only idyll, or Tern's adultery that I dwell on for hours at a time?'

'Silly boy. Tern's infideli'y is her way of coping with your drug habi'.'

'It's the other way round,' I said. 'I use cat because I can't bear to think of her affairs.'

'Pull yourself together! You and Tern blackmail each other . . . but she's more likely t' enjoy i', whereas you hurt yourself t' ge' her attention. You're addic'ed t' sympathy – from Tern, from me and even Saker. Well, i's run out bu' you're still dying. Stop get'ing guilt kicks from asking for help and then rebuffing i'. Stop saving all your pain till later, live in t' real world. I know i's harsh but i's no' as bad as t' damage you wreak on yourself trying t' escape. If you don' break t' vicious circle, Gio will outlive you.'

'Tern left me first . . . She doesn't care about me any more,' I complained.

'Don' argue,' Rayne snapped.

'I'm not arguing. I agree with what I'm saying!'

Lightning stirred and Rayne continued quietly. She turned her back on me and began to sort through phials. I didn't want to listen but I had no option. 'I find tha' selfishness is t' worst chronic disease of Eszai. Tern also suffers from t' condition. She loves you as a daredevil, how you used to be – flying t' Ressond gale, climbing t' cliffs a' Vertigo. Admi' that you're a lo' less beau'iful lying on t' floor staring a' t' ceiling. Sometimes I think t' greatest strain on San is restoring all your livers. Tornado challenges ten men to a drinking contes', Frost sups enough coffee for ten men, and you do both stimulants and narco'ics.'

I wished that people could see and believe my exploits in the Shift. I folded my arms tightly; my sharp fingernails dug into my biceps. I rocked forward. 'It hurts, it hurts. I don't want to do the fast cure . . . I can't kick now. The Empire needs me.'

'You mus' have some now because you're going into shock. I don' wan' two Eszai in life-threa'ening states. Then I ration you, one dose a day, oral no' intravenous, until I have chance to straigh'en you ou'. I can guess a' t' difficulty of injec'ing on a moving ship in a tempes'.'

I nodded, relieved to submit to Rayne's regime. She would look after me. 'It's a deal.'

She held out a hand for my nearly empty hip flask. The whorls on her fingertips were worn smooth through age and she had cured the warts, leaving small brown circles. I forced myself to open my fist a finger at a time and drop the bottle.

'Well done, Jant,' she said approvingly.

Hopelessness washed through me; dread filled me. I gave her a look that would have been puppy-dog if my eyes hadn't been so wildcat. A few minutes later I was rewarded with Rayne's confident grip on my bare arm, and a flick of her finger as she pushed the needle into the crook of my elbow. I felt no pain; Rayne was good. Unlike me she left no time for a red wisp of blood to spring into the syringe and dissipate, be sucked back with the drug. She just pushed the plunger down efficiently. So I got half of the ritual that I so badly craved. She shook her head, shaking her wattles like a bantam. I lost focus of her concerned face. I may look ill but it's beautiful in here. I breathed a week of strife out in one sigh; sleep at last.

I spent the next four days delivering communications. Governor Swallow could only find fifty Select Fyrd whom she could vouch had no sympathy with the rebels, and double that number of reliable General Fyrd. Mist employed a crew but could only find basic supplies, poor quality and meagre quantity: salt fish, three hundred barrels of flour bulked out with ground peas.

Mist came to the deck where I was supervising the fyrd carrying baskets of crossbow bolts up the gangplank. She said, 'Make them work faster, Gio's ships left during the night and they're already out of sight.'

'How many ships?' I asked.

'Three. Well, he took four carracks. Three of them, *Pavonine*, *Cuculine* and *Stramash*, sailed right out through the overfalls at slack water. I don't know the lead skipper, but he's a capable navigator. Gio's braving heavy seas – force-ten gales! But no one will follow him since the *Demoiselle Crane* capsized. I altered the harbour coordinates in the logbook before I so carelessly let a deckhand steal it.' She laughed with asperity. 'The *Demoiselle Crane* hit the Corriwreckan overfalls at flood tide, one a.m. exactly.'

Her thin-lipped expression was unsettling. I shuddered, as an echo of my sea-fear returned.

The loading continued night and day under Mist's impatient gaze, but it took a week before the stevedores' footsteps stopped resounding up and down *Petrel*'s ladders and in the hold. As the gale-force wind filled the sails and hauled us forward, and we began to crash through the storming seas outside the harbour, I retreated below to tell Lightning the news.

I took the first turn to watch over Lightning. When awake, he refused to allow the pain to affect him and was as courteous lying in the sickbay as in his palace. I wished that I had his self-assurance, but I don't have the security that comes from never questioning my place in the world. Rhydanne always see my wings and flatlanders see my cat eyes.

Because wolves track lonely boys, I was hunted out of Darkling in the melt season of the year I later calculated to be eighteen-ten. I was unaware that the high airstreams would carry me to the biggest city of hungry rats, bewildering to a mountain child, and proving nearly impossible to escape. Until I joined the Circle I was always pushed on, only ever seeking to get away from the places in which I was trapped. I became so used to defending myself that in the Hacilith chemist's shop, when I began to feel I belonged, my behaviour left me ruined and homeless again.

After the avalanche I ran down from the devastated valley keeping Mhor Darkling's colossal crags on my right, onto the plateau and warily towards the pueblo. I sneaked into the storeroom of the distillery, desperate to find food, filthy and tottering from exhaustion. I had not run such a long distance on my own before.

I descended a gravel and damp matting slope into the dark cellar and splashed onto a stone floor. It was covered with a good six centimetres of standing water. Drops ran down the dank walls and fell from the ceiling, plinking rhythmically. This was so wrong. Did anyone know the store was flooded?

It was like creeping into a cave. The cellar was stifling with the smell of pounded meat; the freeze-dried pemmican had become a sodden, slimy mass. But I had grown up with the smells of pelts drying and antler soaked in urine to soften it for carving, brown fat spitting on a cooking fire of burning bones, the reek of split long bones boiling to make grease.

I reached up and pulled down one of the baskets of dried berries that were stacked in piles of five. Rhydanne count in base five because it is warmer to keep one hand in a mitten. Besides, five of anything is a lot in the mountains. I ate an entire basketful of bilberries and cloudberries. Then I scooped water from the floor and lapped it out of my cupped hands until I was satiated.

Throughout my childhood in Darkling, I mainly ate meat. So when I reached the city I lived by stealing sizzling burgers from market stalls, which was as near to meat as I could find. When I figured out what fruit was, and how to peel it, I changed to pilfering apples and oranges, loving the intense sweetness, although to start with they gave me indigestion. The first words of Morenzian I learnt were the tradesmen's cries and curses.

I crept back to the distilling room and checked that it was deserted. I dashed out of the stone doorway, left the pueblo and jogged onto the plateau, while biting grit from under my nails. The dull sun shone a white pathway in the overcast sky. A skinning wind blew from the direction of Scree gorge, carrying the roar of the meltwater torrent and bobbing the sparse heather patches. Thick snow lay in hummocks everywhere, receding from dashes of black rock. Muddy blots in the distance were chamois, wandering along the vast plateau. Above them ancient glacier scratches scored the distant cliffs, as if in desperation.

Two Rhydanne sprang out in front of me. I dodged with a cry but they blocked my path. They were adults, I was as tall as them but not as strong. I didn't know the man's name but I knew his reputation. Being the area's fastest runner, he had caught a lot of women and lorded it over the other men. He had married and keenly defended a very desirable fellow hunter, who stood beside him.

A handful of condor feathers quivered in her long matted hair; it was dried back with ochre paste and red daubs stained the hair roots on her forehead. She had a pierced bear-canine necklace, and wolverine claws strung on the babiche lacings of her tasselled puma-beige breeches. She looked old, perhaps thirty-five. They both had knives on their belts and armfuls of plain bangles, prized possessions that confirmed their status. As the mountains grow, earthquakes and erosion sometimes uncover veins of Darkling silver that Rhydanne beat into jewellery.

These hunters were out of their territory, which I knew to be on the other side of the aiguille-lined ridge called the Raikes. They were not at all impressed by the farouche shock-headed boy who, having summed them up, was trying to flee. They strode around me. I couldn't dash between them; I was trapped.

'What is this?' she said with curiosity. Her eyes drilled into me like pale shards of bone.

'He's an Awian. Stocky as he is, he's young.'

'Alone?'

They looked around. 'If he is an Awian he's not old enough to be here by himself, I do declare. An orphan, then.'

The woman spoke slowly, 'Are you an orphan? Or abandoned?'

I said nothing.

'What are you doing here?' the man asked.

With overwhelming isolation I thought, I do two things: I can keep people company or I can leave them alone.

The woman shot out a wind-burnt hand and started pinching my feathers. Her husband gave a laugh and pick, pick, picked at the other wing. I yelped and sprinted away. Why were they doing this to me?

The cold wind lifted my dirty hair. My soaked feet were freezing; my three layers of fur socks had been shredded when I scrambled among the landslide rock shards.

I ran frantically over low outcrops, knocking stones from their frost-shattered surface. The Rhydanne kept pace without quickening their breath and all the time they laughed and plucked my feathers, leaving a trail of the ones they managed to detach. The woman poked me and I staggered; the man shoved me back towards her. I made a break but she leapt and pushed me; I fell over and broke the ice on a snow patch. I got to my feet whimpering with frustration and the numb pain from last night. The woman teasingly flicked my head and tore the hood from my alpaca wool jacket. The man pulled all the horn buttons off and the belt that kept it closed, since I had long outgrown it. They packed snow down my back. If they stripped all my clothes off, I would die of exposure. I thought that was their intent.

I wish I had realised then that my ability to fly would awe all Rhydanne, because it was faster than they could ever run. If I'd known that I would have armfuls of bangles; if I'd known that I would own the Spider, and remind them of the fact with free drinks every year, then I wouldn't have sobbed and darted about in vain attempts to escape, tears rolling down my face.

I wrenched free and ran as fast as I could. The man gave a double whistle. The woman whistled once to show she understood and they spread out on either side of me. They're hunting me, I thought with horror.

I swerved away from her and ran straight. Her mate narrowed the gap and forced me towards her with a laugh of pure joy. The ice inside my collar rubbed my skin raw and was seeping down my neck; the cold air seared my throat.

They easily followed their hunting system and mercilessly passed me between them. For them it was a leisurely pace but I was trembling and close to pissing myself with fear.

The third time around a stack of antlers marking a meat store scraped in the frozen ground I realised that they were deliberately making me run in large circles. I yearned to jump far away from Scree – to leave every one of the Daras and hunters. Blind with tears I swerved abruptly and headed straight for the gorge. They chased me, grinning. The lip of the crevasse loomed far too close. They halted, called, 'Stop!' I heard concern in their voices but I wasn't falling for any tricks.

I spread my wings and glided over the gorge. The ground fell away and I was suddenly one hundred metres in the air above lashing milk-white water.

The Rhydanne clutched each other, their mouths agape. Apart from Eilean, they were the first to see me fly. But I remember terror rather than triumph as I watched their figures shrink into dots. A powerful air current grabbed and hurled me up. The Pentitentes Ridge of Chir Serac lengthened, covered in cone-shaped ice-formations. Mhor Darkling's highest white peak pulled down past my wings; the entire mighty, beautiful massif spread out beneath me.

Above my world, a steady broad slipstream of wind blew to the south-east. I fought for breath in the thinnest air and talked myself calm. 'Then that's the way I'll go. Wherever I land has to be better than this.' I turned with the wind stream and let it speed me away.

'Jant?' Lightning's voice sounded amused. 'Jant, wake up! Are you all right?'

I sighed. 'Yes. Don't worry about me; how are you?'

'Bearing up. Burning, weak. Snatches of music keep going round and round in my head. You look dazed too.'

'I was just thinking,' I said. 'Reminiscing about my childhood.'

The dingy cabin creaked and lurched. The Archer nodded approvingly and said, 'Please tell me about it. It must have been wonderful, living in the mountains and being free.'

# CHAPTER 18

The ocean was a choppy swell laced with lines of foam, a breathing shape over the back of which the *Petrel* rolled. The mastheads were beginning to glow, freezing spray cracked from taut sails, and she listed hard to starboard as she slid rather than sailed down into another trough.

A passing squall blew the surface of the waves opaque and slated rain horizontally onto the gleaming deck. Water dripped off the strips of lead nailed over Mist's cabin door. White rain screamed down so strongly I couldn't see through it. It pounded the waves flat. I really didn't think it could rain any harder.

I slid the forecastle hatchway open on its runners and peered down into the sickbay. Lightning's figure was just visible in the gloom. The bed had been hooked to the padded leather wall and he sat propped up, a glass of brandy cradled in his big hands. He pressed his back to the wall in an attempt to relieve the pain that still immobilised him. I teetered uncertainly on the creaking threshold until he beckoned me down. 'Come in. It's so tedious lying here for weeks. I've either been talking to Rayne or listening to my own heartbeat in the pillow. Close the hatch, please; the chill seems to nip into my wound.'

I dangled off the ladder as the ship lurched unexpectedly, and dropped onto a spare sleeping bag by the opposite bulkhead. 'I was just on deck getting some fresh air – if you can describe sea air as fresh. We keep sliding down the waves sideways, they're like black pyramids. Mist's furious; in the teeth of the storm we're getting nowhere and Gio is increasing his lead. Wrenn hasn't stopped being sick yet. Where's the Doctor?'

'Collecting clean water from the stove. I am in good hands.'

The ship rolled and molten wax poured off the candles in the lantern. The flames jumped up high on their long wicks. Lightning blinked. He winnowed out his uninjured wing to scratch between the contour feathers, then folded it up by hand and tucked it under his voluminous surtout coat. The creamy candlelight cast his face into pallor. He was clean-shaven and, through long practice, fastidiously neat. Living on a ship for three months is like camping at the Front and Lightning knew how boredom, bad conditions and long waiting cause men's discipline and ultimately their behaviour to degenerate. The bandages under his barn-owl-yellow coat were fresh and crisp.

He said, 'I worry about Cyan; I need to see her more. I only have a short opportunity to raise her and I can't depend on Swallow to do it properly. This is such appalling timing; last century the Emperor could have done without me for a decade. Poor Cyan, she always looks delighted when I visit, though she's different every time, she grows so fast. Jant, one day you might find that you rely on prominent features to recognise people from one decade to the next.'

He veered from Low to High Awian, an outrageously complicated language in which every noun has a case, a tense, one of three genders and one of two social classes. Most of the verbs are irregular, and the least slip in the forms of address can cause offence. I am not sure whether High Awian became so intense through its long evolution in their aristocracy or deliberately to discourage aspiring farmers, tenants and Morenzians.

'This is the longest time I have failed to practise. I'll be in a sadly Challengeable state when we reach Tris, but it is my responsibility to catch Gio. This hurts, Jant; it certainly hurts. I can still feel the steel piercing my side – cold and inflexible. Have some brandy. I'm not drinking much, it would be disastrous for my aim, but it really is better than ours.'

'It's the only decent drink on board,' I said. 'Mist left in such a hurry that we've taken Gio's leftovers for rations. My guts are shrinking; I've had nothing but soup and juice all week. Can I bring you any?'

'No, stay awhile and talk. I have a Messenger's errand for you . . .'

'What is it?'

'It is somewhat unusual.' Lightning stared into the centre of the cabin. It was easy to underestimate how debilitated he was, with those overdeveloped shoulders. I waited patiently; perhaps he was rambling. The warm round smell of wax pervaded the berth, making it rather cosy. The rain smelt green; the ship's oakum soaked it up and stank like a wet dog. Thankfully it was difficult to envisage the breakers tearing over the main deck; above us the shredded topsail cracked and plaited. The driving waves caught red dusk like smallpox as sunset flashed under a suffocating sky, transforming the sailors' frantic activity into a series of stills.

Lightning breathed, 'It is autumn again . . . her birthday. I should be with Martyn. Since the Circle was founded I have never missed the date, my long-kept secret. If I could order *Petrel* around and sail for Awndyn, I would.'

'Count me in!'

He gave a bitter smile. 'I knew that at some point I would fail Martyn. It matters not, when Gio is persuading mortals to massacre us. But although my tradition is just a whim, I find breaking it makes me uncomfortable and I fancy she will miss me.' He looked away. 'I suppose you are eager to know what has been eating me up for one and a half thousand years . . .'

Lightning stared into space for a long while. He judged the time was right and suddenly said, 'Jant, I want you to carry a message to a dead woman. If I am killed fighting the rebels, you must visit the mausoleum and speak to her about the circumstances of my end. Explain why I can no longer come to see her.'

He feigned interest in his brandy. 'My cousin's body lies in an aventurine casket near the tombs of generations of my family, in a high-ceilinged sepulchre. You will find it amongst the trees on the man-made island in Micawater lake, in the palace grounds. I visit her once a year; I should be there today. I always leave the door ajar so that a shaft of light falls across Martyn's tomb. She loved the lake, you see. She used to trail her hand in the water, for the suspended mineral flecks that reflect the sunlight.

'You will see one clear track that my steps have made through the dust that lies thickly over every surface, from the entrance to the head of her vault. I sit beside the inscription that I keep free of dust. For the space of a few hours I tell her all the events of the previous year. I say that I visit as promised, because I still love her.

'I always bring balsam flowers. I store them in the underground bow room, which you have not seen. It is near the ice house, a beehive-shaped cellar, a cool, homeostatic store where the bows hang horizontally on stands. The flowers must be white because they set off her magnificent deep red hair so well. They must be balsam, as in the rhyme that no one even remembers any more: balsam for lovers, willows for brides, briar for maidens, lilies for wives.

'When I have finished telling her the news I leave the balsam, gather up the dried remains of last year's bouquet and row back across the lake.'

Lightning rubbed his forehead and sipped at the brandy. In his mind's eye he stroked the glistening green stone, sitting on the plinth while maple leaves fell past the mausoleum portal and doves cooed in the baroque cote.

'Martyn and I were struck with pure and sincere love,' he said very sourly. I was startled, but I suppose nothing causes bitterness so much as a downfall from ecstasy. 'I don't know why. Maids of honour packed my mother's entourage. There were ballrooms full of girls, all very pretty and accomplished, but not one of them was real.

'As a child Martyn was often at the palace. Then one banquet night we noticed each other and everything changed. We fell through into a panorama of hidden possibilities. We stared at each other across the laden table; nothing else existed. Without a word we rose together and left the hall. She was nineteen years old, I was twenty-nine. My conscience made me hesitate; she took my wing and led me to the antechamber, where she pushed me into the cloaks hanging on the wall and allowed me to kiss her.

'We rushed to the stables at midnight. "Don't you want to escape?" Martyn said. She was wild, she didn't care. She charged her white hunter at hedges and ditches, taking the jumps at a mad speed and I galloped beside her.'

An unruly smirk that I had never seen before appeared on Lightning's face. He looked almost boyish. '"Don't you want to escape?" We escaped a lot after that – every opportunity we had.' He held his index fingers ten centimetres apart. 'I was this far from quitting the court, marrying her and exiling ourselves. We were this far, one fistmele, from escaping properly. I wish I had had the courage; she would still be alive today. She would be here *now*.

'I sometimes fought Insects but my lineage shielded me. Martyn and I spent most days in a world of our own. My family never mentioned it but they knew. Oh yes, they knew. The court thrived on Mother's blissful love for Garganey, but my love for her sister's daughter was taboo.

'We talked for hours and rode great distances, far from the palace to converse in the forest. All those long conversations, words came so easily. In dinners we were careful to sit apart. In dances she was serene and unperturbed while I tried hard not to look.

'Martyn was a peerless rider. I remember her perfume, her sepia and sage silk, her strong limbs, pale skin, and her auburn wings that she would spread like an excitable girl. She had seen so many forests the green of them stayed in her eyes.'

I felt like a voyeur in the undergrowth next to Lightning's cousin as she pressed herself against him and lay between the roots of an oak tree. She pulled up her tunic, her necklace's fine links pooled in the hollow of her throat. I peered to see a young Saker kiss her neck and full breasts and repeat her name tenderly and urgently. Her red curls spread on the crisp leaves as Saker mumbled, 'We mustn't do this,' desperately down the front of her blouse.

I felt uncomfortable because I had always considered Lightning to be sexless and celibate; the thought of him shagging Martyn was strange and a bit disgusting.

His deep voice continued: 'I see her again and again. Sometimes a woman's beauty reminds me of Martyn, but she doesn't act the same. Anyway, even the most breathtaking beauty only approximates to Martyn's. If I wait long enough . . . well . . . the types of characters are not endless, and with time they recur. She looked very much like Swallow, but taller, and she resembled Savory too – remember her?'

I nodded cagily. Lightning sent me to deliver his love letters to a fyrd captain called Savory, and she let me fuck her after she read them. I was single, individualistic and hedonistic, so I took it as proof of how wrong Lightning was about women. I now keep the burden of guilt to myself, because for his peace of mind and my own safety he must never know.

He continued without noticing. 'Martyn was as close to perfection as it's possible to be. A happiness so intense can't last long; it's always the case that the arrows we shoot up to the stars fall back on our own heads. The Insects swarmed ever closer, decimating the First Circle, and in the year six-twenty San announced the Games. Martyn watched me win through the hundred rounds in the archery tournament but she did not travel with me to the Castle, where he made us victors immortal. I whispered to her afterwards how nobody in the Circle felt immortal and we hardly believed the Emperor. I established myself, organised my lodging in the Castle, and next thing I knew, San sent us to the Front. The Wall ran on the north bank of Rachis River and we struggled very hard – they stretched the Empire to breaking point. I had no sleep for a week, I fought to the last of my strength. It took years to push the vermin back into Lowespass. It was a harder struggle than that of twenty-fifteen.

'Then San gave me leave. I visited my family, and everything looked different. They were all older.'

Lightning pulled his knees up under the blanket and wrapped his arms around them. The informal gesture made him seem shockingly smaller; I suddenly saw the boy in a man I had thought too old and awesome to contain one.

'The gentry and my brothers gave sidelong glances from the periphery of the courtroom as I knelt before Teale. She raised me to my feet, pinched my cheeks and turned my head. "By god, it's true," she said, with both pride and envy. Their bodies changed with time, mine didn't. The world had seen nothing like Eszai before. I seemed to be a threat although I had no power to intimidate them; I couldn't even age. The stilted politeness of the quality crowd barely covered their distrust. I was keeping their wealthy world safe from Insects but because the Circle was successful the courtiers lost the concept of danger. They took my sacrifice for granted. They drifted, I fought.

'I proposed to Martyn but she could not deny the will of our Queen. She would not leave the court and the country. Although it would have been easy, at the time we couldn't see how. What happened to the carefree rowdy girl in those years I was away? Martyn didn't . . . Now she was older I don't think she trusted what I'd become. I think I frightened her. I wasn't strong enough to take her from the court, and she wasn't as strong as I thought she was . . . or maybe I appeared stronger to the world than I realised. In the blink of an eye she was married, raised a family of beautiful children, was an old woman; she died. She was always very changeable. I admired her ability and loved her all the more. I adored and guarded her until the end, but I never spoke to her.

'Life seems to be more about the choices you don't make. San decreed that I could be Eszai or King of Awia, not both. The throne passed to Avernwater. I threw myself into my work again. Eventually I saw Martyn's own line die out. The bustle and crowds had gone from the palace and I lived there on my own. Hardly anything happened for two hundred years. I had a lot of Challenges because, after all, archery is the national sport. Next time I looked up, I barely recognised the kingdom.'

Lightning realised he was staring at nothing and seemed surprised. He gave me a sharp look and said harshly, 'Never mind. I had expected to outlive you, Comet, but these are not Insects we're fighting now. Will you carry the message to Martyn?'

His confidence overwhelmed me. 'I'll do better than that. I'll bring her balsam blooms and chat to her on your behalf this day every year for the rest of my life, and then, if I can, I'll pass the duty on to another willing Eszai when I die.'

'God, Jant; so generous. I am indebted. Thank you very much . . .' He sighed; he was too exhausted to continue. The silence that followed purged the air. We both knew that we would never mention Martyn again.

I looked at us there: a young and old immortal. The lanky Rhydanne one curled up, safe in his own self-interest, had a bright pride in his eyes because he had the chance to watch over and listen to a prince aged fourteen hundred and thirty-something, talking in a tired attempt to unpick his past. You could peel away shell after shell and still never understand Lightning, because you only get a little of him with each shell. In response I told him everything about Tern's affair, and I asked for advice. 'When Tern's in Tornado's rooms I'm too scared to confront them, because it's his territory, you know.'

Lightning scowled, then surprised me by saying, 'But from the start she was so keen to marry you! I can have a word with her if you like. I can explain how you feel, to show my gratitude for the favour you have promised. I once told Rayne about my cousin, but no one else. You will keep the secret?'

'Yes, of course.'

'You are a good friend.' He lay down, propped on one elbow, and said, 'Leave me for the night. I have to sleep.'

Next morning I waited till the rain dwindled, then ran out of my cabin along the slick bowed deck past the wheelhouse that Mist had constructed around the helm. She had also lashed a copper rod to the mainmast like a lance. Two sailors clinging to the wheel muttered, envying my sense of balance and the way I can relax into the cold.

*Stormy Petrel* barrelled along furiously under full sail, an arrow shot towards an as yet invisible target. The knife-sharp waves scooped up water and rushed forward, all the water slipped off, then up went the peak again, further on.

Every time the *Petrel* bucked up she went 'whoosh', then slammed down 'splash'. This whoosh-splash wound my muscles tight; I was sure it would tear the ship to pieces. When she pitched forward the bowsprit dipped and touched the waves. I waited for it to break off. Water sprayed over the prow, rushed down the deck, sluiced off between railings and down drain holes. I thought we were going to do a headstand on the figurehead all the way to the sea floor. Next second the bowsprit pointed straight at the sky like a flagpole. It described an enormous curve as it crunched down again. The masthead drew a wide circle in the sky as *Petrel* rolled.

Worse, the five-metre waves pushed by the hurricane started overtaking us, and pushed *Petrel* forward a little in time with each tip-up. With each tip-down the bow slammed in the waves and braked the ship, so a stop-start jolting added to the vertical lift and fall.

In Mist's cabin my entrance was met with a nod. She was busy with her charts, while her navigational instruments hurtled from one edge of the table to the other with every whoosh-splash.

'It's been one hundred days,' I said. I wedged myself in the corner. 'When will this stop? You said we should be able to see Tris by now.'

'If there was no sea-fret we could,' Mist muttered. 'How's the Archer?'

'Variable. He can walk but his wound keeps catching.'

Wrenn's voice interrupted me: 'Fret, she says! It's not a fret, it's a hurricane.' He lay abjectly on the bench by the stern windows. His angular Adam's apple pointed at the ceiling. His short chestnut-coloured wings folded neatly to fit under the curve of his spine, so he could lie flat on his back. His face had a greenish pallor; sweat bristled his hair and stubbly razor-cut sideburns. I noticed a tiny lip of fat over the waistband where he used to be trim. The sea crossing was taking its toll. Happily, I thought, I'm better company for Lightning now he's injured. Lightning wouldn't have told Wrenn his secret.

The whole room see-sawed up and free-fell down. I winced at the crash. The Swordsman moaned, 'After I puke I feel better until fifteen minutes later I have to puke again. My nose is full of it. The teeth ache in my gums. When we lift my stomach is left up there. I plunge with a hole in my middle – on the next rise I meet it and god knows what other internal organs.'

'Try flying,' I said merrily.

'Oh, god . . .'

The salt-smeared panes behind him gave onto the pockmarked water. *Stormy Petrel* trailed a green wake. Air bubbles deep inside the waves jiggled and struggled to rise, broke as froth.

The violet rings under Mist's eyes were the same colour as her irises; with her pale hair and fading bronze skin she looked unearthly. She pushed a wooden rule back and forth along the raised rim of the tabletop. 'Patience,' she snapped. 'I can't help that we're hindered by dirty weather, or that *Pavonine* missed it by days. I can't control the seasons! I need to know what Glo is doing. I hope to predict him . . . Against this gale every manoeuvre I make is as pointless as a Circle masquerade.' Her lips cracked as she smiled. She bent over her chart again, preoccupied. 'It's simply chance. I thought I'd find him! I can't run him down with the wind in my face no matter how much sail I fly. The *Pavonine's* skipper isn't better than me. He's just a lucky fucker.'

Wrenn and I remained quiet. The thought that Mist was failing filled the cabin with despondency. She stretched her arm across the table and neatly caught a brass protractor as it slid past. 'Can Lightning draw a bow?'

'He says so.'

'Can you fly in this weather?'

'If I can get above the clouds. Otherwise the rain—'

'Good.' She beckoned me to the chart and stroked her finger along some ruled pencil lines. 'Here's your direction from our current position and we are making just over a kilometre an hour so we'll be at *this* point by the time you return. If Gio reached Capharnaum at the rate I watched him leave Awndyn, he'll have been on Tris a fortnight. We'll have to catch him there.' She sighed and continued almost in a daydream, 'When Gio was Serein, I liked the man, I can't pretend otherwise. We were friends for three hundred years of campaigning. He plays to his strengths so he'll stay ashore. Aye, I recognise that Zascai extreme desperation; they drive themselves so far and so pitilessly they can't survive. There but for San's favour go I. Right. I admit I don't want to deal with Gio on dry land, but I have no choice. I'll let Lightning and Serein take their turn.

'We're coming up on Tris in the next day or so. See? Scout around, Comet, and bring us some intelligence.'

I memorised the calculation and said to Wrenn, 'Don't worry, there's only one day left.'

'Aye, go back to training,' Mist gibed him. 'I want you as keen as a harpooner when I set you on Gio. This surf will break straight onto the rocks. I'm lucky that the Capharnai built such an imposing harbour wall for their piffling little canoes.'

The sky and sea were so overcast that the very light was grey. Cloud lowered to liquefy and make the ocean. The *Petrel* was always the centre of a dull opaque sphere, half-filled with thrashing water. Great spirals of spitty white foam went round and round on the sea's surface.

Waves thumped on the bow and resonated through the whole ship, playing her like a drum. She crashed down, the displaced water spurted up over the figurehead and pattered on the foredeck. Half a metre of white spray stood solid on top of the waves, where raindrops were bouncing back off. Their power smoothed the waves, filled the troughs – the sea was white as a snow field. Spume blew off the wave tops. I was inhaling it; the air was full of salt.

I shrugged my leather coat on over three layers of T-shirts, and shoved my hair down the collar. I drank a mug of hot reconstituted soup with stale biscuit broken into it. Then I set off and climbed unevenly, beating painfully against gusts that came from every direction. Behind me rain fell as a slanting grey strip from a single patch of cloud onto the heeling caravel.

Flickering lightning illuminated the clouds from within. I zig-zagged up, terrified of it. I beat a path with great difficulty through the wind, already waterlogged by raindrops as big as snowflakes.

I disappeared into the cloud base and continued climbing calmly to avoid disorientation. Rain streamed down my coat and cold wisps whipped past my face.

I emerged, pulling up shreds of cloud, into a most perfect, tranquil world – with a population of one. The sky above was a uniform winter blue, a bright sun shone on complete cloud cover beneath me like a second, motionless ocean. Its wan surface was hollowed and carded into static points like a blanket of wool. The light was so brilliant it reminded me of the glare on the Darkling glaciers.

I breathed deeply in the thin air. Directly ahead cumulo-stratus lapped around the summit of Tris's mountain, its charcoal and olive colours muted with distance. Further away the silhouette tip of the second island in the archipelago poked through the cloud. They were like islands in the sky.

I held my wings out in a long shallow glide. On the ground I never had freedom from responsibility, from people, freedom from drugs. This was the ultimate release. Only the dull and earthbound sit in hulking carracks, the humid forest. They will never understand my world because I am the Messenger and I have all this air.

The clouds' surface sped away under me. While *Stormy Petrel* and Capharnaum town laboured under the storm, the setting sun cast the colours of northern lights over my private sea. Meringue cloud turned opalescent blue, pale orange and rose pink; the mountain's shadow lengthened. I loved the uninhabited mountain. The splendour of Tris from my unique perspective filled me with elation, but I wished that I could show it to Tern. I would paint it in words for her if we were ever snug in bed together again.

I reached the mountain's slope after nightfall. The gale concealed my wings' noise, so I descended through the clouds to Capharnaum and circled at height trying to discern detail. It hadn't rained on Tris; the main boulevard and its rotunda were lit but the surrounding streets were completely dark. A few people stood by the crossroads. A group of men walked towards them, carrying lanterns and some sort of polearm. The loiterers started up, slouched downhill towards the harbour and filed into a wine shop, leaving the paved street empty. From the foot of the Amarot crag, a bell pealed ten strokes, and all was silent.

I sailed over the Amarot, seeing its walls lit flame-yellow. About a thousand men were bivouacking on the mosaic between the Senate House and the library. They were Gio's rebels and they had lit a cooking fire right on Alyss' face. The aroma of goose fat rose up to me.

Real food! God, I wanted some of that meat. Shadows ten times life-size reared and lunged on the Senate House columns as they dipped tin mugs and tarred horn cups into an enormous keg of rum and passed them around. Dirty faces reddened by the firelight jeered and laughed. Thousands of hours of effort had been poured into constructing the mosaic, and now Gio's thugs were trashing it.

The night seemed to jump darker by degrees, making me blink; my eyes were adjusting all the time. I made out a small building perched on the cliff edge behind the Senate House. A shape as fat as Cinna waddled out of the dark entrance, buttoning his fly. I bent back my wings to descend. Yes, it was Cinna, appearing like a coagulation of all the lard in the Fourlands.

He sauntered, his hands deep in his pockets. I swung into a standing position and dropped to the ground behind him. Cinna halted in his tracks and turned around very slowly. He said, 'I'm not wanking. I'm just keeping my hands warm.'

'Huh? Shut up and follow me.'

I ran, hugging close against the library wall, to the unlit colonnade that joined the library to the Senate House. I slunk inside and beckoned to Cinna. He reeled; his peacoat was spotted with rum. I grabbed his lapels and positioned him squarely behind one of the columns where he stood less chance of being seen, although he overlapped it on both sides. His red nose was darker than his shocked white expression. Drops of sweat detached from his shiny forehead and rolled down puffed-out cheeks.

I drew the ice axe from the back of my belt and whispered, 'If you cry out I'll kill you.' Cinna gave me a beseeching look, wiped his palms on his knees and pointed at the ground. I let him sit down and lean against the column. I hunkered down too, in shadow and well out of sight.

'What's going on?' I asked. 'Quickly. Why is Capharnaum so dark? The streets are deserted and a bell was tolling. I saw men loitering; there was nothing threatening about Capharnaum before. What's Gio done to them?'

Cinna's frightened whisper was so low I scarcely heard it. 'You saw that, Messenger? Yes, the patrol just called for the next watch. They're not fyrd – the Senate appointed men to maintain the curfew and guard the houses.'

'Curfew? There's a curfew? Why?'

'Because of an Insect that's loose. It's killed eighty people so far. The Senate and Gio have divided the town into sectors and they're searching systematically, even sewers and attics, but they can't find it.

One Insect is causing more trouble than all the swarms of Lowespass. See those posters over there? They warn people to stay indoors.' He nodded towards some sheets of paper pasted on a board at the end of the library. 'They carry a picture of the latest victim. But the fact that Capharnai have discovered The Joy Of Insects isn't the only reason for the curfew. Thieves are roaming the streets. Gangs.'

'Gio's men are desperadoes,' I agreed.

Cinna belched quietly and chuckled. 'Not us. Them. The citizens.'

'But Tris had no crime six months ago.'

Across the square the rabble's voices rose in a raucous cheer and Cinna took advantage of the noise to say, 'It's your fault!'

'Sh!'

'Mist Ata bought up all the spices, didn't she? Now they've nothing to preserve food. So a lot of the Capharnai's stores have gone rotten, it's winter and some food supplies are running low. Prices are steep – The Price Of Spice is like scolopendium, Messenger. The Senate have unconditionally banned trade with the Fourlands and they're endeavouring to ration everything except bread and fish. Well, all I know is they're muttering because Gio's nine hundred men have to eat and they've no choice but to feed us. Those drunks you saw Being Moved On have made themselves a nuisance here all day.'

'I didn't know Capharnaum had drunks.'

'It does now. Those men were the merchants Mist paid. I know, because they hassled me for rum as we were rolling the kegs up here. I don't know how I'm supposed to look like a pusher or a captain if I have to sleep in the outdoors . . .'

'Keep to the point.'

'Well, Mist gave them so many riches they don't have to work any more. Their money is time, and she gave them years of time so now they're idle. I hope she profited from those peppercorns and pickles, the Entrepreneur Of Misrule, like myself.' He rubbed his plump hands together. 'They're not used to rum but they've found a taste for it. They drink it like wine. Because they're armed, they're Creating Trouble. It just goes to show that the only Truly International Language is drugs.'

I began to understand. I prompted, 'They're armed? They'll be armed with the swords and halberds we sold them?'

Cinna nodded. 'Yes, I think so. I was told that the Senate tried to buy up all the weapons from the townspeople to give to their patrols but they clearly didn't get them all because I hear there were armed robberies – at storehouses and the market. Also, young men keep soliciting to buy swords from us. It seems they've become quite a status symbol. Capharnai have never seen quality steel before; it's worth its weight in gold. And of course men have to protect themselves from the Insect.'

'Shit.'

'The Senate are discussing imposing taxes to pay the patrols.' Cinna appraised the Wheel brooch on my patched coat. 'Gio is waiting for you and Serein. Gio wondered if *Stormy Petrel* had gone down in the storm. Of course, he reckoned without Mist's marvellous seamanship. He was thinking about his next move. He told Senator Vendace that we would leave Capharnaum, but he doesn't really mean to. He's safe here; the Senate is In His Pocket.'

Cinna put a special emphasis on Gio's name. He was obviously firmly under the fencing master's influence. Nine hundred men following Gio, I thought. They outnumber us more than three to one. Still, that's better odds than against the Insects. 'If I have to stain my hands with blood, I must admit this rabble is less daunting than the swarms.'

Cinna gaped. 'You think it's just Gio? No, Comet. God, sometimes I believe all you have to do to be immortal is out-arrogance each other.'

'Spit it out.'

'Gio has won over the Senate and he's prepared to lead all Capharnaum against you when you land.' He went on, 'Everyone here hates you, and Gio has been planning. When *Petrel* sails into harbour she'll be surrounded, you'll be seized. There are twenty thousand people in this town.

'Vendace was wary because of the disastrous effects of your visit. But Gio's rhetoric quite convinced him. You should've tried making long speeches in the Senate.' Cinna smirked. 'Gio's here for the same reasons and on the same terms as the original settlers – to leave the Empire and San. Vendace thought he had found a Kindred Spirit. Gio offered to help hunt the Insect and being desperate they welcomed him with open arms. His interpreters are at home with their old lingo. The Senate didn't like the look of us tars as much. They've been discussing it for three days but they haven't made a decision yet.'

I wished for another stint in the Senate. If Gio can sway their opinion simply by talking to them, I thought how much better I could be when it was my turn. Gio may have had two weeks to work on their hearts and minds, but I'd love a verbal battle with him.

Cinna sniggered. 'They are so naïve. Myself and three colleagues could control this town in a year without drawing a sword or promising immortality— Ulp!' I pressed my ice pick to his throat. He gulped: I expected his eyes to pop in like a frog's. I couldn't bear the thought that he could turn Capharnaum into a slum worse than East Bank Hacilith. I hissed, 'You bastard, if you ever bring drugs to Tris, if you even *think* of peddling here, I swear I'll kill you. If you hide your tracks I'll trace them, because I know every link in a larger world than you could ever comprehend. You'll beg to be sent to the Front. You will beg for the wheel. I will have you keelhauled from bow to stern of the *Petrel*—'

'No!'

'You could do with losing some weight. The same goes for if you tell Gio I've been here.'

Cinna wiggled his shoulders, trying to pull away from the pick dimpling his neck. 'Please, Comet. I'm a businessman and San's humble servant. I shall always give a truthful account and say nothing to Gio. In the meantime I've arranged to stay on board *Pavonine* . . . It's the safest place to be.'

'Coward,' I mouthed. I licked salt off my lips.

'Look at you grin. You're enjoying this! Mad Eszai. If *Petrel* lands, Gio will kill you. If you turn tail and run home, you'll starve on the journey. I wonder what San will think when his Circle breaks for Four Immortals At Once? Bet that'd give him a headache.'

I prodded him with the axe. 'Where's Gio now? Does he stay on *Pavonine*?'

Cinna shook his head; the blond hairs on his chin wagged. He pointed up, across the mosaic, to a concertina-shuttered lit window above the Senate House. 'See the end room? Right on the corner past the last column? That's the bedroom of the apartment that Vendace gave him. All the senators have rooms up there. It's very plush,' he added, with a quiet admiration of Gio's achievement. 'Now tell me, Messenger, isn't that a useful piece of information?'

'It certainly is.'

Cinna glanced at the firelight and the rebels singing drunkenly. He pressed a note into my hand. 'Please let me go. I respect Mist. I'd like to help her, the little I can. It's tough to find a way through the surf. I wrote down the details of our approach to the beacon and the position and condition of *Pavonine*. Please give it to her.'

# CHAPTER 19

Midnight on the open sea. The attendant hush of an imminent downpour. I flew circuits over the correct position but couldn't sight *Stormy Petrel* through the rain clouds. A weak glow backlit them; I homed in on it and descended. Mist had festooned every surface, cable and yard with lanterns showing me where to land. *Petrel*'s lights blazed on a yellow ring of water in the impenetrable night. She looked like a party yacht, but she yawed and rolled madly.

Lights attached to the main deck railings marked two parallel lines. I had touched down safely between them. Now, sitting at the table in Mist's quiet cabin, Lightning and I watched her sailors disassembling the lanthorns and hurricane lamps. They were extinguished one by one, until the office and wheelhouse were the only cabins lit.

'Take a good look,' said Mist. 'Tomorrow night we burn no lantern. The wind is dropping and our approach is good, thanks to Jant's spy. You will have the pleasure of sneaking to Capharnaum in complete darkness, through the narrow strait by their beacon islet. You must trust me.'

'Yes, but for god's sake don't trust Cinna. He's a craven liar, he only worships money. Thankfully Gio doesn't know what to ask, or Cinna would tell him everything.'

'Just how did you come to know Cinna, anyway?' Mist asked.

'Let's not go into that,' I said dismissively. I poured myself a quantity of Lightning's brandy and rested my head on my arms.

'Why is Wrenn not present?' Lightning demanded.

'He is too young,' said Mist demurely.

Lightning raised his eyebrows. 'Why isn't Rayne here?'

'She is too old.'

'Simply that they would disagree with your methods,' Lightning said.

'Wrenn is impetuous and idealistic. The Doctor's not a warrior and can bring little to the table. Please let me outline my plans for you clear-headed gentlemen first.'

Lightning said, 'It is the same as when I tried to eradicate Insects from the streets of Micawater. How do we get rid of Gio and his vicious followers without damaging the town?'

'Or making the Senate detest us more than they already do?' I added.

Mist said, 'San gave me the task; I *will* fulfil it. The way ahead is clear. Listen! Lightning, if you were to remove the leader, the rebellion would collapse. Your skill with the longbow makes you best suited to try.'

In the short silence Lightning gazed at his rummer glass. He said amiably, 'You're asking me to capture Gio? Or assassinate him?'

'Saker, think—'

'No.' He looked at her directly. 'No, Ata; I won't do that.'

Mist folded her arms. 'Saker, I'm surprised that you don't want to regain your honour and take revenge on Gio for stabbing you in the back.'

'It would be less worthy still to become an assassin,' Lightning explained. 'I have never killed a man, and if I were simply to hide and shoot him, I don't know if I could live with myself afterwards. I do not want to spend the next few centuries troubled by guilt and introspection. In addition to the fact that it would lose me my esteem.'

'No one on the mainland will ever know. None of your sentiments apply to us in this plight. We're far from home. There are no ingrained traditions, carved beasts carrying pennants, heraldic old charters to say who we are. We're understocked and badly prepared. The Capharnai don't know us and Gio has stacked the odds against us. Eliminating him is the only way.'

'Why?'

'Because it'll save Trisian lives! They're innocent; I don't want to harm them. If we remove Gio, the Capharnai will be peaceable without him. If we set foot in Capharnaum while Gio controls it, we're dead. I think that Gio's lust to rejoin the Circle is driving him insane. You know the saying: Pure ambition seeks one goal only. Don't you think Gio's deeds are a mad panic, rather than a Challenge?'

'I think mad people want to see the madness in everyone,' I commented.

The Sailor ignored me. 'Saker, you *must* stop him. Can you think of a better idea?'

Lightning slowly replied, 'No. Nonetheless, you have my answer. I will not shoot Gio. I do not want it on my conscience for the rest of my life.' Lightning undid the buttons at his collar and pulled the silk down so that we could see a small circular scar pierced front and back through his shoulder. 'See this? An arrow shaft. Eight hundred years ago I beat a Challenger and he turned round and shot me. Fortunately he had a terrible aim and failed to take my life. He spent the rest of his days in the Sturge Prison on Teron Island. There is nothing honourable about assassins; I don't want to be one . . . Anyway, it would look pretty obvious if Gio is found with an arrow in his chest. It is not for me . . .' He trailed off, thoughtfully, and stroked the scar on his right hand.

'Jant—' Mist began.

'Ha! Just because I'm not Lord Micawater you think I have no morals! Besides, Gio's the most dangerous man in the world. Lightning is more capable of dealing with him than I am.'

'But the bastard wounded him. Lightning, your good friend . . .'

'Yes, and the bastard would run me through if he had the chance.'

'Remember all the awful slander you said Gio lambasted us with in his rally? You said you were ready to shoot him.'

I thought privately of how he slurred Tern's reputation and my manhood and dependability. Yes, I had been prepared to kill him.

Mist smiled eerily and prompted, 'Gio attacked the Castle, Jant. There's no doubt but he deserves what he gets. A few drops of the drug you keep injecting yourself with should do the trick.'

I looked at Lightning, who shrugged. I said reluctantly, 'All right, I'll do it.'

'Good!' said Mist. Her leather trousers creaked as she stood up. She turned to her cot and began to delve around energetically inside it. 'If you make it look like he was addicted and took an overdose, we can discredit him in the Fourlands.'

I gave her a flat stare. 'And make the climate dangerous for other people who happen to be users? Thank you, but no. Besides, I need all my supply.'

If an Eszai commits a crime and is caught, the Castle has no power to try him, nor may the Emperor intercede on his behalf. Instead, he is handed over to the court of the country in which the crime took place, to be tried and sentenced there. I couldn't guess how a Trisian court might work, or how severe the penalty may be. Or if I could successfully talk myself out of it.

Likewise, there is only one circumstance in which the Castle may interfere in a country's business – if an Eszai has been attacked or murdered, the assailant must be handed over to the Castle to be tried according to the law of his homeland, as happened with Lightning's erstwhile assassin eight centuries ago. If the murderer is protected by his country, San would forbid entrance to the Circle for anyone from that land, undeniably a terrible threat.

Mist's cot was a box-like bed with a drape of thick ivory lace. It swung as she pulled up the meagre mattress and extracted a bulky white packet – the envelope of scolopendium that Cinna had originally sold me. She tossed it onto the table. 'An additional supply. Use a pinch of powder.'

'But, Ata,' I said, startled, 'you said you'd thrown it in the sea! Wrenn told me you had. You led him to believe . . .'

'I never discard useful assets.'

I stared at her wondering if she had *wanted* me to become addicted. My stash in the coat hem she had overlooked, all the needles and phials on the *Melowne* – I had been surprised there were so many – had she intended me to find them and get hooked so that I would be helpless and corruptible, under her control? And now she bribed me with the drugs I bought myself!

I knew how crazy that sounded, so I said nothing. Without proof, I did not dare to accuse her. I was as lost and confused as in an Awian maze. 'Oh, in San's name, what choice do I have?'

I pulled the envelope towards me gingerly, aware of Lightning's disapproval. The last thing I wanted was Gio materialising in Epsilon. I needed a poison that would kill him outright and quickly, so as not to give him a chance to reach a Shift world. I said, 'Gio might detect scolopendium; it has a distinctive taste. If you're devoted to this course, I can propose a less risky, more efficient substance.' I slipped my wedding band off my fourth finger, and the broader ring that I wore below it – a black star sapphire set in silver. I pushed the stone with my thumbnail; it depressed then popped open. Inside were two very small white tablets. I passed the ring to Ata.

'What are they?'

'Atropine. Extracted from belladonna root.'

'Deadly nightshade! For god's sake – what are you carrying that for?' She returned them carefully.

'I always keep them there. Atropine is effective in treating scolopendium overdose. One tablet would counteract the toxin, although I've rarely been able to take it. Two tablets are lethal. They're soluble and tasteless.'

Lightning made a decision. 'I think I should accompany you, unless you fear I will slow you down. I'll never murder but I will shoot to defend us.'

'Please,' I said gratefully. With Lightning to back me up, I felt I could do anything. Archer and Messenger, we'd share Gio between us. I picked his bottle from its holder clipped to the table. 'I'll decant for Gio a full-bodied draught. Unlike you I don't care enough for it to leave a bitter aftertaste. I know that he won't savour a lingering finish, because atropine will rapidly cause fever, a dry thirst balanced with the aroma of delirium, a sparkling racing pulse, a blend of spicy burning sensations, confusion, convulsions, coma and death. That's what I call a rich vintage.' I swirled the bottle and took a long pull.

'You are a sick man, Jant Shira.'

Mist shrugged. 'So we are decided. We approach tomorrow night at this time. *Petrel* will stay out of sight and I'll row you two to the harbour. I'll wait at the end of the quay. *Petrel* is safe under Viridian's command. I will arrange for her to bring the ship in to retrieve us two hours before dawn. Our hundred sailors and our hundred and fifty fyrd led by Serein will be ready on board if we need them. Lightning, what arms do you advise?'

The Archer pondered. 'Crossbows are better than longbows for fighting in a town, much as I don't like them. I don't want to cause casualties among the Capharnai, and you can take crossbows anywhere, even down tunnels.'

'Good. When Gio's body is discovered, the Senate will have little choice but to talk with us.'

'I hope it works.' Lightning sighed. 'Goodnight, co-conspirators.'

I was about to follow him out of the cabin when the ship slewed. Canvas flapped wildly as the wind changed direction, whistling around the mainmast. Ata shoved past me, stuck her head out of the door and yelled, 'Bring her about! She luffs, you lazy sods! Are you asleep in there? Make use of this wind!'

Cinna's envelope lay forgotten on the table. My mouth dried up. I never have enough cat, I always want more. I couldn't stop myself. I sneaked the envelope inside my coat and slipped out past Ata. ''Bye, Jant . . .' she muttered. 'Faster, *Petrel*. Faster, my love. Gio has nowhere left to flee.'

# CHAPTER 20

I let Mist and Lightning descend the rope ladder first into the tiny rowing boat. It needed testing. I waited till they were settled before climbing down and gingerly feeling with my feet for the planks. The boat bucked. It was ready to roll right over, giving me no chance to fly off. I shuffled as quickly as possible to the middle of the bench-plank at the stern. Ata hefted her oars into the rowlocks.

I advised her, 'Sit still. You're rocking it!'

'Move your legs,' she said. 'You're in the way.'

'I'd rather not.'

'I'll climb over, then.'

'No!' I did not like being so near the water. My feet were actually *under* the level of the scooping waves, which was obviously wrong and shouldn't be allowed. Ata pulled the oars and the dangerous vessel leapt prow to stern. I concentrated on the floor.

'Are you all right?' Lightning asked.

'Of course. But this craft is clearly unstable. A single wave could swamp it.'

'He hates them,' Ata said.

'I'm just being careful.'

She dipped oars, pulled on, leant from side to side and the boat swayed alarmingly. 'You're tipping it deliberately!'

Ata said dryly, 'As if I would. She's hugely overloaded anyway.'

'Stop fooling about. It's not funny.' The rowing boat was completely different from the high-sided caravels to which I had become reconciled. They were designed not to turn turtle but this boat wallowed as Ata rowed. I felt the weight of my two centuries ever more clearly as I searched the extremely close water for Tarragon's fin, but all the wavelets looked like fins. 'Why can't I just fly there?'

'Act your age. Now the storm has died down, the rebels will hear your wing beats,' Ata breathed between strokes.

'I'll glide.'

'And see your silhouette . . . Oh, in San's name!' she exclaimed in terror.

'What?'

'Jant, I forgot the rope. Can you help me? Lend a hand!' She passed me the end of a cable that ran over the side into the water and had been catching on the waves. 'Pull on this line. It's vital! The way she's built, the planks aren't safe unless you keep it taut.'

'Really?'

'Yes – if you let it slack for a minute she'll split into more segments than an orange!'

'I knew this was a death trap! How can you go to sea in a flimsy half-built boat? Shit!' I snatched up the damp rope and hauled on it until drops pinged off.

Ata nodded. 'Good. Now keep it tight or we'll all be in the drink.' Water ran from the blades as she feathered the oars. *Stormy Petrel*'s copper-clad hulk was a vague black shape in the distance. Lights on the three levels of decks were snuffed by the crew, and she vanished.

Lightning talked to the Sailor quietly. 'Eszai are not supposed to sneak around like this. Gio's forcing us to be murderers. I wish I was at the Front fighting Insects.' He had refused to blacken his sword blade even though I offered to do it for him. His concession to stealth had been to remove his signet ring and wrap a black mantle over his dark blue shirt. He held one arm around his new recurve longbow as if it was a lover.

'When the job's done return directly to the quay,' said Ata.

'I'm concerned about Cyan. I hope none of this dishonour rubs off on her.'

'Oh, don't worry. I find that daughters look after themselves.'

'And we have no back-up plot,' he said. 'None of us knows enough to predict the Capharnai.'

'We have our talents. Gio must be frightened of you, Archer. When his followers show their true colours, his lies will become manifest. The Senate will realise we're doing the best for Tris.'

Lightning and Ata fell silent as we came up to the beacon. Its uneven light did not illuminate the whole wide harbour mouth – the furthest point of the marina wall was in shadow. Ata rowed close to it, as quietly as possible. Slimy basalt blocks dwarfed us; thick kelp fronds stirred deep beneath us. I had been straining at the rope for thirty minutes, preoccupied with images of drowning, but I saw the rafts of empty Trisian canoes tied to their floating pontoons, undulating on the waves. In the distance they looked like needles on pine branches. *Pavonine*, *Cuculine* and *Stramash* were monstrous in comparison. At the waterfront, their unembellished sterns faced us, sails furled on skeletal spars, no flags flying. Lights flickered on *Pavonine*'s living deck. Their three tall masts, thinned by the darkness, were only occasionally visible against the night sky. Still, I sensed their bulk and heard the wavelets that slipped in and splashed back between the carracks and the harbour wall. They were rising on their moorings on an incoming tide.

Behind the harbour, Capharnaum's streets interlaced up the dark mountainside. Tris seemed far from fragile but, now we had touched it, it was starting to destruct. What if across the immense sea is an even stronger Empire, more pervasive still, that will do the same to us? San would be furious if he knew that thought. God has not left anything other than us on this world and, since it nominated San to protect the world, San and his orders are right. I will one day announce contests for Capharnai to join the Circle. I will fly over the town carrying their pennant, letting it stream out behind me, and Ata will ride her white horse up the boulevard. Trisian travellers would eventually visit the Fourlands; I could hardly wait to show them the sights.

The harbour lamps reflected in the water. The end of the wall was in shadow, with some canoes upside-down outside a small square building. Ata manoeuvred us towards it past the last pontoon. Lightning whispered, 'I see no guards, but have a care. The wall's very near.'

She braked the oars. Lightning reached both arms over the side and fended us off. He pulled the boat around, long side to the wall. We all looked up to the top, two metres above. 'I don't see anyone.' He stood on the gunwale, palms on the flagstones, and pulled himself up. The boat bobbed and scraped the wall. His face appeared over the edge. 'Pass me my bow.'

'Sh! You should let me go first,' I said, nettled.

'Stop hanging on to the painter, please.' Ata took the rope from me, and gave me a leg up. I scrabbled to the promenade, lay flat on my stomach and peered over. Ata picked the rope from the water, running it the boat's length, then unwound it from the bow post. She threw it up to Lightning, who coiled it on the ground.

I gaped. 'Oh. It wasn't attached to anything?'

She sniggered. 'No. I just needed some way of shutting you up.'

'You—'

'Hush!' said Lightning.

Ata arranged knotted-cord fenders around the boat's hull, then she raised her hands to us. I turned my back, but Lightning took her hands and heaved her up, with a rasp of metal on stone. Her hair showed in a white flash under the hood of her black shawl – so different from the dazzling armour she wore in battle. She whispered, 'I'll hide by this depot. Lightning, follow Jant; he's done this kind of thing before. Jant, for god's sake stop sulking. Remember; return at eight a.m., Starglass time. Good luck.'

I set off a few paces, found myself alone, turned to see Ata and Lightning still looking at each other. She gazed at him straight, and a whole spectrum of unsaid things passed between them. Then Lightning gave a little shake of his head, and stepped away to join me.

The façade of houses along the harbour was dangerously exposed because lamps on posts every fifty or so metres cast light on the paving. They were so bright I couldn't see the stars. We had to dash across the yellow pools and pause in the very narrow slices of shadow.

I reached one of the puzzling black and white posts that had a wooden cross-arm and dangling wires. I crouched behind it. 'Saker, we must keep silence from now on. I know you don't like this and I don't blame you. But, just once, please follow my lead.'

The Archer nodded. He carried his strung bow over his right shoulder, leaving his arms free. His mantle covered the quiver on his back, giving his shoulders a spiky crest, and was pleated into his belt. Nocks and fletchings of fifty arrows projected from the quiver on his left hip, crammed in so tightly they hardly rustled. He hunched awkwardly, trying to hide his broad frame. With an Eszai's determination, he was trying to be a sneak. I said, 'Let's go.'

Oil lamps on the shopfronts lit the entire boulevard. But the grid-streets of Capharnaum were perfect for us assassins; we stole down the adjacent parallel street. I kept near the wall and walked rapidly, ducked into a doorway, waited for Lightning to catch up. The main street glowed on our left every side alley we passed. A statue on a plinth. Sculpin's wine shop; Opah's seafood; Ling and Zingel, grocers, the shutters closed. I ran across the road and continued up on the other side. Lightning piled into the shop doorway behind me. He was favouring his wound. I waved him back into shadow while I took a look around.

Time to change streets. I sped right across an intersection, away from the boulevard and left uphill again. The junctions were sharp right angles, since Trisians don't have coaches. We heard a bell chime, the Senate's patrol calling for the next watch. This street was darker – the buildings were all homes. We dashed past open colonnades and hugged house corners.

If Capharnaum was scruffier and a lot more disorganised, then slinking through it in the early hours would be just like Hacilith: hiding at a corner, giving the constables the slip. Doubling back to be rid of the rival Bowyers gang.

I beckoned the Archer close as we approached a lighted house and together we strode confidently past their front door. When people are at rest in their homes, a furtive movement can alert them, but they don't look twice if they think you're a watchman.

The houses were all of equal size and gave no cover; we walked swiftly. The boulevard's light shone out of the side streets; we sneaked along close to the muralled walls. Behind me, Lightning trailed my movements soundlessly. I value faithfulness among friends. If you have not honoured every childhood oath of allegiance to the gangs that changed every minute; adventuring among the rambling rose, the margins of ponds and darkened streets, you have not been true to yourself. I still have the Wheel scar on my shoulder. I have honoured those intense oaths of friendship, and as a result I am still a child.

The streets came to an end in darkness at the foot of the Amarot crag. Only the lit boulevard continued, climbing it in a zigzag path. A group of Trisians was descending the ten-metre-wide pavement from the Amarot into town. They wore cloaks over loose white shirts and wide trousers; they carried lamps and weapons. If they saw us they would recognise our outlandish Fourlands clothes immediately. We would have to pretend to be two of Gio's brigands, which would be the worst way to meet him. I urged Lightning back with a wave, and we lurked behind the corner of the last house.

The curfew meant that Gio's men were not wandering in the town. Unfortunately they were all corralled on the mosaic at the top of the crag – nothing between us and them but the Senate House itself. We watched the patrol pass by two streets away and descend into Capharnaum.

Lightning said, 'They're going the other way.' I seized his cloak and pulled him back as the previous patrol emerged. They exchanged a few words in a low tone with their colleagues and proceeded up the boulevard. We waited for what seemed like hours until they were thumbnail-sized at the top of the outcrop.

I mouthed, 'Our turn. Ready? Keep a good look round, your eyesight's keener than mine. Remember that bloody Insect. We can't see as well as it can scent us. It can certainly outpace you; it's very well fed.'

For the first few hundred metres, the crag's white boulders were conspicuous. Then we found ourselves stumbling up the escarpments, over the scrubland. I feared there was a scorpion under every rock. A woody smell rose from the damp thyme shrubs, and spiny bushes scraped my shins. Lightning struggled behind me kicking them.

At the lip of the crag there was no cover at all. The stony soil crunched under our boots and a gentle wind gusted down from the mountain above us. I lay flat on the hillside and after a dignified pause Lightning copied me. We listened. Gio's men were obviously on the rum again. They all seemed to be gathered around the roasting fire, lounging and enjoying themselves. Good.

Lightning touched my arm and pointed behind us. Capharnaum was spread out below; the boulevard gleamed like an amber river. Lights shone in the quadrangles of villas, picking out tiny green gardens, lit red-tiled roofs that were otherwise grey, highlighted smudges of colour on the frescoes. The harbour beacon blazed continually in a black strip, a single star under the lowest constellations. I found it hard to believe that, far beyond it, *Stormy Petrel* skulked up and down. Capharnaum was beautiful, but the curfew did not explain a sense of foreboding, an expectant hush. The town waited, but I doubted if any citizen knew why.

The tall outline of the Senate House blotted out the stars. Lightning and I glanced at each other. I tucked my coat back over my sword hilt; he nocked an arrow to string. We climbed as quietly as possible over the edge of the crag and onto its flat summit, into the Senate House's shade, beside the first of twelve columns with square podia that were arrayed along its length. Wind blew the rebels' cooking smoke over the roof ridge. Gio's room was above and round the other side.

Lightning steadied himself with a hand against the stone and looked up. The building towered over us; its columns were fifteen metres high, their edges wavered in the gloom. Lightning patted a smooth corner block, whispered, 'Can you climb it?'

'You do say some bloody ridiculous things sometimes. Look at it.'

'Damn. I hoped our scheme—'

'Well, of course I can.' I grinned. 'This reminds me of when, before I left Hacilith to come to the Castle, I climbed the governor's palace and left a blackmail note on Aver-Falconet's own pillow. It was easy.'

Lightning's volatile sense of morality flared. 'What? I don't remember you divulging that to the Circle!'

'Sh! It's a long story; forget it.'

I had asked for a whole one thousand pounds and I was amazed when Aver-Falconet paid up. I thought it was a fortune; how little I knew. Still, I bought horses and new kit, and kept enough change to make it worth the highwaymen's while when they robbed me of everything not ten hours later on the Camber Road.

'Stand here in the shadow until I return. Don't move. Apart from if the shadow moves, of course.' I took a firm grasp of the stonework with both hands, found a toehold with my leg fully bent and kicked off with the other. Hugging my body close to the stone, my rangy reach gained another handhold and toe. I was fully above Lightning. He kept his arrow nocked and waited flanked by a column. The darkness gave grainy texture to his severe face.

I strained to make out cracks in the mortar. Tiny white pinpoints prickled in my night vision. I folded my wings tight because their weight pulled me away from the wall. I stabbed my strong, pointed nails into the gaps, my fingers clawed. I jammed my boot in, straightened my leg. I raised my weight and stretched out for the next hold. I undercut the grip, cheek to the chill stone, stepped up.

The wind was stronger here. It blew around the exposed corner and cooled off my sweat. I hung on with one hand and both feet, stood up straight and took a break. I exhaled a long breath of admiration at the view: hundreds of houses and twenty thousand lives that Gio had snatched as a stake in his game. Well, now he is dealing with Comet who learnt to climb in the precipitous ice-split chimneys of Darkling's cliffs.

Above me was a narrow ledge. I reached up and felt about in the seagull shit. I secured a good foothold, bent my knees, sprang gracefully onto the cornice. I ran lightly along it, rounded the corner to the side of the building facing the mosaic. I flattened myself against the architrave of Gio's window. The brigands' camp was below, at the other side of the square. If any of them glanced up, they would see me plainly against this white stone. I quickly pushed the shutter open and peered into the room. No one inside, so I hopped over the sill and landed in a crouch, silently on the mint-green tiled floor.

Gio's apartment was enormous. A square bed stood in the centre, no curtains as in the Fourlands, just a taupe silk coverlet. The walls were covered in a *trompe l'oeil* scene of a sumptuous feast. Elegant diners in Trisian robes poised with grapes halfway to their mouths or in the act of raising goblets. Their eyes seemed to follow me across the room as I skirted a wooden screen and approached an alabaster side table on which burned one of the open-flame lamps.

Beside it was a glass half-full of clear liquid and a bottle with a familiar label, Diw Harbour Gin, Gio's tipple of choice. I released the lid of my ring and dropped both aconitum tablets into the glass. They dissolved instantly. I swirled the glass and set it down beside the lamp. The oil lamp was pure gold, in the shape of a breaching dolphin.

Irregular coral in claw fittings and priceless pearl clusters encrusted its base. It entranced me—

'Yeah, right . . .' a voice came from just outside the door, 'which I need like Mica Town needs more coffee shops! Goodnight, Tirrick.'

'Goodnight, Gio.'

Gio! I sprinted back across the room. Gio's foot appeared at the door. I couldn't reach the window. I jumped behind the screen. I was five clear metres from the window. Shit.

Poised to move, I peered carefully though the fine fretwork at the top of the folding partition. Gio slipped his coat off and threw it on the bed. He was wearing the same clothes as when he left the Castle, and though washed they smelt of ingrained mud and brine. He had still not bothered to find a shirt and wore the 1969 Sword slung on a double red belt across the waistband of his blue breeches. His bare ribs and hips were sinewy furrows.

Gio's obsession for revenge might be just another form of despair, but it had kept him disciplined if not hygienic. The scar Wrenn had given him showed as a pale pink incision at the base of his throat.

I wondered feverishly what to do. I was fast enough to escape but Gio would certainly see me and he wouldn't drink the gin; he would send his swordsmen against *Stormy Petrel* and Ata's plan would fail. I kept still. I could stay here until Gio was either asleep or dead.

Beside the bed and ranged against the wall I saw six steel coffers. If they were full, Gio was undoubtedly a millionaire. Stacked on top of the strong boxes were three ormolu jewellery caskets with more primitive locks, because like many Awian mechanisms form is valued over function.

In front of my eyes, the paintings on the screen panels depicted domed buildings, nothing like those of the island. That they were ancient Awian palaces could not have escaped Gio's notice.

He drew his rapier and practised two or three sequences back and forth. He didn't seem satisfied. I watched, excruciating pins and needles prickling my legs. My tight grip on my sword hilt was embossing an image of twisted metal wire into my palm.

Gio held his rapier over his shoulder, pounced to the side table and gulped down his glass of gin. Nothing happened. Gio returned to a cool first guard, began to spar with his shadow, leaving white dints in the plaster. I quietly stretched to see. He should be writhing in paroxysms by now, on the floor, in agony. He should be quickly asphyxiating, tongue too swollen to scream.

I could not for the eternal life of me think what had gone wrong. The poison was having no effect at all. In a few minutes Gio finished his exercises and, looking perfectly healthy, strode towards me. He was coming to close the shutters; I would be trapped inside. As soon as he passes the screen he'll see me. He was just one step away.

I sprang out and made a dive for the window but it was too far. I landed in front of it, facing Gio.

His face was grotesque with astonishment. '*Jant*?' He snatched himself into guard, with me at sword point. His rapier's bright tip hovered a centimetre away from my chest. I shuffled back until my calves pressed the window ledge, the night air behind me. I kept my hands down, in surrender. Gio's crazed eyes were wide, amazement stayed his hand. He checked the doorway – if I was here, the other Eszai might be closing in. 'Where's Wrenn? What were you doing?'

He saw my glance flick to the empty gin glass. I was so confused, I couldn't help but look. No man should stand upright after imbibing that much belladonna. 'Poison?' he whispered; he knew my history. His face went white with fury. 'You cowardly bastard! I'll pour it down your throat! How long before it takes effect? Answer, damn you!' Fear high-pitched his voice. 'What have I drunk? *What is it?*'

I said nothing out of sheer bewilderment; Gio should be very dead by now. My coat leather split at the breast under the pressure of his rapier point. He shouted, 'Tirrick! Help! I've been poisoned! Assassin! Quickly!'

Voices on the mezzanine took up the shout: 'Gio's been poisoned!' 'I knew the Trisians would try something!'

Gio leant forward with a deep, earnest look. 'Comet, do you blame me? Rejected from the Circle, you'd do the same.' He urged me to answer with a manic little nod. I made no move. He suddenly growled with hatred and drew his arm back for the thrust.

I dived backwards out of the window. I fell, back-flipped, spun into a full somersault, fighting to free my wings. Firelight stretched into a blur. Stars below me, white granite above. I forced my wings open. The left one bruised hard against a column. I flapped frantically to get air under them and banked breathlessly over the square. The rebels were all yelling but I couldn't see them. I tried to get my bearings.

I fought desperately upwards to the level of the Senate House ledge. Gio leant out of the window, staring in mute horror. I pedalled my legs, pumped my wings and skimmed the roof above him, kicked off the ridge and glided out over the cliff.

I yelled to Lightning, 'Run!'

Lightning said, 'Oh, no. Hush.'

'Run! We must! Follow me.'

He had no choice; the rebels were staggering to their feet and reaching for weapons. They looked at each other, finding the nerve to cross the mosaic and attack. Lightning dashed round the corner, straight in front of them to the only conspicuous door – the library.

Below me I heard Gio swearing. 'Get me water! Get me the ship's surgeon!'

Was the aconitum belatedly taking effect? I called to Lightning, 'The second floor is defensible. I'll meet you up there!'

Lightning rammed the door open with his shoulder and turned in the entrance to face the men. 'I am' – he loosed an arrow and the nearest one dropped his rapier and grabbed his hand, turned and fled trailing drops of blood – 'Lightning. The immortal Archer.' He let another arrow fly at the largest man in the middle. It went straight through his hand that held an axe shaft. He jumped up with a howl and shook the arrowhead from the skin between his fingers. They all backed off. 'You will find the stairs hazardous.' Lightning nocked another arrow to string. 'I recommend caution, mob. Stay out.' He disappeared into the dark library.

I think he just made it worse. Five uninjured men clustered in. One kicked the door jamb. 'Fuck him!'

He looked up at me; a birthmark half-covered his baggy face, grey in the dim light. Another was ex-fyrd, with Brandoch's white trident badge on his tatty jacket. He called to bring more people round – a big hispid man whose jumper hood hung over his greatcoat; a burly woman, although in the darkness I couldn't be sure.

I went over them low and swept up to the window to bleed off speed. I flared my wings, braked hard, bending my flight feathers right back. My air speed dropped to nothing; I fell. I hit the window's louvre shutters with the soles of both boots. The shutters flew apart. I dropped through and landed squarely on my backside on the floor with my wings jammed in the window.

This storey was pitch-black but I smelt the serious scent of paper and venerable patinated wood. I scraped a match and held it up, seeing that the well-stacked shelves lined a single central aisle obstructed with crates of papers. Lightning ascended the railed stairwell, whirled round with his back to me. 'Comet? Where are you?'

By striking matches and peering through their weak light, I made my way along the aisle. He took deep breaths like a baited bear, stood statue-still, listening to the voices rising from the stairs.

'They're both trapped. You go first.'

'Are you kidding? That's Lord Micawater. *The* Archer. He'll shoot me in the eye as soon as—'

'Lord la-di-da. Rush them.'

'Both eyes, probably . . .'

Lightning snorted.

'They're *immortals*.'

'Then they can wait,' came the woman's voice.

Lightning lowered his bow slightly and sat on a table. I said, 'We're safe here for the moment.'

'Oh, we're safe, are we? Splendid. Shall I just make you a cup of coffee, then? This is *your fault*, Jant! We could have stayed unobserved. I was hidden. I was prepared to steal back to *Stormy Petrel*, whilst you could fly. But no; you cry out "Run!" Now the mob know we're here – and I'm cornered!' He shook a fist under my nose. His face was indistinct in the darkness but I could see he was pouch-eyed from lack of sleep. 'You irresponsible, foundling, Rhydanne—'

'Please don't use "Rhydanne" as an insult.'

'Drug addict. *Well*!'

'Well what? If you'd stayed by the columns they would have caught you. Gio saw me, then everything happened too fast to think.'

'Thinking is *supposed* to be your strong point. So, has he perished?'

Gio was far from dead. I protested, 'I don't understand it. Tolerance to that amount of belladonna isn't possible; there are no recorded cases of recovery.'

Lightning drummed his powerful fingers on the table, sounding like a small horse race. He held his great longbow in the other hand, finger over the arrow shaft across its grip. I lit an almond-shaped lamp and paced to the window. The outlaws milled about below.

I felt queasy knowing that the aconitum was useless. I might have needed it myself at any time. I have never actually used it because scolopendium is such a fast-acting drug that on the rare occasions I overdose I am not in a condition to remember it or operate the ring. I have carried aconitum since I first learned of its effects, fifty years ago. Ah, damn. I haven't replaced the tablets for – how long? Twenty years? And how many rainstorms have I flown through since then; how many long soaks in the bathhouse hot tub? It was a mistake that only an immortal could make. I said, 'The tablets have been in my ring too long. The potency must have degraded. Gio isn't suffering the full effect, if any at all.'

'You have never learned to be an Eszai,' Lightning said quietly, which was worse than his shouting. 'Let me take stock. Item: Gio will be determined to repay our attempt on his life. Item: it is four a.m., so we have a full four hours before *Petrel* arrives. Item: I only have one hundred arrows. Item: I am in considerable pain, and I will not be able to run for a sustained time.'

'What?'

For answer Lightning wormed his hand under the bandages around his waist. He held it up, red with blood, and wiped his fingers over the old scar on his palm. I hadn't seen the stain on his shirt. 'The activity agitated my wound; it has not closed completely. I didn't want to mention it, but it'll hinder me so you must know. Damn it, don't look so taken aback; just go and watch the mob.'

Shrunken by guilt, I turned to the nearest window, swung one shutter open. Lightning said, 'Do you see any of my fyrd?'

'No. There aren't many Lakeland or coast Awians rebelling; they know they need the Castle.'

'Good. I'm grateful for that at least.'

A mass of people filled the plaza between us and the Senate House, red-lit by the bonfire. Their noise was incredible: a tumult of gossip, jabbering fragments of conversation and false rumours – I could use those. I looked down on their heads; hoods, caps and woolly hats. I spotted the mesomorphic woman elbowing her way to the top of the boulevard. There was a general slow flow in that direction, like the start of a landslide. The air thrived with anxiety and excitement. I listened carefully, trying to separate phrases from the chaos: 'Let's go. No point in staying now Gio's snuffed it, is there? You heard what that prat Tirrick said.'

'I would if I could see a bloody thing. If there's two Eszai there'll be more, see? The whole Circle might be here.'

'Gio's *not* dead! His orders are to stay put.'

'I gave up all that order crap last year. Come on, think what we can pick up on our way to the ship.'

Gio Ami emerged from the Senate House hefting a large rectangular shield which had a metal bracket to hold and a big padded hook for his upper arm to bear the weight while carrying it. He immediately sheltered behind a pillar, sword drawn. He seemed dazed and was hangover-pale; I could not decide whether the poison was working on him with reduced efficacy, or whether he was sick with tension. He bent nearly double to yell, 'I'm here! I'm well. Look!'

'Shoot him,' I told Lightning.

Lightning dipped his head, trying to see Gio. I leant out and shouted at the crowd, 'Tornado's coming. Mist is sailing half the Castle's fleet into harbour! Thirty caravels full of fyrd and an Eszai on each ship!'

Gio's adherents drew towards him but the woman beckoned people to join her. 'Come on, we must reach the boats before Tornado arrives.' They surged towards the boulevard.

Gio tried again: 'Come back! Listen, they'll hang you as pirates! I'll pay you an equal share of everything in this town! There are no more ships! Alone, you've no chance against Mist!'

I stuck my head out. 'Tornado's fyrd will arrest anyone who stays with Gio! He'll be brought to justice!' I withdrew rapidly as an axe smashed into the window frame and fell onto the people beneath. I remarked to Lightning, 'Gio can't stop them leaving. I've managed to split them up.'

'Good.' He nodded.

A young swordsman gestured up at my window and babbled something vehemently. Gio shook his head but his friend continued to remonstrate. Gio pointed his rapier. 'No, Tirrick!'

Tirrick looked at Gio, seeing a dirty and dishevelled figure, and he must have realised at the same time as I did that Gio was not poisoned; it was his paranoia making him act as cautiously as if he was really feeling symptoms. I said, 'I think Ata's right – Gio is mad.'

Lightning said, 'Maybe, but fortunately Wrenn is even madder.'

Tirrick glanced at the guards standing by the library entrance, and then ran past Gio into the Senate House.

'Now the fencing masters are arguing between themselves.'

Lightning bit his lips together. 'I have always disliked Gio Ami because he professes to be a man of honour but he only lives by the codes that suit him – like his damn Ghallain traditions. He was married once, you know; if he still was then perhaps we would be spared this. But he feigned respect for the peninsula custom. They receive a candle as a gift on their wedding day. If they argue in the following years, they must light the candle and leave it burning for a time corresponding to the length of the argument. So, when it is burnt down completely, the couple are automatically considered divorced. It happened to Gio. He called his wife a troublemaker, separated her from the Circle, and home she rode to find her friends aged and infirm, or dead and buried. Poor lady.'

I strained to see further down the boulevard. White puffs of smoke like cotton bolls were rising from the base of the hill, where the harbour wall was hidden behind lines of houses. 'I think Mist's signalling. She must have figured that it's all gone wrong. I bet she's burning canoes . . . I just don't know if the signal is for me or the *Petrel*.'

Lightning watched the stairwell sourly. He said, 'Like amateurs we chose a stronger bow than we could manage and missed the mark. If I don't survive, Jant, will you remember to take my message?'

I had never heard a fatalistic word from Lightning before. 'I swear. My duty as Messenger.'

The sky above the Senate was pale grey now; I was able to distinguish the features of the people below. A dark coat became burgundy red, drab showed as light blue, a boy's hair was highlighted with henna. Dawn permeated a pallid, cloudless winter day.

I looked to the sea again and gave a yelp. The beacon islet was now dimly discernible, the surf breaking on its seaward shore. Heeling round it with four masts in full sail was a ship tiny with distance. She headed into harbour at a great rate of knots, her long pennants snaking. 'The *Petrel*! See, the *Petrel*'s coming in!'

Lightning sighed with relief. A few minutes later, some lads in padded jackets hurtled up the boulevard, pushed eagerly to Gio. Gio listened, then waved them aside and called out, 'This is it! We must meet the Castle's flagship. I tell you, there's only one caravel. There are two Eszai aboard and we'll overwhelm them. Let me have the satisfaction of dealing with Wrenn – and your prize is the *Stormy Petrel*!'

The crowd yelled. Gio lifted his shield and hastened across the square, shouting his rabble into a formation akin to a fyrd division. The Ghallain swordsmen he arranged at the front, then the biggest, roughest men, the Hacilith boys and a couple of harridan girls at the rear.

But the swordsmen at the library door refused to move and glowered when Gio beckoned to them. His authority had gone but he pretended that it didn't matter, gave up and returned to the thick column.

Lightning thought aloud: 'I can improve the odds for Wrenn and Ata.' He instantly flexed his bow and loosed. A man at the head of the column reeled with a scream and fell, the arrow through his thigh. Lightning selected another shaft from the quiver at his hip, let fly and the astonished lad behind the first man yowled and squatted to the ground. I could barely see the arrow projecting from his leg above the knee. Lightning started counting backwards from thirty, 'Twenty-eight, twenty-seven . . .' as he lamed each of the men along the nearest edge of the formation, who were arranged like targets in a gallery.

Hearing their screams, the column flashed shields along its length. It surged away from us, bending and abandoning the wounded men, leaving around twenty sprawling and crawling on the mosaic. One man cried loudly as he snapped the fletchings off the arrow and pulled the shaft out through his thigh.

Gio, invisible behind his shield, led his file to the boulevard. They emptied very quickly out of the square, hurried between the slender stone walls and snaked around the hairpin bends. They left the battered mosaic empty; Alyss and the Insects were carious with missing tesserae. Litter was stacked up in the corners against the library and ash blew out of the cooling bonfire into the colonnade. Lightning cleanly and methodically shot down the rearmost rebels in the column, hitting the left thigh of each man. 'You, four; and you, three . . . two . . . one. There. That's all the arrows I dare to spend. Is this not disagreeable work?'

Some footsteps scuttled on the floor below us. Lightning called, 'Join our gathering, by all means. But please introduce yourselves so I know who I'm shooting.'

A movement at the Senate House caught our attention. A swordsman began to back out, lugging one of Gio's heavy coffers between himself and his friend. Another followed, and a fourth, until all the chests and ornate boxes containing Gio's fortune were lined up on the mosaic.

Lightning asked, 'What are those?' but I hardly heard him because I was seething with anger. Tirrick, the goateed little creep, was stealing the treasure and I could do nothing about it.

The senators were next to stumble out of the door at the foot of the pillars. A frightened youth in a pale tunic, then a dumpy old man were corralled by the swordsmen. Vendace came out last, reluctantly, being goaded by Tirrick behind him. The tall, wiry Trisian leant his head at a strange angle because Tirrick held a dagger across his throat. Tirrick shoved him out onto the mosaic, and looked straight up at our window with a bold smile.

# CHAPTER 21

'They're parading the senators where we can see them,' I said.

'Tirrick,' said Lightning. 'I know the type. Privileged but strident and embittered, the youngest son of a minor noble.' He licked his fingers and held them out of the window to judge the breeze. Then his fingertips rasped over the arrow fletchings and settled on the string. Tirrick angled his dagger across Vendace's scrawny neck and called, 'We'll kill one of these for every shot you loose!'

Vendace rolled his eyes and stamped his foot. His brown arms were rigid by his sides.

I said, 'The boxes are full of money. I think the swordsmen will take it to the ship, with the senators as hostages to shield themselves. It's our chance to escape. Oh fuck, no it isn't . . .'

Around twenty swordsmen ran out of the colonnade, carrying lamps and oil jugs with spouts. Lightning drew on them but saw Tirrick's blade bite against Vendace's skin, and didn't loose. The guards around the library door let them speed through. Crashes came up from below, smashing pottery, rustling and tearing.

A heavy thump shook the floor as the men pulled a bookshelf over. I heard them kicking the scrolls into heaps. 'They're going to burn the library!' I darted to the stairs and called down, 'Stop! In the name of San and the will of god. How *dare* you?'

A voice shrugged, 'Come out and be executed or stay there and char.'

But these are books – all the books of Tris. 'You *must* not,' I yelled desperately.

A blue-grey twist rose from the stairwell like cigarette smoke. Within seconds it widened to fill the whole well. From the window I saw the swordsmen pouring out onto the mosaic, shoving the guards back in their haste to escape. 'The fire's caught! Ready yourselves, they have to surrender. It's going up!'

Smoke billowed past me in a thick stream and drifted along the ceiling. Lightning released the tension on his bowstring. 'We have to break out. There are a dozen fencing masters. We can deal with them, but the senators will die.'

'The books!' I wailed. 'I can't leave—'

'Don't be stupid!'

'Maybe there's another way down.' Grey wreaths shrouded the rafters completely and were descending extremely quickly to fill the room. I fumbled through a stack of leather-bound books on the table and slipped them into my coat pockets. I picked up the lantern. 'Wait here. I'll check the far end.'

Lightning began coughing loudly. I called, 'Stoop low. Slouch down under it.' I had been in a burning building before and, as far as I knew, he had not. But my lungs hurt as I sucked smoke and I started choking more than him.

I had to save the books, as many as I could carry. I strode down the aisle snatching them from the shelves. I stuffed one in my waistband, another in my belt. I had no time to translate the titles; I couldn't see with the smoke stinging my eyes. I didn't know what I was snatching. I piled them frantically in the crook of my left arm, discarded a heavy tome, selected two more haphazardly. I thought, I'm rescuing a handful of volumes at random to represent the total knowledge of an entire culture. Which were most worthwhile? Were these engineering, cookery or poetry? Or even bloody fiction? I had no way of judging. I spat out the cloying smoke and the stack buckled in my arms. I reached the end of the library – which was just a blank wall – and I dropped all the books with a series of thuds.

Recognisable but horribly out of place, grey mottled, fibrous drapes strung between the last two bookcases: Insect paper. They looked folded but were as hard as concrete. They curved up from the shelves and blurred into the smoke creeping down from the beams.

Two long, brown forelegs emerged from the nest. The Insect's black spiny foot clicked down onto the floor between my boots, and its three claws articulated shut. I backed into the opposite bay.

The Insect ducked its triangular head and slipped out from between the bookcases. Its eyes' tessellations reflected the lamp-lit swirling smoke. It brushed a fringe on its front right leg over them. It must have pulled out Wrenn's rapier, because the hole through its thorax was now a deep concavity filled with smooth new shell. It had sloughed its skin and was even bigger than I remembered. The high joints of its back legs loomed out of the smoke.

Two club-shaped black palps shuffled like a pair of hands rubbing together. They retracted and the scissor jaws opened and shut. It lifted a foreleg and cleaned its single crooked antenna through filaments inside its knee.

Lightning flexed his bow and spoke with his lips to the string, 'Step aside.' Through the smoke he was just a silhouette blurred by the tears streaming from my eyes. I pressed my coat cuff to my nose and mouth. In another thirty seconds the room would be full and I could hear crackling from below.

'Wait!' The Insect stood still, close enough for me to see the scars and impressions I had made with my axe. A row of black spines four-wide supported the upper surface of its striped abdomen. The pale underside pulsed as it curled its abdomen under itself, pumping air through its spiracles which were wide open.

'Wait. It doesn't like the smoke.'

Its antenna flicked forward, sensing for the clean air. It jolted into an involuntary crouch. 'It's going to run – let it pass!'

The Insect leapt. It hurtled past Lightning, stretched its full length and reached over the handrail, down into the stairwell. Its back sword-shaped femurs kicked and claws scrabbled on the blistering varnish, then it disappeared into the gusting smoke. I ran after it instantly; Lightning seemed bewildered so I grasped his arm and urged him to the steps.

We took deep breaths and plunged down. I patted my hair – it felt so hot I thought it was alight. Lightning held his hand over his mouth and the tip of his bow rattled off the ceiling. The steep steps were opaque with smoke. Perspiration and tears trickled down my face.

We stumbled to the ground floor, onto ten centimetres of fallen books. They slid over each other, making the floor slippery. I led Lightning around the tall shapes of leaning shelves. We crushed scorching scrolls underfoot with a sound like old Insect shell. Even now I was torn with the desire to rake them up. The fire's crackling built into a steady sibilance and its raw orange light leapt behind the smoke, illuminating the surfaces of the billowing wreaths.

Lines of yellow flame spread between the parquet blocks. By the windows, flames began to lengthen and bend as air flow sucked them out of the shutters.

'Can't breathe,' I said weakly. 'Where's . . . the fucking door?' The unbearable heat singed my feathers, my reddened skin stung. The pages of open books on the floor around us were curling and turning brown spontaneously. I saw one burst into flame.

I pointed to the rectangle of pale morning light; we rushed through without readying our weapons. Getting out of the smoke was all that mattered.

The men who had been guarding the door were spilt on the mosaic in a fan of visceral blood. We crossed the threshold with smoke pouring out above us. One had died quickly, eyes open, from a horrible gash that opened his belly to the sternum. Another crumpled in a red pool so thick the Insect must have severed an artery, though I couldn't see the wound. The arm of a third man lay beside a rapier some way off.

The Insect did not pause to clean its mandibles. It was confused by the scents and invigorated by the fresh air. Its six feet left prints, its knee joints bunched and separated as it dashed towards the senators and swordsmen. Their white clothes reflected in its directionless eyes. Their mouths were round in astonishment. Every one of the swordsmen bolted, including Tirrick, leaving the senators in the Insect's path.

Lightning leant into his bow and bent it fully with the strength of his shoulders. The broadhead point drew back to the grip. Across the square the Insect reared up before Vendace. Lightning straightened his fingers, released the string with a crack and the arrow whistled past me.

The Insect's foreclaws lashed the air in front of Vendace, then it fell sideways. It curled on its right side, the arched plates of its abdomen sliding over each other as it coiled and throbbed. A spasm went through it that flexed all its joints and pulled its limbs in, like the legs of a dead crab. They steepled angularly together, its feet drawn up to the six semi-translucent ball joints under its thorax. By the sunken ring at the base of its feeler, Lightning's arrow shaft made a second antenna. The shell gaped around it, an open crack showing an organ of dark brown gel deep inside.

The senators gazed at it, and at the library. All the erudition of Tris was rising with the fire. I faced the intolerable furnace as if it was a punishment and spread my wings to accept and be consumed by it. Rolls of heat belched out, shelves split with creaks and thuds. Tremendous flames raged through the library I respected so much; I felt sick in the pit of my stomach.

'Shira!' Lightning called. 'Come here, why are you standing so close? It's falling apart!'

'No. The books are burning . . . What has Gio *done*?'

'Get a grip! Speak to the senators.'

I was numbly aware of Lightning ushering the Trisian leaders to the boulevard. Behind us, the coffers lay forgotten. I thought, if I live through this I'll claim them. The Trisians would disregard the treasure as dross, so I relinquished it for the time being, avoided the dead

Insect and stepped over three or four agonised rebels with arrows in their thighs, and ran to catch up with them. They were hurrying down the path with appalled backward glances.

Vendace was holding one of the senators tightly, a young lady. She was kicking and biting, frenziedly struggling and pulling in the direction of the library. I ran to help but Vendace snapped at me, 'She's Danio's successor. Don't let her go; she'll run in to the fire. Every time you come here, you put an end to our librarians!'

We tried to calm the hysterical girl. I explained to Lightning, who said candidly, 'I know how she feels. People pass away, there are always more, but the books are irreplaceable. They're the immortal part of Zascai – how many lifetimes are burning to cinders in there?'

I said to Vendace, 'You saw how Gio's men treated you. They're causing this catastrophe, not us. We'll deliver you from them before they destroy the rest of town. Lightning shot the Insect dead. We were sent to protect you from it and from Gio; he's a wanted criminal in the Fourlands.'

Vendace, mystified, turned his pinched, resilient face from myself to the Archer. The Senate had prized Gio's rhetoric so highly that they found it hard to trust our actions. As I walked quickly they pressed close, trying to hear over the sound of the blaze. With an ear-splitting screech and crash, the library roof caved in at its mid-point. Timbers dangled like fingers from both sides. Glowing tiles slid into the fissure, adding to the noise; the rumble grew to a roar. Sparks whirled up and fell on the roof of the Senate House. It was hypnotic.

Lightning said, 'Jant, tell them that I'll see them to a safe place, then I'll clear looters from the avenue as far as the rear of Gio's column.'

I asked, 'Are you well enough?'

'I believe so.'

'Then I'll fly over Mist and Serein, and join you on the main road.'

An elderly senator with a rookery voice coughed. '*What* is going on? Where's Gio?'

I changed language and said, 'He's causing the mayhem – I'm going to find out. Lightning will help you, if you please lead him to a place of refuge. I'm sorry, I am really sorry.'

Vendace pointed a shaking finger at the Amarot. Flames were now lapping on the Senate House roof. Driven to incandescence by the wind, the fire spread to the apartments on its upper storey and began to engulf them. 'No amount of apologising will ever repair that sacrilege!'

When we reached the base of the crag, Vendace directed Lightning towards a road called First Street. I left them, and as soon as I carved into the air I found myself battling against the wind being sucked into the inferno. It whipped round the crag in one-hundred-kilometre-per-hour gusts, causing a swirling column of vertical flame to rise eighty metres above the devastated library.

Smoke layered and drifted out at the height of the Amarot. It completely blocked the sunrise and shadowed the town. Burning embers were falling into the gardens of the villas below. The whitewashed walls looked grey and the boulevard was littered with spoil and broken furniture dragged out by the rebels; here and there lay the bodies of the Trisians who had tried to stop them.

Sleepy residents stumbled into the street, looking up at the crag and trying to understand. At the edge of town, people panicked and began moving towards the harbour. I saw Capharnai of all ages responding to a call to make a bucket chain. About two hundred people filled pails, pans and bowls from cisterns and carried them up the winding road to the Amarot, but the air was unbreathable; the rising heat and wind stopped them before they reached the mosaic. A few of the lamed rebels who were still lying among the boxes of money, writhed as they inhaled smoke. Their clothes and hair caught fire spontaneously.

I soared higher, because I was alarming the Capharnai and they were wasting their time watching me. I lost sight of the peach-coloured sky beyond the edges of the smoke pall. Flocks of pigeons sped round the tiny rooftops, grouping to roost, confused by the eerie eclipse light. Dawn would not end; the light was dim, as if it was still seven a.m.

The looters were fanning out through the top of town, kicking in doors and pulling shutters off their hinges, leaving a wake of debris, barking dogs and half-eaten food.

Pages and whole blackened pamphlets, scroll fragments burnt thin, jostled up in the smoke then fell on the town as hot ash. The residue of hundreds of thousands of books was raining over Capharnaum. The gloaming light and the roar of the library added to the rebels' edginess. It was much louder than the sound of the wind on my wings.

Gio's rabble now packed the lower half of the main street, blocking the wide road as they progressed down the slope towards the harbour. Gio walked ahead of them with his rapier drawn. His column was twice the size of Mist's tight ranks.

Mist's fyrd was marching up the street from the *Stormy Petrel*. The boatswains were drumming; their beats got louder as I dropped height and passed over them. I spotted Mist leading by Wrenn's side; she looked up and raised her hand. She had tied her shawl around her waist, revealing a cuirass and backplate. Wrenn wasn't wearing armour; he was in his fyrd fatigues. He was looking for Gio, dissatisfied with their disputable duel in the forest. He was determined to beat Gio on equal terms and leave no doubt that he deserved to be immortal.

Mist was surrounded on all sides by crossbowmen and a bodyguard of her strongest sailors, all in half-armour. After that came one hundred and fifty Awndyn men carrying halberds and spears; no space to wield pikes. They wore dark green brigandines; their helmets shone like globular mirrors.

As I watched, the rear of Ata's column stopped at the quay and the rest separated and continued up the street. She had left about fifty men, a fyrd lamai unit, to protect *Stormy Petrel* moored, a hundred metres behind Gio's ships. From *Petrel's* forecastle and poop deck, archers looked out. Both her gangplanks were down but coloured shields lined her railings. The longbowmen were tense, watching the rebel defectors who ran, laden with loot, out of the ends of the parallel streets. They raced up the *Pavonine's* gangway to a deck that seethed with drawn weapons; white faces ugly with fear stared up at me. They had turned pirate; they were prepared to defend their carrack to the death.

When Gio's rabble caught sight of Mist's vanguard, rebels in ones and twos began to melt away from his column, down the alleys and into the streets of the grid. They turned left and right along the intersecting roads like counters in a board game. I decided that their movements were too random to be tactical, even before I saw them start smashing shop shutters and grabbing whatever was inside.

Mist's fyrd and Gio's horde stopped with twenty metres between them. There was a second's silence in which Gio, shield on his arm, walked forward of his line and scanned the people opposing him, looking for Wrenn.

The Awndyn Fyrd captain called, 'Crossbowmen! Span. Latch. Loose!' They shot straight into the rebel front at short range, aiming at the fencing masters, knowing they were the most dangerous. The metal Insect-killing bolts cut past shop canopies and statues, burying themselves in men's faces, chests and bellies. I saw black bolt points project from their backs.

The crossbowmen's partners stepped forward with a shout, raised and slammed their green and white shields into a wall, hustling into position across the road. Behind the shields, the crossbowmen began to reload.

Gio's men waited in horror for the next barrage. Heads bobbed up and down as some men split off down the side streets but most were trapped in the centre.

The shields were lowered, crossbows levelled. 'Latch! Loose!' Another barrage flew at Gio's front line. The last of the fencing masters fell, lifeless or mortally wounded. Gio peered from behind his shield; swung his arm. 'Forward! Break the wall! Bear down the shields!'

A wave of three hundred men together started running. The front of the column seemed to flake off, as faster and faster they closed the gap. They jumped high, crashed into the shields at full tilt, hitting them with their shoulders and forcing them down. Their swords thrust over the tops, into the necks and faces of the bearers.

The crossbowmen slung their bows into holsters on their backs, drew their swords and surged forward against the rebels. The confused mass began to shove up and down the street.

I saw that Ata's spearmen were trapped towards the rear of her host. Surely that was a mistake – wouldn't they be better than the crossbows? Crossbowmen had served Ata well five years ago; now she was relying on them too much. The shield wall was perfect but it should be backed by spears. The fyrd are simply following their usual procedure: Insect-fighting tactics. They're wrong but even Ata hasn't noticed the discrepancy.

Both the fyrd and the insurgents tried to outflank each other. From above I watched the side streets filling. As the melee widened, the columns in the boulevard shortened, with Wrenn and Gio in the exact centre.

I called to the fyrd who were exploring the alleys, and led them down the right routes to ambush the rebels, who were more used to fighting in side streets. I landed and directed a group; we surprised five of Gio's men before they could rejoin the main column, and killed them all.

I returned to the air, where I could easily distinguish Mist's bodyguards. I occasionally glimpsed her face but she no longer had time to look up at me. The press was so intense, she held her curved Wrought sword with the convex arc uppermost to thrust rather than slice. Her voice carried – she screamed commands to surround Gio and disarm him. Whenever he could, Gio yelled at his rebels to close in on Mist.

In Lowespass, women soldiers have always successfully fought Insects. The culls follow procedures; the women help each other and men sometimes back them up. The difference in strength was not important when six or seven infantry recruits can tackle an Insect together, or women can join the cavalry and ride destriers. But in this crush they were fighting one-on-one against men, and I gravely feared for them.

Capharnai families peeked from the windows of their houses above the shops all along the street. They were stranded in their homes, witnessing a scene they couldn't hope to understand. They saw the heads of men wrestling and stabbing along the centre line, and behind them, filling the street above and below, a pack of foreigners in strange clothes facing each other, putting pressure on the breathless crush. The strangers were so eager to push forward to the fight that they trampled dead bodies. At the end of the street, flames piled up from the civic centre and smoke boiled like spit in lamp oil. The Capharnai neighbours looked helpless, not knowing what to do. I shouted, 'Stay inside! Don't get involved – they fight each other, not Trisians!'

They saw their own shops vandalised below them. Their faces disappeared from the windows as they began barricading themselves into their upper rooms.

I glanced back; the library was now a roofless shell, the floors were falling through and just the façade was left; with flames leaping in the windows surrounded by blackened stonework it looked like an animated skeleton.

Coruscating sparks and dull fragile ash dropped on us. I beat my wings to dislodge flakes from the feathers, thinking: The town is being covered in burnt knowledge.

Gio was looking for Wrenn, carving his own men aside. I landed on the nearest roof to watch, searching the alleys below for a crossbow to pick up. Gio, wild-eyed, saw Mist's bodyguards and Wrenn beside them in an area of calm because no fighter would engage with him.

Gio raised his rapier and saluted. 'Well, look if it isn't the *novice*.'

'Good morning,' smiled Wrenn.

Gio snarled, 'You could have chosen better last words.'

First-blood fencing in the amphitheatre was just an entertainment; no rules apply in a duel to the death. They watched each other with cool anticipation; Capharnaum didn't exist for them. They were in a world of two people, challenger and challenged.

There are no words in that world. I know, because I have been there.

Gio swept his rapier down in the rage cut. 'You stole my name,' he said. 'I'll be Serein again. I am good enough. I Challenge you, Serein Wrenn.'

Wrenn levelled his blade. 'Just run onto this and save me the effort.'

I took off and climbed above them through the deafening battle's noise.

They dropped the pretence of faking other styles to conceal their own. They flew at each other eager for blood. Gio rushed to chop at Wrenn; at the same time a bystander tried to catch him but Wrenn smashed his teeth with the rapier pommel.

Wrenn lunged at Gio, reprised. Gio swiped it aside with a blow that would have shattered a lesser blade than the 1969 Sword. I thought: How long can they keep this up? But I knew the answer – at least four hours.

Gio pointed his rapier, its lanyard loose around his wrist. He lunged to Wrenn's dagger side. Wrenn swept his rapier across – clash! – disengaged and cut down aiming for the sensitive bone of Gio's shin.

Gio jumped on the spot then attacked. Wrenn parried, riposted, enveloped Gio's blade in quatre, made as if to beat him on the arm and tried to stab him in the forehead. Gio spun away in a move that took me two years to learn. His thigh boots slipped on the pavement. He was trying to predict Wrenn's actions four or five moves in advance.

In a split second Wrenn slid his rapier tip through Gio's swept hilt, sliced the skin off his knuckles, withdrew the blade. Gio's grip became slippery on the freely-running blood. He hid his sword hand with his dagger, so Wrenn couldn't see to predict the direction of the next blow.

Their motions were wide; their heads ducked to avoid being cut in the eyes, watching with the faster speed of their peripheral vision. Their flexed sword arms were close to the body for strength. They hacked at the nearest enemies whenever they had a chance and the melee backed away from them, leaving them in a clear space. The fighting was spreading up and down the street and fragmenting, tussling groups of men dispersing down the side alleys. The densest part of the fighting eddied around Ata's bodyguard; spearmen behind, rebels ahead. Five sailors linked arms, trying to preserve a space around her so she could breathe.

I'm doing no good here, entranced by the duel. I need a firebrand to drop on Gio.

I flew back to find Lightning. It was easy, because he was the only person in Fourlands clothes walking down the middle of the broad street. Behind him, the road rose up the hillside backed by the incredible blaze. He was oblivious to the Capharnai around him, with their crying children, bucket chains and packs of belongings. He sniped unerringly at the small groups of rebels-turned-pirates who were all busy with different intents. Some scavenged like wolves; a man pulled down a gold street-lamp bracket; two lechers were held at bay by a Trisian man defending his daughter.

Lightning limped on his left side, moving slowly. Conserving his energy, he held his mighty bow horizontally with the arrow on top, drawing back the heel of his hand to fit in the hollow of his cheek. He used short-distance arrows, colour-coded with white flights, and let fly at the looters. Anyone who touched a shop shutter or ran from a house with an armful of gold was sent reeling with an arrow through bicep or thigh.

I glided over and called. I landed and ran to a halt beside him. 'Gio and Wrenn are duelling! Ata's caught in the crush – we have to help her.'

I drew my sword and we continued downhill towards the rotunda at the roads' mid-point. Lightning never missed a shot, counting under his breath, 'Fifty-five. Fifty-four. Three . . . Two . . .'

I scanned the windows for any movement that might end with a knife in my back. Beyond the forum we passed a precinct of narrow streets. We looked down the nearest and saw a gang of rebels heaving at a solid door. The first was a weasly man with baggy, low-crotched jeans. He had his shoulder to the cracking panels and the others all added their weight. They noticed Lightning and I but renewed their assault on the building. Inside, women were screaming in Trisian so rapid and full of dialect I couldn't understand. From the first-floor window an elegant lady with ringletted hair, a white chiton dress and red nails hurled terracotta dishes down on the besiegers. They angled their arms over their heads and kept pushing.

'Hey!' yelled Lightning. 'Away from that door! Jant, what are they shouting? What is this place?'

I read a tiny inscription on a stone block set into the wall: *Salema's Imbroglio*

'It's an imbroglio; in Trisian, I mean. A brothel.'

The Archer raised his eyebrows. 'I see. Then we must save the honour of these ladies – regardless of whether they have any honour or no.' He loosed at the thin-faced Awian. The arrow rammed straight through the man's leg and into the wood. Its shaft made a high-pitched crunch of gristle, dimpling his jeans' fabric into his knee, locking it out straight. He tried to step forward but was fastened to the door. He screamed and hammered his fists and free leg against it.

'Are you all right?' said his friend, being slow on the uptake.

He screamed, 'Pull it out!'

'You can't, it's barbed.' Lightning spanned his bow. 'And if you try, I'll kill you both.'

The gang sloped off, then broke up and ran towards the forum. Lightning called to the whores, 'I promise you'll come to no harm.'

'I'm sorry,' the would-be rapist pleaded, leaning forward with both hands over his knee.

'You will be,' Lightning commented, without moving the arrow trained on him.

'Saker, what are you doing?' I said, disturbed by this change.

The rapist's eyes bulged. His left leg kicked, shoe sole scraping the step. He stuttered, 'No, no! I'll—'

'You'll do what, exactly?' Lightning said, driven to fury by the man's Donaise accent. He loosed the arrow; it pinned the rapist's left leg to a panel. It met some resistance at the kneecap but drove easily between the articulated surfaces of the joint behind and split the wood. Its arrowhead was a shiny stud in his flattened and mushy knee.

Lightning selected another arrow. 'My card. Seeing as you need reminding who we are.' He shot again, pinning the man's right elbow to the door. A wedge of broken bone clicked away from the metal point pushing past it.

The rapist howled and sobbed, 'Why? Oh god, help . . . WhataveI-done?' He turned his head and vomited onto the top step.

'You know who we are!' Lightning shouted. 'But still you have to plead, you have to ask! You think Tris is beyond the reach of the Castle! You take advantage of this gentle town!'

Before I could stop Lightning he whipped out a fourth arrow. He couldn't be enjoying this. I dashed in front of him. 'Stop! Are you mad?'

Stony-faced, he aimed over my shoulder. 'The lout has an elbow left . . .'

'Leave him!' I shouted.

'Rape is the worst of crimes,' Lightning muttered. He shook himself and looked up to where the beautiful whores were leaning out watching, some timidly, some brazenly. 'Interpret for me, Jant,' he said, and called, 'All right, girls. Do with him what you will.'

We walked away from the man's beast noise. With his whole shocking strength he made every breath a scream.

The Capharnai watched in horror from their doorways. They couldn't distinguish Lightning and I from the rebels. A young lad, his trousers spattered with somebody else's blood, ran from the piazza and confronted us. He glared and brandished one of our broadswords, holding it like a tennis racquet. Lightning hesitated. I flicked my dreadlocks back, spread my double-jointed hands and wings and roared, 'Raaaah!'

The boy yelled and fled. Lightning looked impressed.

At the next intersection stood one of the unidentifiable poles topped by a right-angled black and white bar. A man stood beside it, manipulating levers that pulled wires to make the plank swing in well-defined motions, somewhat like a flag. He looked up the street to another pole at the foot of the smoke-obscured Amarot and operated the levers to follow its movements. A third device distant at the edge of the town replicated his signals a second later. I realised these were not standards at all; it was a system of communication, and quicker than anything I could provide. Even in the midst of the chaos I thought, I'll make this innovation my own. I'll put this system on the Lowespass peel towers instead of the beacons to monitor Insect advances lest someone else beats me to it.

We reached the rotunda that stood over the main crossroads, a domed folly no bigger than a room. It had round columns supporting arches taking in the boulevard and the north–south road and the boulevard. Someone had hacked great chunks of plaster off the interior walls surfaced with blue gems.

A woman wearing a fyrd greatcoat with the collar up was energetically prising squares of sapphire out of the mosaic. Seeing Lightning's arrowhead levelled at her, she shrank back, tossed up her knife and caught it by the point, made as if to throw it at him.

Lightning swung slightly left and shot at the edge of the nearest pillar. The arrow hit it obliquely, glanced off into the shade inside and she felt the breeze as it zipped past her face. She burst from the northern arch, away between the empty pavement tea shops, her coat streaming behind her. Lightning bowed – he could even bow sarcastically.

The rear of Gio's column was two hundred metres below us on the road. We could see the backs of heads, sallet points or bandanna knots at the napes of their necks. Two men in the last line noticed us, nudged their friends and the motion rippled out until everyone at the rear turned round. They were only inclined to watch us until one man, with a look of hatred, pulled a bolt from his bandolier, cocked his crossbow and raised it to his shoulder. Nine or ten others followed suit; I dodged inside the rotunda but Lightning stood still, in disbelief. I urged, 'Come on!'

Lightning shook his head as the men pulled their triggers and a barrage of bolts flew at us. Out of range, they dropped and struck the pavement, and the broken pieces skidded, stopping two metres from Lightning's feet. He stepped forward and kicked them, as if to check they were real and he wasn't imagining it. He sounded aggrieved. 'What have I done to warrant all this? They think they can outshoot me. I'll attempt to confer with them.'

'*Talk* to them?' I stopped because Lightning took a handful of distance arrows, long thin shafts with stiff triangular red and yellow fletchings. He held them together with his bow grip, and shot rapidly along the line. 'Twenty, nineteen, eighteen.' Another handful. 'Seventeen, sixteen, fifteen.' The rebels ran like their arses were on fire, but they all ended up lying on the ground moaning or yelling. People in the next line pointed us out then made a break for it, forced to run towards us to reach the side streets' empty entrances.

The horn tips of Lightning's longbow shook. He lowered it, breathing deeply, gazing downhill to the churning front of the fray where Gio and Wrenn appeared and disappeared. His legs were trembling and he was pale with pain.

I watched the Sailor's bodyguards, in dark blue and steel, hacking at the rebels with Ata close behind. From the midst of Gio's rabble a spear looped up, fell steeply onto them. It hit Ata, impacting on her breastplate. She staggered, unhurt but knocked off balance. The mob surged forward and she fell under their feet, out of view. Her bodyguards lurched back, tried to stay upright by grabbing each other and the soldiers around, but simply pulled people down together, opening a hole in the crowd.

'Get up,' I said. 'Quick, Saker; shoot!'

Lightning now shot to kill, aiming at the rebels standing over Ata, in the most accurate volley I had ever seen: an arrow every two seconds.

'Get up! Get *up*!' he muttered.

The rebels fell around the place where Ata had gone down. He picked them off in the solid crush, no space between them. They couldn't even raise their shields. The arrows started to hit the same men again and again; dead bodies kept upright in the crush were filling with them, their heads and shoulders pinned with the bicolour flights, but Ata and the men stabbing her were underneath. We couldn't see her.

The bodyguards tried to shove forward, stabbing the rebels facing them in chests and stomachs. They shouted and tugged at the clothes of the men to either side, urging them to push ahead.

Lightning hissed in exasperation, 'I can't get a clear line of sight. Nine. Eight. Seven. Move out the way!'

His quiver was nearly empty. The ends of his bow vibrated; rapidly his right hand reached down for the short nocks, pulled one up and fitted it to string. Hooked the string with three bent fingers. Drew it past his ear to the side of his head, swinging his shoulder back for a couple of extra centimetres.

He shot with unflagging speed but dimples appeared around his pursed lips. 'Five, four. Jant, brace yourself; the Circle is going to break.'

Zascai are slaughtering Mist. And there's nothing I can do. I tried to feel it starting – couldn't – and it hit me. Time rushed past us; I felt torn across the middle. My awareness raced out, expanding in all directions. It stretched, flattened, spread thinner and infinitely thinner until my own identity and individuality vanished. I lost consciousness of my surroundings. I ceased to exist. The Circle reformed with a snap. I woke and blinked around at the battered shopfronts and blue domed ceiling overhead.

It happened so quickly I was still on my feet but I had dropped my sword. I felt cold, very aware of my body and the battle's noise.

'Three, two . . .' Lightning stopped with an arrow at string. 'I . . . I am still here,' he said deliriously. We looked at each other, appalled that Ata was dead.

'Killed by Zascai,' he whispered.

At the battlefront crush, Serein Wrenn staggered. New to the Circle, he didn't understand what had happened. Gio, on the other hand, had known it well. He took advantage and cut at Wrenn's forehead, drawing a red line across his temple to blind him with blood.

Wrenn came to and tried to defend himself but, concentration lost, all he could do was retreat. Gio pushed him back, slashing at his face to further unnerve him.

'Serein!' Lightning raised his bow again, arced an arrow up high over the entire rebels' column.

I just had time to see that someone had grabbed Wrenn from behind. Wrenn, still confused, struggled to free himself. The arrow came straight down into the top of the assailant's head; he crumpled up.

'One.' Lightning fitted his penultimate arrow to the binding on his bowstring. Behind Wrenn a man in a painted leather jacket brandishing a curved falchion leapt at him. Lightning drew and loosed; the arrow pierced the man's forehead and his body fell, knocking Wrenn. The crowd realised that anyone who closed with Wrenn received an arrow between the eyes. They left the duellists alone.

The Archer gasped, 'Serein is an Eszai and must win his own duel. But I made it an even fight; there won't be two Eszai murdered today.'

His shirt hem was soaked with blood; it was spreading to the tops of his trousers.

At the place where Mist's dismembered body was being trodden underfoot, someone raised a halberd, her head on the spike. I could only tell by the short white hair, because it was crushed and gashed. The pole turned and the head jigged round to face us. Its indigo eyes were turned up, its mouth open, its nose flattened and bloody.

Lightning's legs buckled. He staggered back to the rotunda wall, sat down against it, then collapsed sideways leaving a smear of blood. I helped him sit upright with the bow across his knees. He pulled the leather tab off his right hand with his teeth and dropped it. His face was ashen. 'The animals. How could they do that – tear her apart? An Eszai, and Cyan's mother . . . Immortality is pointless in the crush. We're too used to Insects. They don't throw spears. Damn, don't you feel like you've died? I hate feeling someone else's death and the years I've cheated catching up with me. You know . . . we all become a second older before San mends the Circle.' He bowed his head. 'You know that with me it adds up to minutes . . .'

Lightning hugged arms around his waist and squeezed his eyes shut in agony. I crouched and laid a hand on his shoulder, trying to bring him round because he was drifting and talking to himself. 'They killed her. Her schemes were useless . . . I don't know what they'll do next.'

He could not fight in this condition, and the rotunda gave sparse cover. Lightning knew this and made a tremendous effort. He nocked his last arrow and eased his short sword loose in its scabbard though it took all his mettle to lift it.

'Wait and gather your strength,' I said.

He nodded. 'Yes. I'll try to make my way back to Rayne . . . I'll meet you at the *Petrel*.' He sighed, chin on his chest. He was thinking about Mist; the reality hitting him was as incapacitating as the wound. 'You and Serein must persevere. Kill Gio, for Ata . . . for me. You are Eszai and that is your purpose.'

He looked so ill that I didn't want him to tangle with any more rebels. 'Don't stay here, those bastards will come up. Go all the way to the end of Fifth Street before you turn down to the harbour. The roads are quieter at the edge of town. Saker, I really think—'

He spoke through gritted teeth. '"Saker, I really think" nothing. Into the air and *stop this fight*!'

He watched me pick up two jewel-encrusted pieces of plaster, one in each hand. I ran to take off.

I dived at Gio and dumped both bricks on him. They hit him, one on his tow-head, one on his forearm, and he reeled. Wrenn jumped forward and thrust.

Gio's neat last-minute parry saved him – the rapiers clanged hilt to hilt. Their blades bound, they wrestled. Gio kicked Wrenn's shin. The muscle fluttered in Wrenn's calf but he threw the taller man back and wiped blood from his eyes.

'Shoot him!' Gio bellowed at a crossbowman. 'Shoot him, someone, why don't you?'

In return Wrenn spat at Gio and swiped low behind his knees to sever the hamstring. Gio pivoted on the ball of his foot and let the soft thrust go past.

A bruiser of a man offered his rapier to Gio. Gio fluidly slipped his dagger into his belt and snatched the sword from the man's fist. He levelled both rapiers at Wrenn. They must have had different hefts but I couldn't tell from the way he handled them.

Instantly at a disadvantage, Wrenn hit at the new rapier's side. Gio parried and at the same time attacked. Wrenn stood his ground. A sailor tried to pass his sword to Wrenn, but Gio severed his hand still clutching the hilt. Numbly, the sailor bent to retrieve his sword but he had no hand to pick it up with.

I circled above Wrenn, calling encouragement. He looked desperate; blood flowed down his face. He searched out the last of his strength and stood tall as if he had found hope, but I thought he was acting because Gio didn't respond. Wrenn feinted. Gio attacked with a move like a sneer. Wrenn evaded, left his dagger arm exposed, too low. Gio's rapier penetrated between his fingers, slid through his hand and up his arm under the skin. The point issued from his elbow in a patter of blood. Wrenn's hand opened, his dagger fell.

It's over, I thought; but Wrenn had trapped Gio's sword. Wrenn's rapier forced Gio's other blade far to the left, disengaged and thrust. His hilt slammed into Gio's chest.

Gio hunched; about a metre of bright steel projected from his back. A red patch darkened his coat around it. Wrenn pulled the hilt down, tearing his lungs. Gio staggered, blood spitting from his mouth. Wrenn couldn't hold Gio's weight on the blade and dropped it, leaving him sprawling transfixed by the rapier. Gio's blade snagged in Wrenn's arm tore out through the muscle making a gaping wound.

Gio lay curled up. He coughed around the blade. Blood sprang from his mouth onto the pavement, dribbled from his lips. He didn't breathe in again. Died.

Awndyn soldiers rushed to Wrenn and supported him. His fingers scrabbled, trying to stick the edges of the gash back together. Blood ran down into his mouth and he smiled. He had deliberately caught Gio's blade in his arm, in a furious variation of the same attack that had won him immortality a year ago.

Wrenn struck out with his fists at the soldiers trying to calm him. He fainted, so they picked him up and I led them to the *Stormy Petrel*.

I picked up a sheaf of arrows and a bottle of water, and my horn that I sound to give commands on the battlefield. I flew back to Fifth Street and landed near Lightning. He looked exhausted but grateful as I sprinted past, called, 'Gio's dead!' dumped the ammunition and bottle while still running, took off.

I swept low over the rebels and shouted, 'Gio has fallen; give yourselves up!'

The whole front of the column who had seen the duel, and several more, especially the girls, surrendered to the Awndyn Fyrd. The rear dissolved, rebels becoming looters or fugitives. Many became disorientated and I saw them running further into the meshed streets. But the leaderless centre of the column and the men who had killed Mist knew they were doomed. A new sort of aggression flared among them, affected by desperation, the strangeness of Capharnaum and the rum they had drunk.

There was a tangible atmosphere of possibility and menace. Instantly the five hundred rebels in the main street acted as if they were a single being, powerful, euphoric with it, and mad. I sensed their vigour and my pulse raced. Anything could happen; everything was happening – the riot obeyed no laws at all. The youths were at home with it; it was their atmosphere. They ran in large ragged groups. They all thought: why not take the wealth that surrounds us, in an abundance we've never been allowed before? The strength of individuals was nothing compared with the violence of the crowd – they tore the shopfronts apart. They were bent on spending every-thing in the town in one hysterical surge. They brought out bakers' trolleys and smashed them into caryatid statues. They infected each other to screaming pitch rejoicing at their own bodies' force, their freedom and their sudden riches. No future prospects Capharnaum could offer them were as good as the fun they could have trashing it. From the air I saw a mass of people sweeping away from the boulevard. They spiralled around ransacked shops like the eye of a storm.

The burning crag's jumping unnatural light lit the quay. Gio's men were now just pirates, plundering the surrounding houses. They dragged out tables, threw lamps into sheets and bundled them up. Fights broke out between them: men stabbed and punched each other over any precious-looking metal. They broke furniture and hefted the pieces as clubs.

Bricks were hurled against the houses' upper windows, and when a Capharnai man leant out and shouted, they threw bricks at his face. The pirates gathered cutlery and amphorae but discarded them when gold gleamed. So much gold, it was like the Castle's treasury. They hastily lashed together enormous packs of objects with their belts. When each had plundered all he could carry, he set off to the *Pavonine* leaving wailing and raging Capharnai families behind them.

Some Capharnai defended themselves. A group of fishermen threw a huge weighted net over thieves escaping from a house. As they struggled under it, the fishermen stabbed them with marlinspikes and tridents that sloughed dried white scales.

A group of Trisian lads came out of one house carrying sacks to loot food, kicking the door of a restaurant. Thick olive-oil smoke ribboned from its cellar grating. Little fires had been kindled at irregular intervals on the boulevard. The rioters set alight waste bins and chairs; I could see no reason why, apart from the lust to cause as much havoc as possible. I yelled, 'Stop destroying this wonderful town!' The ones that heard me started laughing.

There was no hope of catching the rioters without abandoning our own wounded men. I ordered the fyrd to pull back to the *Petrel*. At the foot of the gangplank the Awndyn unit had formed a barricade. They levelled pikes above a shield wall. Some fyrd regrouped there, but in equal numbers those who spied the gold were unlinking their shields and deserting to join the looters. Archers on the *Petrel*'s fore- and rear-castles sent sporadic volleys down at the pirates crossing the quay, who had no choice but to run through the hail of arrows to the *Pavonine*.

Thieves poured up the *Pavonine*'s gangways carrying their prizes or dragging their wounded friends. I flew over the *Stramash* and *Cuculine*, puzzled; their decks were on the same level as the water. They had been scuttled; they sat empty and perfectly upright, their keels on the sea bed. Their main decks were swamped with lapping waves, from which their castles projected like four square islands.

The crews of all three ships were at work unfurling and setting the *Pavonine*'s sails. Others, yelling, waved their friends aboard. Poleaxes and spears looked like metal hackles standing up on the ship's back.

I glided above *Pavonine*'s deck and saw Tirrick, and Cinna. Tirrick had Cinna Bawtere at rapier point, forcing him to steer the ship. Cinna clung to the wheel, shaking visibly, his porcine face set in a grimace. Tirrick, however, smiled rapaciously. He shouted, 'Climb aboard! We'll sink the *Petrel*, then pack provisions and sail for Awndyn! I'll be the next Serein and fatty will be the next Mist!'

Cinna glanced up at me and scowled. He had a length of chain around his middle, worn by fearful sailors so if they fell overboard their suffering would have a quick end.

I shouted, 'Cinna, don't you dare leave!'

He told me to go and do something unspeakable with a goat.

Sailors on the harbour cast *Pavonine*'s mooring ropes loose and swarmed up. The ship grated along the quayside with looters still chucking bags onto the deck and catching lines to haul themselves up.

Those left behind turned their attention to the *Petrel*. Small groups of rebels gathered out of range on the villa verandas; they began to coalesce, ready to attack the *Petrel*'s gangway in a desperate bid to hijack her. I thought of Rayne; I would not let anyone hurt the Doctor. She was my adviser, Lightning's confidante and devoted friend. Lightning would be even more shattered than he already is, if anything happened to Rayne.

I have seen Mist die and Serein badly wounded. I have left Lightning faltering his way through the outskirts of town. The only books to escape the firestorm are in my pocket. I don't know how many Trisians have succumbed but their houses, their shops and the harbour are despoiled. Cinna was sailing off with their belongings, surrounded by pirates and protected by Tirrick. The remnants of Gio's men were completely beyond control. Our forces were disheartened and either retreating or deserting.

I needed everyone in the riot to listen to me, to stop and look up so I could shatter the hysteria that gripped them. I must attract their attention with a gesture more powerful than Gio's last stand. But how? None of my battlefield horn signals mean anything now. I couldn't drop rocks accurately onto *Pavonine* from above the archers' range.

I shouted, swooped acrobatically and landed on the main street, but although the rebels heard me they paid no attention and simply ran away. What was I to do – pursue them one by one? Infuriated by our failure, realising that we were stranded, I felt my scolopendium clock running down. A cold shiver washed over me; the long muscles twitched in my arms. Oh god, not *now*. If Tarragon surfaced she could soon put an end to the *Pavonine*, but that wouldn't stop the fighting on land that second by second was becoming bloodier. I needed Tarragon, her car or a congregation of Tine, a sea krait . . . A sea krait! Did I dare speak to the kraits? I thought: I can *use* the Shift to stop the sacking of Capharnaum!

I flew to *Petrel* and landed on the half-deck. Rayne had transformed the main area below me into a field hospital, and she was extremely busy. Wounded men were being brought in and laid on camp beds between the masts and hatchways. Rayne bent over one, whose blood pooled in the brown stretcher. Her assistant struggled with the breastplate strap, having to pull tighter in order to release it through the buckle. Rayne said, 'No! Tha' sucking wound – ignore the res'.' She slipped a gauze pad under the edge of his armour and pressed on a jagged gash in his ribs. The soldier struggled. Rayne grasped his hand firmly and he lay still. Then his hand relaxed out of hers.

I watched as I retrieved my envelope of cat from my cabin, and I saw it all. Rayne looked into his eyes as he died. She often did that with the mortals for whom, no matter how hard she tried, she could not prevent death. She wants to glimpse the change as their eyes set. I once thought her obsession was compassion, now I think it's just her insatiable curiosity. She wants to see what they're seeing, she wants to know all that they suddenly know. It's understandable because people are always inquisitive about what they can't do. Or maybe, and although it's morbid I wouldn't rule it out, Rayne is fond of being the last thing a man sees as he quits the world. One day her curious face might fill my field of vision, through a blood-red filter.

I ducked into Ata's office; the bottle of brandy stood on her table.

Through the stern windows I saw the *Pavonine*, nearly stationary against an onshore breeze. Her sailors swarmed on the high aft castle, adjusting some timbers – the long beam of a trebuchet. I said aloud, 'Bloody fuck, not another catapult.' It could even be the one we saw being dragged along the Remige Road. It had two large wooden treadmills set upright on either side. A sailor crawled into each wheel and walked them around; others on the outside pushed to winch the arm back. It was so long it overhung the poop deck steps. Another pair of men lowered a ball into the sling. Tirrick gave a shout, the arm kicked up to one side of the mizzen mast, and the stone flew through the air.

It overshot *Petrel* and crashed into the roof of one of the harbour villas. Cinna's sailors busily set about winding a windlass to decrease the trebuchet's throw. Shit, if we ever needed Lightning's professional opinion it was now.

I dashed out of the cabin and called to Rayne, 'They're taking potshots at us! Move down below – and stay there till I bring reinforcements. Don't abandon ship unless they hole the hull. If you must go to land, ask the officer of the Awndyn Fyrd lamai to give you some cover.'

I heard Rayne ordering that her patients be taken to the living deck; I did not have much time. I tipped a fistful of cat out of the envelope. It ran like fine sugar between my fingers as I sifted it into the brandy glass. I tapped my hand on top to knock the powder out of the damp lines on my palm. Then I uncorked the brandy and sloshed it in. The crystals eddied and spun. I drank it down right to the dregs of undissolved powder where the brandy had not penetrated between the dry grains. I put the glass down with a click.

That was a massive overdose. Through the windows broadsword fighters battled at the junction of the boulevard. Pikes held the gangplank secure but only one line of fyrd remained behind them.

The metal clashes muted suddenly, as if at a distance; the bustle of the surgery shrank to background. My own breaths boomed loud and blood pressure rumbled in my ears. It is coming on.

*Pavonine* turned her slender stern to me and the flat towers of her soot-spotted sails. Her reflection vanished. The image of the quay wall and houses ripped away. The sea moved, silver but featureless. It wasn't reflecting; it should be mirroring the sky.

The waves slowed to the consistency of treacle. *Pavonine* lifted and fell again hours later. Another round shot slowed until it was almost floating; it tracked a lingering trajectory through the air and disappeared at the water's surface in front of the window.

I'm going under. I slipped to my knees, trailing my fingers down the dirty panes. If I concentrate on breathing I'll never remember how to. I could no longer kneel. I lay down, one arm extended. The bracelets on the other wrist pressed into my cheek, my sword belt dug into my hips.

Black haze filled my vision from the edges to the centre. I thought with a sudden flush of panic: I haven't taken anywhere near enough. This will never work. I need more—

# CHAPTER 22

I set off flying over Epsilon's savannah towards Vista Marchan and the old Insect bridge. Hundreds of metres below, Tarragon's gold car left the edge of the market and followed, accelerating until it was directly below me. The car kept pace, a tiny shining rectangle on the immense plains, leaving a straight dark green track as it flattened the grass. I could see Tarragon in her short red dress glancing up at me.

I slowed, let the car race ahead and then swooped down, speeding faster as I lost height, and catching up with it from behind. I swept over it, lifting my legs so my dangling feet didn't hit the headrest, and then lowered my pointed boot toes onto the front seat next to Tarragon. She looked ahead, keeping the car speeding straight. I crouched and pulled my wings in unevenly, wiggled to sit down. I pointed at the grey Insect bridge. *'Go!'*

Tarragon clenched the wheel, rocked her body forward and slammed her foot to the floor.

The towers of Vista Marchan shimmered and cohabited the space where only the flourishing grassland was supposed to be. A warm wind blew directly from them, drying my eyes. Nowhere in the Fourlands has such a parched, relentless wind. Tarragon glanced at me, complaining, 'I've been looking everywhere. What's happening, Jant? I swam into harbour and saw stones falling through the water around the hull of your boat.'

'We're under attack. The other ship's throwing them. Rayne's on the *Petrel* – and so am I.'

Tarragon gnashed her Shark's teeth angrily. Her shape flickered violently between being a prissy lady and a vicious fish. 'What a waste of scholarship! I will flip their boat into flotsam!'

'It's even worse: the library's on fire – one thousand years of wisdom lost forever. We'll never know what essential works are gone for good. Mist Ata's dead. Oh – was that gargantuan shark you?'

'Yes. I followed a schooner that I sent to sail alongside your ship on a Shift sea. You asked me for help so I chartered it as a guard.'

'God, Tarragon; you're big.'

'Big-ish. Do you want me to bite your enemies' keel out from under them?'

'Even if you do, the pirates ashore will keep fighting and they're killing the islanders. The Trisians will still resist the Castle after this. No amount of talking will bring them round because after Gio's lies they're never going to believe any Fourlander again. We can't win. The only way I can think to take control of this riot is to stage a spectacle so incredible that both sides forget their differences. Sea kraits live far from land, don't they?'

Tarragon said, 'Yes. They wouldn't eat humans, not worth the energy. They live in the deep ocean; when they slough their skins they scratch themselves on the continent's roots shelving up from the abyss.'

'Well, I want a sea krait.'

'You want to save them! Are you sure?'

'Only if they agree to the deal. The stinguish told me their ocean dried up, and you said they needed a safe haven. Kraits can come to live in the Fourlands' sea on the condition that they obey me.'

I braced myself as we rushed onto the wide bridge. Our wheels hummed as they sped over the irregular surface. I could see the striations where individual Insects had added their masticated wood pulp. The bridge's stringy supports of hardened spit whooshed by on both sides. Looking between them I saw the savannah drop below us as we laboured up to the apex.

We crested the summit buffeted by Vista's breeze that blows across worlds, and for one glorious moment I could see the whole of the sprawling market.

Then it had gone; we were in the world of Vista. The wind howled through the top of the bridge. Below us, it blew the top layer of flaking sand across the wasteland as fine crystal dust, drifting onto high dunes against the base of the sea wall.

Many white tracks converged on Vista Marchan city; from up here they resembled the rays of a star. Its cluster of pale blocky towers appeared suspended in mirages and pooled in bent light across the entire wasteland.

I had not seen any place like this before. We descended past the towers that I realised were higher than the Throne Room spire. I was overawed and shaking as we rolled to a halt on top of Vista's great sea wall. On either side of us were empty, sand-choked dockyards and piers with long, dry barnacled ladders that stopped short of the ground.

I looked out over the salt flats, to see Epsilon as a translucent illusion, a lush plain and thriving market lying at forty-five degrees through the white wasteland.

Tarragon said, 'Aren't Insects fascinating creatures? That's the Vista desert. It used to be the ocean floor.' Her car's wheels pulled the grit into tracks as we drove along the top of the immense wall. The salt-bleached streets were devoid of movement. The only living things in Vista were myself and Tarragon; her fin annoyingly brushed my thigh as she operated the controls. Paper Insect cells meshed between and hung like grey lace around the worn concrete buildings.

'I'm sorry to bring you so far,' she added. 'Your trip home will cause you substantial distress.'

Rust stains ran down the dock wall from flaking iron rings bolted into the top. Sea-level markers and fading numerals were stencilled in a script twice my height. We stopped and stared out at the vanished ocean. The white sky and sand stretched away as far as I could see: two parallel planes meeting at the horizon. Occasional patches discoloured the dunes' glaring surface, chemicals and oil seeping up from below. A stagecoach that must have belonged to a recent tourist lay derelict and half-full of sand. The tops of its spoked wheels showed through the surface of a hard-packed ridge.

Behind us was the city, faceless towers and blanched walls abraded with centuries of wind-blown sand. Spiral steps emerged like spinal columns from their broken shells. Rusted girders jutted out of the fortieth floors – metal thinned to perforated wafers. There was no sound but the breeze skipping salt crystals over the dry ocean floor and concrete promenade. It was completely outside my experience. I said, 'It's not beautiful. It's . . .'

'A desert, Jant. Lots of sand.'

'Tarragon,' I said impatiently. 'Capharnaum is burning!'

She tutted but moved quickly, taking a gold pocket watch from a box that was part of the car's fascia. She clicked its glass case open and I saw that it wasn't a watch at all. Inside was a gold mechanism and a wire gauze that securely held down a fat black fly, twice the size of a bluebottle. It buzzed energetically, sounding as if it was trying to drill through its gold cage. Tarragon said, 'It's amazing what you can purchase from the Tine in Epsilon market if you have enough meat.'

'What is it?'

'It's a Time Fly. They have a way of avoiding being squashed or eaten. They can jump a split second back in time, up to the point at which they emerged from the pupa. This Time Fly hatched in Vista Marchan and has been imprisoned here ever since. I'm taking you back there; we will turn back time until the tide comes in. Wind it for me, will you?'

I turned the contraption's little gold key, just like a watch, and the gauze began to put pressure on the trapped insect. It felt threatened and tried its method of escape, but because the mechanism snared it, it carried its threat along. It took us, too, and it went *fast*. Really fast.

For a few minutes, nothing changed. I twisted round and looked behind at the town. The buildings could be a little less grey, less dilapidated.

There was a blurring at street level around the car, as if I could see coloured air swirling. Tarragon said, 'They're city people, in their everyday lives or fighting Insects, moving back in time too fast to see.'

She patted my arm and pointed to the horizon. Prodigious steel ships began to rise from the areas of oily discoloured sands. Sand dusted away from them, revealing masts and wheelhouses then unearthed long hulls lying on their sides. The sand's surface darkened to pale grey and began to glisten. Then shallow blue pools appeared in the lowest linear sand ripples, where I had not noticed hollows before. The long pools swelled and coalesced, turning the summits of the sand ripples into islands and building up around the dunes. Water ran together around them, darker blue as it deepened.

The ripples were all covered, the sea level climbed, the dunes were dispersed islands. Just a few islands left; then the sea covered the final dune. The ocean kept rising, closer to the bottom rungs of the ladders, bearing upright the drab metal ships.

Colour poured into the sky. From monochrome it became pale, then bright blue. The automobile's highly polished gold chassis reflected it. The Time Fly in the watch whined with effort. It was now a young imago, its wings crumpled and damp, as it had been when someone imprisoned it. Its six thin legs scraped against the watch's shiny inside surface.

Suddenly the Insect bridge vanished. Fresh paper, it disappeared in jerky stages from the foot of the arch to its zenith. Waves hit the harbour wall and climbed its sea-level gauge, higher and higher. The steel ships disappeared instantly; instead the ocean spat out white boats that bobbed at anchor. The rings in the dock wall were glossy; Vista Marchan's towers were complete and spotless, glass walls reflecting the sun. The buzzing in the watch stopped abruptly, and everything was clear and still. It was a beautiful day. Men and women in orange tabards and yellow helmets went about their business at the docks, blissfully unaware of the annihilation that will happen when the Insects' bridge crashes through.

Tarragon showed me the watch; it was empty. She said, 'In a factory in Vista, the Time Fly's just been hatched.'

An almighty wave reared from the middle of the ocean and cascaded into harbour, diminishing every second, until it lapped at the wall as a gentle ripple. A vast green snake's head and upper body erupted from the ocean, spattering us with spray and blotting out the sun. Its head was four times bigger than a caravel, the solid muscle trunk of its monstrous body as thick as one of the towers behind me.

The glossy green snake lowered its flat, pointed head onto the promenade. The harbour workers seemed annoyed but were too polite to say anything. Tarragon and I climbed out of her car. 'God-who-left-us,' I gasped.

'No, it's just a snake.'

'Shit . . . How many are there?'

'Sh!' Tarragon chided. 'Their population numbers less than a thousand.'

The sea krait's bulk stretched into the distance. It meandered in colossal hundred-metre curves like the Moren River. A ship steered away from its side, panicking and belching smoke. Around half a kilometre from shore, the krait dipped underwater and the same distance further away a striped blue and green conical island trailed back and forth in the frothing sea – the flattened tip of its tail.

We stood in front of the snake's slightly domed yellow eye. Its vertical slit pupil was the height and width of my body. Its head was covered in bright scales the size of a table-top. Black skin showed between them, looking like stitching around the square scales on its closed lips. A deeply forked black tongue darted out of the tip of its snout and flickered around us. It didn't touch me but I sensed the motion of the air a centimetre away from my face and I felt its moistness. The snake darted its tongue back into the hole in its top lip, which was big enough for me to have crawled through.

Tarragon said, 'Jant, may I introduce you to the king of the sea kraits?' She addressed the beast: 'Your Heinouss, this is a messenger from the Emperor of the Fourlands who could soon be your Emperor too, if you agree to his terms . . . Jant, talk to him; he can hear you with his tongue.'

The snake turned its enormous head on one side like a keeling carrack, and rubbed its closed mouth on the promenade. With the grating of a thousand millstones, it scraped great grooves into the cement and uprooted the iron mooring posts on either side. Its eye moved back and forth, appraising me.

I declared, 'Tarragon will show you the direction to the Fourlands' ocean. You and your people can live there if you promise me three things. First, destroy the ship called *Pavonine* afloat in the centre of the harbour, that Tarragon will show you. Second, after that don't damage any other vessels or harm any people. Live in the depths and stay away from the shoreline, so you'll be less likely to cause accidents. Third, our world is threatened by the Insects too; that makes us allies and in the future I might call on you for help again, via Tarragon.'

All the time, the krait's pennant-tongue flicked in and out of its long colubrine smile, picking up vibrations in the air. It was tasting my words. It twisted its head looking for Tarragon and slithered dangerously close to crushing her car before she ran round in front of its eye. It hissed, and I felt its hot, fishy, miasmic breath blow from the arched hole in its lip.

'What is it saying?' I asked.

Tarragon said, 'He wants to know if your sea is of sufficient size. I don't think the Fourlands' ocean is roomy enough to hold every one of the sea kraits. I will tell him that there's only space to allow a few of them through. That way at least some will escape the disaster and their species will survive.'

The snake's glistening body writhed along its whole visible length. Tarragon gave me an encouraging look. 'The King accepts. He is convinced of your honesty; he says he can taste it.'

'How do I know whether to trust a sea snake?'

Tarragon laughed. 'You have a Shark's word that you can.'

The meanders of the krait's kilometre-long body drew tighter and closer together as it pulled its head back and smoothly submerged under the water. I stared at it, open-mouthed.

'You will see him once more,' said the Shark. 'Goodbye, Jant. I have to act as their guide and we have rather a long way to swim in this delicious water. Still, we've plenty of time.' Her red dress turned grey, and stippled to continuous sharkskin all over her body. She walked to the very edge of the massive wall, hooked her bare toes over and raised her shagreen hands above her head.

'Don't leave me here!' I cried. I was not only in a completely unknown, alien world, but somewhere in its past.

She turned a shark's cold eye on me. 'Have you not been practising? You should be able to will your way back by now! I advised you to study and I expected you to learn. Well, this is an excellent opportunity to try.' She leant forward, gave a little jump, and fell through the air in a perfect dive. She splashed into the crystal-clear water and did not rise again.

I might have to stay here forever, I thought in panic. I might have to *live* here. Berating myself, I examined the stinking abandoned car but it was already beginning to rot. I kicked it. The dock workers had left when we were talking to the King krait, and I was alone. I sat down and for about an hour, though I had no way of measuring time, I tried to copy the feeling of my return Shifts. I imagined the pull – a plausible path to the Fourlands – growing stronger, solidifying. I grasped it, and dragged myself through.

I lay somewhere that smelt of feathers. Darkness surrounded me. I felt nothing. My body was paralysed; I couldn't move. 'Because you're dead,' a heavy voice pronounced in my ear. I screamed with no sound. This is the wrong world; I've no body to return to. I struggled and thrashed and forced myself awake.

I came to lying on the worn carpet in Ata's cabin, by the linenfold panelled walls and brocade bench on which Rayne sat in front of the stern windows. 'Well done,' she enthused. 'You saved us!' The windows behind her were completely black. 'Shame i' killed you, though.' She smiled and her mouth widened on both sides. She smiled and smiled and smiled. I'm still not home. I'm still not awake!

I squeezed my eyes shut and fought desperately. I then saw a louring landscape with ruined bridges, fortresses, windmills all benighted backlit with raging fire, vast buildings with stone stairways running in every direction. I did not set down there. Someone's fingers were on my face, probing like worms in my mouth; they forced my jaw open and rammed down my throat. I simultaneously woke up and vomited helplessly.

I opened my eyelids to two slivers of glazed-green iris but lay otherwise inert. Rayne's pair of bloodstained pumps and Lightning's thick-soled buckled boots stood in front of my face. God, I hate it when I wake up lying in the recovery position.

'He's no' responding,' said Rayne. I felt her thumb my eyelid.

'I am,' I said, but it came out as a breath.

Lightning's voice sounded very weak. 'Well, bloody *make* him respond.'

Rayne made a sound like a shrug and slapped my face. 'His pupils are so thin they're like threads. Can you feel t' Circle working t' hold him?'

'Yes, damn him.'

Rayne slapped my face again and I gasped and spat.

Lightning said, 'Ah, Jant. Everyone fights to survive but you wipe yourself out! You couldn't poison Gio but you do a bloody good job of poisoning yourself! We need you to fly above and drop missiles on the trebuchet team. I know you prefer to be comatose under heavy bombardment; are you hoping to be revived by the cold water when we sink?'

I rolled into a kneeling position and blinked at him. He half-lay on a chair, still shaking with pain. Instead of his longbow he held a smaller bow with pulleys that could be kept drawn effortlessly.

Rayne said, 'Lightning, don' make him feel bad or you'll give him an excuse t' take another dose.'

'The gamin wretch! I'll—'

I whispered, 'You're wrong. You told me to stop the riot and that's exactly what I am doing.'

A ripple jolted *Petrel* hard against the harbour wall, throwing Rayne off balance. The snakes have arrived. I swallowed dryly, then I stumbled to my feet and out of the cabin. Rayne hurried and Lightning struggled after me, up the ladder to the poop deck where I gazed from the rail. The quayside was littered with bodies; its pavement was cracked and the walls of houses demolished where *Pavonine*'s shot had struck. Our figurehead and forecastle had been smashed into a mass of splintered wood. I took it all in with one glance, not knowing if I had really woken. The sky was dark – was this Fourlands or still Shift?

Looking down to the lower level through an open hatch I saw Wrenn sitting on a rope coil, drinking a canteen of water voraciously. Rayne's assistant was sewing the gash that was open to the bone in his arm. The sight brought me back to earth. He knew that Eszai can take wounds – although *not* wounds as serious as that. He must have badly misunderstood what I told him about the Circle.

The *Pavonine* continued her bombardment. Cinna spun the wheel, keeping the ship's stern towards us, rudder at full lock. Tirrick commanded the sweating pirates scurrying inside the treadwheels to ratchet the catapult back. They stacked its sling with slimy rocks from the ship's own ballast.

The *Pavonine* jolted. An unnatural ripple circled her. The water on either side of her hull began to churn and bubble; waves lapped in every direction. Behind her, between her and the beacon island, a long black ridge surfaced. It was domed like a whale's back but it rose higher and higher out of the water, passing the height of the *Pavonine*'s rail. It was the King krait's top lip.

Lightning and Rayne stared, stunned. The men on the *Pavonine* ran about in confused terror as the ridge continued to rise. Two curved sharp fangs emerged parallel with the waves. Longer than pikes they projected from the black arch on the far left and right. The sea krait's jaw showed its green and blue stripes and the water seething as it emerged glowed with phosphorescence.

A hundred metres away from the top lip, in the water between us and the *Pavonine*, the slick lower lip crested up. Men by the catapult shrieked and pointed; on the main deck they ran from one side to the other, unable to fathom what the arches on either side of them could be. The krait's open mouth ascended, its teeth curved towards the *Pavonine*. The ridged black skin of its upper palate faced us, twice the size of the mainsail and glistening like tar. Water sluiced off its smooth bony head.

The smoke-filled sky resonated with the pirates' screams as far as the town. I had the impression that the whole sea bed was ascending. Water thundered out of both sides of the krait's open mouth; in the rocketing froth between its upper and lower jaws the *Pavonine* danced and spun like an eggshell in boiling brine. The cocked catapult went off, hurling shot vertically into the air.

I heard Cinna screeching. The snake's lance-long teeth reached the height of *Pavonine*'s foremast, curving above the ship and caging it in. *Pavonine* canted over so far the crow's-nest on its mainmast slapped the water, now on the port side, now the starboard, throwing off men. The krait's bottom jaw obscured the ship. Its yellow eye emerged, surrounded with wet black skin, waves battering against it.

For an instant the water inside its mouth was carried higher than the harbour water. The snake reared out of the sea, bearing the *Pavonine* up. Sailors clung onto the ropes, dropped off with raucous screams.

Foaming brine spurted out both sides. The sea krait closed its mouth, with one sickening crunch.

In the sudden silence, the bitten-off masthead of the *Pavonine* tumbled to the surf. It floated, no bigger than a matchstick, beside the diamond-shaped snake's head projecting straight up from the waves. Its body rose to the surface, blocking the harbour entrance, and the length of it extended to the horizon. The King krait lowered its head and turned to look at us.

Lightning scrabbled for an arrow, stammering, 'What is that . . . ?' He flexed his bow, aiming directly for its yellow eye.

'No!' I put my jittery hand over the arrowhead and forced it down. 'Don't shoot!'

Lightning gaped at me, striving to understand. 'Why not? Its carcass won't block us in. The sun will rot it. It will rot away.' He yelled at the sea krait, *'What are you?'*

The snake's long mouth stayed closed but the black tongue whipped out like a pennant at the summit of its snout, curling down to our railings, licking slickly in front of me. I assumed the krait was tasting the air for my scent. I actually admired its beauty and overwhelming incalculable strength. I waved my arms to it, grinning madly with gratitude. 'Thank you! Thank you in the name of the Emperor – now go find a home!'

It tilted its head to the side, but as it sank it scanned the *Stormy Petrel*'s deck with its great amber eye. The sea rushed back with a noise like rolling boulders, closing over the snake's eye, upturned mouth, pointed nose; the nostrils last to submerge. An enormous V-shaped ripple formed where, underwater, it began to haul its massive body and retract its head from the harbour.

I swear there was a gust of wind as everybody on the *Stormy Petrel* exhaled. The quay was silent for a second – it *was* silent, the fighting had stopped. I heard weapons fall and clanking as bags of loot dropped to the ground.

Pandemonium broke out as, shoulder to shoulder, some soldiers and pirates moved closer to the waterfront to stare, rapt, at the floating topmast, the broken pieces of canoes and pontoons where the krait had been. The rest, especially the Trisians, tried to run as far from the sea as possible, back into town. The rioting on the quayside and all the way up the boulevard had completely ceased; everybody was watching the ocean.

'Did . . . ?' Lightning stammered. 'In the name of . . . god's arse . . . I can't believe I just saw that.' He turned on me. 'Why do you keep stopping me from shooting monsters?'

'It saved us, Saker; it's a friend.'

On my other side Rayne spoke calmly. 'You were in too deep, Jant, if you reached Vista Marchan.'

I goggled at her, but she simply smiled.

'How did you know that *thing* was going to appear?' Lightning demanded.

I seated myself on the deck; I was too nauseous to question Rayne. I moaned, 'Oh, please let me lie down. They've stopped fighting. I halted the riot; we've won.'

'We los' so much, Jant, tha' I doubt you could call i' winning.'

Lightning nudged me with his boot. 'I see Vendace and the senators approaching the gangway. At the moment I don't think relations between Capharnaum and the Castle could be any worse. Can you address them?'

Rayne said, 'Jant is very disorienta'ed; I don'—'

I nodded. 'Yes. I will speak for the Castle.'

Scavenger smoke rifled across the sky. The moisture of the sea breeze condensed on the library's fumes to form a thick cloud descending over the crag; we gradually lost sight of the blackened, burnt-out Amarot. The air was filthy and muggy, unfamiliar to the senators. They stood huddled together, coughing. The sea krait had rendered them speechless and their eyes were downcast; they were in mortal fear. Lightning and I walked unsteadily down the gangplank to the corniche which was littered with debris. Vendace's tunic and unruly grey hair were soot-stained. He looked at the blood on Lightning's shirt, the puke on mine and the ash on us both. He faltered, 'We saw the serpent. Can you communicate with it?'

'I just did,' I said.

They conferred between themselves; they all had a tone of defeat. Vendace said, 'This is so much worse than legendary Insects coming to life. We had no idea that such a serpent existed. How did you summon it?'

'What are they asking—' Lightning began.

'One minute!' I said to him. I gathered my thoughts and addressed the senators. 'Yes, I summoned the snake to stop the battle and save your homes. I don't want to call up any more but the Archer is furious and unmerciful. You heard us arguing on the ship; he wants to show you what we can do. I'm trying to make him agree not to encircle the island with giant snakes.' I turned to Lightning and addressed him gravely in high Awian. 'We must look like we're conferring. I'm bluffing, but the senators will appreciate the Empire after this. Pretend to be angry and speak to me; quote theatre or something.'

Lightning was quick to understand. He shook his head and said in a stern tone, 'Well, in that case – balsam for lovers.'

I enquired, 'Willows for brides?'

'Briars for the maidens,' Lightning retorted. 'Look, you will explain this afterwards, please?'

I patted his shoulder as if in agreement, 'Oh yes, but I am positive you won't like it. And to wives we give lilies. Right.' I switched back to Trisian and said, 'My friend and I have decided not to summon the snakes, and to let them abide in the deepest ocean where they will be no threat to your country again.' I extended my hand to Vendace. 'There are many more wonderful things in the Fourlands. We're your allies; please join us.'

Vendace and the others seemed doubtful. His lean shoulders were sagging. 'If all the trials to face Tris from now on will be this arduous, then we cannot resist them alone. We'll give you a message for' – he paused and blanched – 'for San, now he has done to us what he did to the Pentadrica.'

'What?' I said.

Vendace looked at his associates for support, shrugged. 'Everybody knows that centuries ago San let the Pentadrica be destroyed so he could seize power. He deliberately contrived that unfortunate Alyss be slain, and now he's done the same to us.'

I shook my head. 'No, no. San was only an adviser. He would have told Alyss not to visit the Insects' enclave and she must have ignored him.'

Vendace glanced at the murk covering the Amarot, through which glimpses of the blackened library walls came and went. 'That is not what Capelin wrote. I have read the manuscript, many of us have, but now . . . how do we prove it? It is ash with the rest.'

I didn't know what to say or who to believe. I searched around for more evidence of our goodwill, took the books from my pockets and gave them to Danio's successor, who was still choking back sobs. 'Here . . .'

'Oh, thanks,' she said sarcastically, looking at the titles.

'The Castle's Doctor is here; she'll help your doctors with the wounded Capharnai. Her knowledge and supplies will be useful. We'll repair the damage that has been done, as far as we can. If you need grain ships I shall send them. The Circle is at your command; whatever you think about the Emperor's history and motives, I promise you we will work day and night.'

I thought, we have brought them misrule. Our presence has made Tris grow out of childhood to delinquent adolescence. But scolopendium was still hitting me in waves of sickness and bliss. I was simply glad to be alive, one of the lives remaining.

Our soldiers, seeing Lightning on the quayside, approached him. But he was feverish, so he simply sat down and left me to give the commands while Rayne tended to him. I told the Awndyn Fyrd captain to round up the rebels and put them in the hold. Then came Viridian, Ata's daughter, who had collected the gory pieces of her mother's body. She insisted that Mist Ata Dei be buried at sea, with the respect that was due to a famous explorer and the Circle's Sailor.

I said, 'It's terrible that Mist can never know how Tris turns out.'

Lightning glanced over the broken paving stones, the trebuchet shot and abandoned gold loot on the harbour pavement. His gaze loitered on the sea that splintered the dawn light. He was now as suspicious of the ocean as I used to be, and I loved it because it was not the same sea now the kraits swam in its depths. 'Yes, it is, Comet. And I wonder if the Empire will ever regain a vestige of normality.'

# CHAPTER 23

## The Castle, January 2021

The paths under the Finial arches were slippery with snow that had partially melted and then frozen again. The translucent footprints preserved the detailed marks of boot treads and hobnails. Frost rime edged the stone leaves on the Architect's Tower, and icicles so long you could spit Insects with them hung from the Bridge of Size, which took the cobbled Eske Road across the Moren River. On the lawns between the Simurgh Wing and outer wall, two centimetres of snow were sealed beneath a centimetre of sparkling ice, blue in the early morning light.

I waited outside the Throne Room in the small cloister, staring out of one of its pointed glassless windows. I was contemplating the fact that if you put the world's finest – athletically or intellectually – into one Castle and let it stew for a thousand years, the results will not always be palatable.

Looking south between the outer wall and palace, the roof had been rebuilt on the Harcourt barracks, where the Imperial Fyrd are based. Men were repairing the Dace Gate barbican, and all along the curtain wall flags flew at half mast.

Next to me, on the spandrels between the little arched windows, were green-men carvings, dead faces with branches growing out of their loose decaying mouths. Their sole purpose was to remind us that one day we will die and be nothing but plant food. It is a thought that spurs Eszai to keep their places in the Circle and mortals to do great deeds and join them, or be remembered for their great deeds alone.

Tris would take years to recover from the damage Gio caused. Lightning, Wrenn, Rayne, Viridian and I had left the island one month after the riot. I last saw it diminishing in the distance under a sunset pink from the amount of soot and burnt book dust high in the air. 'Ata's sunsets,' the Capharnai have come to call them.

Lightning was staying at Awndyn convalescing, and with Wrenn's help he was arranging for a monument to be built on Grass Isle in honour of Ata. Thousands of her extended family had gathered there;

I found the way her whole network had clung together rather alarming. But most of all I felt sympathy for Lightning because he also had to find some way of explaining it to Cyan.

I had spent yesterday relating the battle to San, the ensuing riot and the debt we owe to the fifth land: Tris, manorship of Capharnaum. I was now to answer for giving the sea kraits a lodging in our world.

I looked up as Rayne emerged from the Throne Room. 'Now i's your turn,' she said. 'I told San everything I witnessed.'

'You told him about Vista Marchan?'

'Yes, but I couldn' tell if he was surprised.'

I said, 'It's hard to believe I'm not the only Eszai who knows about the Shift. And to find out that *you* have taken cat.'

Rayne grinned like a crack in a walnut, showing mottled gums. 'When I were a girl. I was a lass once, Jant; isn't tha' amazing? Rumours were rife a' t' university about i's effects. I only experimen'ed once, in a spiri' of scientific enquiry; I didn' like t' hallucinations because they were extremely intense. When I saw t' snake I though' i' were like t' krai' I saw when I dreamed I was walking in Vista. Then I though': hmm, that was under the influence of t' fern scolopendium too. Jant, I *wanted* t' go t' Tris. I wanted t' keep abreas' of new discoveries. But t' mos' interes'ing thing I learned wasn' Trisian; I have reconsidered my hypothesis.'

I sighed. 'People can learn to meditate their way through the Shift worlds. I doubt I'll ever be successful at it, but you might be able to – you're good enough to feel the Circle.'

We looked at each other, wondering if the Emperor himself might have visited the Shift. For all we knew, he might walk there nightly, observing the Insect hordes preparing to burst through into different parts of the Fourlands.

'I have no desire to go back to the Shift, Rayne. Ever since seeing the King krait, how powerful he was, the beauty of his striking colours, and how content and happy the stinguish are, I feel freed from my craving. I'm ready to straighten out. When I'm through withdrawal and recovered from the trauma, I'm going to spend Gio's treasure on Wrought.'

'For t' stability of Awia.'

'To win Tern back.'

'You know, Tern felt t' Circle break. She said tha' she worried herself sick with t' though' tha' i' was you. She asked t' Emperor if you had died and if she was aging, bu' he wouldn' tell her.'

I was aware that San was waiting. I pointed to the Throne Room door. 'Come with me. I don't want to walk in there by myself.'

We progressed down the scarlet carpet and through the portal in the screen like a couple about to be married: Rayne in her shawl that had seen better days at the turn of the millennium and me in a new shirt and waistcoat, with a long velvet scarf, fine black eyeliner and my hair cut so short it was cruel to my sharp-boned face.

Rayne curtsied and seated herself on the bench and I knelt before the dais. The shining sunburst behind the Emperor's throne reflected light in all the zestful colours of the stained-glass windows.

'Comet,' San said. 'You brought serpents from the Shift to infest our ocean. I cannot think of anything more dangerous and irresponsible than your playing with the boundaries and indigenes of worlds.'

I bowed my head. 'Tris is part of the Fourlands; the Fourlands is part of the Shift. They've always affected each other. As far as Insects, maritime creatures and . . . and myself are concerned, it's a continuum.'

'The snakes will pose as big a problem in the sea as Insects do on land!'

'My lord, I assure you they won't attack us. They only eat the huge whales that never come near land.'

'And do we not need the whales and shoals? Furthermore the sudden appearance of a sea serpent will threaten people's very perception of reality.'

I was still desolated that Capharnaum library and its precious manuscripts had been lost. I looked up to let the Emperor perceive my anger. He couldn't expel me from the Circle so soon after Gio's rebellion. Although there was much less unrest in the Fourlands now, a bibliophile Messenger can be just as dangerous as a vengeful Swordsman. The Emperor needed me, a Trisian scholar known to the Senate and the sea beasts, and, though unwilling, his loyal servant all year. He sent us out to deal with battles and infernos and he offered no reward, just the measly Castle grant and yet more lifetime. I wondered again about his motivations, but no matter how much I cared I could do nothing. If I angered San he would make me mortal, and without him the Fourlands would be swamped by Insects.

I thought of the picture in the history book, showing San as an unassuming sage-turned-soldier. I spoke with determination: 'I know that my decision was best. It saved us and Capharnaum. We stopped Gio, and the Senate will be governors of Tris. You gave me to understand that we should use whatever means necessary, and calling the kraits was the right thing to do . . .' My voice crawled slower and slower and dried up like a snail on a dirt track.

'You sound unrepentant, Comet.'

'My lord.' I fixed my gaze on the apse where the fifth land's column should be.

The Emperor understood and regarded me for a long time. 'Whatever happens, we can do little about sea kraits at the moment. If mariners and whalers sight them, hopefully they will believe that kraits have continually inhabited our sea. There have always been legends of monsters.' He paused. 'Comet, you will not tell anyone of the Shift.'

'I promise.'

'I doubt a debauchee such as yourself can keep his word! How many times has the Circle brought you back from the Shift when you would otherwise have died? Immortality was not meant for that purpose, Comet. Next time I am afraid the Circle will not be able to hold you. One more fatal overdose will indeed be fatal.'

The rest of the world would believe that scolopendium had at last killed me. I fiddled with my earring, thinking that anyway my private playground was somehow spoiled, now that I knew other Eszai had visited it. The meaning of Epsilon had changed and I no longer had a yearning to go there, especially after my experience trying to Shift home. I didn't think I was going to miss it.

I said, 'I can do without it. I don't want to be addicted any more; I want to be cured. The last thing Mist said to me was, "Stop sulking, Jant."'

Rayne stepped in on my behalf: 'I'll look after him and treat t' condition. I don' think he will go back to scolopendium again. T' prognosis is excellen'.'

The Emperor said with a warm tone, 'Well, I thank you, Comet. Despite your injudicious decision with the sea kraits, your service to the Fourlands has been invaluable. Now go with Rayne, and in the fullness of time you will invite the Trisians to compete in a games for the Sailor's position. You will send mortal emissaries who weren't involved to talk at length with the Senate, to invite them here and reduce tensions in Capharnaum.'

I bowed and took my leave. I paced past the screen and the first of the Zascai benches. San's voice called from behind me, 'What of Gio Ami's fortune?'

I stopped dead. *Damn.* I turned round slowly and slunk back, as the Emperor continued, 'That which you salvaged from the Senate House square? Rayne told me that she saw you leading a retinue of servants dragging metal coffers up to your apartments.'

Was there nothing San didn't know? I imagined my hard-won plunder disappearing into the Castle's vaults, or being divided up into projects that I would never see. I sighed, resigned. 'My lord, what do you want me to do with Gio's treasure? I intended it for Wrought.'

'In that case, Messenger, I believe it would be best if you keep it.'

## CHAPTER 24

Tern walked through the ruined square, the walls of which are now just shapes of drifts. Snow piled up ever higher by the Northwest Tower. She climbed its staircase, cased in ice. The door of my apartment closed and she let her long coat fall to the floor. I lay naked in bed and watched her. I have plenty still to fight for but also plenty to celebrate.

I had arranged Gio's treasure around the room. Gold chains hung from the mirror, silver plates gleamed on the mantelpiece. Stacks of bar silver armoured the fireplace, constellations of coins glittered on the rug. I had draped the four-poster bed entirely in jewellery. Tern came to examine the riches; she stroked them and she began to smile.

Her fingers on my skin left delicious tracks of sensation, like sparks. I told her she was beautiful. She ducked under the sheet, tented it over her shapely shoulders. I threw my head back and howled.

A little while later, someone rattled the door handle, but it was locked.